WHERE THE BULBUL SINGS

Serena Fairfax

Acknowledgments

Many thanks to the late Maureen E. Mahon (London) who nobly read and re-read the drafts, to Anglo-Indians in India and of the diaspora and to an Indian Princely family (all of whom wish to remain anonymous) who shared memories with me.

***

Historical events/incidents have been slightly re-jigged. Any errors are all mine.

ABOUT THE AUTHOR

Serena Fairfax spent her childhood in India, qualified as a Lawyer in England, and worked in a London firm.

Some of her novels have a strong romantic arc although she burst the romance bubble with one quirky departure. Other novels pull the reader into the dark corners of family life and relationships. She enjoys the challenge of experimenting and writing something different.

Her short stories and a medley of articles feature on her blog, and she reviews crime fiction and thrillers for a blog.

For more information please visit her website: www.serenafairfax.com

'A ripened peach and just seventeen, man. She'll be heartbreaker and trouble stirrer, yawl see,' the railwayman muttered to a workmate their gaze locked on Hermie Blake as she propped up her black Raleigh bicycle against a betel-stained wall of Ajeemkot's two-storied mustard and red brick station building and un-looped a basket from the handlebars. Then, tucking her broad brimmed khaki solar topi under one arm, she hurried, her bronze tumble of hair lit by sunlight, up the dusty, stone steps to the arched entrance. After a humid night that promised the monsoon, the temperature had climbed. That June day in 1939 was cloudless with a slight heat haze and above the raucous bustle of the station the chimes of the town's Victoria Jubilee Memorial clock danced across on a spice-spiked breeze.

Eight o'clock! Hermie – christened but seldom called Hermione - glanced across for confirmation to the station clock, accurate to a second, courtesy of its German manufacturer, and gave a gusty sigh. She wiped her damp forehead, grimly conscious that she was late again for work and mentally hurled invective at Bishu, their absent chokra.

'Girlee. Wait! That jungly boy has hopped to the bazaar forgetting Pa's tiffin as usual.' Hermie's mother, Noreen, had buttonholed her, as she was about to leave home. 'And mind, yawl know Pa's a picky eater. So drop this in for him on your way.'

Noreen was pin thin, her frame that of a distant forebear – an English infantryman in the pay of the East India Company, once a mighty London based commercial venture with its own private army. Three hundred and fifty years ago in a battle waged in Bengal mangrove swamps against a local ruler, he'd survived to marry his Indian village sweetheart and stayed on, never to return to the green meadows of home.

To cement allegiance the Company tossed a gold mohur coin to every India born child of an Indian mother and European father and from such beginnings the hybrid AI (AI) community evolved. This was the community to which the Blakes belonged, its distinct genetic footprints leading back to European ancestors in the male line of descent who'd flocked to India to seek fame and fortune – and found love.

AIs were English speaking and Christian; their skin tone ranged from fair to swarthy, hair colour fair to black. They bore European names and adopted the customs and traditions of the British. Most inter-married within the tight-knit, mixed-blood circle; few married Indians.

After a scandal-busting probe the Company, whose trading crusades had led to terror-ridden land-grabs, was ousted by the British government - the Raj – that gained direct rule of India, its jewel in the Crown. Applying divide and rule, it accorded AIs preferential treatment in subordinate jobs on the railways, tea and coffee plantations, mines, hospitals, schools, post and telegraphs, customs, the police and government service.

The Raj turned India into its very own treasure-trove, and the AIs- a buffer engineered by the Raj between itself and its Indian subjects - spurned its ancient Indian heritage yet won scant social acceptance from its colonial masters who were scornful of its mixed-race. There were AIs who yearned to go *home* – to the Britain of which they were not born, did not know, had never before visited, but which they considered, by virtue of tenuous links to long-dead kinsmen, to be their natural homeland.

'Why should I do Bishu's chores, Ma? Tell me that, eh? Hermie's cream skin oval face had sharpened with indignation. 'It's the second time this week and just once more and I'll suffer. Yawl know the Bank's rule – three late days on the trot means half a day's leave docked.' She wondered why Ma tolerated the feckless chokra, who'd come to them bearing a testimonial that read, *without any reservations we can recommend him as a thoroughly useless servant.*

'Just this once, pet.' Light brown eyes peered anxiously at her.

'All right, as a favour to you,' Hermie's resolve faltered and her voice softened affectionately, 'but mind, never again. There can't and won't be a third strike. I'm fed up of making allowances for him.' Her singsong accent, like that of Noreen's and characteristic of AIs, ended on a note of finality.

Noreen, who gave the impression that she might disintegrate in a puff of wind, seized on the grudging assent and hastened to the hot, soot-walled kitchen returning with a large wicker-lidded country basket. Muttering under her breath, Hermie had reluctantly borne it away. She knew what it contained - an aluminium, three tiered, lidded tiffin-carrier containing wholemeal parathas, spicy pork bhoonie, a generous helping of omelette-rice, Ma's spicy cucumber pickle, a portion of banana cream, and a thermos flask of condensed-milk sweetened tea.

Hermie slackened pace along the crowded platform skirting passengers squatting on their bedding rolls, eyeing, with a sharp twinge of envy, an English woman's smart cream linen outfit, and gloomily comparing it with her own bazaar-made floral, mid-calf cotton skirt, the matching pin-tucked blouse and plain brown Bata sandals.

Resentment resurfaced. *Will I ever savour the rich pickings? Everyone's talking about the winds of change and the call for Independence is as loud as the call to Morning Prayer from the minarets. Even President Roosevelt supports the exit of the Raj and then who knows what will happen?*

Beyond a huge hoarding that pictured a woman, hair coiled into a big bun, flashing an impossibly white smile asking coyly, *Did You Maclean Your Teeth Today?* Hermie passed the Ladies Waiting Room and the European Refreshment Room and at last came to the Stationmaster's Office that led to the Guards' Rest Room.

About to push open the door marked NO ADMITTANCE EXCEPT ON DUTY it was snatched from her hand by a sandy haired English subaltern. Hot air poured in and the creaking ceiling fan circled lazily bringing scant relief. Hermie's heart leapt. Ooh, he's handsome, and she smiled encouragingly. The soldier's eyes narrowed, liking the shapely legs and the nice way Hermie's skirt moved but immediately setting her down as one of those chee-chee AIs who hung around outside the Europeans only Devonshire Club. He turned his head away and swiftly transacting his business with the wrinkled chaprassi, swivelled out of the room dashing Hermie's hopes that he'd introduce himself to her.

Hermie eyed his retreating back with some distaste, angry not just with him but also at her own vulnerability. *Just you wait and see. It's not always going to be like this,* she promised herself. *I won't be excluded.* Thrusting the basket at the chaprassi who'd taken it all in with his usual impassivity, she snapped in kitchen Hindi, 'mind you give this to Guard Wilburt, ek dum.'

'Achha'.   He nodded and Hermie, feeling virtuous at a tiresome task duly completed, rewarded him with a smile that had turned many a male head.

Sounds of angry bellowing made her spin round and she dashed outside, the door banging shut behind her. 'Hello? What's the hullabaloo?' What's all this tamasha?' It was the sort of commotion that rendered it somewhat different from the usual station hubbub.

'Hey sonny! Where's your ticket? Come back here, mind.'

Hermie glanced sharply up and down the platform and saw an angrily gesticulating ticket collector and, further along, with startled recognition, the running figure of a skinny brown lad, fifteen year old Frank Gannon, AI like herself, an altar boy at St. Columba's Church. Frayed shirt tail flying, he dodged in and out of the throng of jabbering coolies squabbling over luggage.

She paused, then put on a burst of speed. 'What are you doing here, eh? What's up, Frank?' Sweat trickling down into her collar, she'd caught up with him and seized his arm. 'Mind, you ought to be at school. Go on, what's happened?' She stared at him disquieted. He stank; the spotty, unwashed face, with its hint of black down was more bitter than she'd ever seen, the religious medallion, never worn except at Mass, dangled from a long chain round his neck.

Frank's gaze dropped to his tattered sandals. 'I don't want to talk about it. I can't. Not to you. Not to Bernadette.' Bernadette, his sister, was Hermie's best friend and like her worked at the Ajeemkot Central Bank.

'Come on Frank, I'm like your big sister. Somebody ticked you off and you're running away, right?' Hermie put an arm round his shoulder. He stiffened, saying nothing with such a blank look on his face that she wondered if he'd heard her.

'Pa can't afford to buy me a watch. Pa can't afford anything.' He rubbed his knuckles against red-rimmed eyes then went on in a tight singsong, ' I'm always going to be poor, always going to be a chee-chee, blackey-white, anglo-banglo, off-white, half-caste, Eurasian....'

Hermie winced a little as he woodenly parroted a litany of pejorative names that the British called AIs behind their back. He stared miserably at the ground, his features dissolving into uncontrollable sobs.

'There...Now mind, you listen to me...' she said gently stroking his bowed head, adding reassuringly. 'Things are set to change. The Raj needs us even more than ever. They can't go on without us. We've got the upper hand at last. We'll...' She raised her voice above the shrill whistle and the hissing of steam from the approaching express, her muffled words borne away on the wind.

Frank shook himself free and his face froze. A large black fly was settling on his head. Hermie could hear his quick, hard breathing. Then whipping round, with one swift, frenzied twist he pitched himself onto the track and into the fury of the oncoming train. The driver hadn't a chance. The sickening screech of brakes tore through Hermie. There was a clanging of wheels as the footplate heaved and stilled. A moment's sudden hush.

'Hai Ram!' An appalled gasp rose from those who'd witnessed what had
happened. Instinctively they surged forward only to ebb back with a low moan at
the gruesome sight of mangled body parts scattered along the line.

'No, Frank, no.' When Hermie found her voice at last it was scarcely more than
a whisper, and glancing round she saw that nearly every face bore much the same
sense of shock and horror that she felt. 'Oh my God, no!'

Passengers' heads appeared at the windows demanding to know why the train
had halted so abruptly; whistles blasted as uniformed railway police ran onto the
crowded platform and brandishing brassbound lathis pushed through the
pandemonium. The ashen-faced AI engine driver, sweat pouring from him and
visibly shaken climbed slowly down from the loco, to be immediately engulfed
by officialdom.

Sick to the stomach, Hermie recoiled, stumbling to the nearest bench and sat
down heavily, her thoughts raw with disbelief. She shut her eyes and kept them
shut in a vain effort to erase the memory of the grim scene, swallowing quickly,
the sour taste in her mouth nearly choking her. She was shaking all over, her
heart bumping and knocking against her ribs and staring down at her hands saw
that they were trembling. For several minutes she just sat there utterly numbed, a
great sorrow welling up for Frank and the grey despair that must have prompted
the suicide. Then anger stabbed sharply through her. *Was there to be no bright
future for an AI like her?*

 As a junior clerk in the Ajeemkot Central Bank where the better paid and
managerial jobs were reserved for British staff and domiciled Europeans
(Europeans born, raised or settled in India but lacking Indian forbears), Hermie
knew only too well that the prospect of promotion to a higher grade that she knew
she richly deserved was remote. Like Frank she felt bitter and trapped. *Unlike
Frank I'm made of sterner stuff and I'm going to shut the door on all this,* she
told herself. Steadying herself out of her turmoil she wiped her sweating palms
on her skirt and elbowing her way through the throng, unlocked her bicycle and
pedalled shakily in the direction of the Bank. Her first thought was for
Bernadette. She chewed her lip. *Poor, dear Bernadette. God, what am I going to
say?*

Frank was interred the next day. His last desperate words ...always going to
be a chee-chee reverberated in Hermie's ears as the cheap coffin, a dark trickle of
blood seeping from its cracks, was lowered into the gaping grave, hastily dug

during the night by the light of a kerosene lamp. Unlike Hermie's family, who were nominally Church of England, the Gannons were staunchly Roman Catholic. *Roaming Cutlass* as Bishu put it.

Not for Frank a Requiem Mass, decided the Monsignor, a well-fed English cleric who boasted of patrician connections, conveniently ignoring the fact, Hermie thought angrily, that the Gannons were among the most devout of his parishioners. The emptiness of the committal and the futility of it all brought a deep melancholy to her. Who knows, she thought, what repentance Frank had experienced at the last moment of his life. Was not God all merciful? Nevertheless, Frank had taken his own life, and in the eyes of the Catholic Church   that was a mortal sin undeserving of the Lord's forgiveness and grace, which meant that Frank's remains must be consigned to un-consecrated ground.

Beyond a 1920s grotto that housed a plaster representation of the Crucifixion, the scene echoed her despairing mood - the grey, rock-strewn earth parched and dusty, treeless; the black-clawed scavenging kites soaring in the still, hot air. Hermie fanned herself with a paper fan with as much vigour as decorum permitted. The sombrely dressed Gannons, Frank's parents and siblings, mahogany faced Vincent, a seminarian, and Bernadette, a plump, timid brunette with an olive complexion, dabbing her eyes, huddled together with their rosaries. Sobs punctuated murmured Hail Marys as a grief-stricken, care-worn Mrs Gannon linked arms with her swarthy husband while the thumb -sucking, fairer-skinned six-year-old twins clung to their mother's skirt. In this painful pilgrimage to the graveside the family resemblance was striking in spite of the marked difference in hair and skin tone.

Two of Frank's teachers from the Order of Irish Christian Brothers, the scorching sun beating down on their starched white, emerald-sashed soutanes, and more compassionate than the absent Monsignor, opened their prayer books:

Give him eternal rest, O Lord, and may perpetual light shine on him forever.

'I'm very, very sorry- if there's anything I can do...' Hermie's voice tailed off lamely and she wiped away her tears. She could find so few words of comfort. She turned to Mrs Gannon and put an arm round her hunched shoulders, and stroked Bernadette's back. 'I'm here for you. Yawl know that.'

Bernadette chewed her sodden handkerchief. 'Yes. We knew you'd come.' She didn't need reminding why Hermie's family was absent. Their relationship with the Gannons was strained, despite the long friendship of Hermie and Bernadette through school and the YWCA stenography course since Hermie's father regarded Mr Gannon as a feckless loser who lowered the tone of AIs and fed the stereotype that AI men were good-for-nothing drones.

'You were there for him, in his last moments. You comforted him. And now you're comforting us. Thank you, dear.' Mr Gannon said, passing a hand over his eyes. He seldom had much to say and now seemed on the verge of collapse as he shuffled forward to lay flowers.

'Only wish I could've done more - saved him. Are you all right?' Hermie said in a choked voice, aware that he and Vincent had spent several tormented hours hand-digging Frank's grave.

'Yes.' He squared his shoulders pulling himself together with dignity. 'We have lost our wonderful Frank, but we'll have to manage. And you're away now?'

She hesitated fractionally. 'I have to.' She didn't but that they wanted to be left alone to grieve in private for Frank was plain. Mumbling a few words of commiseration to Vincent and nodding at the Brothers, she consoled Bernadette and Mrs Gannon with hugs and walked dispiritedly through the cemetery, her sandals rustling over the dry, bleached grass to the entrance set between Ionic columns. The poignant image of the crushed Gannons refused to budge.

'Tonga wallah!' There were several thin-ribbed horses with their lethargic drivers waiting outside, smoking foul-smelling beerees between cupped hands. Hermie climbed in. 'Chullo. Number 22 Loco Quarters.' She leaned back and feeling absolutely drained clutched her handbag tightly in her lap.

The tonga wallah pulled up the tongas's faded red canvas hood providing a welcome angle of shade and, with a flick of the whip, the animal broke into a trot its hoofs rhythmically clattering along the dusty tarmac road bordered with huge neem trees. Loco Quarters was on the far side of the town of Ajeemkot, in the Railway Lines, an area where railway employees were housed. There, in a small, semi-detached bungalow, Hermie lived with her parents Wilburt and Noreen, and her older brother, Ashley. As long as she could remember Pa had worked on the Rajputana-Malwa Railways as a conductor-guard and Ashley, seven years older than her, was doing well as a junior loco driver.

As the tonga bowled along, harness bells jingling, Hermie gazed idly about her at the all too familiar scene, her thoughts still dwelling on the funeral and the injustice of the Monsignor who'd denied the Gannons the consoling ritual of a Catholic service, yet hadn't hesitated, not many months earlier, to accord a full-blown Requiem to a certain English major found with his brains blown out, his service revolver in a limp hand.

Her thoughts switched to a certain day a few weeks previously, recalling an incident with no pleasure in some detail.

'No, Hermie, I'm afraid I can't make an exception for you. Y' know club membership is restricted to Europeans only and you're not eligible to play in the inter-club tournament.' Mr Armitage, Hermie's English boss and, as Manager of the Ajeemkot Central Bank, Honorary Treasurer of the Devonshire Club, glanced away from his clerk's pretty face out of the window to where a red-breasted copperpot was hollowing out a branch of a wide leafed tree.

The Club! How these half-castes who had neither the virtues of the East nor the vices of the West all pined in vain to join.

'As a guest, I could,' Hermie who was a keen tennis player reminded him with a sweetness that did not match the sharp defiance of her eyes.

'Correct.' Mr Armitage dropped his hands to his side aware that she was staring with some repulsion at the patches of sweat at his armpits soaking through the cotton shirt. 'But you'd need to be invited,' he added, quite sure she knew of no one who would do. He'd heard Hermie Blake played some classy ground strokes, and young Smith in securities was in need of just such a partner if he was to win the mixed doubles but... no, he couldn't ask her. He wished she wouldn't stare at him in that bold fashion, hoping to shame him into changing his mind. His watery blue eyes swept over her - she was immaculately turned out as usual, and that sensuous mouth - she was a sight for sore eyes all right, in spite of a lick of the tar brush.

'I'm hoping you'll do the honours, sir.' Hermie switched to a stereotypical AI servility she did not feel. 'Besides, the club was only too pleased to rope me into to help with Empire Day.' She couldn't resist the dig. Moreover, Hermie knew the powers of her charms and that it would take just one more visit to the club to ensnare a Brit and put her on track for **home.**

Mr Armitage hesitated, wondering for one wild moment if he could pass her off as 'one of us.' At stake was the honour of the Devonshire, trounced two years running by a team from the Somerset Club, the defeat rendered even more humiliating by the knowledge that the victor was from a mofussil. He closed his eyes momentarily to visions of an amazing comeback and the silver tournament trophy resting once again in its rightful place in the Devonshire. True, Hermie had proved a natural with the kiddies last month on Empire Day when she'd helped organise the egg and spoon and obstacle races, the fancy dress and tea party, and the youngsters sing-along and march past the Union Jack to the rousing, patriotic finale of Rule Britannia and There'll Always Be An England. Beating time with his fountain pen on the leather trimmed blotter, he hummed the words under his breath.

'Sir, that's a yes?'

That voice of hers marked her as an outsider. ' No. Most definitely not and I should be obliged if you would not mention it again. And anyway,' Mr Armitage added lamely 'Empire Day was a commemorative occasion for us all and quite a different kettle of fish. Now, Sharma has prepared an important set of quarterly figures he wants typed up today, so be sure to collect it from his office.'

He unscrewed his pen cap as if to signal that their meeting was at an end, wincing as she swept like a gale out of the room slamming the heavy door behind her.

***Ruddee** pig, Hermie muttered to herself in the safety of the corridor leaning heavily against the wall, resolving never again to volunteer her services to the Devonshire, given that her last effort had signally failed to provide the entrée she craved. She had visions of herself one day, the doyenne of society, when they'd be clamouring for her patronage. Nursing the grievance, she reluctantly made her way to a door marked Deputy Assistant Chief Accountant.*

Mr Sharma, a bespectacled Indian, looked up. 'This is urgent...' he held out a sheaf of papers covered with figures and footnotes in his spidery handwriting.

Hermie slapped them down on the desk. Mr Armitage's refusal still stung. 'I will not work for Indians so long as there's a drop of English blood in me.' Her voice quavered and she turned on her heel.

Mr Sharma rolled his eyes and shrugged. He'd simply ask Mr Armitage to consign it to the typing pool. Willy, nilly it would get done. He'd heard it all before. But it wouldn't be for much longer. Gandhi-ji and Pandit Nehru saw things quite differently. Everyone knows that the present decade has seen the start of serious civil disobedience campaigns, strikes and labour disputes. It is increasingly evident the British can't continue to hold India except at very high cost. Already they've been forced to give ground by according us political and administrative rights. Jai Hind! The sun will soon set on the Empire. Independence is accelerating and then we'll be boss. We'll have the last laugh.

'Watch it, tonga wallah,' Hermie cried. Flung about in the seat, her thoughts boomeranged to the present. The quiet of the cemetery and the orderliness of the Cantonment and the Civil Lines with their broad shady roads and large creamy bungalows set in well-tended gardens, the spire of the Anglican Church of St. George's rising behind it, had unrolled away. They'd passed The Albany, the town's premier hotel that boasted: *Entirely European owned and managed. Spacious bathrooms fitted with bathtubs and a daily supply of fresh produce*, and the commercial centre of the town was beginning to close in.

The piebald slowed to a more leisurely pace as they approached Kingsway, the busy main artery. The featureless exterior of the mighty Britannic Life Assurance Company made her shudder, dwarfing as it did, the equally non-descript Ajeemkot Central Bank. There, but for Frank's funeral, she'd be working alongside Bernadette in the regimented rows of the typing pool, rat-tat- tatting away on a gleaming black Remington Rand typewriter.

From her desk by the window, a spot much coveted that she'd bagged quickly, she had a clear view across the street of Kumar Foto Studio, sandwiched between the New Era Book Depot and Lakshmi Cloth Mart, where, decked out in a hysterical mix of purple and orange, fascia lights flashing, it did a thriving business.

They veered into a narrow ribbon of streets and the familiar smell and colour of the bazaar swept up to her - the spicy, pungent odours, the somewhat cloying scent of perfumed hair oil, the beams of glinting brassware, the many corrugated iron roofed, open-air stalls, the babel of hawkers' cries above the sweet warble of caged mynah birds. Cursing and shouting, the tonga wallah angled his way through, skirting Hermie's favourite bangle stall which today held no charms for her, eventually pulling up outside the Blakes' small, flat-roofed, semi-detached bungalow.

Hermie escaped out of the fierce sunlight through a neat, small garden and up a shallow flight of steps to the deep, front verandah, involuntarily reaching out to touch the horse-shoe hanging from a rusty nail on the oiled door-frame. She felt drenched; her armpits damp, the cotton dress clinging limply to her back. Was it, she thought irritably, too much to expect that Bishu had remembered to lower and water the tatties? She stepped inside. It was not! The air was cool, the welcome shade and fragrant scent of dampened cuscus grass coming up thickly and mixed with lavender, and she was slightly cheered by his apparent spurt of initiative.

'Bishu, char leeow!' Hermie shouted for a cup of tea in kitchen Hindi, banging the fly-mesh screen door behind her. There was no answer. He was nowhere to be seen, so she supposed she would have to put on the kettle herself, but she could nurse her thoughts, still chained to the grisly memories of yesterday, in secret.

Tossing her topi onto the heavy, black wood hat-stand, she slipped off her sandals, and went into the stone-floored bathroom. She stripped off, turned on the tap and filling the metal bucket, poured water over herself with a long handled brass ladle, gasping slightly as the first cold drops hit scorching skin.

Bishu was singing to himself on the back verandah, sliding nasally up and down the scale, as he lit a charcoal fire under the hamaam that supplied the hot water for their nightly baths. Pa must have had a go at him she thought with some satisfaction for he seems to have turned over a new leaf.

Altogether much refreshed, Hermie stretched out on the bed resolutely shutting her mind against recent raw events. She supposed she must have dozed off, for when she opened her eyes Noreen was standing at the foot of the bed in a patchwork apron she'd made herself from pieces of left- over cotton.

'Hermie, Hermie!' Noreen's shrill tones hid solicitous concern. She shook her daughter.

'Are you all right, **girlee?** You've been asleep for far too long. Get up, rouse yourself now, otherwise who knows what'll become of you.' Ma held the theory that excessive sleep shortened one's life. 'And tell me WHO was there?'

Grumbling, Hermie sat up in a wisp of embroidered lawn, a creation of Ma Webb, a local AI seamstress. 'It was dreadful. I hope I never have to endure that again. Ma Gannon was beside herself. And as for Bernadette, you know she's been half-thinking of joining a convent and this might just push her over the brink, right.'

'Oh no! Mrs Gannon has already sacrificed one child to the Church. Look, don't you go telling your Pa, but when he goes out on his next shift, I'll slip over to the Gannons with some of my coconut cake. I can't imagine what I'd have done had it been you.' She shivered. 'But I mustn't think like that. Oh no, no, no. It's only tempting fate.'

'Well, not my fate,' Hermie said forcefully, 'far from it. I'm nothing like Frank.'

'But I fear for you, dear. You've never stopped moaning about this and that since you went to work in the Bank. Nothing seems to your liking – so different when you were at school.'

Hermie considered for a moment. Ma was right. She'd enjoyed the routine of school days high up in the Nilgiris. Railway and service personnel families like the Blakes were frequently transferred the length and breadth of India, so offspring were deposited in boarding schools for an uninterrupted education from March to December.

From the age of seven to sixteen, Hermie was absent from home, although Ma journeyed to visit her every eight weeks combining it with a visit to her hospitable brother Bruce, Hermie's gruff but kindly uncle, who lived in Ooty, not from the school. It was there, in an Inter- Schools Athletics Competition, that she'd met Bernadette, a charity pupil at a Catholic run boarding school. Yet even among AIs discrimination flourished. Hermie shared Bernadette's pain on hearing that Ma Gannon, having taken her to the school of first choice, was turned away and advised to try elsewhere as her daughter's skin tone was considered too dark.

'Then I had something to look forward to, or thought I did. It's all turned out dreary and disappointing now,' Hermie said.

Noreen blinked and wisely bit back a retort. It didn't do to row with **girlee,** who had a mouth on her, least of all in this black mood of hers. She walked to the door, 'Don't you be long now.'

'I'll join you when I'm ready.' Hermie said tartly, stifling a yawn. She slid her feet to the floor, and then going to the bathroom dashed cold water over her face, and changed into a sleeveless cotton blouse and Madras check skirt. As she applied a slick of Coty's rose-pink lipstick to her full mouth she subjected her face to a critical appraisal and smiled to herself as she deemed it perfect.

Sunlight poured into the short narrow passage that led to the parlour - a sitting cum dining room. Hermie hoped against hope that Pa and Ashley wouldn't be home to tea since their clashes had become more frequent and bitter. They were. Pausing momentarily at the door, with a twirl of her skirt, she crossed the room to the circular teakwood dining table, sliding into her usual place opposite her brother.

Noreen bustled in and out of the kitchen, driving herself like a galley slave for her family and berating Bishu. Wilburt, barrel-chested, a half-smoked cigarette between stubby fingers and buried behind a newspaper grunted an acknowledgment. Ashley and his fiancée Iris Quinn, a member of their AI and a nurse at the Civil Hospital, were dressed as though they were going out - he in that muddy brown suit that matched his skin tone offset by a blue shirt and striped Railways tie, she in that livid bottle green dress that did nothing for her weak-tea complexion - and deep in some soul searching conversation, probably the price of mutton.   Their heads came up when they saw her and Iris smiled a greeting her pale brown eyes widening speculatively at Hermie's crisp, obviously new skirt and the cream leather belt that emphasised the wasp waist.

'Splashing the cash again?' Ashley shot her a condemnatory glance but then that was nothing new.

'What's that to you? I can do **what** I like, **when** I like, with **my** money.'

Iris said quickly, seeking to defuse the atmosphere. 'Listen Hermie. Saving never hurts. Changes are afoot. These Indians have Home Rule now. Who knows where this is leading, how it'll all end. I've seen what's going on at the hospital. More Indian doctors and Indian staff being appointed to senior positions, and Uncle in Customs in Bombay has noticed the changes there, too. God knows what those Congress Party firebrands will do to next. Will there be jobs for us? That's what so worrying.' She ran her tongue over her lips. 'You can't just bury the facts like a dead cat. Whether we like it or not, we'll all be affected by these changes - for better or for worse. You may not think so now, but you'll thank me when you've saved the down payment on a passage *home.*'

It was the longest speech Hermie had ever known Iris to make and it made good sense but she'd be the last to admit as much. She decided to ignore her. 'I'll just have some char.' Hermie flicked crumbs from the striped tablecloth and shook her head as Noreen pushed over a plate of homemade cake and guava jelly sandwiches.

'But **girlee,** everything's your favourite and cooked specially for you, especially for today, especially after what's happened.' Noreen sounded mortally insulted. 'Take a bite, pet and keep your strength up. Don't you go wasting away. That won't bring him back.' Frowning slightly, she re-adjusted the black Kirby-grip in her lank, mousy hair.

In things such as this Hermie had long since discovered the futility of protest. She lifted a shoulder and reached across for a slice of orange pound cake. 'Dreamy.' She licked her fingers. 'No one makes it quite like you, Ma.'

Ma glowed at the compliment. She was still on her feet, frenziedly fussing round them without regard to the heat.   Hermie's gaze moved about the room and the clutter brought her up short. Over-furnished, it was as if she was seeing it for the first time. The outsize shiny-black glass fronted showcase in one corner, adorned with numerous family photographs marking all stages of family life, was crammed with lovingly polished silver-plated trophies of Pa's hockey playing youth, Ma's collection of china dogs and miniature liquor bottles. There was a worn, fringed carpet. A couple of small brass teapoys with ebony barley-twist legs stood on either side of the black, cane-backed sofa.

Above it, on the plain-whitewashed wall, the King and Emperor of India George V1, and the Queen Empress with their two daughters, the Princesses Elizabeth and Margaret, smiled benignly from a framed photograph. Facing this, below the stuffed head of a fox, was a colour print, cut from last year's calendar, of Constable's *The Haywain*, its composition deeply evocative of 1820s English rural life during harvest time. Her eyes moved to the window and beyond it she could just see the small square of coarse grass now dry as tinder, edged with trees drooping in the sun and the heat-stricken remains of a once colourful herbaceous border.

Wilburt threw down the paper and reached for a sandwich. 'Mind, that boy would never have amounted to anything.' From what he considered his elevated position on the Railways, Wilburt Blake looked down on the more humble Gannons. Hermie saw him glance sideways at her and she knew he couldn't just leave it alone. 'Why you went to his funeral beats me.' Like Frank, he had a clipped accent, the tone strident and accusatory. A sallow man, with arms like legs of mutton, he'd lumbered over to fill the comfiest easy chair by the open window, a fly swat at the ready.

An unnecessary item if ever there is one, Hermie thought wearily, her eyes turning to the sponge steeped in lavender oil lying on the window ledge, a household tip for repelling flies, gleaned from Aunty Al.

His tortoise-black eyes came back to her. 'It's a mercy our Ashley wasn't the duty driver yesterday. That poor chap's confined to bed with shock, and the miserable prospect of an enquiry. Yawl know very well Frank was buddhu, a complete dunderhead, a chip off that china pombula Pa of his.' He belched loudly, blind to the misery that had driven Frank to take his own life.

Hermie's mouth tightened and she reached for a cigarette, ignoring Iris' frown for in her book only loose women smoked. 'Your callous indifference to the misery of others is sickening', she cried. 'You've never questioned your own way of life - '

'No reason to,' Wilburt retorted.

'And Ashley's no better.' She could cheerfully have slit Pa's throat. 'Well, yawl ought to. I always have and will.'

'Show some respect for your elders and betters.' Iris jumped up. 'I don't want to hear anymore of your tirade. Come on, Ashley. Let's leave her to her own devices.'

'He wanted to better himself. What's wrong with that? The trouble was he'd no idea how to go about it,' Hermie continued more quietly through a curl of smoke. She poured herself another cup of tea, which tasted dark and very strong. Not that Ma was generous with the tea leaves but she knew the economical trick that adding a spoonful of sugar to the pot opened up the leaves, and drew out the flavour. Hermie replaced the padded tea cosy, decorated with a felt cut out of an English country cottage surrounded by pink rambling roses, a parting gift to Noreen from a fellow AI who'd recently sailed *home.*

Ashley, a younger version of Wilburt, gave a quelling snort. He jerked his head at Iris who subsided into the chair. 'What's it to you?' He spoke rapidly in the same singsong tones. 'Right, the Gannons are hard up, but Frank had his life ahead of him, right? He was OK – ready to leave school - the Brothers had found him a job as a mechanic, right. He could've made what he chose of himself, right?' He straightened his tie with nicotine-stained fingers and smoothed his brilliantined dark hair. 'Now look at me...' He had a highly developed sense of his own merit.

'I am looking,' Hermie held the cup with her pinky finger crooked, a mark of gentility she'd been led to believe, 'and I don't like what I see.'

'Hermione!' Noreen's seldom-used long form of the name signalled a reproof.

Hermie refused to feel guilty and briefly closed her eyes. She felt only sorrow for Noreen who she saw as an ineffectual, downtrodden woman, happy to be dominated first by her husband and now by her son, with the same creamy colouring as that of her daughter.

'Can't yawl even sit down to a meal without picking a quarrel? I go to such trouble to make things nice and yawl do nothing but snipe, snipe, snipe like pi-dogs. Now mind, don't you go talking to your brother like that. What has got into you lately, eh? Show some respect.' Noreen's lower lip began to tremble.

'Respect must be earned.' Hermie drew a sharp breath and said shakily, 'yawl ganging up on me. Yawl are so smug and self satisfied. When will yawl realise that we AIs mean nothing to the Brits? All right, we speak English, we go to

English churches, but we don't bond with them. We're in bondage to them, and they sneer at us, calling us blackey-whites and country born behind our backs.' She threw in a firecracker. 'Yawl know Gidney has warned us the Brits will hang us out to dry'. As Leader of the All India AI Association, AIs held Sir Henry Gidney in high regard. Her pain at the Club's rejection was like a dagger in her heart. 'Don't yawl want something different, something better?'

Somewhere off in the trees, bulbuls twittered breaking the sudden vacuum of silence. Ashley pushed back his chair, looking the pugilist he was - the All-India Inter Railway light heavyweight champion. 'And I suppose you do?' His tone was nasty. 'Sis, this is as much our country as it is these Indians and Brits. Remember that. Talking like this, you must have fallen out with that Mervyn of yours, right. It's time you settled down and got married, like Iris and me.' He shot a loving glance at his fiancée, a witness to yet another Blake family spat. 'That'll keep you out of devilry.'

Hermie said violently. 'Don't yawl tell me how to run my life.' She resented being reminded of Mervyn to whom she'd decided to show the door. 'Yawl won't get me marrying him.'

They stared transfixed. 'If yawl think I'm going to scrape along as the wife of an AI telegraphs clerk with a brood of kids, yawl got another think coming.'

This was tantamount to heresy. 'No girl of mine will talk like that,' Wilburt bellowed. 'Shut your mouth or you'll get a good tight slap.'

Ashley picked up Pa's theme. 'Yes, you've become a **bloodee** snob. What's wrong with us AIs, then?' We've got good jobs, right. We're doing the things that make this country tick, right. We're called the wheels, the cranks, the levers. We're valued. Look at my Iris, right?' He squeezed her hand, his gaze full of worship. 'What nobler work is there than nursing, eh? A job that no Hindu lets his wife, daughter or sister do because of that rigid caste system of theirs and distaste of bodily functions.'

Iris's sweet face broke into a serene smile. *Miss Mealy-mouth*, Hermie thought. 'It's nice to know I'm appreciated. I know I do an important job. I agree with you, dear. Hermie must learn to be content with what she's got and not cry for the moon.'

Iris lived with her parents, who were Wardens of Bishop Forrester's Home. This was an orphanage, one of several of the same name located in various places throughout India, founded by an English cleric, Bishop Forrester, at the turn of the century to care for orphaned and illegitimate AI children.

'Yes, the jobs the Brits won't do. I want something else. I want...' If she couldn't beat them, she must join them; it was a thought that had recently begun to echo loudly in Hermie's heart.

'...To be a Memsahib?' Ashley lashed out with a malicious laugh. 'Ma, it's all those trashy magazines she's forever poring over. *The Lady, Homes and Gardens,* right? They're responsible for all these cock-eyed notions and airs and graces of hers.' As a railwayman used by his British superiors to move men, materials and supplies across the vast sub-continent, he was less sensitive than his sister to the slights of the ruling class. 'And where do you think that'll land you, eh?' Pointing out other people's failings was a duty he rarely shirked.

Hermie felt cornered but checked the impulse to empty the teapot over him, pushing the several thin gold bangles up her arm with a savage movement, and struck out. 'Anywhere but Ajeemkot. You're an insensitive prig, Ashley.' She leaned her elbows on the table. 'You've planned your life just like one of your blooming railway journeys, no deviations, no unscheduled halts.' This time it had gone too far. She couldn't bear it any longer. No one understood her. Or wanted to.

Their scowling eyes met across a vase of marigolds and she knew that things could never be the same. She didn't want to spend another moment with her boorish father and brother. 'I'm getting out of here. I'm getting out of Ajeemkot.' She sprang from her chair, her fists tight balls.

'Girlee!' Noreen stared blankly at her for a moment or two then her face crumpled and tears rolled down her cheeks. **'Girlee,** my baby, you mustn't go away.' Hermie was the apple of her eye.

Wilburt lumbered over to his wife and put a clumsy arm round her thin shoulders, his eyes flickering between his son and daughter, as he sucked air noisily into his nose.

'Just yawl try and stop me,' Hermie said shakily and fled out of the parlour, brushing through the bead-strung curtain, hearing it rattle and click behind her, her nerves stretched to snapping point. She slammed the bedroom door and bolted it, half-comforted by the familiar smells of scent, face cream and powder. Flopping into the cane bedside chair, she thought unhappily of being condemned forever to scraping along on the Bank's pittance, of the non-fast, Indian cotton dresses run up by the Muslim durzee, so different from the creations featured in imported women's magazines. Of the way AIs were treated by their British masters who pretended to hobnob with them yet privately despised their mixed ethnicity and isolated them from their social lives.

It mustn't go on. Hermie knew she possessed looks and charm and that she could employ that to the best advantage was something she knew she must do. But as to how was rather more difficult. The rows with Pa and Ashley had been constant since she'd begun to earn her living after leaving school and joining the six months Pitman's shorthand and typing course run by the local Y.W.C.A. Almighty rows over her coming home in the small hours, rows when she was found canoodling with Mervyn on the settee. Her views were ignored by the men folk; her actions minutely criticised and analysed. The endless whys and wherefores, the endless post-mortems. Only Ma, dear Ma, with long practice understood and was there to soothe and appease. But Ma was of the patience is a virtue and everything comes to she who waits school of thought.

She heard a soft step. 'Pet... Come on **girlee,** open up now. Forgive and forget...' Noreen's plaintive tones became shriller as she rattled the doorknob and knocked, first a light tap, then several thumps each getting progressively louder.

'LEAVE ME ALONE. '

Ma seemed about to say something else but changed her mind for there was the sound of retreating footsteps. Hermie remained where she was staring blankly out of the window until she'd reckoned the Blakes had gone out. Ashley and Iris, both avid picture-goers, to the flicks at The Rivoli - *where coolness adds to comfort* - to see *Lost Horizon* directed by Frank Capra and starring handsome Ronald Coleman. Released in the USA in 1937 it was rumoured that it had so utterly beguiled President Roosevelt that he'd considered naming his Maryland retreat after the legendary land of Shangri-La it portrayed.

Hermie and Bernadette, equally star struck, had laughed themselves silly at Carol Lombard's comical antics in *Nothing Sacred.* She knew Ma wouldn't miss her weekly canasta and mahjong evening with her cronies for anything and Pa was probably at the Inster (as the Railway Institute, the hub of AI social life from which Indians were excluded, was familiarly termed) sighing contentedly into his second pint of Murree beer as he marked his housey card. The bungalow was quiet save for faint sounds from the kitchen where Bishu was scouring pans with cold coal-ash.

I can't go on like this. I'll go mad. Hermie was past waiting. Her one desire was to go - to get right away. *I'm all alone in this.* Bernadette, placid and contented with her lot was bewildered by Hermie's chafing at the bit.

Now as never before, Hermie felt she couldn't share her dreams with Bernadette, bereaved as she was. Suddenly she remembered Al Caston - universally known as Aunty Al - whom Noreen and she had met at a neighbour's tea party the previous year. After a swift, friendly clash of wills with Hermie, Aunty Al seemed to have taken to her, perhaps seeing in her slender figure and lively spirit, Noreen supposed, something of her own beloved daughter, a lovely girl it was said, and her only child, who'd succumbed to TB at much the same age.

Aunty Al was a legend. Every AI and beyond knew the stout, tiny woman, or, Hermie felt, ought to. Married to Cedric Caston, six years her junior, who she publicly addressed as Mr Caston, he was her third husband, the previous two having died from tick fever. Hermie remembered her as an olive skinned woman with bright brown eyes in, she supposed her late forties, with an all-consuming interest in people, and a passion for clothes and hats. She was always smartly dressed, not a pin out of place. Despite personal tragedies, her strong Catholic faith never faltered; she was pillar of the Delhi AIs and choir mistress, possessing the celestial voice of an operatic soprano, who brooked no slacking at the Cathedral of the Sacred Heart.

Aunty Al took in lodgers. Not just anybody, she was quick to tell the Blakes. Oh no, she was more selective than that, for her choice was quirky and uncoloured by mercenary considerations. It was more of a hobby for she didn't really need the money. That she made from breeding her cats whose pedigreed mates she chose with the same level of eccentricity as her choice of lodgers. Her sole criterion was like at first sight. If one failed this test one was unlikely to be favoured, no matter what the inducements.

Hermie laid plans, did sums, then crossing the passage to the parlour that still seemed to echo with the tensions of the day rummaged in the old walnut wood roll-top desk and taking up a pen wrote to Aunty Al. She'd surely be sympathetic. By the time Hermie had sealed the envelope and stuck on the stamp that bore the head of the King, the violent intentions she'd felt towards the world in general and Pa and Ashley in particular had seeped away, replaced by elation at her bold move. Freedom beckoned!

CHAPTER 2

'What's this about, **girlee?'** Noreen grimaced slightly, brandishing Aunty Al's letter welcoming them to Delhi. 'Bishu!' The sound reached the kitchen. 'Fetch a tonga, we're going out.'

Yes! Hermie's heart gave a joyful leap. Noreen frowned and tapped the envelope with a thin finger. 'Yawl know your uncle Bruce in Ooty is expecting us.' That he was a bachelor with a nest egg from teaching and a soft spot for Ashley and Hermie was not lost on the Blakes. 'But let me see... I suppose there's no reason why you and Bernadette shouldn't go. You'd be company for each other, and after what she's suffered I'm sure she could do with a break.'

This was definitely not what Hermie had in mind, fond though she was of Bernadette. 'Bernadette?' she said on a high note. 'Just where does she fit in?'

'You know - ' Ma began mildly.

'This,' said Hermie sharply, 'is what I know and that is, my youth's slipping away. I want to go ALONE. SOLO.' She'd hoped that three months away would enable her to find her feet although she'd not clearly identified what she'd do. The future was still an agreeable haze but one in which she featured as the most gracious of players. 'There'll be some paid leave' she fudged, hoping Noreen wouldn't probe, 'and some unpaid. I persuaded boss to let me borrow from next year's entitlement and he has promised to keep my job open for me, as I'm a good worker.' This was scarcely even a half-truth, for Mr Armitage had merely reluctantly said he'd look into the possibility of it but could give no guarantees.

Ma mopped her neck and gave Hermie a searching glance.

'Please.' Hermie switched to the sweet reason tack. 'Aunty Al will look after me so yawl have nothing to worry about.'

A tonga pulled up and it creaked fit to bust as they climbed in, Ma shouting about domestic chores to Bishu. 'And make sure boxwallah leaves a dozen curry puffs.' Bishu nodded woodenly but plainly had no intention of doing anything, Hermie thought irritably. With the two ladies away, he'd chat and smoke beerees with his equally idle cronies on the back verandah.

Noreen glanced skywards. 'Looks as if the monsoon's about to break.' Bloated iron-grey clouds had been gathering for the past few days. 'Three months absence and what do you mean unpaid?' The significance of Hermie's remarks suddenly registered.

'I've been saving hard.'

Ma gave a little laugh. 'You're all for squandering Miss Hermione Delicia Blake, but you're a proper little miser when it comes to anyone else. Now don't you take this as a foregone conclusion as you know I'll have to check with your Pa.'

Seeing the advantage slipping away from her, Hermie added quickly, 'How can I expect to meet a suitable boy if I'm always twinned with Bernadette? She's so serious-minded and holy they're scared off.' She knew she was on to a winner here as Noreen, although friendly with Ma Webb, privately considered her daughter a cut above Mervyn Webb.

Lantern-jawed, twenty-three year old Mervyn worked in Posts & Telegraphs. Of medium height and slim build with jutting cheekbones in an oak brown face, she'd met him when she was crowned Inster Queen of the May a year earlier. Sunny natured with a singular lack of ambition, his energy was focused on billiards and carrom rather than on bettering himself. They'd been to the flicks, the Saturday night jam sessions at the Inster, listened to Glenn Miller records on the gramophone, and much else besides, even Mervyn unbuttoning her blouse - Ma would've had a fit had she known - and it was taken for granted they'd wed.

Noreen's expression became thoughtful and meeting Hermie's eyes she smiled and briskly placed her doubts, with the letter, in her pocket. 'Mind you, they say Aunty Al has a wide circle of friends...' She broke off to scream at the tonga wallah. 'For God's sake man, slow down! Are you trying to murder us? Now **girlee,** what's that they say about Al?'

Aunty Al had friends – even better, **VALUABLE CONNECTIONS**, as she herself put it - in every corner of India. There was quite literally no one in the AI or beyond that she didn't know or make it her business to. From the hard up Gannons, in their three noisy, hot rooms in the bazaar, to those well- to- do Powleys and Reids who occupied those big bungalows crouched round St George's, Aunty Al knew them all.

'Leave your Pa to me.' Confident that **girlee** would find someone in the AI, notches above Mervyn, through Aunty Al's select introductions, she was already nursing happy visions of Hermie returning home on the arm of a nice young AI professional - one of the Powley boys, perhaps, both graduates with first class degrees and now employed in Delhi. They were a catch having done very well and joined the elite Indian Civil Service. The heaven-born, as its chosen were called. Or there was Dr Reid's only boy, a promising lawyer, recently London returned, having been called to the bar of Middle Temple. Noreen was deaf to the sound of the furious ironing of frocks that their prospects had generated with AI girls of marriageable age.

Sympathetic to her daughter's aspirations, Noreen was aware that Ajeemkot was, admittedly, somewhat of a backwater and besides, and she'd be the first to acknowledge this, the Blakes didn't move in the right circles. Nevertheless, in Delhi **girlee** would have every opportunity, and she knew her Hermie well enough to know that she'd seize it. So, while the prospect of the next few months without her was grim, she wouldn't dwell on it. Hermie would fulfil her own long-buried dreams and the good marriage Noreen envisioned for her daughter was within grasp.

'Just you leave your Pa to me,' Noreen repeated confidently. She knew how to cut Wilburt some slack when angling for favours. She conveniently overlooked her last bruising encounter with Mrs Powley when the latter had monologued on about her own well-settled family and her equally (well, almost) well -settled friends in Ajeemkot, Cal, Jubbulpore, Puri, Poona and Meerut and much else besides. She'd made it plain to Noreen and Hermie by her continual asides to her canteen of sterling silver cutlery, her Edinburgh crystal decanters, the brand new imported saloon car and the squadron of servants in the large Ajeemkot bungalow that she considered the Powleys vastly superior to the Blakes (indeed how could they even be mentioned in the same breath?).

And while Hermie, for the sake of a good marriage, might have been prepared to put up with her sons Winston and Marcel, who even Bernadette had found baoth putani – snooty, she'd not been prepared to toady to Ma Powley whose thin-lipped face she'd dutifully kissed and who was, anyway, thought Hermie derisively, and drawing comfort from it, as black as beetle resin.

It was Delhi or bust and Hermie's heart sang.

'Tonga wallah, pull over there.' They alighted outside Lakshmi Cloth Mart renowned for the quality and variety of its fabrics. Ma was a great believer in making an early start on their Christmas finery, so as to avoid being caught short by a run on the durzee's services, as had happened last year when she and Hermie had found themselves with nothing new to wear. It had been a drama of some proportions.

It was cool inside and, to Hermie's delight, for it was a popular rendezvous for the dress conscious of Ajeemkot, they were the only customers and would be assured of the salesman's undivided attention. Behind polished wooden counters lay deep shelves stacked high with the stuff of dreams - bolts of soft velvet, rustling taffeta, rich brocade, filmy French chiffon, the metallic sheen of organza, every known material in rivers of colour.

'Can I help you?' A middle aged Indian salesman with black brilliantined hair and an inch tape round his neck moved slowly towards them immediately identifying them as chatakaran.

'We'd like to see some of your slub silk,' Hermie said cheerfully.

'Any special colour?'

Hermie turned to Ma and grinned, 'Oh, royal blue for me, and what's your fancy, Ma?'

Noreen pondered for a moment. 'The shell pink... or is that too youthful?' she dithered, all set to change her mind if Hermie so much as hinted. She relied heavily on her daughter's innate dress sense.

'Get on with you. You're not past it, yet. Pink it is now and purple when you're a ripe old age.'

The man nodded, steadied a stepladder and was reaching up for their selection when a booming voiced Englishman and his blancmange faced wife entered. Taking one look at them over his shoulder, the salesman promptly hopped down and turning his back on the Blakes glided over to the newcomers with the speed of an ice skater.

'Hold it!' Hermie bleated. 'What do you think you're doing? We aren't finished yet.'

The salesman was deaf to her pleas and Hermie, incensed, could hear and see him fawning over his English customers with much unctuous sahib-ing and memsahib-ing.

'This won't do. Now look here.' Hermie raised her voice rapping coral fingernails on the counter. Her bangles jangled and the voices across the room momentarily stopped. Customers and salesman stared sharply across. Then, after a charged silence, resumed the task in hand.

Thus snubbed, she'd have marched across to challenge them had it not been for Noreen's restraining hand.   'It's all right, dear,' Noreen whispered weakly. 'We aren't in a hurry. We can wait.'

Fuming Hermie drove her fists down into her pockets, staring pointedly at her wristwatch and it was not until nearly forty minutes later, after the salesman had shown the couple out and dealt with another British customer that he sauntered back.

'At your service.'

'And about time. And if it's not too much to ask.' Hermie said in a voice shaking with rage.

He gave a hugely unapologetic shrug and said something quickly under his breath in Hindi, which she didn't catch but judging from his expression was most probably impudent backchat.

It was galling but the salesman knew only too well as did they that it was the British who had the financial muscle, even though the latter's purchases on this occasion were modest.

'Mission accomplished!' Noreen said gleefully as they found themselves on the pavement, their arms full of brown paper parcels tied round with twine, its future use already earmarked since she possessed a highly developed sense of economy. They headed to *Giuseppe's* - a coffee shop run by a moustachioed Italian – whose sundaes and milk shakes played havoc with a girl's figure - but who cared? 'Isn't it nice to have something new? I'll send for durzee next week and ask him to bring his new pattern book. He'll need to re-measure me, since I think I've lost a bit.' She enjoyed her chats in kitchen Hindi with the Muslim tailor, a fount of local gossip, who'd sit on the back verandah and run up new outfits on his treadle Singer sewing machine.

Their gaze roamed over the menu that they knew by heart. *Comments on our service are welcome and will be conveyed to staff. Complaints will be investigated and a remedy sought.*

'Don't work so hard for us, Ma,' Hermie said, still very piqued, 'or you'll fade away.' She dug a spoon into her rich *Rocky Mountain*. 'That Bishu's the one who should be jumping through hoops.'

'Yes, yes.' Noreen hastily changed the subject and concentrated on demolishing the *Coupe Jacque*. The Blakes lived modestly and Bishu was jungly for the very reason that they could ill afford anyone better. 'Oh, and we need to order more of that Ayurvedic ointment for Ashley. It's already done wonders for him.'

Hermie laughed at the memory of it. 'And for Mervyn. Not that either's a Cary Grant but still... I've reminded Bishu to fetch it from the bazaar and drummed it into him that he must personally witness the paste is freshly prepared by the hakim with the best ground black peppercorns, tamarind leaves and sesame oil. Not some rubbish that's been gathering dust on a shelf for weeks that the old rogue wants to palm off on us.'

A few days earlier Noreen and Hermie had returned from a fruitful evening of planchette with friends, having communed pleasantly with several long-dead relatives, to find Mervyn and Ashley slumped round the dining table somewhat the worse for wear.

'What's happened?' Noreen cried. 'I thought yawl had gone to the Inster to play billiards.'

'We did,' they chorused, raising their heads.

Hermie screamed. 'Just look! Yawl have been in the wars. And it's not a war of words.'

They were black and blue, their eyes half-closed, and Mervyn, sporting a torn shirt and somewhat more battle-scarred than Ashley, was trying unsuccessfully to staunch a bleeding nose.

'We were minding our own business sis, having a beer when, lo and behold, these rowdy tommies storm in.'

'Nothing wrong with that,' Hermie said cheerfully wishing she'd been there for Mervyn hadn't exactly inspired real passion. She'd cheerfully have deployed her charms on a British soldier and the prospect of *home* would be just that much closer.

Mervyn's voice was muffled, a handkerchief pressed to his face. 'Nothing wrong! There's plenty **bloodee** wrong! Gate crashing private premises and swinging the lead with our girls.' Jealousy had got the better of the young AIs.

'So we closed ranks and pitched into them,' Ashley said with grim satisfaction. 'We squared up to them good and proper. I floored one limey with a lightning left upper cut and we bashed the hell out of the others and sent them crawling back to barracks. It was quite a dogfight, man. They won't try it on again.'

'Yawl ought to have fetched the police instead of taking the law into your own hands,' Noreen said apprehensively, wondering if the bar brawl would have disciplinary repercussions for Ashley.

'What **bloodee** rot!' Ashley was belligerent. 'They had it coming to them, thinking they can sniff round our girls.' He groaned. 'God, I feel lousy. Sis, make us some char.'

Our girls were only too happy making eyes at the tommies who seemed always to possess deep pockets unlike Ashley, Mervyn and their buddies.

***

Soup simmered away in a thick-bottomed, handle-less pan over a charcoal fire, ready to be served when Wilburt ended his shift. Noreen heard heavy footsteps on the verandah and a door banged. Wilburt was washing away the grime of the day. Then he came into the parlour, saw her and grunted a greeting.

'Hello dear,' Noreen said cheerfully and shouted instructions to Bishu. Her pretty face was flushed, her tip-tilted nose shiny from her day in the kitchen demonstrating the mysteries of baking a sponge cake to Bishu who'd proved surprisingly receptive. She ladled out a generous helping of velvet soup, a nutritious blend of raw eggs and tapioca that Wilburt was partial to even in hot weather.

He took a spoonful and there was another grunt that she knew signalled a sign of appreciation, so she decided to take up where she had left off the previous day, when he'd proved remarkably difficult to budge.

'Hermie's capable of anything if we don't let her go,' Noreen said with soft persistence.

'Rubbish,' Wilburt said, helping himself to a hot chappati. 'As far as you're concerned she can do no wrong. Three months absence from work is three months too long. The devil has work for idle hands.' He added unexpectedly, 'You've gone and done something to your hair.'

'Do you like it?' She'd had it cut and permed and soft curls framed her face.

He nodded. 'Like when we first met. Takes me back to the Noreen I courted.' He reached out and patted her hand. They ate in companionable silence and the aroma of coriander wafted through the air as Bishu served the main course.

'I wouldn't want to be responsible for the consequences...one can't be sure what she might do...' Noreen gave her husband a measuring glance. 'We can't risk another Frank. And she maintains her youth's slipping away.'

Wilburt gave a hollow laugh and helped himself to a golden fillet of masala - fried fish. 'Dear, she's a drama queen who winds you round her little finger and doesn't spare a thought for us. But I know her little tricks. Now, don't think I haven't considered long and hard.' He popped some ghee-fried wedges of potato into his mouth. 'Right, if it's not Mervyn she wants and seeing the way he behaved with those tommies, I'm bound to say he's proved a disappointment, like that boozard Pa of his, then shouldn't we steer her in the direction of that teacher training college in Poona – St Mary's, isn't it? That'll put her on the right track to a rosy future.'

Noreen's head jerked up. *This isn't something my Wilburt is capable of devising on his own. I reckon he and his cronies have dreamed it up.* She could just see them huddled together over glasses of rum and ice at the Inster.

'And I think we can just afford it now that the policy we took out when we married has matured.'

'I thought that was earmarked for her wedding.'

Wilburt sighed. 'Well, that doesn't look at all likely right now seeing (a) how high she's set her sights, and (b) what a surly little devil she's become. Maybe it would be better spent on furthering her education, and after that she'll be able to fund her own big ambitions.'

Noreen was nonplussed. She knew **girlee** well enough to know that she wouldn't care for the plane the conversation had shifted to. Earning her living as a teacher or anything else for that matter was not something Hermie envisaged as a long-term goal. She wanted the greatest gain for the least effort. And teaching was not that.   Nevertheless, Noreen saw her chance and took it. 'That's an excellent idea, dear. Why didn't I think of it? I'm sure **girlee** will jump at it. She's always flourished away from home. Remember the good grades she achieved in the school-leaving certificate? And Al knows the Principal of St Mary's and could pull strings.'

'Eh?' Wilburt patted Noreen's hand and they smiled at each other in silent acknowledgment of a united front. 'And maybe Al could wangle a reduction in the fees.' His voice suddenly roughened and he pushed back the chair. 'I'm going to give our Hermie a hisaab book so she can keep track of her spending. But mind you tell Al to keep a sharp eye on the cheeky monkey. Yet...'

'Something troubling you, dear...?' She noticed a sudden droop to his shoulders.

'I'm worried about Hermie with all these airs and graces - turning her nose up at us.' He added a little resentfully, 'it seems we aren't good enough for her. That our values aren't hers. That she feels she doesn't belong here. Where did she get that sharp tongue? Not from you, dear. How's she going to keep a marriage together? Eh? Look at our Ashley with his head screwed on and his little Iris and his pride in his savings account. You've got to hand it to him. He knows what he's doing. Hermie's brain cells have turned to sawdust.'

'Don't take on so. She's bound to outgrow it. It's just a phase,' Noreen said quickly, although she knew she couldn't persuade him otherwise. For once Wilburt had seen beyond the family quarrel, and his hurt at Hermie's rejection of him and the home he'd worked so hard to provide for them made Noreen's heart ache. She got up and sat in his lap and let him fondle her breast. 'She's at a difficult age. A little lost girl is entitled to a few yearnings and rebellions. Just wait and see. She'll be home when she's realised we were right all along about everything. You'll be whistling when you're a grandpa, bouncing her kiddies on your knees and forgetting their names.'

***

'Good morning. There is ship soon going Australia, yes?' The English was halting.

The young clerk in the dark, oak- panelled shipping office in the City of London's Fenchurch Street raised his head. A German accent he decided, his gaze settling on a tall, angular, poised woman in her twenties with a flawless skin and fair hair tied in a long plait who had approached the counter with her dark-haired male companion.

'I can tell you without checking that the next P&O sailing to Sydney is in mid-August via Bombay and the *s.s. Moloja* is fully booked.'

'Is nothing sooner? Edith Müller half-turned to the lean man beside her. From what he recalled of his schoolboy French the clerk thought he heard her mutter, did you hear that, Jean-Claude?

'I'm afraid not, madam. And, as I said, the passenger list is closed. There's no vacancy unless a cancellation occurs and that's as unlikely as Christmas in July.'

'Surely not! It cannot be. What is the reason?' Jean-Claude's fingers gripped the edge of the counter draining the knuckles of blood, a note of desperation creeping into the quiet tone.

'Sir, it's that time of year. Personnel on leave returning to duty in India and the Colonies. That sort of thing. The sailing has been sold out for weeks.'

'Please to check again on availability.' There was a hint of steel in his tone. His eyes took in the man's bitten fingernails and cheap brown suit. 'Edith...' He took her arm and drawing her to one side they went into a whispered huddle. The clerk pretended to run a check on vacancies and his straining ears caught a rapid exchange of French and German that he couldn't follow.

'Maybe this is a sign that we ought to stay together.' Edith said clutching his hand.

'Not a bit of it,' Jean-Claude retorted briskly. He'd mentally prepared himself for her leaving believing she should sit the war out in safety in Australia. 'You're on your way and there's no two ways about it. Here's what we'll do...'

They returned to the counter. 'It's vital my friend catches that boat,' Jean-Claude insisted, almost harshly.

The clerk spread his hands in a gesture of helplessness. 'Sir, I'm no miracle worker. My hands are tied. There's not a cabin to be had.'

Jean-Claude pushed over a bundle of crisp pound notes. Edith hesitated then leaned over and the clerk caught a whiff of her eau de cologne. Her voice was soft and coaxing. 'I hope this will loosen those ties.' Her knees were shaking and she was icy-cold.

The clerk shot a nervous glance at a glass-panelled door marked MANAGER and clamped a hand over the money. He averted his gaze from the piercing cornflower blue gaze that bored through him. 'I'll see what I can done... I suggest you return in half an hour.'

Jean- Claude shook his head, his mouth a straight line. 'We will wait.'

There was a sharp ping as the street door opened and the clerk looked up as a couple on the cusp of forty crossed the floor. A bear of a man in a trench coat removed his brown hat and his grey eyes crinkled. 'No guesses why we're here today', he said in an accent that immediately identified him as American.

'Good morning, Pastor Addison, Mrs Addison. Yes, I was told to expect you. If you'll take a seat, I'll fetch your tickets. They're ready.'

'Thank you.' The couple sat down and beamed at Edith and Jean-Claude.

In a low voice, the clerk motioned the younger couple over and took down some details.

'Are you going on a voyage too, Mam? Mrs Addison had an open, red-cheeked face.

Edith exchanged a glance with Jean-Claude, 'hopefully, to Sydney.'

'That's nice. We're bound for Bombay on the *Moloja*. She's a comfortable old tub.'

'That's encouraging. And what takes you there?'

Pastor Addison laughed. 'Oh, we're old Indian hands and into our second seven-year tour of duty. We've been home on twelve months furlough in Scottsbluff - '

' Nebraska,' Mrs Addison interjected. 'By the way, I'm Martha and this is Greg. We're with the American Baptist Mission and we're returning to our mission not far from Calcutta. We crossed over to England from New York a month ago - my, I've never known it be so choppy. After a brief stopover in Bombay staying with friends, we'll head on by express train. I run the Sunday school and help in the dispensary as I trained as a nurse.'

'And help me so very much in doing the Lord's Work,' Greg said squeezing Martha's hand.

Edith warmed to the two kindly Americans and introduced herself. 'So it seems we're be travelling companions for part of the way.''

Martha's homely face lit up. 'Did you hear that Greg? Isn't that so nice? Well, the sailing to Bombay lasts about three weeks, so we're sure to have a ball together.'

Edith's curiosity got the better of her. 'How do you make yourselves understood in India?'

The Addisons exchanged a smile. 'Easily. From the very first we made it our business to learn Bengali and Oriya and now we're word perfect.'

Just then the clerk returned handing the Addisons a large manila envelope addressed to The Reverend Dr Gregory Addison, D.D. that Edith managed to sneak a glance at and another that he passed to Jean-Claude.

The Addisons rose and thanked the clerk. 'Goodbye until we meet on deck, Edith. God bless.'

The clerk waited until the door had shut firmly behind them and turned to Edith and Jean-Claude. 'It's all there. A one-way ticket in the name of Miss Edith Müller. *s.s. Moloja.* Single cabin. Sydney via Bombay.'

Jean-Claude ripped open the envelope and slowly and carefully examined the contents.

'It's all present and correct.' The clerk was on edge. 'I promise you. Please, please hurry.'

'The ticket is legitimate, yes? We don't want any issues.'

'Me neither,' the clerk retorted. 'The procurement was, shall we say, somewhat unorthodox, but there's nothing dodgy about the ticket. Miss Müller will have absolutely no problems boarding.'

'She'd better not.'

'Thank you very much. Edith intervened hastily and inclined her head. Her heart raced. The die was cast. With Jean-Claude's hand in hers, they vanished into the golden summer's day.

***

Standing on tiptoes, which added an inch or so to her medium height, Hermie lifted a small tin trunk down from the top of the almirah.   The locks were rusty, but between stages of washing and dressing as Bernadette sat on the bed among a scatter of clothes, her round face giving out waves of longing, Hermie spruced it up. *Wear this, pack that or should it be that? Arrive looking your best. And remember to pack the Kotex that transformed life after leaving school, freeing me from those cumbersome, coarse linen sanitary pads that each month we secreted in bags to be flailed clean by women servants for subsequent re-use.*

'Wish I was coming.' Bernadette had a tiny mouse-like voice. 'I've never been to Delhi.'

Hermie reached for her brush and comb. 'I visited ages ago although I can scarcely remember any of it.' Her tone was excited.

'I don't suppose I'll ever be able to afford a trip like yours.' Bernadette's peat brown eyes were doleful.

'Don't be silly. Of course you will.   In the meantime, do as I did, save the paisaas and the rupees will look after themselves.' Hermie was in the seventh heaven and not averse to dishing out unsolicited advice.

Bernadette gave a disbelieving sniff. 'You don't have youngsters to look after.' Mrs Gannon was a housewife, although far from house-proud, Hermie realised. And what with Vincent in the seminary and Mr Gannon's chronic diabetes (although Pa was sceptical of that) disabling him from undertaking anything other than light, casual work, Bernadette was virtually the only breadwinner. 'Not that I mind,' she added hastily.

Hermie put her arm round her friend's shoulder. 'Be happy for me.'

Bernadette, shocked out of her phlegm by Hermie's accounts of the rows with Wilburt and Ashley, wiped her eyes. The Gannons, close-knit but impoverished, never raised their voices to each other and pulled together.

'Of course.' She got up and gave her a hug. 'But I'll never forgive you if you don't write me with news. It'll be a long three months and the Bank won't be the same without you.'

'Not long enough for me, though,' Hermie said. 'Boss with his miserable debits and credits isn't something I'm going to mourn.' She gathered up her handbag and shouting to Bishu to take her trunk, cast a last look round the room, stooping almost as a matter of course to top up the water level in the cigarette tins in which the bed legs stood to thwart the dreaded red ants crawling up into the mattress.

The pearly rose flush of the brief twilight had replaced the day's harsh glare. Bishu manhandled the trunk into a waiting tonga and Hermie got in. Noreen opened her handbag and pressed an envelope into Hermie's palm closing her fingers over it. '*Girlee,* here's a little something for you that I kept back from the housekeeping.' She'd promised Wilburt she wouldn't cry.

Hermie flung her arms round her neck. ' Oh Ma. You shouldn't have.' There was a terrible lump in her throat and she fought back a flurry of emotions. Ma must have pinched and scrimped. And here she was duplicitously concealing from dear Ma that she'd no intention of ever coming back. 'I'll do you proud, you'll see. No home's the same without a Ma like you.'

Hermie's remarks brought a broad smile to Noreen's lips rather than a tear to her eyes. 'Now don't you go getting sunstroke. And make sure you drink lots of water.'

The shortcut to the station took her past yapping pariah dogs and cow-dung heaps, through alleys reeking with the stench of rotting vegetation. As the daughter of a railway employee, Hermie enjoyed concessionary travel facilities and possessed a rail pass.

'Going on holiday eh, Hermie?' The ticket collector, AI like herself, waved her through. 'Delhi, I suppose? My, you've chosen a lively spot.'

'Mmm,' Hermie murmured, 'train on time?'

He looked affronted. 'What'll your Pa and Ashley say if they hear talk like that? Of course it's on time - always is, isn't it? Don't they say you can set your watch by our trains?' No wonder she'd gained a reputation for being Wilburt's difficult daughter.

'It wasn't that day those Congress wallahs incited their supporters to lie down on the tracks.' Civil disobedience campaigns orchestrated by Congress Party activists to exert pressure on the Raj for the grant of independence had caused havoc to the railways in recent months. She nipped smartly away before he could air his views about *those Indians* daring to stir up trouble.

The train drew in, the carriage facing her labelled First Class. Hermie took a deep breath, determined to escape, come what may, from the life into which she'd been born but with which she seldom felt at ease. A new life, a new future started now and, with that heady thought, she shook off the sense of guilt at concealing her true intentions from Ma.   She peered through the window. A young, kind faced Englishman and a curly, auburn-haired woman she assumed was his wife smiled at her. She took this to be a good omen and with scant regard to her eligibility to travel in that carriage - Pa's rank entitling her only to second class - she returned the smile and greatly daring turned the handle and climbed in, motioning to the coolie to stow away her trunk.

'Good evening,' Hermie said politely and comfortably installed in her seat gazed around taking in the luxurious upholstered compartment with its white headrests, tinted windows, furled green blinds and wall mounted electric fans.

The man was casually dressed in an open necked shirt and a crumpled, grey cotton suit, his rangy body showing an easy strength.

'What sweet kids!' Hermie's opening gambit was perfectly timed. Mention children and people immediately opened up. And that's what she wanted.

The woman had a lovely speaking voice. 'My darling tot, Vanessa newly minted. And here's Timmy and Adam. Say hello, boys.'

'Hello!' chorused Timmy and Adam who were six and five respectively. They solemnly held out their hands.

Hermie smiled. 'I'm Hermie Blake.'

'So sorry, Hermie I'd shake hands if I could but as you can see they're full. Oh, how remiss of me. I'm Jennifer Oakley, and this is my husband Peter who isn't wearing his clerical collar today.'

Peter Oakley reached over and took Vanessa in his lap then shook Hermie's hand, his grey eyes scanning her face. Hermie glanced across at plump, freckled Jennifer Oakley, plainly dressed like herself, in a blue seersucker gathered frock, buttoned to the waist, her pale, bare legs in white, open-toed leather sandals. Both she and her husband were pukka, she thought approvingly.

'Are you going the distance?' Peter raised his eyebrows. They were so fair she thought as to be almost indistinguishable from the colour of his skin.

Hermie nodded. 'Although I must admit I haven't been to Delhi for a while. But one can never forget the magnificence of Lutyens or the twisting lanes of the old city. Do you know it well?'

A whistle shrilled on a long note, the flag was lowered and the train began to move, rolling and snorting out of the station.

Jennifer laughed, adjusting herself in her seat like a mother hen. 'Not a bit, but we intend to. It's completely new to us. We sailed from Southampton and for the past few weeks we've been staying with friends in an outstation getting acclimatised. Peter has been appointed vicar of St. James, Kashmiri Gate. It's a promotion, you know.' She beamed proudly at her husband.

Peter was bubbling over at the prospect of his new parish. 'They say it's a beautiful old church dating from 1836 with a domed roof and handsome pillars in a magnificent setting.'

Hermie leaned forward with an air of what she hoped betokened interest, unaware that Jennifer was trying to place her.

'Ooh! That sounds interesting. Tell me more.'

'Sikander Sahib built it. He who was the legendary Colonel James Skinner - for the men of his cavalry regiment, Skinner's Horse - entirely with his own money and to fulfil a private vow....'

Vanessa began to cry. 'Feeding time. Here we go again.' Jennifer opened a wicker tiffin basket and reached for a large tin of Ostermilk, vacuum flasks and feeding bottles.

Hermie gently disengaged the howling Vanessa from Jennifer's arms. Peter's harassed expression relaxed but Jennifer scrabbling through the baby paraphernalia looked up and bit her lip, dismayed.

'Lordy, ayah has forgotten to fill the flasks with boiled hot water. I can't do without it. We're stuck.'

Hermie's thoughts raced. 'I've an idea.' She rocked the infant as Jennifer measured out the milk powder.

'What?' There was desperation in Peter's eyes as Vanessa's squawk reached fever pitch. Timmy and Adam glanced up then returned to their drawings, oblivious to the undercurrents. The train was now speeding through the dark night chattering over the points, the carriage swaying rhythmically.

Hermie smiled and passed the child back to her mother. 'Just wait and see. I'm sure I'll be able to manage something at Walipur, the next station down the line, if you can manage to hang on for a while.'

Jennifer and Peter took it in turns to rock Vanessa but nothing would silence her.

'And you've organised a meal for yourselves?'

Peter nodded. 'At the railhead our host telegraphed an order down the line to Kevin's'-

'Oh, you mean Kellners. They're superb dining contractors and their caramel custard's quite simply the best.' At the sound of caramel custard the boys' heads shot up. 'Yummy!'

'Is that so? We hadn't any idea just what to expect and you know how finicky kids can be. Now did I hear you mention the princely state of Walipur where Prince Sanjay, the heir apparent, was invested as Maharajah?' Peter asked as they roared past a vast emptiness of thorny scrub.

'You're well informed. It was earlier this year,' Hermie said, 'although the Political Agent made a great to-do about the expense, on top of what he described as a long period of careless living.'

'That makes the Maharajah sound fat and fifty.' Jennifer ruffled Timmy's hair.

'Far from it.' Lives of the movie stars and of the rich and famous were meat and drink to Hermie and she waxed lyrical. 'There were photos of the enthronement ceremony in all the papers. His Highness, who's about twenty-five, looked rather resplendent flanked by courtiers.' Hermie saw HH as a personable, handsome man greeting the guest of honour, the Viceroy. 'And -'

Peter exchanged an amused glance with Jennifer as Hermie recalled every detail.

'So that's...oh, here we are.' The train had cranked into Walipur. 'Won't be a jiffy.' Hermie jumped down with the flasks and darting in and out of the knot of bawling char wallahs, sweetmeat vendors and purveyors of sugar cane juice working the platform, hailed the loco driver, AI like herself, who was leaning out of the loco cab smoking a cigarette.

'Hello! I'm Hermie, Driver Blake's sister.' She smiled, adding softly, 'I'd like some hot water from the engine if you can spare it.'

'Pleased to meet you at last, Hermie. Of course, anything to oblige. Pass my best to Ashley, mind. We're swapping routes next month.' The driver picked up his kettle, filled the flasks with boiling water and Hermie stirred in Ostermilk before making her way back to the carriage.

'You're the eighth wonder of the world.' Peter exclaimed gratefully as Vanessa sucked greedily. 'What brings a resourceful girl like you to Delhi?'

A tray bearing their meal had been delivered to them by a white- jacketed turbaned bearer, the starched white napkins, crockery and heavy Sheffield cutlery all stamped with the insignia of the Railway Company, and the boys tucked in with gusto.

Hurtling through stations and flashing in out of tunnels the train bore Hermie further and further away from Ajeemkot.   Hermie had sensed the Oakleys growing curiosity. What a young domiciled European, as she perceived they imagined her to be, was doing travelling alone. She seemed decent enough - if somewhat overly composed - neatly turned out in crisp, striped cotton dress - presentable and well mannered.

Hermie gave a light laugh. 'I'm having family problems and I thought a change of scene might help, especially if I can get suitable employment.'

'That's very enterprising. So you decided to strike out on your own?'

'I had to.' Hermie's mind scurried and unleashing a graphic account of abuse at the hands of a crusty uncle who'd housed her, an only child, when she was orphaned after her parents were felled by malaria, she wallowed in the Oakleys' sympathetic murmurs.

The four hundred miles that divided Hermie from Ajeemkot closed and ahead of them, all at once, blazed the lights of Delhi. Hermie's heart thumped at the prospect of change.

CHAPTER 3

The air smelled of a thousand spices, trees in full leaf glittered in the moonlight. A car from the barracks met the Oakleys as Peter had been appointed Army Chaplain in addition to his other duties.

'Be sure to look us up,' Jennifer called from inside the car, a drowsy Vanessa in her arms. 'We keep open house.'

Timmy and Adam broke off from savaging each other just long enough to wave furiously to her.   Hermie returned their goodbyes thinking she'd never met a nicer English family and, as the car pulled away, turned with a swirl of her dress and hailed a tonga. Once past the teeming old City and its crowded bazaars, New Delhi's cosmopolitanism and the illuminated shops of Connaught Place promised to deliver.

The tonga lurched to a stop outside a modest semi-detached bungalow with a cared for look about it and a small patch of front lawn bordered by weed-free beds and low hanging bushes. In the cold weather Hermie imagined it was a garden of scent and colour, and even now Aunty Al defied the heat in the showy blooms of zinnia set against snow-white flutes of cosmos and purple-top Brazilian verbena attracting many butterflies. Hermie flung herself out of the tonga and quickly crossed the springy grass.

'**Welcome**!' Aunty Al had seen her and, beaming broadly, appeared on the brightly lit terrazzo- floored verandah.

Hermie dived into her arms through a row of red earthenware tubs. 'It's been a long time coming.'

Unlike Bishu, the Castons chokra, Deepak, was lying in wait and unbidden unloaded her trunk.

'We've been **looking forward** to having you, my girl'. Aunty Al smelling of gardenias pinched Hermie's cheek hard. She stressed her words that gave her singsong lilt a bounce of its own. Hermie gave Mr Caston a hug and hunted in her purse for loose change.

'Put that away now, mind. I'll take care of it.' He opened his wallet and paid off the tonga wallah, dodging as the horse relieved itself in a strong smelling burst. Quiet and bespectacled with a chocolate-brown face and carefully arranged thinning grey hair, Mr Caston was a book-keeper in government service and adored his lively wife who he shared with an aviary of budgies that happily coexisted - a triumph of hope over experience - with several over-indulged seal point Siamese cats that shrieked like banshees.

'Come in, come in. You **must be hungry and tired** after that journey.' Aunty Al shepherded Hermie indoors.

'I'm far too excited.' She gave a quick sideways glace at Aunty Al. 'You look marvellous, you haven't changed a bit.'

Aunty Al gave a bark of laughter showing perfect white teeth. 'This is **certainly** your night for charming me. And you're **blooming.'** The kind little dark eyes surveyed her. 'I can see I'm going to have my hands full with you. You'll have the boys **buzzing** round you like wasps round a jellaybie.'

'I can't wait.'

'But don't let that go to your head.'

'As if you'd let it.' Hermie and Aunty Al grinned at each other with a certain sort of understanding. 'And before I forget, Ma's sent you a little something. Not a gift as such - that's still in the trunk'.

'Let me see!'

Hermie rummaged in a holdall and handed over several eight-inch crocheted squares.

'Bless her heart. Noreen's **always** so thoughtful. Just the **job** for cleaning all the daykchies Deepak slaves to shine.'

Noreen had knotted together the lengths of twine she'd hoarded and crocheted them into dishcloths.

'There's **nothing** quite like this.' Aunty Al spoke as though she'd come into a fortune. 'They **won't** scratch the surface of my daykchies and precious bone china, yet the knobbly bits will remove **all** dried food remains. Now,' she propelled Hermie towards her room, tiny but spick and span with plain dark-wood furniture and a striped cotton dhurry and smelling of freshly ironed sheets, overlooking the front garden.

'When you've freshened up **come** and meet the others.'

Hermie threw a bucket of water over herself and changed into a dress the colour of vanilla ice cream, renewing her make-up and lipstick. Somewhere out in the dark an owl hooted. Nearly midnight but the Caston household, unlike the Blakes who'd have been tucked up in bed by now, showed no signs of turning in.

'That's it my girl. There's a seat for everyone and yours is over there.' Aunty Al had arranged her lodgers round the dining table like pieces on a chessboard. 'Now on your right, please meet...'

Hermie's eyes roamed round the large but cluttered parlour. Deepak must have his work cut out dusting, she thought with a stab of sympathy. Endless little knick knacks, bowls of cacti, family photographs going back to the farthest collateral and a bevy of gaudy plaster saints, one of whom she immediately recognised from the abundance of arrows as St. Sebastian, fought for every inch of space.

Of the two lodgers, one was an elderly AI bachelor, Mr Turton Jones, a semi-retired violin master cum piano tuner, in straitened circumstances, with a wistful smile and the beleaguered air of one who has shouldered a heavy burden all his life. Aunty Al housed him out of the kindness of her heart because he didn't exactly pay for his keep. She'd turned a corner of the back verandah into a room for him and cosseted him, instructing Deepak who, unlike the jungly Bishu, was trained by her to the highest standards of a bygone age, to run his errands.

'Hello! Hermie smiled and shook Mr Turton Jones' outstretched hand. It was dry and very bony.

'I've visited Ajeemkot.' He had a throat disorder that rendered his voice a hoarse whisper. 'But you'll find Delhi quite something else.'

'And this is...' Aunty Al gestured without enthusiasm to the willowy woman opposite.

'I am Bettina-Lorna Douglas-Drummond.' An upper-class English voice drawled, slicing across Aunty Al. 'How do you do?' She radiated all the charm of minor royalty greeting a lesser mortal.

The interruption was rewarded by a swift glare from Aunty Al from under her thin black brows that was enough to tell Hermie that Bettina-Lorna was not one of the chosen. As Aunty Al was later at pains to explain, Bettina-Lorna was there, on sufferance, against her better judgment.

'She was foisted on me', Aunty Al sketched an unforgiving gesture, 'by the Archbishop. She was abandoned in Delhi by her surgeon husband who just beetled back to England with his theatre nurse – a much younger woman.'

'Really?' Hermie was agog. 'She's rather coy about her age'.

'She won't see fifty again,' Aunty Al dropped her voice, fully launched on her denunciation of Bettina-Lorna.

Bettina-Lorna was languidly handsome, Hermie admitted, with a flawless milky complexion and that night her large green earrings set in gold brought out the leak-green lights in her protuberant eyes. Her abundant corn mane was arranged in a French pleat.

'Mark my words, it's bottled', Aunty Al had sniffed contemptuously.

'Takes one to know one,' murmured Hermie under her breath, gazing innocently at Aunty Al whose own jet-black hair, invariably worn in a fine hairnet, had grown darker with the years.

'I heard that, you bold child. Lower your eyes.'

With the air of one who is biding time until the tide turns, Bettina-Lorna had told Aunty Al that she was of Scottish-Belgian parentage, had been educated at an exclusive school in Brussels, and boasted of her aristocratic connections. That cut no ice with Aunty Al to whom she was always *that woman about whom everything rings true except the facts.*

***

Delhi's sociable AI Association was keenly supported by Mr Caston and Aunty Al who never missed the Saturday dances and the whist drives, but Mr Turton Jones was seldom persuaded to abandon his wind-up gramophone and classical music records for the beat of Fats Waller, Irving Berlin or the latest Glenn Miller played with verve by the talented AI band.

And Hermie made it her business to lose no time in joining in the AI's social activities. Trailing clouds of Houbignant's *Lily of the Valley* loaned by Bettina-Lorna in a rare access of generosity, Hermie donned her prettiest frock resolving to be the prettiest girl on the boarded, French chalked dance floor. To preserve their creamy complexion, she and Noreen were privy to the hakim's closely-guarded secret formula paste – an uplifting blend of oils, flower extract and turmeric - that arrested the formation of skin darkening melanin - and maintained a glowing complexion. Other AIs, sceptical of the hakim's concoctions, resorted to a lotion of hydrogen peroxide that produced disastrous patchy results.

'What do you think of Arthur Rubinstein?' Winston Powley bellowed in her ear above the drums in a flat, slow voice. He may be God's gift to the Indian Civil Service (ICS) Hermie thought, but he's no Fred Astaire. He held her at arm's length, stepping on her toes, and making her wince, muttering one, two, three, one, two, three under his breath, completely out of sync with *Moonlight Serenade.*

He wasn't the husband material she'd dreamed of. His small, hard eyes were level with hers - still, swallowing her disappointment, Hermie smiled sweetly into the podgy, dark face. Maybe, she could make him over... she burned to be delivered from her marginalised life.

Hermie paused, flummoxed. The name meant nothing to her. She bestowed her best Vivien Leigh smile on him. 'Is that Polish or Russian vodka?'

Winston halted in mid-step, arms dropping swiftly to his side. 'Are you being funny?' His eyes registered her bemused expression. 'No, I see you aren't .' His voice rose, 'well I'm amazed you know nothing about the brilliant Rubinstein.' Shaking his head, he ungallantly stalked off leaving her stranded.

Hermie ground her teeth and swiftly made her way off the floor relieved that his abandonment of her had apparently gone unobserved. The band had stopped for a breather on a resounding clash of percussion and Hermie, sizing up what was on offer, having rejected his brother Marcel whose pockmarked face was turned to Aunty Al by whom he'd been reluctantly inveigled into the church choir as a bass baritone - 'I'm fed up with tenors -' Al had declared, wondered if she could locate tall Gerald Reid, the lawyer, who she'd persuade to fight his way to the bar for her.

'Can yours truly get you a drink, pretty woman?'

Hermie swivelled round and met the easy, late night smile of a tousled-haired AI in his twenties with a scar across one nut-brown cheek, the trousers a shade too tight, the bow tie a shade too loud, the feet thrust into white buckskin shoes, recognising him as Barry Maddox, the compére. With his fast-talking, confident manner and cheeky ad-libbing, he was a born entertainer, always making the evenings go with a swing.

'Ooh, that sounds lovely. I could shift a gimlet.'

He raised his eyebrows.' Kicking over the traces, right?' AI girls of Hermie's age were considered fast if they drank anything other than shandy or a brew of lemon and port. 'If you can handle it, it's coming up. What's upset the high and mighty Winston? The oaf looked more pouting than usual.' Barry was soon back balancing in one hand a tray laden with three bottles of Murree beer for himself and two gimlets for Hermie. 'Let's nab that table.' He glanced round, whisked off the *Reserved* sign and stuffed it into his pocket.

Hermie giggled. 'Oh, you're the devil himself. I've been warned about men like you who don't miss a trick.'

Barry tapped the side of his nose. 'Hear all, see all, and say nothing. That's the motto of yours truly.'

Hermie crossed her hands over her heart. 'I'm innocent. Arthur Rubinstein's guilty.'

He gave her a quizzical look. 'You've lost yours truly.' His eyes were the colour of a blackbird's feather. 'Have a smoke?' He flourished a cigarette case and flicked a tiny button.

'Thanks, I've been known to have the odd one.' Hermie leaned over and examined it closely. 'That's a cute case-cum lighter.'

He lit her Capstan cigarette and one for himself, blowing a cloud of smoke into the air. 'Smart of you to notice. This is Ronson's Double Decker, 1937. Case and lighter combo. Enamel with a double hinge. In short supply.' He didn't say where he'd acquired it and Hermie's curiosity got the better of her.

'Don't ask. Now tell.'

Hermie launched into her story.

'Damn good.' Barry brimmed with laughter. 'I'll work on that and use it one of these days, mind.' He leaned across the table and took her hand, raising it with gentle mockery to his lips. 'You're my muse. And I don't know any man who's a better judge of beauty than me.'

'Just what are you on about?' Hermie demanded, determined to share his amusement. 'Stop your jesting. What's the matter with you, eh?' She pulled her hand free, but he seemed not to mind.

Between amused snorts, he enlightened her about Arthur Rubinstein and Hermie, first appalled at her ignorance, was persuaded to laugh at herself.

The band was tuning up again, and Barry downed the last glass of beer in one gulp. 'Love you and leave you, Hermie. See over there? You'll be in very good arms, mind.' He gently pushed her forward. 'Shorty's coming to claim you.' It was his nickname for Gerald Reid.

Someone had requested a waltz, and good-humoured groans broke from the younger couples. Gerald, with skin that resembled parchment and carefully brushed black hair drew her away, hovering somewhat melancholically above her. Although they'd never been introduced, he recognised her from Ajeemkot.

It occurred to her that he was dressed with an odd formality, as if before the Bench - in black, pinstriped trousers, fob and watch-chain and wing collar.

'Barry says he hasn't seen you around for some time.' For someone so gangling, Gerald was lighter on his feet than Mervyn.

'It's hectic in the High Court. I may have to depart any moment now to seek an injunction.'

He took her questioning, upturned face as a cue to embark on a rambling account of a commercial case he was handling that involved breach of contract of an order for bailing hoops. His pale brown eyes narrowed in recollection and she nodded and smiled at what she hoped were the right moments.

When he stopped to draw breath, she said quickly, 'I realise law's tricky, but it's the way you tell it that makes the issues come alive,' her gaze never leaving his face but he was too absorbed in his account to notice, and about the only thing she'd caught was a reference to his opposing Senior Counsel, the handsome Muslim politico, Mohammed Ali Jinnah.

'And he's on a massive daily retainer.' Awe crept in Gerald's voice at the undreamed of riches.

But it was all beyond Hermie, or perhaps it was more to do with how he told it, in his rather dry monotone. But clearly he had a bright future ahead of him. Maybe she could be part of that.

'Whew!' She'd give anything for a date with him. 'And you're terribly clever making sense of all the ins and outs. I know it would be beyond me.'

'I've a trained mind,' he said modestly and gave a cautious smile. Hermie's hopes rose in optimism of a breakthrough. 'I'm delighted to explain the finer points. No, don't apologise it's really no trouble at all. Now first...'

'Oh, please ...' Hermie didn't think she could bear it. The waltz moved into a fox trot, one of Hermie's favourite steps, and Barry breathed one of his famous double entendres into the mike that had them all in gales of laughter.

'Barry boy's born to hang,' Aunty Al said with a laugh as she swung by on Mr Caston's arm.

'You're like a feather,' Gerald told Hermie happily. 'When I was a student in London, I made it a point to attend the dances at the Y.M.C.A. and by gum, sometimes I thought I was toting a ton of rice.'

He wasn't as retiring as he liked to make out, Hermie decided. 'And you're so fleet of foot,' she said with total sincerity, hoping he'd consider the common interest as the starting point for a relationship.

'That's nice of you.   I'll go home on leave when the trial ends; maybe I'll see you there. By the way, aren't you a friend of Bernadette Gannon? I've seen you both together at the Inster.'

She registered with a sinking heart the way his cadaverous face seemed to plump out at the mention of Bernadette. It was the closest she'd seen him get to a look of pleasure. She'd not realised they'd met, for Bernadette had said not a word. They moved in different circles and Bernadette was no beauty.

'When I'm home, I make it a point of doing my bit for the Paulines. Bernadette...'

So that was it. It made sense. As a volunteer for the charitable Society of St. Vincent de Paul, Gerald would have visited the Gannons with donations of second-hand clothes and household goods.   He droned on, Bernadette's name punctuating the music like a throbbing heartbeat. It was hideously obvious he was smitten with her. 'She's an angel and so interested in my work. I wrote her a long letter the other day.'

Bernadette has certainly kept choop, Hermie thought in a state of some resentment. 'The Gannons are hard up, to say the least,' she said a little spitefully, hoping it would make him think twice about Bernadette,

But Gerald was well into his stride. 'Such a shame they're struggling as they're all very nice. Wasn't that just terrible about Frank? That really cut them up.' He stared into space. 'But Bernadette's been so plucky and as hardworking as ever keeping the family together. Oh, she's such a little saint - just like her namesake. She's just meant to be worshipped.' There was tenderness in his tone. 'Ma has taken to her.'

The band played on, Gerald whirled Hermie round the floor and then Barry bounced back to the mike. 'That's all for tonight, folks and if there's anyone out there that I haven't insulted, I apologise!'

Mortified by the Rubinstein episode, Hermie sought out Mr Turton Jones. 'You'll see how well-travelled I am,' he said cryptically, and delighted to be of help, escorted her to the concert halls of Prague, Vienna and Salzburg, to the opera houses of Paris and Milan, to the castles of the German Princes and the courts of the Medici.

***

Monsoon rain fell in torrents from the dun coloured sky, turning the dusty streets to a muddy skidpan, driving Bettina-Lorna from her daily fix of gin and tonic at the exclusive Delhi Gymkhana Club to a cane chair on Aunty Al's verandah.

'Sit here.' Bettina-Lorna, wearing one of her many diaphanous frocks that showed to perfection the outline of her long limbed, firm body, gestured imperiously to Hermie. 'Tell me what you've been up to.' She closed her eyes. 'Oh, this never ending rain makes me want to scream.'

Hermie, confident that that Bettina-Lorna would impart a few time-honoured tips about nabbing Gerald, began, 'I'm rather aggrieved Bernadette said nothing to me.'

Bettina-Lorna considered. 'He's spoken for, dahling.'

'But...' Hermie was dismayed. These weren't the pearls of wisdom she expected to drop from the lips of the worldly-wise Bettina-Lorna.

'Take it from me. *God grant me the serenity to accept the things I cannot change, courage to change the things I can, and the wisdom to know the difference.* You're wasting your time trying to lure Gerald away from Bernadette. Listen, dahling, he's bound to have an eligible friend. Save your energies for that.' She nibbled her third samosa.

From someone whose own life was scarcely characterised by delaying gratification, thought Hermie, Bettina-Lorna's advice was breath taking, but she decided not to press it. She changed the subject. 'How you keep your figure is amazing. I have to watch my weight like a hawk. What's your secret?'

'I make sure I get plenty of exercise.'

'Exercise!' Hermie squeaked. She'd not seen Bettina-Lorna lift so much as a little finger.

'Sex. There's no exercise quite like it.' Bettina-Lorna gave a roguish laugh. 'And three times a bride.' She was flattered by the way the impressionable Hermie hung on her every word; it was so long since anyone - man or woman - had been so attentive and, all of a sudden, she felt unsure of herself when, not so long ago, she'd handled life with the air of one who was born to rule. 'Unfortunately, none worked out - men are quite impossible,' she added after treating Hermie to one of her many cliff-hanging confidences. 'Why does one put up with it?' She gave a deep sigh. 'But can one manage without one's little bit of rough?' she drawled, examining her long Pompeii red fingernails.

Yet Hermie was comfortable in the improbable friendship she'd struck up with Bettina-Lorna who only the other day Aunty Al had dismissed as being *all fur coat and no knickers.*

'Let me show you something.' Bettina-Lorna jangled the bell at her elbow and Deepak hurrying in was ordered to fetch something from her room. 'And before you ask, dahling, this is Fraser.' She hugged to her breast a silver photo frame containing the snapshot of a man with a dazzling smile, not unlike the Hollywood heartthrob, Errol Flynn. 'He's the son of my first husband who, I might add, traces his lineage back to 1066. My dear Fraser's now serving as a District Officer in the Gilbert & Ellice Islands.'

'He's a dreamboat.' Hermie's eyes widened as she pondered on his availability. 'Where does he spend his annual leave?'

Bettina-Lorna sighed. 'Alas, not in India. The government will only defray the cost of home leave. We usually try to co-ordinate our visits back to England, but since my recent little *un manqué d'argent gênant* our reunion has hit the buffers.'

Hermie had no idea what the French expression meant but equally didn't want to expose her ignorance of the language. It sounded like a nasty tropical disease but Bettina-Lorna was bound to overcome it.

'Would you marry again?'

'I never say never, dahling. Meanwhile I keep in trim exercising to keep the juices flowing, and so should you. Use it or lose it.' Bettina-Lorna needed no prompting to regale Hermie with tales of past glories: stepping ashore at Cannes, racing at Royal Ascot, the hunting lodge in the Highlands, black tie dinner parties in the Kensington townhouse overlooking a leafy garden square, ski-ing in St Moritz, the smartest cocktail bar, the swankiest restaurant...Hermie nearly swooned.

'Bah! He's blind drunk most - no, I tell a lie, all – the time,' Aunty Al told Hermie roundly when she asked her what she knew about Fraser. 'Why do you think he's never been promoted away from that God forsaken outpost?'

It was a complete mystery to Hermie how Aunty Al came to know such things. She was accurate to the last degree.

***

'Do you good to get out of the house, my girl.' Aunty Al had said but what she meant, Hermie realised, was away from the clutches of Bettina-Lorna. 'Come with me.'

They set out for Connaught Place. 'Madam Olga lives in a flat up there, right at the top,' Aunty Al pointed to an eyrie high above the shops. 'Look, the window's open. All the better to shove Trevor out...' she murmured under her breath. 'It's a long climb but you're a young thing.'

She trudged up the dingy, narrow staircase, with Hermie close on her heels, stopping at each windowless landing to catch her breath. Halfway up, a middle-aged, mud-coloured, simian faced AI man, in sweaty vest and shorts and in need of a good shave and a bath, came hurtling down with an untidy mongrel, almost knocking them for a six.

'Good morning to you, Trevor,' Aunty Al said with as much dignity as she could muster when one's flattened against a peeling wall.

Trevor stopped, as did the dog, both breathing rather heavily; the dog unkempt like its owner and barking loudly in an unseemly fashion. He jerked a grimy thumb upwards. 'Olga's expecting you. Can't think why she makes such a fuss, though.' There was no love lost between him and Aunty Al. He caught sight of Hermie, and his bleary look steadied. 'Oh ho. What tasty morsel have you here? Had I known about you, young lady,' he leered at Hermie, 'I'd have made it my business to stay put.'

'Hermie, we're almost there.' Aunty Al sallied upwards, in the process stepping on the dog's tail. It gave a high-pitched yelp.

'Watch it!' Trevor yelled disagreeably. 'He's my best friend.'

'And your only one,' Aunty Al snorted, despite being exposed to human and canine bad breath at short range. They'd reached the top and Aunty Al, somewhat out of breath by now, motioned Hermie to knock. 'That was Olga's hubby, a right boochee,' she trumpeted, not caring who heard. 'She keeps him going. He's a skirt-chaser and rather too fond of the bottle. He used to do odd jobs, but he can't even manage that now. If I were her I'd have him and that ugly brute of his put down.'

Madam Olga flung open the door and fell excitedly on Aunty Al. 'When you see what I've got lined up, you won't go away empty-handed.' To Hermie, she said, ' I've heard all about you. Nice things, mind. Come, my girl, come quickly.' She grasped Hermie's arm in a wrestler's grip. 'There's not a minute to be lost. There's no time like the present. Don't put off to tomorrow what you can buy today.'

Madam Olga, who had a face like a hippopotamus, dragged Aunty Al and Hermie inside chirruping all the while in an incredibly fast singsong, her voice rising and falling like a ship on a storm tossed ocean, and in spite of her exotic sounding name, the nearest she'd got to Russia was eating chicken Kiev at one of Aunty Al's musical soirees.

'I've got a customer for each and every one of my creations.' Madam Olga was nothing if not a positive thinker.

Aunty Al slanted a glance at Hermie and muttered under her breath, 'perfectly true - if you live to be a hundred.'

It was hot and airless within. Hermie stumbled behind the short-legged Madam Olga down a long narrow passage lined to overflowing with a collection of lampshades.

'A new side line, Olga?' Aunty Al, making it her business to find out these things, stopped to finger a sequinned, feathered number. She knew Madam Olga was forever experimenting with new ventures that would supplement her meagre earnings.

Madam Olga beamed showing few teeth. 'Now, I'm expecting a rush of takers, although they're rather expensive, I don't mind admitting. You'll have to be quick off the mark if you want one.'

She didn't see Hermie, who'd never seen anything so awful, shudder. Aunty Al didn't like the implication that Olga had something she couldn't afford and wasn't to be outdone. 'If it's quality... then one must expect to pay.' It was one of those ambivalent remarks she was master of.

Hermie subsided into the chair and glanced round. The room was stuffed with millinery accessories - hat boxes in one corner piled high to the ceiling, reels of multi-coloured hat-bands, tins brimming with pins, fabrics and felts, hat-racks, and surrealist plastic hat-moulds. A framed verse embroidered in needlepoint hung on a wall:

> *Where did you get that hat?*
> *Where did you get that tile?*
> *It's a Madam Olga creation*
> *And always the fanciest style!*

'Now, Al, dear. Here's the new season's collection, and as my friend and favoured customer, you're privileged to have a preview.'

They went into a huddle. Aunty Al tried on one after another, while Madam Olga cooed, *wonderful, charming, and just perfect.* She was a persuasive saleswoman and Aunty Al would have gone away with the lot had she not had

her wits about her. Hermie had nothing but admiration for her self- control.
What it must have cost her.

'No. **Oh no, no, no.** I look like Sherlock Holmes in that. And that **won't suit,**
dear, it's like that hat Gandhi wears. Olga, **don't** prematurely age me. I'm still
in the first flush of **youth.** Remember, I won **first prize** last year in my Cleopatra
fancy dress? Surely you have something more **alluring** for the **temptress** that's
me?'

Hermie giggled.

'And I'm only here for the **one** chapeau, Olga dear. Greed's a deadly **sin.'**

Madam Olga frenziedly unveiled an enormous cream velvet hat sporting an
ostrich plume.

Aunty Al gazed critically in the mirror. 'This is the job.   It spells **taste,**
exclusivity.' She didn't ask Hermie what she thought of it and Hermie was
relieved, for she'd have been hard pressed to say that she liked it. To her mind it
was reminiscent of the headgear worn by English Cavaliers and overwhelmed
tiny Aunty Al who could only just be glimpsed beneath it.

'Mr Caston won't recognise you!' Madam Olga said. 'Now you're next young
woman.'

Hermie was horrified. She did not like, or want, any of Madam Olga's
creations. 'I can't afford it,' she mumbled.

'Nonsense!   I shall treat you.' Aunty Al announced, patting her hair into
place.

'I've got the very thing.' Madam Olga, sensing another sale, was rummaging
about in a cupboard. Her voice was muffled. 'Won't be a tick.' Moments later,
she withdrew, beaming. 'Here we are.' She held something up in both hands like
a trophy.

It's really not too bad, Hermie thought with some surprise. She wondered if
Madam Olga had made it herself or, uncharitable thought, had purloined it from
an Englishwoman returning *home.* It was a charming, wide brimmed cream
straw hat with a corsage of pink silk roses sewn to the hatband.

Hermie tried it on. 'I love it.' The reflection that stared back at her was a
mixture of innocence and coquetry. Farewell topi!

'You look a picture!' breathed Madam Olga. 'There, Al, a true professional like
me possesses an unerring instinct.'

'Mm,' said Aunty Al critically. '**Very** winsome indeed.   We'll take it, Olga.' She didn't actually ask Hermie if she wanted it, but Hermie supposed she didn't need to, judging from the expression that was probably showing on her face.

While Madam Olga, chattering inconsequentially, sought out hatboxes Hermie discovered that it was she who'd permed Aunty Al's hair with one of those home-perms. This was yet another of Madam Olga's sidelines. I ought to have guessed, Hermie told herself, for in a corner stood an ancient salon-type hairdryer on a rusting stand.

'I could do you, Hermie,' Madam Olga offered, tilting her head expectantly. 'At a special price as a favour to Al. It'll be a bargain you'll never, never find cause to regret.'

Or forget. Hermie felt herself go cold. Not in a million years would she let her loose on her locks. 'No thanks, I don't need a perm as my hair has a natural wave. Anyway, Ma won't approve.'

'And **when** did you ever do what your Ma wanted, eh?' Aunty Al sniffed, raising her eyebrows.

'I'd want to discuss it with her first,' Hermie said, determined to win this round. Her eyes met Aunty Al's with cool composure.

Aunty Al glanced at her watch rather than be seen to have given way. 'Your **old man's** bound to be back soon, so we're off. Take care, Olga.'

As they picked their way down the stairs and emerged into the sunlight, they saw Trevor shuffling along with his cur. Seeing Hermie, he quickened his pace.

'**Hurry,** my girl! Into the *Blue Danube*,' Aunty Al hissed. 'His type isn't **welcome** there.' Over her shoulder she flung him a glance that was about as friendly as a cup of hemlock.

CHAPTER 4

'Idiotic pin brains.' Barry scowled at Aunty Al's budgies. 'Give me a warm blooded reptile any day, and now let's go for a walk, my beaut.' He'd dropped in not so much for the pleasure of Hermie's company as to scrounge off Aunty Al. He wasn't disappointed. Plump, honey-brushed apricot buns and nutty, roughly-scored semolina nankaties warm from her newly acquired Valor perfection stove, which burned kerosene on an adjustable wick flame, lay temptingly on lace doyleys on her best willow pattern china.

'In this weather? You must be joking - just look at the lightning,' Hermie objected, glancing out at the leaden sky, split by a sudden flash from which, even as she spoke, fat raindrops were descending. 'Besides, I'm not going to get far in my new shoes. They're pinching.'

Hermie was deliciously aware from Barry's glint that she looked fetching in the sleeveless, scalloped neck candy-striped cotton dress that showed off to perfection her pretty arms and bosom, and a pair of white, high-heeled peep toed sandals. His attentions boosted her femininity and she saw Aunty Al eyeing him from the corridor with a kind of sour speculation. The straw hat Hermie had tossed ever so casually on a side table.

'Well, we're not exactly going to scale Mount Godwin Austen, although we can have a crack at the *Blue Danube*. I need my daily caffeine fix.' Muscling in on the last of the cookies and abandoning the wreckage of a tea-stained tablecloth and brimming ashtrays, he seized a large, black umbrella prudently propped up in a corner of the verandah.

'You can't take that,' Hermie cried. 'It's Aunty Al's.'

He was shameless. 'So what? I'm warped and twisted. She knows that. I know that. COME ON!' He unfurled it and took her elbow.

Crouched over a table in the coffee shop Barry said, 'I've had a number of short term re-incarnations, the last as a PT (physical training) instructor.' He fumbled in his back pocket and withdrawing a hip flask splashed some brandy into the coffee pot.

'And what's the current day job?' Hermie sipped cautiously. 'This stuff peps it up no end.'

'Well now I'm with All India Radio.' He was watching her through a thick cloud of cigarette smoke.

'Broadcasting? How thrilling!' She leaned forward. It reeked of glamour. Of long limbed men in bespoke tailored suits with chiselled profiles, impeccable manners and pukka voices.

'You bet...'

'All these Americanisms ...'

'Oh, I pick them up from the movies.'

'I bet that's not all you pick up,' Hermie put in swiftly, and smiled.

He gave the sort of smile that must have disarmed a host of pressing creditors. 'We digress. As I was saying, yes, radio...I'm really a lowly sound technician.'

No matter. To Hermie it was LIFE.

'When I first came to Delhi like you I roomed with Aunty Al, then she evicted me to my current lodgings. Pa, Ma and my married sister live in Bareilly.'

'And that's?'

'Far enough.' He grinned. 'Roughly 250 miles north-east of Delhi, where the loveliest roses bloom.' He flicked cigarette ash onto the floor. 'When a guy tells a gal, as I'm telling you now, that she's a Bareilly rose, it's a hell of a compliment.'

'Flatterer.'

Barry was twenty-one and as long as he could remember, he'd hankered after a job in entertainment.

'It's in your blood,' Hermit said warmly 'you're a natural. You've the gift of the gab.'

'Is that the plain, unvarnished truth?' Barry said a little anxiously then relapsed into badinage. 'You're not just lusting after my body?'

Hermie burst out laughing. 'Listen, you're a brilliant presenter - that other dreary fellow isn't a patch on you.'

'You've made my day. I don't compére just for the dough.   Well, all right, I tell a lie. It comes in handy - supplements the radio station pay, if you can call it that. It's so low, ' he added without rancour, ' for us AIs as to be almost illusory. But I'm never happier than when I'm out there, on that stage, behind that mike.' His eyes lit up. 'It gives me a buzz, right. There's nothing quite like it 'cept ...'

'Except what?'

His eyes twinkled. 'Is your lipstick kiss proof?'

'BEHAVE, Mr Dangerous.' She wasn't averse to flirting with him, but suspected he might be an elusive man.

'And this dame's sitting opposite me is dynamite. And talking about danger, you know war's rumbling on the horizon. If Britain gets involved, India will be dragged into it and blokes will be expected to join up.'

She shuddered. 'I'd no idea the situation was critical. Do you really think war's on the cards?'

His mouth turned down. 'I'm no politician. All I do know is there's talk of nothing else at work and they say it's more go than touch.'

Until then Hermie had not interested herself in the world at large. In Ajeemkot there'd been the usual routine between home and the Bank; she'd smash a tennis ball over the net and go on outings with friends, or dip into a thriller, borrowed from the Inster library where light fiction predominated. Rarely did the Blakes, when they weren't bickering, discuss anything other than the most parochial things - the next pay round, a cousin's wedding, why so and so had sacked the chokra, the cost of mutton, who did what to whom, and when, how and where.

'Do you think you'll enlist?'

Barry's expression became sombre. 'I expect so. Hey, your hair looks different.'

'It's a new hairdo and definitely not one inspired by Madam Olga.' She'd copied it from a picture in an American movie magazine and it made her look like Vivien Leigh. 'Do you like it?'

'Yes. But I like this better.' He reached across to extract an ivory comb and her hair would've tumbled to her shoulders had she not jerked away.

'Keep your thieving hands to yourself. You're misbehaving over a simple cup of coffee.'

'That's the best idea you've had so far. Can I count on your being my misbehavee?'

'I'm saying nothing,' Hermie giggled, 'or I might incriminate myself.'

'Hells bells.' Barry glanced at his watch and made a sharp sound of exasperation. 'Time's wingeth tonga draweth near. I've got to skedaddle.' He flung some coins down on the table, ground out the cigarette stub on the floor, and rushed her out.

Torrential rain cascaded from a slate-black sky. Barry's eyes scanned left and right but every taxi and tonga was full. Muttering under his breath, suddenly he darted into the middle of the road. A tonga pulled up with a terrific rattle and creak and a volley of oaths from the tonga wallah, then Barry was press-ganging its bewildered occupants into vacating claiming that Hermie urgently needed to be transported to hospital. He bundled her in, roaring with laughter, and dropped her back, still speechless, before reporting for duty at the radio station. 'So long, my beaut. Be seeing you.'

The more Hermie saw of Delhi the further Ajeemkot retreated and felt less like home, although she was grimly aware that unless she found a paying job, she'd be on the first train back when the holiday ended. That evening she sat down at the small dressing table and began to brush her hair long and hard, something she was inclined to do when things overwhelmed her. *Oh God what am I to do?* She dropped the brush and rested her elbows on the table top, staring unseeingly into the mirror, fighting a rising panic.

She must have fallen asleep for the next thing Hermie knew she was waking to the sound of a clanking milk churn. She went to the window and looked out. Deepak was already up, making sure the doodwallah didn't adulterate their milk with water. Another day in Delhi had begun and she'd make the most of it, forget about those terrible imaginings. But unknown to her, Aunty Al had been nursing ideas of her own, and she was galvanised into action as Hermie, nicely turned out as usual and undeterred by the throbbing humidity, set out for Connaught Place, almost believing she was born to be a lady of leisure.

***

That Hermie was **husband hunting**, Aunty Al was well aware for Noreen hadn't so much as hinted as spelt it out in words of one syllable.

'**Nothing** wrong with that, Cedric,' she remarked. 'But **something** tells me,' she tapped her heart, **'that the girl will be difficult** to suit.' She knew Hermie and Winston hadn't hit it off, that Marcel wanted nothing to do with his brother's reject and Gerald, who'd not warmed to her, was in pursuit of Bernadette.   'And I **don't** approve of the girl **aimlessly** hanging about with that Romeo'- Barry's name hung unspoken on her lips - 'and **wasting** what little she has on fripperies.'

Aunty Al watched approvingly as with neat movements Mr Caston changed the water in the budgies drinking bowl, and sprinkled birdseed in the cages. 'She'll only come to **grief,** and Noreen will **never** forgive me.'

'There you are my angels. Yes, dear.' He looked across from the feathery clash of colours and started at the purposeful gleam in her eyes. 'You've gone and fixed something up for her.'

'**Indeed** I have, Cedric ' she said with relish. 'Marie and I had an **interesting** chat about our little madam.' It was only to Mr Caston in private that Aunty Al referred to her old school friend by her baptismal name. To everyone else, she was Reverend Mother St. Xavier, the Mother Superior of the best fee paying school in Delhi.

Mr Caston looked uncomfortable. ' Dear, wouldn't it have been...er...better to have broached it to Hermie first?' He hated scenes especially those that he considered could well have been avoided.

'Hermie,' Aunty Al said, not without a certain satisfaction, 'has **no** option.' She seemed to consider the matter closed, but unlike Wilburt and Ashley, it was one of Aunty Al's qualities that she sensed that Hermie would respond better to persuasion than to coercion.

The next day, Aunty Al sealed a blank sheet of paper in an envelope and addressed it to REV. MOTHER SUPERIOR. CONVENT OF THE HOLY MARTYRS. BY HAND. PERSONAL.

'My girl, run along to the convent. Now mind, you're to hand it **personally** to Reverend Mother and no one else. Is that understood?'

'What if she's out?' asked Hermie glancing at the address before tucking the envelope in her handbag, the usual grumble forestalled since the errand wouldn't involve a detour as the convent was located near Barry's lodgings.

'You're **bound** to find her there. During school hours, she's nowhere but. ' Aunty Al turned to busy herself with Deepak, allowing herself a small smile.

Hermie was ushered into the convent parlour by one of the domestic Sisters. She looked around with interest, for unlike Bernadette, she'd not attended a *Roaming Cutlass* school. It was spotless, the terrazzo floor scrubbed to a high sheen she could have put on her makeup, off its reflection.

In a niche stood a statue of a rouged and lipsticked Our Lady, a Mona Lisa expression etched on her pale face, clothed in a sky blue gown, a sparkling tiara nestling within golden tresses. I wouldn't mind wearing that myself, Hermie murmured. Facing it was a picture of the Sacred Heart, and alongside a large wooden Crucifix. But in spite of the religious symbols, there was no odour of sanctity but rather of carbolic and furniture polish. She arranged herself in a comfy chair with a starched, head-back, idly watching through the window a bevy of girls playing netball. Footsteps sounded and Reverend Mother bustled in with a rattle of black rosary beads that drooped in a great loop from her waist. Hermie jumped to her feet.

'Sister says you've come with a letter for me,' Reverend Mother prompted. 'And be seated, child.' Reverend Mother cocked her head as she opened the envelope. 'So, you're on holiday in our fair city. And what do you make of it?'

'It's glorious,' Hermie enthused. 'I love the variety and the fancy shops.' Aunty Al had mentioned that Reverend Mother was a friend of long standing from the AI but she wondered how the nun could tolerate that wimple with its tight cigarette pleats and the starched white ankle length habit, so unflattering.

'So you fill the days of leisure easily?' Reverend Mother fingered the silver pectoral cross. Barely five feet, a firm-bodied dumpling with fair, clear skin, the hazel eyes were shrewd, the mouth-line amiable. Hermie's gaze was drawn to the broad gold ring she wore that signified her spiritual marriage to Christ. A natural-born entrepreneur with considerable flair, the convent school provided the big-business opportunity, which, as a female and an AI at that, she would've been denied in secular life.

'Not entirely,' Hermie confessed with a slight sense of shame. 'I wouldn't dream of admitting it to Aunty Al but there're too many days when I'd like to be getting to grips with something, what with Barry at work, Bettina-Lorna at the club, and Mr Turton Jones nobly giving violin tuition to some talentless youngster.'

'Some of those talentless youngsters are at school here,' Reverend Mother said dryly, but Hermie's careless remarks had given her the entrée she was looking for. She pounced.

'You seem a capable young woman. My kindergarten teachers could do with some assistance.'

'Well, er, I don't know. I'm not qualified. I've just got my Senior Cambridge Certificate,' Hermie protested weakly, but she had, nevertheless, achieved excellent grades in seven subjects in the school leaving exams.

'Oh, you won't be required to teach; just supervise the little ones - girls and we have a few small boys, as well. Play games and sing-along with them, help in the artwork and handicrafts hour, and hear their reading. Take them to the lav. That sort of routine thing - nothing arduous,' Reverend Mother said briskly, glossing over the grind involved in looking after small children. The girl had a pleasant speaking voice of which the parents would approve and seemed interested, although not wholly enamoured of the idea.

'I...'

'Good. You're sensible to give it a try.' Reverend Mother cut through Hermie's indecision, the autocracy sheathed by the dimpled smile that had coaxed many a skinflint to donate generously to the school's laboratory refurbishment fund. 'The convent will provide a mid-day meal and you'll have the company of the other teachers.'

She'd said nothing about pay, Hermie noticed. 'All right, I suppose.' Hermie was surprised by the speed of it all. 'Thanks. Er, er, how much will I get?'

Reverend Mother's eyes blazed. 'Money's the root of all evil. You'll find the training ample recompense.'

Hermie was determined not to seem a pushover. 'But you do know it's only temporary?'

'Understood.' Reverend Mother glanced at the mahogany cased grandfather clock and was on her feet with the swiftness of a bullet that was at odds with her tubby frame. 'I'll expect you tomorrow then, dear,' and before Hermie could demur at the haste of it, she found herself ushered out of the room, and as she walked through the well-kept grounds, the sweet chimes of the Angelus seemed to call her back.

Aunty Al nodded almost absent-mindedly when Hermie reported her conversation with Reverend Mother. **'That'll test her nerves**, Cedric' she said gleefully that night as she hung up his suit.

The next morning Hermie was leisurely sipping Darjeeling tea and contemplating a stroll to the school when there was the loud screech of a horn.

'Hurry, my girl. That must be for **you**, and remember **don't** be pert,' Aunty Al called out from her altercations on the verandah with the dhobi who'd run remarkably quickly through the soap she'd supplied. She suspected he was using it to service some else's dirty laundry, charging that customer for it and making a tidy sum for himself on the turn.

Reverend Mother had said nothing about sending transport for her. Now that was a nice gesture. Another long blast prompted Hermie to quicken her pace. Then she nearly fainted. Pulled up outside the gate, its engine running was a large school bus, filled with little faces pressed excitedly to the windows.

'You're late.' Hermie recognised the stringy, sharp-featured AI woman as Thelma Lord. From her seat behind the driver she was tapping the face of her wristwatch. 'Five minutes late,' she whined. 'Don't you know you're supposed to be waiting here on the pavement? Don't you know Reverend Mother won't allow the bus to wait for anyone? Don't you know she'll brain you if you're late again?'

'No one said I was going to be collected,' Hermie retorted as she swung herself onto the bus. 'How could I have known that? I'm not psychic.'

Sporting the school colours, orange and white, the polished coachwork bore the legend RAPHAEL.   The word was repeated above the driver's mirror, which was flanked by a small picture of St. Christopher, and a larger one of a fluffy-feathered, winged celestial being.

'Good morning, Miss,' the children piped.

Hermie recovered herself sufficiently. 'Good morning, boys and girls. Now what's all this Raphael business?' she asked eyeing Thelma's white pique, bolero-topped sundress.

She was rewarded with a supercilious smile. 'Don't you know...?' Basking in the reflected glory of her father's rank, a naval Commander, Thelma invariably thus opened her conversation with Hermie. 'He's one of the Archangels. The school's other buses, which ply different routes, are Gabriel and Michael. 'Stop that at once, do you hear...'

Thelma turned round to remonstrate with some kids who'd picked a fight with another and were cruelly chanting: *Fatty, fatty bombalati ate up all the ghee chapatti.* 'For heaven's sake, Hermie Blake, they're sitting right beside you - can't you even keep them quiet? They're up to all kinds of mischief. '

'You need eyes in the back of your head,' Hermie countered good-naturedly. 'Ssh children - ' she began ineffectively.

'Anticipation! Don't you know that's what the job's about?' Thelma's tone was shrill with the superior knowledge of one who'd graduated from St Mary's and was now embarked on teaching practice. 'Driver, driver, don't go so fast. Slow down at once or I'll report you to Reverend Mother. Really, *these Indians* are the limit. What can one do with them?'

Hermie let out a long sigh and her eyes strayed to the passing scene and the waves of cyclists on their way to work. The day had scarcely begun and already, as minutes later, they reached the school gates, she felt drained.

In winter school started at eight-thirty a.m. sharp; in summer an hour earlier. If a pupil was late she was reprimanded by Reverend Mother who, depending on her mood and the degree of unpunctuality, either sent her home to repent or allowed her to remain but marked her absent for the day.

With amiable disregard to the different religious persuasions of the students whose ages ranged from five to sixteen - no parent was ever known to protest - Morning Assembly was swiftly dispatched with *Come, Holy Ghost Creator, Come* all seven verses gabbled in English in sixty seconds flat by the senior girls, a musical interlude of either *Jesus Loves Me This I Know* or *All Things Bright and Beautiful* although Reverend Mother whose own family background was modest, firmly censored the fourth verse:

> *The rich man in his castle*
> *The poor man at his gate*
> *He made them high and lowly*
> *And ordered their estate*

There was seldom a pep talk as staff was instructed not to waste teaching time, for which parents were paying through the nose, and then to the sound of military band music, which ranged from *On the Quarter Deck* to *Entry of the Gladiators* played on a new radiogram, the serried ranks of uniformed pupils about turned and by the left quick marched out of the Assembly Hall to classrooms.

At the end of the five-hour day Hermie trotted round the sprawling building, clanging a heavy bell, her hands slippery with sweat. She was then last off the bus, stumbling from it worn-out, having seen the children safely home.

***

'How's it going Hermie?' Aunty Al asked after the second week, turning from the task of initiating Deepak into the mysteries of converting a starched table napkin into a swan. 'I heard from your Ma today and she **can't** get over the news that you're helping out at the convent. Who'd have thought **girlee** could be tamed, she said.'

Hermie laughed and looked up from her nails that she was painting the same pimento red as her lips. 'It's not too bad, I suppose. The Order's supposed to have taken a vow of poverty but you'd be forgiven for thinking otherwise if you saw Revvy's fine bone china, her valuable stamp collection, their downy beds and the brand new chauffeur driven Dodge. I wouldn't mind joining the novitiate myself.'

Surely Hermie's pulling my leg? She's far too secular, not sufficiently pure in heart - definitely not convent material. But then with Hermie, quite anything was possible. Aunty Al threw her a sharp look over her shoulder, and saw her wicked grin. 'You little minx. For a minute you had me worried. **Paagal,** I thought. And as for Reverend Mother she's a firm believer in quality,' she retorted, sticking up for her friend. 'She says it always pays to buy the best because it's more economical in the long run.'

Hermie slipped into a routine and enjoyed tiffin, at the brief meal break, provided by the convent kitchen, in the pleasant company of the other teachers drawn predominantly AIs. Mrs Durie whose dubious claim to fame was that every pupil could sing *Shrimp Boats are A Coming*, pious Mother Imelda, doddery Miss Williams with a mole on her chin from which a hair sprouted who, when Hermie asked her in all innocence what the word fornication meant having read it in one of the fire and brimstone religious magazines lying about, drew a sharp breath and muttered: *it's being naughty in bed.*

Mrs Munsiff, the Maths teacher was a middle-aged Parsi widow with, it was rumoured, a considerable private income who never wore the same sari twice, and who was firm friends with Mrs Carvalho, a breezy Goan who taught chemistry.   Hermie knew by sight, from the weekly dances, the Misses Casey. The younger cleaned her nails with a black Kirby grip plucked from her hair and her older sister wore dresses with armholes so deep that Hermie could see right through from bosom to bosom.

Porridge faced Miss Randall fancied anything in trousers and had achieved the ultimate - an engagement to an Englishman - a spotty clerk in the Public Works Department - whom she'd pursued like a dog worrying a bone - and was going **home** at the end of term. Even frightful Thelma Lord began to thaw and on the one occasion she and Hermie went together to a Stewart Granger film, they timed his kisses. There was also a little Punjabi postulant, Sister Veronica, who did all she could to please. They encouraged Hermie to enrol at St Mary's and she was pleased they thought she was up to it. Although perhaps not just yet... she told herself.

***

The roads dried up, the monsoon tailed off and September slipped into October. Hermie threw herself into the celebration of Corpus Christi, deferred from flaming June to a more agreeable time of year. She scurried round supervising a dozen senior and junior girls decked out in gowns of cream organza. Wearing   coronets of white jasmine they swung bamboo baskets brimming with strongly scented pink and white rose petals. Processing in double file through the grounds of the convent, the adjacent Catholic boys school and the Cathedral in the wake of choir and clergy chanting prayers and singing hymns, they lobbed the petals over their shoulders as they whispered *Sweet Jesus I Love You.* A senior girl from a Brahmin family was a picture as the Madonna.

Diphtheria – and there was said to be a carrier amongst them – later descended on the school and Hermie helped line up all the pupils for throats to be swabbed. The carrier was identified and whisked off, her name being uttered thereafter in hushed tones.

***

A return to Ajeemkot loomed for Hermie had confessed to Noreen that she wasn't ready to apply to St. Mary's. 'Aunty Al?'

'In here, child.' She was in the pantry in a check apron pickling red cauliflowers with a fierce concentration.

'Ajeemkot's not for me,' Hermie declared.

Aunty Al rinsed her hands and gave Hermie a withering look. 'And **why not,** pray? She decanted the pickle into tall, glass jars.

Hermie found a fork and speared out a piece, eating it rolled up in a hot chappati. 'Mmm, tasty. Nothing you cook's a dud. I want to better myself and there aren't the opportunities at home. I'll only rot there.'

Aunty Al didn't mince her words. 'There're **plenty** of chances in Ajeemkot, only you're **blind** to them. And you've passed up the **grand** opportunity of training college when your parents are keen to have you go.'

Hermie tilted her head defiantly. 'I've applied to Grindlays Bank in Delhi and they've placed me on file.'

'Have you now? And you'll be **waiting** till kingdom come.' Aunty Al lifted the lid of the tea caddy decorated with a picture of Big Ben and spooned leaves into the teapot.

Hermie refused to let her see that she was at all bothered. 'Something's bound to turn up. I'm also answering every advert.'

Aunty Al gave a derisive sniff. 'My girl, you're **not** the only one job-hunting – there are **hundreds** of other lasses doing likewise now that our boys have volunteered to join the forces.' The worst had happened; Britain had dragged India and the Empire into the war with Germany.

Hermie fell silent, a cold wave of despair hitting her as she realised that Aunty Al had no intention of letting her stay on beyond the original timescale unless she paid her way and if nothing materialised she saw herself doomed forever to Ajeemkot with scant prospects of escaping again.

61

Aunty Al peered at her and relented, drawing her pencilled black brows together. 'I'll speak to Reverend Mother. Perhaps she'll pay you something if you're prepared to stay on until after Christmas. That's a **busy** time of year for them - what with the nativity play and their forthcoming presentation of *The Mikado.'* It was not as generous an offer as it sounded for Reverend Mother had already broached the subject to Aunty Al and she'd rejected it, believing it only right that Hermie should return home.

Almost in the next moment Hermie remembered the Oakleys. They might know of someone who'd need help of sorts. She sprang to her feet and reached for her bag.

'Where are you running off to?' Aunty Al demanded as Hermit powdered her nose. She gave her one of her speculating looks. 'If it's to visit who I think, just you tell him **nothing** below the neck, **nothing** above the knee.'

Hermie gave an exasperated snort. 'I hardly think that applies to the Reverend Oakley.'

Aunty Al appeared to accept this as an incontrovertible fact but it was apparent from her face that she wondered why Hermie hadn't spoken of him before. 'Well then, my girl, bring back a **nice** leg of **mutton** from those Muslim butchers in Kashmiri Gate.' She wasn't one to pass up an opportunity.

CHAPTER 5

Two white-cheeked black-eyed bulbuls whistled a medley in a peepul tree as children played on the front lawn of the Oakleys off-white bungalow under the lackadaisical eye of a plump, very dark ayah who stared at the visitor, but made no attempt to ask what she wanted. That was the bearer's department.

'Hermie... My word!' Jennifer heard her voice rise in some surprise. She hadn't really expected to run into her again. 'How nice to see you. Do come in,' she added warmly, wondering what brought her there.

She steered Hermie into a large, plainly furnished sitting room relieved by bright chintz curtains. 'It's a bit of a mess I'm afraid, but you know what it's like with children.' It was very much lived in; a cheerful clutter of toys, a jumble of books on a table, a sewing basket by an easy chair, a tin of toffees on the window-ledge.

'Oops!' Hermie stumbled over a teddy bear. She stooped down and propped it against a wall.

'Life treating you well?' Jennifer asked pouring tea from a brown pottery teapot. She hid a smile at Hermie's careful, *refained* pose - knees firmly together, legs crossed at the ankle.

Hermie sipped her tea crooking her pinky finger. 'Ah, Darjeeling – the Queen of teas,' she drawled. 'I'm having fun.'

'Well, you seem a lot happier than when we last met.' It occurred to Jennifer, unaware that Bettina-Lorna's was Hermie's paradigm that Hermie's accent had changed considerably and, even as she spoke, grew more aristocratic by the minute. And talking of holidays, right now, I could do with a break.' She bent down and tossed some model soldiers into a cardboard box. 'Oh don't get me wrong,' she added hastily. 'I love my kids but things are rather fraught at present as Nanny, who we inherited from the previous incumbent, has been ordered home by the medic, suffering from chronic dysentery. So we're at sixes and sevens, with the children milking the situation for all it's worth.' She brushed a wisp of hair from her face and crossed to the window watching the ayah running after Adam who was wriggling through a hole in the shrubbery just like the mongoose.

Hermie told Jennifer what she'd been doing for the past few weeks.' Could I replace Nanny?'

Jennifer who hadn't been prepared for anything so direct was so startled that it took her several moments to collect her thoughts. 'Well... er... we do have ayah and other servants and Peter had a notion that we might try and get by without, although I have my doubts. I'll have to discuss it with him. He's at the BMH (British Military Hospital) at the moment but I'm expecting him back for lunch. May we leave it until I've spoken to him?' She glanced across at Hermie and felt instinctively that she could be just what they were looking for.

The door flew open and Timmy and Adam tumbled in. 'Mummy,' said Timmy staring round-eyed at Hermie, 'it's the nice lady from the train.'

'Yes, darling.' Jennifer ruffled his blond head. 'And she's going home for her lunch.'

But Timmy wasn't to be hurried. 'Will she come again, Mummy?'

Hermie stood up and looked round for her bag. Jennifer gave her son a non-committal smile. 'You never can tell.'

Feeling rather flat, Hermie strolled in the direction of her favourite bangle stall, recklessly blowing Noreen's parting present on several fine gold bangles. She'd completely forgotten about her errand for Aunty Al and had to endure the sharp end of her tongue.

'You're the **giddy** limit.' Aunty Al's gaze flickered over Hermie. Some guilt about the bangles must have shown in her face. 'I know that bangle wallah. He's an old **rogue.**' She weighed the bangles in her hand. 'How do you expect to put money aside for college if you fritter it away like a Maharani?'

Aunty Al liked nothing better, Hermie knew, than to order her life and she'd realised that she hadn't minded that if it meant finding her a husband, but telling her how to spend her money, what to do, or not to do, well, that was another thing.

'You will take them back **at once.'**

Hermie jangled the bangles.

Aunty Al said grimly, 'don't **cross me,** my girl. If you don't return them, I will.'

'As the devil loves holy water.'

'**Button** your mouth you sly puss. I know what they're really worth. So how much exactly did he cheat you out of this time, eh?'

Hermie was in no mood to humour Aunty Al. 'One gives one's all for a pearl of great price.'

***

Over roast lamb, Jennifer, who'd been rather tied to the house since Nanny's departure, looked hopefully at Peter.

Peter sharpened the carving knife. 'Does Hermie have any nannying experience?'

'Technically no, but she has had a lot to do with small children and somehow I think she'll be every bit as good as, if not better than, Nanny,' Jennifer said. Jennifer hadn't taken to the sour-faced woman and wasn't sorry she'd left. But she liked Hermie. 'She seems very pleasant, if somewhat over-impressed with us English,' she observed shrewdly. 'And she has the advantage over Nanny - that of knowing the country like a native.' She added hastily, 'only don't let's say that to her face.'

Some members of Peter's congregation were AI and the Oakleys had soon realised that Hermie was not domiciled European but AI, experiencing all the difficulties and tensions that the mixed-heritage involved.

Peter said slowly, 'I rather took to Hermie. No harm in giving her a try. Ring the Reverend Mother, darling – I gather she's no fool - and get a reference from the horse's mouth.'

***

A few days later Deepak handed Hermie a letter from the Oakleys suggesting a start date. Hermie's heart pounded with excitement. The pay was adequate but the situation was all found and if she were careful, she could save hard and eventually go **home** with the Oakleys. *I've done it!* She resolved to collect her belongings from Ajeemkot, say a proper goodbye to Ma, and steel herself for the inevitable showdown with Pa and Ashley.

Aunty Al sharply reminded her that she couldn't join the Oakleys until after Christmas as Reverend Mother expected her to stay on until then. Hermie was tempted to say she'd do as she pleased, as she was nobody's slave but decided against it. After all, once the school day was over, the rest of the time was her own, whereas with the Oakleys she'd be on the bit almost constantly.

***

'**NO,** Noreen.' Wilburt shouted. 'That girl stays under my roof till she marries or comes of age. This time I intend to put down my foot with a firm hand. Can't you see you'll only be another **bloodee** servant, Hermie? All this fine talk of bettering yourself and here you are, just a glorified ayah.'

When that didn't shift her, he accused Aunty Al of aiding and abetting (although his bluster didn't extend to a face to face confrontation), and threatened to withhold his consent, as Hermie was not yet twenty-one years old.   Inevitably it was Ma who soothed him and made him realise that the experience of working with small children would stand **girlee** in good stead when she ultimately joined the training college.   But in their heart of hearts they were only too aware, although fearful of admitting as much to themselves, that this was just a smoke screen.

'You'll visit us often **girlee?'** Ma put up a hand and brushed away her tears. 'I'll miss you dreadfully.'

'I'm always here for you.' Hermie got up and gave her a hug without actually saying that so long as Pa and Ashley behaved badly she was through with them. 'But I can't ever live in Ajeemkot. Not after Delhi.'

'Yes, **girlee,** I know that. You've sipped from the fountain and found it to your taste. It's a magical place, and…'

If she was any judge of the signs, the question was coming up now, Hermie thought.

'...Have you found the man who'll keep you in diamonds and caviar?' News of Barry had not so much filtered as flashed back.

Hermie met Ma's eyes with a broad grin. 'Not yet, but it's only a matter of time.'   Barry was attentive, he was fun, but she sensed he was stardom-hungry and until he'd grabbed that, everything else was peripheral. Besides, he wasn't pukka enough for her.

'Girlee, I know you'll do well and be a credit to me. Better than ever Ashley would, but that's our secret so don't go letting on to him what I've said, mind.' Ma perceived in Hermie the spark that was missing from her son. 'Now I've a surprise for you.' She got to her feet.

'Where are we off to?'

Ma tapped her nose. 'Patience, patience. Bishu, we're going out. Now listen up. Don't forget to get those saucepans re-lined or we'll die of copper poisoning.' A pedlar who was due to call that day did the job twice a year. 'And the stuff in that corner's for the bikri wallah.'

Intrigued, Hermie allowed herself to be hustled out of the house into a cycle rickshaw and through   familiar teeming streets to where Ma Webb lived downwind from the stench of open drains.

'So Delhi has snatched you from us, a little birdie tells me.' Ma Webb looked and moved like a grasshopper. Pa Webb's whereabouts was a mystery. A boozard, he used to thrash his wife with a hockey stick until one day Mervyn, then sixteen, had wrestled him to the ground. Pa Webb had slunk off never to be seen again. Hermie caught the look of complicity Ma Webb exchanged with Noreen.

Glancing through a window to garments airing on a washing line slung across the back courtyard, Ma Webb's sideline was revealed. Unable to afford dry-cleaning prices, but determined to keep up appearances, she'd doused her clothes in rectified spirits of turpentine bought cheap in the bazaar. It had worked wonders for she and Mervyn were immaculately turned out.   Emboldened by this unexpected success, Ma Webb was taking in other people's dry-cleaning, in the process undercutting the Sikh-owned drycleaners in Kingsway that, until then, had enjoyed a rare monopoly. It had retaliated by slashing its prices, and a savage price war was being waged.

'Over here.' In the best traditions of amateur theatricals much indulged in by her, Ma Webb flung open the door of her small bedroom. On the floral counterpane that covered a sagging charpoy lay lots of little parcels, wrapped in many layers of rainbow coloured tissue paper, hand-tied with coloured ribbons and bows and decorated with pompoms and tassels.

Hermie gasped.

Noreen and Ma Webb beamed. 'For you.'

Hermie's hand hovered uncertainly then closing her eyes momentarily pounced on one at random and tore it open. 'It's gorgeous!'

Noreen had commissioned from Ma Webb sets of slinky lingerie and nightwear; petticoats and knickers in silk voile and satin, some appliquéd with roses, poppies and sweet peas, some embroidered with lotuses and Kashmir lilies; some shot through with lace, tiny beads and mother -of -pearl; pure silk pyjamas in iridescent blue, a housecoat dappled with hand-crafted wool work.

Hermie pressed a garment to her cheek savouring its delicacy, allure and vampishness. 'It's divine.' There was a lump in her throat. Darling Ma was so thoughtful.

'Only the best's good enough for **girlee**.' Ma kissed Hermie and they held hands, Hermie fighting the tears that threatened to spill over.

'And we hunted this down especially for you,' Ma Webb twittered, hoiking a large, square cardboard box off the floor.

'You shouldn't have. But give me a clue.'

'Well,' Ma Webb gave a little squeak. ' Remember that Afghani furrier who favours me by selling my wares in his shop on an agency basis?'

Hermie pulled off the lid. 'Oh!' Completely at a loss for words, she stroked the rich softness of the dark fur jacket. It was so stylish, so film star-ish. 'I can't wait to try it on.' She slipped it round her shoulders and stepped to the mirror. 'I feel like royalty.'

'You look like royalty. My princess! Delhi can be so cold in winter and you'll want to be nicely dressed when some nice young man comes calling in the evenings,' Noreen said, a little tactlessly, having already consigned Mervyn to oblivion.

'Thank you, thank you. Ma, you're the best in all the world.' Hermie flung her arms round her. Noreen had made everything perfect. Reverently she replaced the jacket in the box, wondering if Ma had bought it on tick for her savings could never have run to buying the gift outright.

'Now, not a word of this to your Pa or Ashley. It's our little secret.'

***

As Loco Quarters faded out of sight, Ma with her arm encircling Hermie in the tonga was red-eyed all the way to the station. Ashley and Wilburt still nursing a grievance had refused to see her off. Mervyn sat nervously beside Ma; the whole business had left him bemused, and in Hermie's present mood, he hadn't dared to ask her if they had a future together. Mother and daughter embraced, Ma promising to spend Christmas with Hermie and the Castons.

'Cheerio.' Hermie offered Mervyn her cheek and raced to the train. She didn't look over her shoulder to wave goodbye to Noreen again for she knew that if she did her resolve to leave Ajeemkot would be completely undone.

***

'Revvy was nowhere to be seen today,' Hermie remarked to Aunty Al. 'She's playing truant.'

Aunty Al was grim faced. 'You're bound to hear sooner or later, so I might as well tell you now. She's gone to June's funeral, and plans to be away for a few more days supporting the grieving family.'

Hermie was flabbergasted. She remembered June - or rather Juanita as she'd rebranded herself - as an attractive pregnant brunette in her late twenties with a lily-white complexion who'd recently paid a visit to her aunt, Reverend Mother. A super efficient secretary who'd acquired a smattering of Spanish, June had headed to Calcutta five years earlier from an unremarkable town and passing herself off as Castilian became PA to the English Manager of a jute factory. He'd fallen deeply in love with her, they'd married and their life together was magic.

My Juanita has married up, her mother gleefully told Reverend Mother

'June looked blooming; I'd no idea she was ill.' Hermie was all agog. 'How did she die?'

Aunty Al frowned as if to say Hermie could've put it rather more delicately. 'She gave birth to a typical little Indian boy, the colour of burnt almond.'

Hermie gasped and put a hand to her mouth.

'Yes, a throwback. There'd not been a soul like that in the family for generations. Against Reverend Mother's better judgment, June had kept choop about her AI origins. Her husband had no inkling she was AI. He visited her and their baby son in hospital and told her he didn't mind about his colour; he promised he'd love and cherish her and their child forever; he vowed to stand by them, but June was inconsolable. She didn't believe him, wouldn't, couldn't believe him. She said her future was lost to her.'

Aunty Al took a big gulp of sherry to steady her nerves. 'Forty-eight hours after labour, June and baby went missing, sparking a massive hunt. Then just days later their lifeless bodies were pulled from the well into which she'd flung herself.'

Hermie shuddered. Suppose nature played the same cruel trick on her?

***

Aunty Al's preparations for Burra Deen – Christmas - began early and accompanied by Hermie and Deepak she descended on the bazaar to select the plumpest raisins, the juiciest sultanas, the choicest currants and candied peel and to do annual battle with the bania whose price of dry goods rose in proportion to seasonal demand. Bottles of rum were delivered by the crateful, for Aunty Al was justly famous for her milk-rum punch. It took dedication, patience and family involvement, but the proof of it was in the drinking.

'Make yourself useful, girl.' Aunty Al pulled out a dining chair and up-turning it tied the corners of a dampened piece of muslin securely to the legs.

'What do you want me to do?' Hermie said. Back home, Ma had lamented that brewing punch was too fiddly for her.

'Fetch that large basin and stand it under the muslin and then...' Aunty Al proceeded to strain the punch that had taken eight days of preparation to reach this stage, through the muslin, a cupful at a time, occasionally stirring the mixture. Hermie did as asked, watching fascinated as a clear liquid dripped through the muslin into the china basin. One batch was followed by several and Aunty Al prevailed on Mr Caston and Mr Turton Jones to decant it into bottles that were then tightly corked.

But there was to be no reward for their labours. 'No, not even a sip. You'll have to wait the fortnight it takes to mature,' Aunty Al said wickedly. 'But the cook's obliged to sample it.' She filled a wine glass to the brim and swallowed, a look of sheer bliss crossing her face. 'Well up to standard.'

Coloured crepe paper was purchased from the bazaar; Hermie and Mr Turton Jones cut short lengths that they twisted and flour-pasted into streamers; balloons were blown up and the warm smell of herbs and spices filled the air. Christmas cake ingredients were mixed, stirred and poured into cake tins and shipped off for baking by a local bakery for Aunty Al lacked a large enough oven. Then, perched on a large metal plate and boldly labelled CASTON for God forbid they got entangled with another family's inferior efforts, they were delivered back by tonga.

On Christmas Eve Aunty Al, in yet another new outfit and a Madam Olga creation, and Mr Caston set out for Midnight Mass. The Cathedral choir had been rehearsing carols for weeks.

Noreen arrived that day and flinging her arms round her, Hermie realised how much she'd missed Ma. Mr Turton Jones, a self-confessed agnostic, stayed home with Hermie and Noreen, who claimed that the long journey in second class had rendered her too exhausted to join the service, and the three conspirators sat in the parlour round a glowing coal fire cracking nuts, quaffing ginger wine and munching prawn puffs. Freed from domestic drudgery and the heavy presence of Pa and Ashley, Noreen became skittish in the glow of Mr Turton Jones' charm and *olde worlde* gallantry.

Christmas morning dawned bright and cold. A soft tap on the door heralded Deepak. 'Mary Kismet!' he said and, smiling shyly, slid in bearing a coconut and garlands of rose petals and tiny white chrysanthemums threaded between tinsel. Noreen and Hermie were sharing the room recently vacated by Bettina-Lorna. Only days earlier, Hermie had witnessed the inevitable falling out between Aunty

Al and Bettina-Lorna whose demands had become increasingly unreasonable. A bigger room... breakfast in bed... monopoly of Deepak...

'Negotiate negotiate. That's all she ever does.' Aunty Al had stormed. *'Well she's tested me too far. She's negotiated herself out of this house.'*

The breakfast table was dotted with miniature bouquets of mixed blooms and maidenhair arranged with perfect artistry all by Deepak himself.

'He's so creative and multi-talented,' Hermie kicked off her slippers under the table, implying that Bishu was bereft of both.   Presents were exchanged with the rest of the household and replete after porridge, hot chappatis smeared with butter and rolled up with lumps of gur, curds, onion omelettes, French toast and fishcakes, and they drifted away to prepare for the lunch party.

The leaves of the dining table had been extended for a buffet and Deepak was busy laying the best silver and china on a starched damask tablecloth.   Ma had finished dressing and Hermie thought she'd never looked more fetching in the pink slub silk suit.

'My, Mrs Blake you   look a picture!' remarked Mr Turton Jones. Natty in his best brown suit and check bow tie he wasn't normally given to making personal remarks.

'Thank you. And may I return the compliment.'

Aunty Al was unruffled despite the arduous preparations of the past few weeks that she'd juggled with charitable works and choir commitments.

The trickle of guests swelled to a flood. Scotch whisky, brandy, gin, and beer flowed like the river Jumna and they couldn't have enough of Aunty Al's famous punch.

'It's well worth the wait,' Noreen was saying, somewhat squiffily, after her third glass and Mr Turton Jones was by her side in a trice with a steadying arm. She'd forgotten how potent it could be, and how delicious. 'It's a million times tastier than the finest amontillado, and it certainly packs a punch.'

Mr Turton Jones cleared his throat and said carefully, 'All the best things in life are invariably well worth waiting for ...um...Noreen,' he boldly ventured her Christian name.   Noreen had flopped into a chair, and he perched himself on the arm. She was enjoying herself without Pa and Ashley, refusing to feel guilty about leaving them, for the first time ever, to fend for themselves. Besides, some woman in the AI would jump at the chance of ministering to them, she'd decided - no doubt that ghastly spinster next door who was forever knitting those shapeless pullovers for Wilburt. Not like Mr Turton Jones who'd re-titled his new composition An *Ode to Noreen.*

The Castons AI friends swarmed in joined by a few Armenians, and Indians of all faiths, although some of Mr Caston's high caste colleagues snubbed them by declining the invitation for they were unwilling to eat with the lower caste, taking particular offence at the presence of Deepak lest his untouchable shadow loomed over them.

Pungent smells of Indian home cooking fit for a Maharajah filled the air and Aunty Al also paid homage to the unique specialities of the AI. Heaped platters of ox tongue, salt meat, but not, as in other AI homes that day, brawn, because made from the brain of a pig, it would offend Muslim guests; thick mutton chops with macaroni, panthe kaukwswe – a chicken dish swimming in noodles that gave a clue to its Anglo-Burmese origins - plump pumpkin fritters, pickled damsons, apple pickle, mutton soufflé, salmon kitcheree, spicy chunks of chicken country captain and stacks of steaming chappatis. The sweet toothed were dazzled by mouth-watering desserts - bibinca, rosa cookies, crisp kul kuls, and dhol-dhol (the AI counterpart to Christmas pudding made from black puttoo rice), ice creams in every hue and flavour and rose-essence flavoured rice phirni sprinkled with pistachio nuts.

'Wonderful grub.' Barry, working his way through a third helping, materialised at Hermie's side. ' I'm doing serious damage to Al's chicken biriyani.'

'She certainly knows how to party,' Hermie said with admiration as she quaffed punch that was all the more enticing after her modest contribution to the effort.

'Seems a fitting occasion for yours truly to say *au revoir.*' Barry raised his glass. He explained that he'd joined the Indian Air Force and, although just an aircraftman, he'd be one of the guys the pilots depended on to keep planes airborne. 'Number 1 Squadron IAF has three flights all located in Ambala so initially that'll be my base.'

To her surprise, Hermie realised she'd miss his company.

***

On New Year's Day, Reverend Mother telephoned asking Hermie to stay on for a few weeks as a number of staff had succumbed to flu. Hermie, groggy after a night of revelry at an Old Year's Night dance that featured an AI crooner in a long, slinky dress, the last wisecracking appearance of Barry who was given a rousing send-off and a noisy rendition of *Auld Lang Syne,* uncharacteristically found herself agreeing. But eventually, in February, Hermie arrived at the Oakleys bearing a tuck box brimming with Aunty Al's goodies.

'Am I glad to see you.' Jennifer smiled warmly as Timmy and Adam bounced out of the house to greet her. 'I thought this moment would never come. Peter has nipped across to the Aliens Internment Camp but has asked me to say welcome on his behalf.'

'I'm thrilled to be here.' The first hurdle was over and, despite the clouds of war and the chaos of lively youngsters, this was where Hermie sensed she could look forward to a new future. There'd been another bitter clash with Pa and Ashley but Hermie, torn between Ma and a determination to catch the running tide, had stood her ground.

CHAPTER 6

From her cane chair by a window of the so-called library of the Aliens Internment Camp, a former army barracks on the outskirts of Delhi, Edith Müller glanced up from her sketch book and saw Peter Oakley striding across the parade ground, bordered by ranks of scarlet and yellow cannas, to the Commandant's office. She studied him afresh - a tall, athletic figure, not handsome but pleasant looking with warm slate-grey eyes and a square jaw that belied his sensitive mouth - and felt oddly glad to see him again. It helped relieve the monotony of waiting for news of her family in Germany, and especially Jean-Claude, whose photo stood on her bedside table and who'd written saying he'd managed to slip safely back into Paris.

Beside her was a letter from the Addisons with whom she'd struck up an unlikely and lively friendship. They'd disembarked in Bombay and eventually reached the Mission near Calcutta, unaware she'd been ushered to one side by British security forces that had boarded the *Moloja* as she'd docked. Learning of her internment the Addisons had harried government officials to secure her release, but to no avail.

Photos they'd sent suggested a crimson-brick, steepled Baptist Church with a bell tower and pitched tile roof standing in a compound filled with many trees and   colourful flowerbeds. The Mission house, a high ceiling, two-storied flat roofed brick affair, had deep verandahs back and front, electric fans, a large garden planted with seasonal flowers and vegetables and tennis and badminton courts shared with sporty members of their congregation.

Edith uncurled long, white drill trouser legs and strode out into the compound, deftly side-stepping a column of black ants scurrying across her path.

'Good morning.' Peter raised his hat and smiled, drawn to the self-possessed German woman with a fine, fair skin, and fair hair tied back from her face with a blue ribbon that matched the colour of her eyes. 'It's another perfect day and,' he sniffed appreciatively, 'something smells good.'

'I expect it's the little lamb I saw frolicking in the grass yesterday.'

He laughed. 'Heartless woman. If my sense of smell doesn't deceive me, it's mulligatawny soup.'

'Yet again.'

Peter caught her dry tone. 'Well I won't argue with that - you're undoubtedly the expert. But it's nourishing all the same with those tasty chunks of meat, rice and lemon. 'Jennifer says your English is coming along very well.' His wife, a former teacher, had volunteered to instruct those of the internees who were interested in learning English, and they knew Edith as the energiser of activities at the Centre.

Edith lifted a shoulder. 'Thank you, but my neck under the yoke is not easy to bear.' She smiled briefly, buttoning up her hand-knitted wool cardigan against the chill of the bright, February morning.

'Understandably so,' Peter felt himself flush and he cringed inwardly; both he and Jennifer viewed with distaste the British government's haphazard policy of detention of all these German and Axis nationals, some of whom he'd learned had been successful businessmen in India for many years and refugees - fleeing to safety abroad, only to be interned. It was quite absurd, he thought, for they hardly posed a threat to the defence of the realm.

'I'd no idea north India could be so cold in winter.' Edith's charming voice bore unmistakeable traces of her origins but her English, after five months in the Centre, was almost perfect.

'Indeed. We light a fire in the evenings and it's almost like being back home in Wiltshire.' From the Commandant, Peter had learned that Edith had fled Germany in the spring of 1939. 'Tell me, if I'm not being inquisitive, what brought you here?' He'd chatted briefly to her on previous pastoral visits, wondering what quirk of fate had brought her to India, or, for that matter, how the other internees - a broad mix of mostly professional people - came to be there.

'It's complicated but I had to get out so... I stowed away on a freighter leaving Hamburg and after I reached England, I managed, but not without paying Dane geld, to secure a passage on the Moloja that set sail in mid- August last year, bound for Sydney.'

'So you'd planned to settle Down Under?'

'Only until political sanity was restored back home.' But when the ship arrived in Bombay and before she could continue her voyage, war broke out...'

Peter knew the rest. '...And that prompted the promulgation of various Foreigners Ordinances, the upshot being that you so-called enemy aliens on board were served with restriction orders and handed over to the military.' Ill at ease he looked down at the grass, avoiding Edith's cool, steady gaze.

' Correct. And so here I am.'

'And if you weren't, I'd never have had the good fortune to make your acquaintance.' He looked up and met her eyes. 'It's an ill wind...Shall I be seeing

you at evensong? You're very welcome.' He shared pastoral duties with a
Catholic priest and an interned Rabbi.

Edith gave a low gurgle of laughter. 'Padre, that's the last place you'll find me.
I haven't seen the inside of a church since my baptism in Stuttgart's Stiftskirche...'
her voice shook a little '... but I've seen the inside of a German gaol and that
doesn't earn golden opinions.' It was there, she'd come to realize, that she learned
how to confront the current crisis.

Peter sensed that she was wondering whether her earlier record of detention
had anything to do with the present internment, for the other restricted women
and children were allowed to live out in supervised, civil accommodation, subject
only to reporting conditions. It must have been a political imprisonment he
decided; Edith didn't strike him as a common criminal. From her papers he knew
she was twenty-three, some ten years younger than his Jennifer. 'But you can
commend other things?' His eyes probed the bony face.

'Ja wohl. Marx, Lenin... Their ideology is despised and feared by the Nazis.'

So she'd been gaoled for her Communist affiliations he realised with a sudden
jolt. It wasn't what he'd have expected.

'And it's flawed.' Peter's grin robbed his reply of its abrasive edge.

A quiver of exasperation, quickly suppressed, crossed her face and he saw the
sudden snap of her eyes. 'You know, I could make you change your mind about
that,' she said slanting him a humorous look.

'I'm certain you can't, but I'm always willing to listen.'

'Oh yes. Ever reasonable, ever ready to lend an ear but never to be persuaded
from your deeply held convictions.' She spoke a little fiercely.

'I couldn't agree less,' Peter said with asperity. 'If it's right I'd be the first to
admit that.'

'Right and wrong. So you want to talk about the true meaning of that? You
know, I read philosophy at Göttingen University so I'm sure we'd have a very
interesting discussion.'

Peter could sense the excitement of intellectual combat flaring in her and it
made him recall something she'd once said - that it was so long since she'd
revelled in the freedom of expression, sitting up all night over bottles of wine at a
pavement cafe. Would those heady days ever return, she'd wondered.

'I'll hold you to that and… oh, there goes the Commandant. I'll catch up with
him.' Peter rubbed his jaw with his hand. 'I'm sure to see you again. But

goodbye for now.' He'd dearly have loved to stay to talk to this extraordinary woman with the mobile face. They shook hands and Peter turned and walked away towards the other man, aware of Edith's gaze and sensing how much she envied his freedom of movement.

Edith gave a resigned shrug and rubbing her hands in the cold headed slowly across the dew-wet grass to the Common Room that the Commandant dignified by the title *Recreations Wing*.

The scene there was a replay of the previous day and the day before that but she'd not really expected otherwise. Dr Becker and Herr Neurath were crouched over a chessboard. Edith waited for the game to end as others had done - in an almighty row.   Edith suspected it was no different from the scene in Dr Becker's expensive Hanover residence before the war. But it wasn't difficult to feel sorry for them for like a small number of other Jews who'd managed to flee Hitler's Germany, Edith knew that the Beckers and the Neuraths, hastily abandoning their comfortable homes, had bolted simply with their prayer shawls, Sabbath candlesticks and ten marks in their pockets.

Across the room the chords of a piano concerto thundered away as Valentin, a Bulgarian carpet dealer tormented Chopin. He smiled as Edith paused by him. 'I play it again, Edith, just for you, and you'll turn the pages for me, yes?' A polyglot, he'd impressed her with his encyclopaedic knowledge of dies and wools, and bore his detention with equanimity.

'You know,' he said proudly, 'I'm employed by the famous Atiyeh Brothers of Kerman. We're a byword in the trade for goods of quality.'

'How on earth did you end up here?' Edith asked.

'I'd like that to be a long story but regretfully it's not.' He executed a trill on the piano.

'I prefer short stories,' Edith said with a smile.

'Along with my customers - a compatriot and a Hungarian bacteriologist...' He began to laugh as he saw the sceptical twist of Edith's mouth ' ...no, seriously, I don't joke. We were apprehended in a Tehran restaurant just as we were tucking into the main course and hustled to India. Even with pressure from people of influence - my uncle had been Prime Minister of Bulgaria and my father an Ambassador to Austria, I'm still not released. But one day I promise myself I'll go back - perhaps with you, my dear Edith,' he gave her a soft look, 'and do justice to that unfinished meal.'

'Mein Gott. If I had my way, I'd sentence you to life imprisonment for defiling the music of a genius.'

Valentin's hands slipped to his lap and he lapsed into a shocked silence as the speaker, a thin, pre-maturely bald man in his early thirties flung down his newspaper.

'Ulrich!' Edith reacted sharply. 'SHUT UP!'

'I've been searching for you all over the place. I thought you'd absconded. Sit here and let me have the pleasure of your company. I'll find myself another chair.' Ulrich was charging off before she could remonstrate with him, probably sensing the danger of it. Edith dropped into the easy chair exchanging a deprecatory glance with Valentin and to her relief his face broke into a broad, no-hard-feelings smile.

Edith shifted in her seat, silently reflecting on her fellow internees. Their foibles had once seemed quirky, almost endearing, but now they'd become tiresome and today her frustration was even more benumbing than ever. In the relative safety of the Internment Centre, with plentiful though plain food, far from the deepening crisis in Europe, they'd accepted its routine and, overcoming its petty restrictions, they'd reverted to type. But oh, how the days trickled by.

Her gaze swivelled across the room to the two van Meuwen brothers chatting quietly to each other in an obscure Indonesian dialect. She'd tried out her smattering of Dutch on them without success. They resolutely kept themselves to themselves and had been shipped to India from Java where they'd gone from Salem in the mid thirties. First interned in the Straits Settlement, they were impenitent Nazi sympathisers and had made no friends in the Centre, although another internee, young Father Jurgen of the Society of Jesus, a gentle man from Carinthia, whose nose was buried in a Jesuit periodical *Stimmen der Zeit* had tried his best to build bridges.

Ulrich is taking an inordinate time, Edith thought drowsily. *What's keeping him? It's not like him to be side tracked.* A mathematics teacher at a high school, she'd known of him slightly through a faculty acquaintance who had shared his passion for mountaineering. An exceptional climber, Ulrich told Edith he'd left Germany last summer holidays to lead an expedition to the Kulu and Lahul districts of the Himalayas.

Outraged that the outbreak of war had curtailed the trek, he'd complained bitterly over and over again to Edith until she was heartily sick of hearing it and told him so.

We learnt at base camp on l6 September of the outbreak of hostilities and that was it. We were expected to report immediately to the nearest police station. Can you imagine such nonsense?

Edith could but sensed Ulrich was the sort of person who'd never have dreamed of disobeying an order, however absurd. He wasn't a companion she'd have chosen to be saddled with. But then, Edith sighed, she'd had no choice. But once she was out of here...

She let her mind dwell pleasurably on the prospects of release, consoled by the knowledge that only last week, the architect Herr Friedrich, two young clock mechanics from Aachen on a tour of duty in India servicing railway station clocks, and a German geophysicist employed by Burmah Oil, had all wangled an early discharge.

The slap of leather-soled sandals on the terrazzo floor prompted her to open her eyes. Ulrich was looking down at her, chair-less but smirking. It was, she realised, the first time ever that she'd seen him smile. And if she was honest, it wasn't a pretty sight. He looked positively lunatic with what was left of his hair flopping over his forehead and those half moon spectacles.

He cleared his throat to speak but only incoherent sounds, like that of a man being slowly strangled, emerged.

'What's got into you?' Edith demanded impatiently.

He flapped a sheet of paper weakly at her. Edith snatched it from him. It was the permit for his release. Something pitched in her. But what about me?

Eventually Ulrich blurted out, 'I bumped into the Commandant; he was about to summon me to give me the news...' The excitement made him sweat. 'That's what took me so long...Oh...'

'My God.' Edith was no longer listening. Jumping to her feet and circumventing the circle of Ulrich's arms, she ran the length of the corridor passing the kitchen with its smell of boiled cabbage and rounding a corner slithered to a stop at the Commandment's office.

'Miss Müller! There you are! Come right in. We were just about to call for you.' The Commandant was an austere, over-age British Colonel yanked out of retirement for a task he found distasteful at times.

'I've been... in the... Common Room...what is it?' Edith faltered, catching her breath, her heart sinking apprehensively.

He gestured to a chair, aware that she was the sort of woman who said little and wasn't one to make a fuss but registering that she was under a great strain. 'Won't you sit down?' He smiled across at her - a genuine smile of goodwill - and she sent up a prayer of wild hope. 'I'm pleased to inform you that your internment is at an end. He cleared his throat. 'I'm very sorry - it was all er...er...a mistake. You're free to leave whenever you wish.' There was a note in his voice that indicated deep regret and anger at the bureaucratic bungling.

Edith managed to nod, staring at the discharge papers, her eyes skimming over the formal, official words. She clasped them to her heart and closed her eyes tightly overcome with joy and relief. Never one to express her emotions, she could have wept.

Dimly she heard herself saying, 'Thank, thank you. I've dreamed of this moment for so long.' She moved forward and planted a kiss on the surprised Colonel's cheek.

***

Emboldened by Peter Oakley's friendly overtures, the next morning Edith, after writing up the journal that charted her life from the *Moloja* onwards, gave Ulrich the slip and cycled the few miles to St. James' Church. Overhead powdery puffs of cloud in the grey-blue William Daniel watercolour sky arched over beds of crimson hollyhock, velvety blue pansies and creamy lilies.

'Look who's here,' Peter said to Jennifer as a flash of red appeared round the corner of the house. 'It's good to see you,' he shouted to Edith.

Edith threw down her bicycle near a maroon Austin bought for the Oakleys by the diocese, sensing beneath the warmth of their welcome their complete surprise at the unexpected visit.

They rose quickly to the occasion and, ushering Edith indoors, Peter produced a decanter of sherry and three glasses.

'What can I do for you?' Peter asked, hardly believing she'd come for religious solace.

Not one for small talk, Edith was swiftly despatching the preliminaries. 'Padre, can you help? I'm a free woman and what I need more than anything else is a job.' She added bluntly, 'I have to earn my living now. Even with the loss of liberty, it's been an odd few months, being fed, watered and sheltered at no effort or expense to oneself.'

Disarmed by Edith's directness, and full of respect and admiration for her spirit triumphant in adversity, Jennifer felt she deserved whatever help they could give.

'What do you think, darling?' She glanced across at Peter knowing that he felt exactly as she did about Edith.

'You've boasted of your close acquaintance with Hegel, Schopenhauer, Locke and Nietzsche, but they're rather rarefied so what else, Edith, could you offer?'

'They're my best friends,' Edith said dryly, warming to the Oakleys. 'But I'm also something of a linguist. German, Russian, French and, dare I add, English. And I can dance, ride, fence, swing a tennis racquet, ski, ice-skate....'

'Oh yes, plenty of opportunity for that when the Jumna freezes over,' Peter said.

They laughed and Jennifer lifted her eyebrows. 'And a Francophile, like ourselves. How marvellous! We honeymooned in the Loire Valley and just adore it. I expect you often visited France given it's so easy to cross the border from Germany.'

Edith felt a faint flush creep into her cheeks.   'I spent a lot of time with a Frenchman, Jean-Claude.'

' Is he here with you?'

'If only. But he recently sent news to say that he has managed to cross back safely into France. And there's nothing like love, or war, to make one speak a foreign language like a native.'

Aware from Peter's expression that he'd had a brainwave, Jennifer grasped Edith's hand. 'She'd be perfect, wouldn't you say, darling?'

'Padre, don't be so irritating, you've something in mind?   Come on, give.' Edith looked from Peter to Jennifer.

'Oh, do call me Peter.' He got up to replenish her glass. 'I know the princely house of Walipur has been looking high and low for a tutor –'

'Maybe...' Edith wasn't going to show she was about to go overboard at the prospect.

'Edith, you're priceless!' Jennifer declared, leaning back in her chair. 'You're being maddening about something most women would give their eye teeth for.'

'This is about the size of it, then,' Peter said briskly. 'The new Maharajah of Walipur, HH as he's quite happy to be called, succeeded to the title last year on the death of his father.' He paused and took a sip of sherry. 'The ADC- you know, the *aide de camp* - a sort of equerry and private secretary- was in the Mess the other day so I got to hear the woes. Both the nanny and the tutor handed in their notice and beetled back to England just after war was declared. The gap has to be plugged as HH has several younger cousins who need a firm hand before

they're shipped off to boarding school.' He broke off to admire a crayon drawing
Adam rushed in with. 'It could almost have been tailored for you, but be warned,
the pay itself isn't exceptional as it's all found.'

Edith heard him out in silence. 'So I wouldn't necessarily be based in Delhi?'
The prospect of exploring other parts of India that, despite the internment, had
cast its spell over her, appealed enormously.

'Correct, but there's no hard and fast rule. It's all a matter of HH's whim, I
gather. He doesn't disguise his love for Delhi because it's so jolly but by and
large he holds court at the principal palace in Walipur... '

'... Although during the torrid summers the entourage decamps to his country
estate in Sivalik, a ravishing hill station in the Himalayan foothills,' finished
Jennifer.

'Well, he seems to have a fun time. How do I go about applying for a share in
it?' Edith had sensibly determined to take the first reasonable opening that came
her way.

The Oakleys were regarding her with amusement and affection. 'I'll put your
name forward and, if I can, arrange for you to meet the ADC,' Peter promised.
'The rest's up to you.' It really was, he thought anxiously, wishing that they could
do more for Edith but they'd no real influence.

Edith inclined her head slightly. 'Wunderbar and thank you,' she said huskily,
touched at the Oakleys kindness to a complete stranger - a stranger whose
country was at war with theirs. 'But...suppose I'm found wanting? What would
I do then? I suspect there aren't many footholds in India for a woman and a
German at that...' Her voice trailed off uneasily, her perpetual optimism taking a
sudden dive.

'It's just a formality,' Jennifer put in quickly. 'They've been hunting for ages
for the right person.'

'And you think I'm that?'

'Yes,' the Oakleys chorused and Peter added, 'we'd be delighted to give you a
testimonial, only...' he paused '...may I offer you a piece of advice, Comrade -
keep mum about your manifesto.'

Edith gave a deep sigh. Subterfuge wasn't her style, yet she understood the
prudence of keeping her political views to herself. To survive, she had to be
practical, even if that meant being a closet card carrying member of the Party.
One day, and she was sure that day wasn't far off, she'd be free to unveil her true

political allegiance. She arranged her features into something resembling compliance. 'Naturally. You're right, of course.'

Jennifer threw her a sharp look from under her thick brows. 'It's a matter of expediency.'

'When is it not?' Edith gave a resigned shrug. 'But believe me, I won't tempt fate. I hear what you say. And my secret's safe with you, is it not?'

Jennifer nodded, her curls bobbing up and down and Peter made a sawing motion across his throat.

Shrieks of laughter had been drifting from the garden and prompted them to the window. Edith glimpsed a young woman playing energetically on the lawn with the children. Jennifer followed her gaze, grinning and waving furiously to the little group.

'I spy Jennifer!' The woman's voice rang out cheerfully.

Returning the greeting, Jennifer said to Edith. 'That's Hermie, our new nanny. She's an absolute treasure. We'd be lost without her.'

'You brought her with you from England?'

Peter gave a lopsided grin. 'Listening to her accent now, you'd have thought she'd been bred in the purple. But no, she was a most amazing find – an AI runaway from a difficult family situation in Ajeemkot, oddly enough not a million miles from Walipur, but for some personal reason, she doesn't like that widely known.'

'And you took her to your bosom, like me. So you've a genius for collecting the flotsam and jetsam of life.' Edith liked Peter and Jennifer more and more.

'No. I wouldn't call it that,' Peter said quietly. *'More like full many a gem...full many a flower... and all that.'*

'Look,' Jennifer said, inspired, 'come and say hello to her on your way out. She's really awfully pleasant. I can't think why some nice man from her community hasn't snapped her up.' She gave Edith a hug. 'We're keeping our fingers crossed for you; do let us know how you get on with the ADC.'

'Oh, there's just one more thing...I've a confession to make...'

The Oakleys stopped dead.

'I can't cook and I can't bake *apfel strudel.'*

***

'But Edith, surely you've made some plans for the future?' Ulrich was stuffing his belongings, which included bulky climbing gear, into a rucksack. 'Why don't you come down south with me? We'd be company for each other. After all, we've shared many experiences, have we not?'

'No, on all counts.' Edith had no intention of telling him about the Walipur appointment of which she'd received confirmation the previous afternoon, neatly typed on expensive Royal household writing paper bearing the Walipur crest - crossed scimitars above which stood an elephant poised on a globe of the world. She'd opened it with trepidation for it had been a week of suspense in which Edith, who wasn't normally given to negative and dark forebodings, had agonised, after the unpromisingly brief interview with HH's ADC, Major Naidu, a taciturn, clean-shaven south Indian in his thirties.

But now she was happy, so happy when only a few days ago she was almost drowning in misery and she wanted nothing more to do with Ulrich into whose company she'd been unavoidably thrown.

'Ah, Edith - that sigh. It speaks volumes. I know. It's seldom easy to say goodbye.'

'Not for me.' She was very discouraging. If Ulrich harboured secret desires for her, she was determined to undermine them. There was no one for her but Jean-Claude of whom she had worryingly no further news. 'Now you really ought to get a move on or you'll miss your train.'

'But...Now see.' He was visibly taken aback. 'Here's my address. I'll write to you and you'll reply, yes?'

'Of course.' The white lie tripped off her tongue. With a bit of luck, he'd soon find himself a nice girl and she'd be history. 'Look, I'll give you a hand with that.' She forestalled further questions by heaving his rucksack to the waiting lorry.

Ulrich had landed a post teaching mathematics at a boys school in Madras, although she'd wondered how comprehensible he would be with his guttural English accent – he'd absolutely no ear for the language. Still, she supposed the language of mathematics was universal.

'Auf wiedersehn.' He bent to kiss her mouth but Edith experienced in such things adroitly shifted her head slightly and his wet, pale lips caught her cheek instead.

'Good luck!'

Outside, several grey-winged bulbuls sang lustily in the trees. Edith blew kisses to the other released detainees – the Bavarian agronomist off to manage a fruit farm in Kashmir; the Viennese pastry-cook to re-open his high-class

patisserie in Simla. *This internment affair has practically ruined me,* he'd
stormed, wringing his hands and cursing the British; the radiologist couple from
Hanover resuming duties at an Agra hospital - all of whom she'd got to know and
like.

'Take care.' There was an unexpected lump in her throat.

CHAPTER 7

Sitting beside the ADC in the rear passenger seat of a Pacific-blue Citroen tourer behind a chauffeur in pinky-mauve and white livery, her meagre belongings stowed in the boot, Edith felt she was entering another world.

Outside the window, the changing landscape unrolled like a bale of muslin - rich farmland giving way to ruined temples, a harsh wilderness of rocks and mottled hills, the flash of jade green bee-eaters through tree branches, the ADC's detached remarks occasionally punctuating the brooding silence. But she was appalled by the sight of naked, pot bellied children; of peasant women in tight bodiced skirts of scarlet and orange burdened with heavy loads of bricks or bent double in the fields of wheat and sugarcane, yet their dignity impressed her.

'We're almost there now, Miss Müller,' the ADC said against the distant throbbing of drums from burning ghats when, after several hours, it seemed to her that the journey to Walipur would never end.

As they snaked uphill on a hairpin bend, Edith gave a spontaneous gasp. 'Oh!' A tingle of excitement rippled through her making her catch her breath.

Rising dramatically from a rock, and fortified by a high encircling wall was the palace, its windows winking white fire in the morning sunlight, a dream in rose-pink sandstone, a private realm at the summit of a hill defying the encroaching desert.

The car swooped up to the front entrance and, as it slowed to a halt, the chauffeur leaped from it and opened the passenger door with a flourish.

Edith swung herself out and stood stock still looking around, dazzled, in spite of her resolve not to be. The gold of the sunshine was captured on the stonework. Around her rolling velvet lawns encircled creamy lotus ponds and several fountains and although the proportions were immense, it welcomed rather than intimidated.

Preening peacocks fluttering turquoise feathers brushed past Edith and it occurred to her that this magnificent scene must be almost unchanged for over four hundred years.

For a moment there was no sound but the splash of water spouting from the trunk of a large bronze statue of Ganesh. Then, through an archway, a liveried servant scampered towards her and garlanding her with marigolds retreated with a respectful namastae.

'How romantic.' So different Edith thought from that other welcome - well, it could scarcely be described as that - when the *Moloja* docked in Bombay. She buried her nose in the heady scented blooms.

'Ah. Excellent. Here's Dhawan. I'll leave you in his capable hands.' The ADC bowed slightly and marched away, his relief at handing her over to someone else almost palpable, Edith thought with amusement.

'Greetings and **welcome** Miss Müller. Welcome!' A tubby man, Mr Dhawan, the Comptroller of the Royal Household bounced towards her down a wide stone step that curved round the front of the building, his hands outstretched. He pronounced it like mullah and Edith gave a little giggle. 'I do hope you had a **pleasant** journey and that Naidu took good care of you.'

'I couldn't have asked for a smoother trip, but it's even more pleasant to have arrived,' Edith said cheerfully, shaking hands.

He laughed uproariously as though she'd cracked a huge joke. 'And **most** pleasant to see you. How **delighted** we are that you've graciously consented to join us.' He made it sound as though she was doing them a favour. 'His Highness is **so** looking forward to meeting you. Now come with me. I'll **personally** escort you to your quarters.' The way he said it made Edith realise that she was indeed honoured. 'And remember, you **mustn't** hesitate to ask for anything that you require or desire. We'll be only **too glad** to assist, and if by some remote chance, we don't have it, we'll be only **too happy** to procure it for you **forthwith.'**

'I'm sure you've thought of everything.' Taken aback at the effusiveness of his greeting as if she were a visiting potentate, Edith began to wonder if HH was of the same stamp.

' Follow me if you please.'

Edith, thirsty and tired, realised how very ready she was to be persuaded. She accompanied him, matching her longer stride to his shorter one, her shoes rattling along endless airy, marble floored corridors, lined with glass cases filled with stuffed birds, stuffed rhino, pangolin and a black bear, and moulting stags' heads and antlers. They seemed to be a long way from the front entrance and Edith tried desperately to orientate herself as he chatted away.

Eventually they reached a heavy wooden door studded with brass bolt heads. 'I trust you'll find the accommodation to your liking. It's our **greatest** wish that you make yourself **at home.'**

It was some time later that same day and Edith had bathed and changed in a colossal mirrored bathroom that not so much as echoed as surpassed the splendour of some rococo ballroom. From the graceful arched windows of her light, spacious three - roomed suite, its elegant furnishings complemented by a Bechstein grand that had obviously never be played, she had a view of clipped topiary, a sense of Versailles in Walipur, and due east the distant perfection of minarets, temples and domes. *I'm a part of all this,* Edith thought as she curled up in a high-backed chair of carmine velvet sipping a nimboo pani. She lifted her head to smell the fragrance of orange and myrtle brought to her on the breeze and laughed out loud. Seldom had she felt so unburdened, so cosseted.

***

After the enthusiastic welcome, for several weeks Edith found herself wandering through the palace and its luscious acres, quite un-noticed and seemingly ignored by HH as if she were invisible. Did he know she'd arrived, she wondered? Should she introduce herself? Silent-footed servants regularly appeared unbidden in her quarters with delicious meals; there was an occasional telephone call from the ADC who enquired if she was settling in, and when she happened to bump into the Comptroller, which was seldom, he was extremely solicitous and charming. It was a distinctly odd set up, she decided.

Occasionally she'd catch a glimpse of what she supposed were younger royal cousins, riding ponies or generally misbehaving; hearing the roar of laughter and the squeal of brakes as a fin-tailed Chevrolet, driven with careless abandon by a satin-skinned man she took to be HH, spun to a halt. Once she'd even been within a yard of him as he sailed through double doors in aviator sunglasses and flying outfit, a trim, officious looking European man sporting a black eye-patch in his wake.

It's all very nice and calm, all fine and dandy, Edith told herself, burying her nose in the rich smell of the red morocco bound volume of *Die Lieder des jungen Werthers* by Goethe in the extensively stocked library, but when am I supposed to start work? She itched to invest her energies in a challenge, and this all seemed mad and scatty.

Then, quite unexpectedly while she was debating how she'd spend the rest of the day, with the chota hazri a servant brought a message from HH asking her to accompany him on his morning ride.

'What? This minute?'

Edith was nonplussed; she'd no formal riding clothes with her but thinking quickly she improvised and rummaging through a carved almirah, the size of a small house, pulled on brown corduroy trousers and stout shoes. A glance in the mirror and she was running a comb through her hair, disdaining a much-hated topi as she hastily made her way to the stable yard. Although she'd not ridden recently, she thanked her lucky stars that she'd spent many summers on an uncle's farm with horses.

'My dear Miss Müller, good morning!' HH bellowed.

'Hello, HH!' Edith ventured boldly.

'Walipur bids you a hundred thousand welcomes. I do hope you're comfortable here.' HH wheeled round his silky flanked mount and trotted towards her with a broad smile, his teeth very even and white against his smooth walnut complexion. He leaned down and shook hands, his grip firm and dry, the tangy smell of his Roger & Gallet cologne almost knocking her to her knees.

'Do call me Edith.' Blinking in the sunlight she regarded him with interest, having heard some horror stories about Indian princes. She realised she'd conditioned herself to expect a pot bellied man with rotting teeth and bad breath, but here was this amiable, handsome, broad shouldered personage, of above average height, with a head of thick, glossy black hair, military moustache and an engaging air of indolence.

'Edith - as in Edith Cavell - the English patriot of the last war?' He was watching her, his olive black eyes sparkling with candid appraisal.

'And I hope I don't end up like she did, confronting a firing squad at dawn,' Edith said tartly.

HH threw back his head and laughed, a rich deep sound. 'I like your attitude - I can see we're going to be good friends.' She wondered what exactly he meant by that. 'The only firing at dawn you'll hear, my dear Edith, is when I raise my guns at the duck rising over a lake on a cold winter's day. And now...'

He   clicked his fingers and a syce led her horse forward, a grey with a tail like a plume. It lowered its head and blew and Edith slid a hand over its neck. The syce busied himself with stirrup leathers then held out a hand and with one mighty heave she was astride.

'Ah!' HH gave a small grunt of appreciation. 'You have a wonderful seat. I shall make it my business to see that you're always happy here.'

Edith felt herself go bright pink and then as he beckoned she twitched the reins and moved alongside him.

'That's much better.'

'You look v-e-r-y elegant yourself,' and so he did, in gleaming tan boots and perfectly tailored jodhpurs on a black, proud-necked mare, obviously worth a mint.

'Then we are a mutual admiration society.' HH gave her that smile again pleased with the effect he'd produced. 'I'm delighted you're an accomplished horsewoman. I must confess it's no fun at all with a rank amateur and I've a theory that my horses would prefer me to spare them that.' He nudged the mare with his heels and with Edith a head behind him was clattering out of the yard accompanied at a short distance by the ADC and a bodyguard.

As they rode alongside deep into the countryside Edith gazed about her enjoying the fresh morning scenes. It was dewy and green and tranquil. The glint of a silver stream tumbling over water-worn stones, the subdued light, farmers working their fields, the scent of cool, crushed leaves, the hum of bees over a blaze of poppies and everywhere purple creeper festooning the trees. A carpet of wild laurel and strobilanthes silenced hoof sounds - she'd almost forgotten that a forest could smell and look like this - then suddenly she became aware of the chorus of bird song as they halted at a group of villagers waving petitions.

HH smiled and acknowledged their respectful greetings. The ADC clearly accustomed to such incidents was pressing forward into a trot, and drawing level with them reached down and took possession of the requests.

'Tell them I'll make sure their grievances are properly investigated and addressed,' HH instructed him. He caught Edith's eye and added smoothly, 'you know these rides are more than mere occasions of fun; my father always took them very seriously because he wanted to develop closeness with our people, and I've maintained that tradition.' His hands – slim, sensitive hands, Edith thought, with well-shaped fingers - lay loosely on the reins.

'Can anything be done for them?' She asked dubiously as they ambled through a dappled glade, hoping he wouldn't take offence.

She saw straight away that he did not. HH sighed and lifted one hand in a slight gesture. 'Occasionally yes, but all too often unfortunately, no. But they don't expect miracles, and the mere fact that they've met me and been given my personal guarantee that the problem will be looked into and is, gives them enormous relief and satisfaction. It's a weight off their minds.' He radiated confidence.

And off yours, she told herself on a sudden burst of irritation, suspecting it was all window-dressing.

'We're on the homeward track now,' HH said as they trotted into a large sunlit clearing and glancing at her watch, with some surprise Edith realised that they'd been riding for some two hours.

Without warning HH turned down a path that forked off to the left and suddenly plunging his mare into a canter threw over his shoulder, ' race you back.'

Startled, Edith shouted back, 'you've got a head start on me you cheating, conniving devil.' The sound of his laughter trailed across the widening gap and the grey lunged forward nearly unseating her, its canter lengthening instinctively into a gallop.

They hurtled out of the woods onto a well-made road and then the palace rose into view and they burst through a gateway. Syces ran forward and as Edith swung herself out of the saddle and dismounted, from somewhere the lyrical phrases of a reed flute, some strange strings and drums soared through the air.

 Breathless from the sudden effort she wondered if she was hearing things but somehow managed to say, 'What on earth's that?'

HH was looking decidedly pleased with himself and taking her arm, jerked his head to a point above the gate. 'That's what we call the naubat khana, or rather the drum house, where the court musicians have their quarters, and its very location is designed so that the music can be enjoyed not only by us but also by the public. My father was a great patron of the performing arts, and on my investiture I made a solemn vow to support our rich heritage of classical music and dancing. 'Just listen to that!' He put his hands on his hips and   listened intently his head rocking from side to side. 'Wah, wah!' he shouted, applauding loudly when the music died away. 'Wah, wah!' He beamed at her. 'Did you like that, Edith?'

'It's very different from Mozart and Beethoven but I'm sure, given time and familiarity, it will hold the same charms for me,' Edith said tactfully. The rhythms were complicated to the western ear but the melodies infinitely haunting.

'Let's have breakfast. I've worked up an appetite.' With a start, she realised that HH was inviting her to join him. 'This way...'

And there were other things that Edith couldn't get to grips with. The opulence of Carrera marble, rooms crammed with gleaming crystal, many pieces, Edith discovered to her horror, still languishing unpacked in tea chests ten years after purchase.

A jumble of daggers, axes and antique pistols, HH's collection of swords – one for each day of the year; a solid gold double barrelled shotgun, erotic Japanese netsuke, pictures and yet more pictures – moth-eaten mythological canvases, portraits of mutton-chopped Victorians, mysterious Armenian beauties, sentimental ones of the chickens, puppies and kittens variety and one of a hefty Maharani ancestress astride a black horse entitled *The World's Greatest Woman Pig Sticker* - ormolu clocks, rare Meissen, antique silver, over-stuffed French furniture, portfolios of priceless Mughal miniatures, strings of polo ponies and the lines of deferential liveried servants were a complete mess, contrary to all her socialist beliefs, and although she knew she'd be well treated and would lack for nothing, she realised she'd be constantly at HH's beck and call, however delightful he was.

'My foreign friends love that Canaletto,' HH said carelessly, pointing to a picture whose sole function was to conceal damp, flaking patch of wall. 'But I can't think why. I'd swap it for more horsey pictures any day. Now you'll want to meet some of the family.'

He introduced to her several young cousins ranging in age from seven to fourteen - two thoroughly indulged boys, and three doe-eyed girls. They were disobedient and spoilt and Edith found them an obstreperous lot, freed as they were from the shackles of discipline, and she'd almost come to the conclusion that they were un-teachable and unmanageable when, to her intense relief, help arrived not so long after she'd embarked on her struggles with them, in the shape of a boot-faced English martinet in her late thirties who, Edith learned, had defected from the service of another princely family and, to her delight soon had her charges toe-ing the line.

* * *

If there was a war elsewhere it impinged not at all on palace life. One month moved smoothly into the next and if it wasn't for the newspapers that Edith read avidly, and the radio, she might have been on another planet. But if she could do nothing for the war effort she felt she ought to do something for the people of Walipur. She was possessed with baffled anger at the way the miserable, struggling villagers, indebted for generations to moneylenders, had to scrape to pay rent to their Landlord, the Maharajah, in sharp contrast to the profligacy and extravagance of the court. How the poor at their looms earned only a few rupees a day for weaving a sari that would fetch several hundreds.

HH had no understanding of these things and, although Edith pestered him to improve the lot of his subjects, she could make no headway with him.

But if blind to their social conditions he didn't, Edith was quick to realise, stint himself. He threw himself into learning French and German with the sort of alacrity undemonstrated in his undergraduate days at Cambridge, which he'd left without taking a degree. Ever the playboy, by moonlight he romped with nude, big-busted European blondes in a lotus covered pool brimming pink champagne and during the day concocted endless petitions to the Viceroy to upgrade the number of his gun salutes.

'Your interest in modern languages is rather more than academic, HH,' Edith remarked amused when she heard that yet again he was entertaining foreign women with gusto.

'I'm inviting them here for conversation only,' he declared solemnly.

'I don't believe a word of it,' she retorted having been woken by the nocturnal comings and goings. 'Your activities don't require a very extensive vocabulary.'

Another dazzling smile and he was cuddling to his chest Tinkerbell and Pixie, his pug-faced Lhasa dogs whose honey-blonde hair fell over their eyes like a Chenille curtain. Bred in a Tibetan Buddhist monastery they'd come to him as puppies, and the pit- patter of their paws along polished corridors signalled to Edith that HH wasn't far behind.   He neither wanted not expected deference from her and in spite of the battering she meted out to him about his people, there were no barriers between them.

'I find your company invigorating and stimulating.' His glance was affectionate and he placed an amorous hand on her knee. 'You can have anything you want; you've only to say.'

Edith shifted away slightly; she was still emotionally tied to Jean-Claude about whom she'd only just had scant news through the Red Cross that he'd been forced into hiding in rural France.

***

Safe and well with her past dangerous experiences behind her, Edith found herself beginning to tire of the hot house atmosphere of the palace and longed to be able to make contact with ordinary people.

'I'm holding you to your promise to give me anything I want,' she said brazenly.

'Of course - what is it?' HH said indulgently. He lit a cigar, plucked from an elaborately carved cigar box that tinkled a tune from *The Merry Widow* when the lid was lifted. 'No, no, let me guess. You want to learn to fly my three-seater. Oh what fun! You shall be my co-pilot and we'll roam open skies together.' He clapped his hands excitedly. 'I'm sure there'll be no problem - I can deny you nothing.' His large, dark eyes - passionate eyes - Edith thought, were searching.

She doubted if he knew what she had in mind. 'Wrong - a hundred times wrong. But if I'm to be of any use to you,' she began cleverly, 'I think I ought to...' Edith looked straight back into his good-natured face for a long moment before she continued, 'learn Hindi. The women of the household don't speak any English and I feel rather cut off.'

HH looked startled and a little disappointed then let out a loud guffaw and slapped his thighs. 'Surely you're joking? Why go to all that trouble when I can provide an interpreter?'

'That's not the same thing,' Edith put in quickly inwardly groaning at the idea of the ADC constantly at her elbow putting his own gloss on every word. 'No, that won't do at all.'

He stopped laughing and gave her a puzzled look. 'It's a crack brained scheme. Won't you have some more cognac?'

'Don't try and change the subject.'

'I'm only being the perfect host.' But he had enormous tolerance towards what he labelled her eccentricity. 'Oh, very well, if you must.' He was sure the novelty would soon wear off. 'I'll see to it that you get a munshi.'

Warmed by his quick acquiescence, prepared as Edith was to wage a battle to persuade him to her point of view, she did, nevertheless, expect a long period of inaction that she'd realised typified most things in India, and said as much to Parvati, a lively and handsome older woman and celebrated exponent of Indian classical dancing who'd been in the service of HH's late father. Her connections with the palace remained significant, being a regular houseguest at Walipur and the royal family's other retreats, and Edith, finding Parvati in many ways to be a kindred spirit and stimulating company, warmed to her.

HH surprised her. The next morning on the dot of eight, Pandit Lal, a slight, bearded, self-effacing man in his thirties wearing steel-rimmed spectacles, tight trousers under a spotless white achkan and a Gandhi cap, who doubled as the court astrologer, materialised.

'Namastae.'

'I'm so pleased to see you.' Edith felt her spirits lifting and she began Hindi lessons with him, two hours a day.

She called him Pandit-ji and he addressed her as Müller memsahib. They got on famously, taking long walks together so that she could practise conversational Hindi, and then tiring of her halting sentences, they'd lapse into English.

But even he couldn't have prophesied the hapless state he'd find himself in one day. Edith glanced at her watch and frowned, and crossing to the window looked out. Unusually for Pandit-ji, he was late. She was used to him arriving promptly every morning from his village on an old bicycle, a pile of Hindi textbooks and her exercises in a bag attached to the handlebars. He'd dump her homework, marked in his minute handwriting, on the table instead of handing it to her because to him, she was untouchable, in spite of being a memsahib.

'Müller memsahib, I am begging forgiveness for tardiness.' A breathless voice came from the doorway and she turned round. Pandit-ji was profusely apologetic and looked so dazed that she thought some dreadful calamity had befallen.

'Take it easy, and drink up first. Then you can tell me what's wrong.' She handed him a cup of strong very sweet tea, her concerned gaze travelling over his dishevelled state so different from his normally neat self.

He sat down gingerly and washed down the tea in one noisy slurp. 'Porcupine is assaulting and battering me.'

'Oh!' Edith smothered an exclamation trying hard to keep a straight face. 'Are you sure, Pandit-ji?' She wondered if he'd drunk too much toddy.

'Are you sure, are you sure?' he protested excitedly. 'Not only am I sure, but I am also very, very certain and positively sure. I am pedalling lickety-split and not scrutinising large porcupine crossing road. I am colliding with abject beast and falling on top of it and it is grievously bodily harming me on my buttocks before it is bunking away.' He patted his behind.

'How very painful.' Edith bit her lip to conceal her mirth. 'I'm so sorry. Let's see if there's anyone who can anoint your wounds.' She reached over and rang the little hand bell on the side table.

Pandit-ji rose cautiously as a servant appeared and was whisked off, emerging soon afterwards, a muted approximation of himself, smelling of Dettol and

Mercurochrome, and thereafter spent the rest of the lesson perched gingerly on the edge of his chair watching Edith mournfully out of the corner of his eye.

CHAPTER 8

Hermie couldn't remember how or when it happened but the Wiltshire of the Oakleys - much-loved and, during burning summers much-longed for - with its wild-flower meadows, damp days, and gauzy mist became as much, if not more, home to her as it was to them. In the manner of memsahibs, Jennifer and the children escaped to the refreshing cool of Simla, the summer capital of the Raj, where, from April to October, the Viceroy and his bureaucrats governed the sub-continent from the baronial-style mountain-top edifice of Viceregal Lodge, and holidaymakers from the plains got up to high jinks.

Ajeemkot and the Railway Lines were tied to a part of Hermie's life that was over and remained out of mind until springing, all too uncomfortably, from the mauve- tinted, lilac-scented writing paper Ma had a weakness for.

Hermie's heart went out to her and she felt a twinge of homesickness, writing that the Oakley set-up suited her perfectly and that she occupied a large, quiet bedroom with its own bathroom overlooking the back garden. And if the grit in the nannying oyster had so far failed to yield the pearl of memsahib-ship, she didn't and wouldn't admit as much to Ma, and less so to Pa and Ashley who, she suspected, were poised to exploit any sign by her of regret or repentance.

Behind the Oakleys airy bungalow, at a fair distance, were quarters for several servants. There was kaansama, an elderly, bald Bengali Buddhist, who'd worked as a young kitchen hand at the 1911 Durbar of King George V. Occasionally Jennifer found him dead drunk on the kitchen floor on payday, but she overlooked his lapses as he produced amazing culinary extravaganzas. There was the bent-kneed mali immaculate in a white cotton dhoti under whose green fingers the garden flourished, the bearer, ayah - an Indian Christian who was no better than she ought to be - Hermie suspected, the sweeper, whose jharoo could be heard dusting the floors at daybreak, and a chowkidar who slept at night on a charpoy on the front verandah flanked by a kerosene lamp and armed with a heavy, wooden lathi to deter intruders.

The surrounding shrubbery was four feet deep and inhabited by a mongoose that made short work of the occasional snake that strayed in from the outlying jungle. At night, a solitary jackal prowled in the garden in search of bones that the two liver-coloured dachshunds, Putch and Suzie, left lying around.

The Oakleys didn't interfere with Hermie's links to Bettina-Lorna although it hadn't taken them, or Hermie for that matter, long to realise that Bettina-Lorna was a scurrilous gossip.

Husband-less, status-less, living on the fringes, Bettina-Lorna was an inveterate social climber and if one wanted anything disseminated, one told it to her first. Evicted by Aunty Al, and possessing as much teaching experience as she had of playing baseball, she'd wangled a job teaching French at a private boys school in Delhi and rented a poky, shared room in a working girls hostel where the state of the lavatories sorely tested her airs of refinement. Through the Addisons, Edith kept abreast of American public opinion that clamoured to keep America out of European strife.

***

Bernadette, in Delhi shopping for her wedding trousseau as Gerald was generously underwriting all the expenses, and Hermie huddled over ice creams in the *Blue Danube*.

'You mean you don't want to see your Ma again? Jhut phut! '

'That's not what I said or meant. All I said is that I don't want to attend Ashley's wedding next November. It's not the same thing.'

'Oh my God, there'll be hell to pay,' Bernadette warned. She'd not been invited but had scarcely expected to be.

Hermie was a little defensive. 'They'll only pressure me to stay and I just couldn't face that.' She toyed with her spoon and said in a rush. 'Now don't you go being a marroeur of gup, but I miss Ma more than I ever imagined possible. She's like a big sister to me.' It wasn't only Ma that she missed. It was, though she scarcely cared to admit it, the familiarity and warmth of the AI community maddening thought it was. 'The Oakleys are super, but life with them, however thik thak, can be a strain and can't be compared with number 22 Loco Quarters where -'

Bernadette said shrewdly '– you're not expected to be reasonable and calm or anything other than a ruddy nuisance.'

Startled, Hermie laughed at the insight. 'Well yes, and to my surprise I've quite missed the bickering that kept us on our toes.'

***

Traditionally the cold season was the wedding season and in November 1940 Ashley married Iris. A week after the wedding Ma paid a visit to Aunty Al and

98

Hermie joined them for lunch, remembering to eat rice with a fork, instead of a spoon, à la Bettina-Lorna's table etiquette, that drew a considered glance from Aunty Al.

'Look-see, I've brought you a slice of wedding cake. Yawl know Iris' mother baked and iced the three tiers herself,' Noreen said happily.

Hermie reluctantly acknowledged that Ashley cut a dash in a smart, chalk-stripe suit sporting a pink carnation in his buttonhole whilst Iris on his arm on the steps of St. George's, was transformed into a beauty that seemed to float in a silvery-white wedding dress encrusted with seed pearls artfully adapted by Ma Webb from a *Vogue* pattern. Hermie stared at the photo for a full few minutes, pierced by a sour pang at the evident happiness on her sister-in law's face radiant under a coronet of yellow jasmine.

The dowry custom was on the wane in the AI community and the reception, paid for by the bride's parents, was hosted at the Inster.

'It was the best do in years,' Ma reported with satisfaction. 'We danced the night away and gave them a grand send-off on honeymoon to Mount Abu. Iris will make our Ashley a good wife. And now when is my **girlee** going to surprise me, eh?'

'I've struck lucky with the Oakleys who, unlike many of the British serving in India, treat me more as a member of the family than the hired help.'

'So they should.' Noreen put in swiftly. 'Don't expect otherwise,' although she knew exactly what Hermie meant.

But having torn herself loose at seventeen, Hermie had grander designs in mind for herself. 'When all's said and done, Ma, you know I think of nannying only as a staging post to you know what...'

'Well, don't you go making it too far a journey. You'll have to buck up. I'd great hopes for you when you left Ajeemkot. Won't be long before **girlee** is settled, I thought.' Noreen waggled a finger. 'Mervyn disposed of. Ditto the well-placed Powley boys and why you didn't put yourself out for them is a complete mystery.'

'They're too puffed up and I didn't like them', Hermie put in firmly.

'Like, like**?** What's **like** got to do with it?' Ma said crossly. `You don't have to like them. And Gerald came along, destined for a bright future. All slipped through your fingers. My **girlee** is still unmarried and who knows what'll become of you.' Hermie had never seen Ma in such a mood. 'That wily Mr Jinnah, with whom Gerald clashed in a recent trial, is a rabble-rouser what with his demands for a separate country for Muslims. People will think there's something wrong with you, and I'll have to shoulder the blame for have failed in my duty to find you a nice boy.'

***

With the Japanese raid on the US Pacific Fleet anchored at Pearl Harbor in December 1941, America entered the war, its neutrality already weakened by the supply of money and arms to Britain under the lend-lease agreement. A year later in 1942 when the Quit India movement was in full spate and the imprisonment of Gandhi-ji met with rioting, Ashley and Iris became parents. Ma sent Hermie a photo, taken at Kumar Foto Studio, of her granddaughter swaddled in a lace-edged ivory christening shawl cradled in Iris's arms whilst a doting Ashley hovered over them. *For Aunty from your loving niece, Delphine* he'd scrawled across the reverse. Hermie felt curiously detached. If she missed anyone at all it was Ma who paid visits to Delhi to spend time with Hermie and Aunty Al and, Hermie suspected, although Ma wouldn't admit it to herself, to bask in the gentle, innocent attentions of Mr Turton Jones.

***

Sunlight shafted across the bungalow, the grass closely shorn and sweet smelling.

'Hello there!' Spotting Hermie on the front veranda Edith dismounted from her bicycle. Had she known it, Hermie regarded her as a rare creature that conformed to none of Hermie's pre-conceptions about memsahibs, yet was obviously so upper class and so unheeding of it. Hatless as usual, the bulky topi long since relegated à la Lawrence of Arabia, to the fire, Edith adjusted her sun specs and crossed the lawn.

'The court's in Delhi for the winter so I thought I'd look up Peter and Jennifer. Are they in?'

'They've gone out with the kids. Anything I can do to help?' Hermie wound up the gramophone and placed the needle-head to the groove. The opening bars of the *Emperor Concerto* showered a million jewels into the air.

'Ooh,' gasped Edith, ' that brings back memories.' She shut her eyes tightly.

'Nice ones I hope.'

'The best. Let me see. It's a spring evening. I'm holding hands with my Jean-Claude, he's a research chemist, you know, in a packed concert hall and Maestro Fűrtwangler is conducting the Berlin Philharmonic Orchestra.' The pain of happy times was so sharp it made Edith catch her breath. But firmly she brought the

100

curtain down. 'Sorry - idiot me, I'm wool gathering. Actually, I'm here on the off chance. HH has gone to play polo but I thought the Oakleys antics would be infinitely preferable to watching his.'

Her *lesè majesté* brought forth a nervous giggle from Hermie. 'I hope you won't think my company's a poor substitute.'

'Well you shall prove that it's not.'

'Then first you must have something to drink. Coffee?'

Edith shot her a quizzical glance knowing they'd both taken risks with their lives - Edith's careless defiance, Hermie's weighed and contrived. Who could say which was the better way, she mused watching Hermie's dancing eyes.

As Edith lifted the cup to her lips, she saw Hermie's eyes watchful on her face. Then Hermie was saying, 'I want to show you something.' She seemed suddenly overwhelmed by a need to confide in someone, and Edith got the impression that Hermie felt she could trust her who she probably regarded as untrammelled by the prejudices shown by memsahibs. 'Wait here.' Hermie hastened indoors.

Intrigued, Edith leaned back in the basket chair, her thoughts returning to Jean-Claude and the last romantic cycling trip they'd taken together through the Black Forest. Those half-timbered inns where they'd stayed and made love. *Liebling, come back to me safe and soon.*

'Well?' Hermie waved two photographs under Edith's nose.

Edith held them up to the light with interest, and after a long pause said, 'That's your brother, isn't it, and, let me guess, his wife and their baby?' She took in Hermie's slightly flushed face.

'Yes, little Delphine.'

'And you're the black ewe?'

'Listen...' Hermie began a little belligerently then the family history poured out. 'I'm the one who got away,' Hermie finished.

'To what?'

'To all this, of course,' she said startled sketching a gesture as if to say couldn't Edith see how different it all was from Ajeemkot, 'and helping Peter and Jennifer organize whist drives, dances and soirees for the church-going troops.'

'To being a glorified ayah.'

'I had to start somewhere and this was as good a place as any,' Hermie said impatiently, after a pause. 'Besides, ' she added running her hand through her hair in the manner of someone embattled, 'your own position is not so very different.'

'On the face of it, no.' Edith got up abruptly and went over to the edge of the verandah, looking across the compound to where Putch and Suzie were thirstily lapping water from a bowl, 'although I've never regarded myself as anything other than a complete equal of the Walipur royal family.'

She stopped and gazed across to a flight of plump, iridescent Imperial pigeons. 'Stop your darned cooing, birdies, or you'll end up in a pigeon pie. 'In fact,' she gave a slow, crooked grin, ' if I'm honest, I'd say that I've the edge owing to my superior intellect.' She waggled her index finger at Hermie who was by now looking faintly incredulous. 'The difference between us is the one that'll keep you back - attitude. I don't give a damn, whereas you're overly concerned with - how shall I put it - keeping up appearances. That's so bourgeois. '

Hermie shifted uneasily in her seat. 'It's all very well for you. You've had every advantage.'

Edith resumed her seat and said in a quiet voice. 'And what do you think it's like to be parted from the man you love, to wake up cold and hungry in a damp, overcrowded prison cell fearing that each day might be your last, to huddle under rough canvas on a heaving cargo boat when every footstep could mean your unmasking, your undoing, to sail to freedom only to be interned?'

Hermie gave a little gasp. 'Sorry', she mumbled. 'I'd no idea.'

Edith's eyes met hers. 'Fine manners and a fine accent are nothing without self-confidence and an unshakeable belief in yourself. Remember that and the rest's easy.'

Hermie looked close to tears and Edith wondered if she'd been a tad too brutal with her and her voice softened. 'You've done well to make a start, instead of just dreaming. I know some people might accuse you of redefining yourself but look at it this way. You're going places where you've never been before.' She jumped to her feet. 'And now before I depart, I'll do a spot of Teutonic plunder.' She swept to the flowerbeds and gathered up an armful of blazing African marigolds, purple-faced pansies and as many strongly coloured zinnias as she could shift, happily aware that Hermie was staring at her with an expression of condemnation and admiration.

'And,' Edith straightened up with a grin, 'over there's something that'll suit me just fine - amaranthus caudatus.' She hovered over the scarlet pendulous tassels.

'Get on with you, you show off. What's that when it's at home?' Hermie said a little crossly, flummoxed by the botanical Latin.

'Love - Lies- Bleeding.'

***

Japan invaded Malaya and Singapore fell in February 1942. Tuning into All India Radio, Hermie followed the frightening developments from the safety of the Oakleys, horribly aware that within a short space of time, Japan had secured for itself all the rubber, tin, oil and other strategic products it needed and having gained footholds in the Andaman Islands and New Guinea was poised to bring the British Empire to its knees even as cyclones and floods wiped out crops in Bengal, already suffering from eight years poor harvest.

Where are you now, Barry? She prayed he was safe.

The active Burma Campaign the following year when British and Indian troops took on the Japanese sent shock waves through the Indian sub-continent; much of Mandalay was raised to the ground. Hermie read chilling accounts of the influx of refugees, who trekking to India through infested jungle arrived, if they'd survived, stricken with malaria, cholera, smallpox and dysentery. Rice imports from Burma were blocked, millions starved in the Bengal famine and prices there rose six hundred per cent in six months.

At Walipur House in Delhi Edith slit open a letter from Martha who was an assiduous writer. *Seeing that we're not far from the Bay of Bengal, everyone's nervous given the territorial ambitions of the Land of the Rising Sun. Greg has brought forward the evening service to four o'clock so that the congregation can be safely back home when darkness falls. The durzee has run up blackout drapes. Stacks of sandbags are propped up in great heaps against government buildings, and if you're caught photographing, however innocently, the docks, bridges or anything sensitive you're sure to be fined. For a long time we'd no mail from home but eventually it reached us and the censor has had a field day. As for air raid practice, the siren still makes me do a high jump!*

This contrasted with the situation in Delhi and Walipur, where it was business as usual. Cut off from Europe and America by enemy action, India had to become self sufficient in supplies and there was rationing of a kind although nothing on the scale in Britain. Using the Oakleys permit, Hermie shopped for the family at the Officers' Shop, a cornucopia of provisions and delicacies, supplementing the servants flour and rice quota, and delighting Jennifer by her innovative use of

RAF (Royal Air Force) issue blue blankets which she ran up as warm dressing gowns for the children.

Enlisted by Peter in the rehabilitation of wounded Indian troops at the Indian Military Hospital, where volunteers were few, Hermie caught a crowded, rickety bus from the Secretariat Building, played netball with limping soldiers, distributed parcels of fruit and sweetmeats and helped men with injured arms to pass the time operating fretwork machines, or embroidering in multi-coloured wools on special frames the regimental badge.

'It's therapeutic and said to be just the recipe to soothe shattered nerves.' Catching the sceptical glint in Jennifer's eyes Hermie grinned, as she took pleasure in putting the finishing touches to one of her quirky patterned, knitted pullovers for a soldier whose leg had been amputated that day.

Despite the reverses of war the minutiae of life in the bosom of the Oakleys kept Hermie amused. It occurred to her that her value to them lay in her intimate knowledge of India. Jennifer had quickly grasped the nature of this and it gave her the edge with some of the other British women who were inclined to swing the lead with the Padre's wife.

Hermie saw to it that the servants boiled the milk and water, that fruit and vegetables were washed in potassium permanganate crystals that turned the water pink and that drinking water was stored to cool in large, earthenware narrow necked chatties rather than the new HMV refrigerator, pointing out, when Jennifer queried this, that over-chilled water brought on a sore throat. Woollen clothes were wrapped in newspaper, packed in tin boxes and covered with bitter-tasting neem leaves to deter the worm-like *woolly bears* that would otherwise have ravaged them. And one memorable day as the sky darkened, Hermie shouted that they must seize whatever   pots and pans they could lay their hands on. They charged into the garden making a terrific din; the children screaming, whooping, and wildly ringing their bicycle bells, Putch and Suzie barking non-stop, in order to beat off a dense black cloud of swiftly advancing locusts bent on ravaging the garden.

Jennifer mopped her brow. 'Rescued in the nick of time. Nasty little perishers.' She shuddered 'I'm not sure locusts and honey would be the meal of my choice in the wilderness. But you're a blessing, Hermie.' They grinned as moments later they heard a similar commotion from a neighbour.

'Oh, it's nothing, Hermie said modestly. 'You've only to listen to the locust forecast on the radio. It broadcasts the movements of the swarms.'

If Jennifer had a weakness, she'd be the first to confess that it was for the box wallahs who arrived on bicycles piled high with tin trunks; she sat happily for hours on the verandah inspecting their wares, as they squatted smiling and patient, saying, *You only look-see memsahib, no need buy.* They were very persuasive, never in a hurry, always made a sale and were happy to extend credit of which she partook by signing a chit.

'Steady on, dear,' Peter cautioned as, with mounting horror, he riffled through a pile of IOUs. It was the end of the month and the reckoning had come. 'You'll land us in the bankruptcy court and the Bishop will have me transferred to some miserable outpost.'

Dubbed *cakie wallah* by Adam and Timmy, who lay in wait for him, there was the box wallah who sold mouth watering sweetmeats, fudge, halva, burfee, pastries and the inevitable curry puffs laid out in layers of grease proof paper on tiers of tin trays, and the most heavenly pink and white melt-in- the- mouth candyfloss to which they became hopelessly addicted.

Temptation was personified in the shape of yet another box wallah who sold hand embroidered table and bed linen, and fine silk underwear that   poignantly reminded Hermie of poor Ma Webb struggling for survival in a back room. Hot on his trail came a wizened Chinaman who made snakeskin shoes to measure. Jennifer would   slip off her sandals and stand barefoot on a sheet of paper and he'd draw round it with an indelible pencil.

'Be careful about gypsies and snake charmers.' Hermie struck a note of warning knowing that Jennifer had become accustomed to itinerants beating a path to her door, for she was known as an easy touch. 'They're said to hypnotise women into parting with their jewellery.'

'Heavens. Peter would have a fit.' Jennifer's hands flew to the pretty, single-row of cultured pearls she invariably wore. 'This was his wedding present to me.'

Hermie quickly brushed aside a sudden twinge of envy; one day she told herself she'd have more than pearls. 'But you simply mustn't send a sadhu away without giving alms. It's considered very unlucky.'

After the fall of Rangoon in 1943, a Japanese sea borne invasion of India was expected. *Everyone within one hundred   miles of the coast*, wrote Martha, *is readying themselves for an emergency evacuation, and that includes missionaries. Our Consul-General has told us Americans to inventorize and estimate the value of our personal belongings and household goods. All week Greg has been trying to figure out our worth and reckons we're paupers!'*

estimate the value of our personal belongings and household goods. All week Greg has been trying to figure out our worth and reckons we're paupers!'

The seasons slipped by. Now and then Hermie felt   uncomfortable and a bit of an impostor, sitting with Jennifer and the children in an airy pew in the body of the church, alongside Europeans and British government servants, since Peter, following long established custom, had unwittingly allocated the murky, sweltering seats behind the pillars, out of sight of the pulpit, out of reach of the fan, to Indian Christians and AIs.   With new eyes and after years in the milieu of the Oakleys suddenly and painfully Hermie realised how AIs stood out - conspicuously over-dressed in their Sunday best.

Wednesdays were Hermie's days off and she spent them wisely - in the swimming pool of the Delhi Gymkhana Club the Oakleys had joined and on its tennis courts - with young British servicemen who she met through the Combined Forces Weekly Dances.   But they were only briefly in Delhi for rest and recreation before being posted to other theatres of conflict, and had no time to engage in any permanent attachments.   Often she'd retreat with a bagful of knitting wool and the challenge of a tricky pattern to her favourite spot in the tranquil tree-filled Lodi Gardens, a large park dominated by bat infested tombs, where homesick young Italian POWs, transferred from Abyssinia, strolled, chatting to her in broken English, and calling her *bella Signorina.*

I've escaped the Ajeemkot trap only to end up in another snare, she moped. *I'm twenty-two next year   and my steno skills are rusty and all I'm fit for at home is more domestic service.*   It dawned on her that the acquisition of status and security that she'd craved was not as easy as she'd once optimistically imagined. The problem was what to do next and how to set about the business of getting what she wanted if her life wasn't to become a recurring decimal.

From Bernadette, now a very contented Mrs Gerald Reid, Hermie learned that American GIs transiting in Ajeemkot had become fair game for AI girls, being offered considerable cash inducements for marriage. *Shame on our girls!* Bernadette had said with some scorn.

Mervyn, seizing the chance to make something of himself and longing to be called to the colours in any capacity, had enlisted in the Royal Indian Navy Volunteer Reserve.

Hermie's thoughts steadied. At least she wasn't as broke as she was when she'd left home. The pay was not exceptional, but she enjoyed free board and lodging and she'd acquired the habit of putting something away each month. She contemplated with some satisfaction her modest but slowly mounting savings account, but the reality of her unrealised dreams was like a big fist in front of her and the buoyant mood of material benefit in her pocket and the right to do what she liked with it, collapsed in the chatter of self-doubt. Not for the first time she wondered if she ought to cut her losses and sign up for the training college.

***

Drifts of cotton were borne away on the breeze when, from the compound a few days later, a familiar twang of the pinjara wallah reached Hermie in her room, reading letters and updating her Royal Family album, gluing in pictures of British and Continental royalty interspersed with the occasional Maharajah or Nawab, neatly cut out from magazines and newspapers.

Dated a month ago, yours truly wrote in high spirits, telling Hermie that she'd been ousted by his new pin-up, the glamorous Rita Hayworth.   He was now with his unit in a secret location. NO TWO WAYS ABOUT IT, when war ended he meant to carve a career for himself as a performer, adding that he'd wangled himself onto the team that organised stage lighting for entertainment of the troops.

Barry's a man after my own heart, but Hermie though attracted to him would never have cast her lot in with his, for he wasn't pukka enough for her. She'd have been stung had she known that he saw himself as a free spirit opposed to monogamy and domesticity.

Getting up, Hermie crossed to the window and leaning her elbows on the sill looked out, and then slit open the second envelope with an ivory paper knife. Proud of her long, shapely fingers, she took care not to chip manicured nails that that day glowed with the colour of Kashmiri saffron. She stared uncomprehendingly at the unusual brevity of it of Ma's letter. There was a passing reference to her recurring bouts of indigestion and extreme fatigue, which so far had not responded to the hakim's remedies. She told Hermie that Pa and Ashley, who'd always played a vital part in transporting troops and supplies across India, were working twenty hours a day for the war effort as well as carrying out sentry and patrol duties as part of the Auxiliary Forces. An unexpected feeling of pride welled up in Hermie, but with a pang she read that Ma would have to curtail her visits to Delhi since she felt it wouldn't be fair, in present stressful circumstances, to leave the men on their own. Something she didn't recognize as fear squeezed Hermie's heart. Immediately she picked up her pen and urged Ma to have Iris organize a check-up at the hospital and urging her to visit Uncle Bruce in the Nilgiris as the fresh hill air would do her good.

***

The *Quit India Movement* had unleashed big clashes with the army and the police, a rebellion of farmers in Bihar and the United Provinces, and mass strikes. Congress Party leaders were arrested and jailed. Biking around the capital, Edith was hissed at by cycling clerks, and passers-by shouted *Quit India*. The Movement was contained by March 1943, put down by repressive British government measures. In a leaked confidential telegram to the British Prime Minister Winston Churchill, the Viceroy reported that *it was by far the most serious rebellion since 1857, the gravity and extent of which we have so far concealed from the world for reasons of national security.*

Although Indians resented being dragged into a foreign confrontation, many thousands volunteered to fight with the Allies and sacrificed their lives in horrific battles overseas. Support of the Axis powers came from the Indian National Army, founded by the firebrand Congress Party rebel Subhas Chandra Bose, and some Indian POWs in Japanese detention camps made a pact with their captors to wipe Britain off the face of the sub-continent.

Edith sighed and buried her face in her hands. When the German army overran Paris she'd learned from Jean-Paul that he'd joined a Resistance cell. From time to time, letters smuggled out suggested he was keeping one step ahead of the enemy. But for the past year there'd been no further news, even through the Red Cross. It did occur to her that he might have fallen in love with someone else, but somehow she doubted it. Anyway there was little she could have done about that. He was a straightforward person who wouldn't have hesitated to say that his affections were otherwise engaged.

***

As Hermie contemplated her future, the year 1944 opened and Edith found herself involved in HH's plans to celebrate, in style, his thirtieth birthday that fell on 1st March.

'If I need an excuse for a party,' said HH, 'this is it'. He paused and eyeing Edith wickedly added, 'and before you say that it's just another irrelevant frivolity, it's also meant to mark the Chindits successful penetration far behind Japanese enemy lines.'

'Really?   Surely that was a while ago?' Edith was deceived not a bit. 'Neither the war, nor those   ragbag Indian National Army renegades nor the gaoling of Congress Party leaders and freedom fighters has interested you one iota. You're frittering away your talents,' she said roundly, 'instead of applying them to better the conditions of your people.'

But she realised that, as always, her stern denunciation fell on deaf ears.

HH gave a little laugh. 'As usual you're right, but what can compare with the thrill of hooking the mighty mahseer in the rush of a mountain fed stream?'

And he'd disappear on shikar for days at a time, occasionally managing to persuade a reluctant Edith to join him in hunting cheetah, antelope and, on one occasion, which made her laugh in spite of herself, a loudly snoring tiger, the tethered bait - a goat - having been primed with opium. She deplored the slaughter, deplored the way he tore right through fields of ripening corn and told him so.

'But you must see it from their perspective,' HH had cried. 'Every farmer considers himself honoured and privileged when I drive across his land.'

That left her speechless although she couldn't help but admire the way he could shoot to perfection with one hand, while steering the jeep at break-neck speed with the other.

'One's only young once and there'll always be an opportunity to do good in India,' HH opined. 'The issues won't vanish.'

Standing behind HH, the ADC covered his eyes with a hand in a gesture of despair. From him Edith learned that HH's father, who'd reigned for sixty years, had been formed from an entirely different mould. A true pioneer, he'd established   a Representative Assembly, inaugurated hospitals, engaged in famine relief – visiting stricken areas on camel and horseback and personally directing relief operations - launched reforms in the state judiciary and irrigation; introduced the state postal service, where a state stamp still bore his profile, and championed the cause of female education and compulsory schooling for all. An enlightened ruler he'd capped the Privy Purse and seldom drew more than 15% of state revenue for himself.

'Too true,' Edith said a little explosively, 'and as I've said often enough, my job here's done.'

HH's eyes stood out on stalks. 'What? No, no, you must forget such nonsense. I can't be hearing right. I shan't allow you to go. I need you for my son and heir. '

'Of which, currently, there's no sign,' Edith put in slyly, 'unless...'

He cocked his head and she saw the glint in his eyes. 'Why are you looking at me like that?'

He gave her that grin that made even her go weak at the knees. That he was a dedicated womaniser was an open secret and Edith knew of his weakness for girls who made no emotional demands, suspecting that his frequent assignations took place at a select address in old Delhi, operated with considerable panache and discretion by the vibrant Parvati, now in her fifties, she supposed, although she concealed her years artfully. HH, loving intrigue, made Parvati his eyes and ears.

'...You know something I don't.'

'That's complete rubbish.' HH retorted cheerfully. 'I have no children...at least none that I know of and you know all my secrets. Now that's out of the way, let's concentrate on the party.'

When he has ever thought of anything other than partying, Edith wondered leaning her elbows on the table.

'It goes without saying that you're welcome to invite a few guests of your own. My priority right now, however, is to attend to some rather important Treasury business.'

Edith took that as a hint to leave and was on her feet, but HH waved her back into her seat, shaking his head. 'No, no. Don't go. I'd value your advice.'

Intrigued, Edith sat down again rather heavily and HH was saying something to the ADC that she didn't catch and about five minutes later a seemingly endless train of liveried servants materialised, each bearing on his head a steel-grey metal box stamped with the royal crest. One by one, keys were turned, boxes unlocked with a somewhat theatrical flourish, contents carefully disgorged on a felt covered table.

After years of palace life Edith thought she'd seen it all but this was really something. She heard herself drawing a long breath watching the light play on the dazzling array of jewellery. She lost count of the many ropes of pearls, knotted with diamonds. Pearls the size of marbles and several strings of rare, black and blue-toned ones. Pendants blazed; there were bangles of gold and silver overlaid with enamel work in brilliant hues; turban diadems sparkled like frost on a fir tree, heavy glinting anklets, earrings and necklaces in every precious and semi-precious stone that the earth could yield, each surpassing the other in radiance; buckles and brooches and buttons that shimmered and shimmered.

'W-e-l-l!' Her mouth and eyes widened. 'What an arsenal. Alibaba and the forty thieves would kill for a slice of this haul.'

HH laughed. 'Ah, but they'll have to overcome the slight problem of Fort Knoxipur.'

Fastening a diamond horseshoe brooch to her blouse, Edith slipped a pair of lion-headed bangles over her wrists. 'It's history in the making - all this acquired over the centuries. What events they must've marked – plunder, thanksgiving, sacrifice, dynastic union.'

'Indeed.' There was deep satisfaction in HH's tone.

'Truly astounding,' Edith heard herself say several times over, hoping he'd take the hint and invite her to choose a bauble or three for herself, perhaps one that matched the colour of her eyes, but no such offer was forthcoming, although he was smiling broadly at her evident appreciation, obviously tickled that here at last something that he possessed had impressed her.

Then he was snapping his fingers. Once HH got started there was no stopping him; no end to the boxes, no end to the gems and jewellery some of it quite simply tasteless junk, she thought privately, but all literally priceless.

'Now my friend,' his mouth curved, ' is the *piece de resistance.*' Nestling in creamy velvet beneath a square of chamois leather, was an enormous holly-red ruby, its beauty almost making Edith reel. 'We call this ancient heirloom, the Jewel of Walipur and it's been in the family for generations. For the last few hundred years it has brought us nothing but the best of luck. And now, advise me, which of these lovelies shall I wear to the party?' He pounced on a heavy gold bracelet set with emeralds, the size of ostrich eggs. 'I am guided by Pandit-ji who tells me that, according to astrological configurations, green is an auspicious colour for the occasion. 'And I can't do without this,' he added, slipping on a platinum signet ring.

'Enough's enough.' Edith slapped his wrist playfully as he began to toy with a collar of diamonds. 'You'll cut quite a dash as it is, but it won't do to outshine the Vicereine.'

'I suppose not,' he said rather wistfully, but perhaps I may venture just one other little indulgence.' He slipped a solid gold Boucheron cigarette case into his jacket pocket. 'Thank you, Edith - as usual, you've been most helpful.'

***

How I love to hear about your life in the lap of luxury - so very different from ours! Martha wrote to Edith in Walipur. *But I know that doesn't compensate for*

****

Gold-edged engraved invitations to HH's birthday party, much sought after and
fought over, summoned guests to Walipur House, Delhi. Constructed in the
1920s, it reflected the character of the State in its intricately carved stonework
and it was across its fabulous ballroom that Hermie, Edith's sole guest that
evening. Peter and Jennifer had regretfully   declined believing it inappropriate
for them, as clergy to attend such a lavish function, was to remember seeing HH
in the flesh for the first time.

Under the baton of its conductor, an excitable Romanian in tails, the Walipur
State Orchestra decked out in royal livery was playing excerpts from Gilbert and
Sullivan, when the panelled doors to the ballroom were flung open and HH,
escorting the Vicereine, the principal lady guest of the evening on one arm, a
gimlet-eyed falcon on the other, strolled along the richly carpeted entrance-way
threaded with topaz and pearls.

Hermie was spellbound. HH looked sensational in a rose and gold brocade
diamond buttoned sherwani and ivory silk churidar trousers, a jewelled sword at
one hip. Any other person, Hermie thought would have looked comical, like
something out of a B movie, but HH was a natural and with his bearing carried it
off with matchless grace. Hard bodied and muscular with his strong, beaky nose,
smooth open face, and dark, liquid eyes that sparkled with fire and mystery, he
was the most physical man Hermie had ever set eyes on, radiating glamour,
power, money, status.

'I'd introduce you if I could,' Edith said to Hermie, acknowledging HH's regal lift of the hand in her direction, 'but as you can see he's surrounded.' With some amusement she'd observed the stunned expression on Hermie's face.

'You do look elegant.' Hermie managed to drag her gaze away from HH. It was one of the rare occasions Hermie had seen Edith in anything other than trousers; that night she was soignée in an ankle length apricot chiffon gown.

Edith blushed and lightly patted her hair, which she'd rolled up into a French pleat revealing her long, slender white neck. 'The palace durzee ran this up from a sari I found in the bazaar. And you look very nice yourself, which is only what I'd have expected!'

Hermie knew she did but it was even nicer to hear it. Her thick, dark hair fell in a deep curve to her shoulders; the low cut, full-length, cerise taffeta ball gown cleverly copied by the Oakleys durzee from a French fashion magazine completely transformed her, her favourite gold bangles giving emphasis to her slim wrists. Behind her ears she'd dabbed some *Soir de Paris* for it was all she could run to, reluctant as she was to approach Bettina-Lorna for her cache of French perfume knowing that the price - wangling an invitation for her to the party - was beyond her. She'd learned that Bettina-Lorna had, by dint of scheming, quickly managed the impossible - a favoured corner suite all to herself, in a new wing of the hostel, with a ravishing view of the city.

'It's like a fairy tale.' Hermie's gaze was drawn upwards by the blue dome of the ceiling. Viennese crystal chandeliers sparkled like fireflies floating in a night sky and across the room, through open double doors, she glimpsed the dining room banked with orchids from Kathmandu. The silver shone; there was Dresden china bearing the Walipur crest and Sevres bon bon dishes. Liveried, white-gloved servants moved silently with sure footed efficiency, and beside each lady's place, there was a fragrant posy of fresh flowers and a little keepsake - a porcelain figurine, perfume perhaps, or a pretty trinket.

But Hermie was not so overwhelmed that she could not engage in pleasant small talk with the attentive male companions on either side of her. Lubricated by vintage champagne, chilled sherbet and thundar, a refreshing drink that Edith and Hermie consumed in large measure, later learning from the po-faced ADC that it was brewed from cannabis, and fortified by a lavish range of dishes ranging from the finest Maine oysters to the best of Rajasthani and Mughal cuisine, it was an unforgettable occasion.

As the ADC, there under compulsion as he didn't share HH's love of the high life, whisked Edith off into a lively quick-step, a young Englishman in tails bowed and asked Hermie if she'd like to dance.

From then onwards he was her constant companion and, after dinner, when they'd drifted into the starlit garden, fragrant with orange blossom, frangipani and jasmine, he put his arm round her waist in a lover-like gesture and whispered in her ear, 'Where have you been hiding all this time?'

Half way through the evening HH, who was an ardent amateur magician - and not a very good one Edith privately thought, who had suffered his jadoo performances before this - entertained them all to his sleight of hand. His party piece consisted of transforming water into flames of fire. His audience oohed and aahed and clapped enthusiastically, if somewhat dutifully, and encouraged, he was treating them to a juggling trick with glass balls as an encore.

Edith and Hermie retired briefly to the ladies room and as Hermie clicked open her compact and was powdering her nose, a stylish sari-clad woman applying lipstick recognised Edith in the mirror and turned round.

'Edith, my dear,' she exclaimed, her voice attractively husky, 'you look just divine! Isn't HH's party fun?' It was Parvati, smooth skinned and lissom in a cobalt blue, shot silk sari and wearing just the right amount of diamonds. Catching Hermie's eye, her gaze lingered on her, her full-lipped mouth curving in an enigmatic smile as if she were satisfied that Hermie measured up to some secret criterion of hers.

'It's months since you were last in Walipur.' Edith kissed Parvati on the cheek. 'And so very nice to see you again. I thought you'd abandoned us.'

Parvati smiled. 'Not at all. It's just that more pressing concerns in Delhi have preoccupied me somewhat.'

Edith introduced them. 'Oh, by the way, Hermie's a friend who has been helping out the Oakleys.'

Parvati inserted a cigarette in her ruby studded cigarette holder, her small dark eyes lancing through Hermie, missing nothing. 'Of course, that delightful English couple with the three small children not a million miles from me. Well, if for any reason you find it's no longer working out, and I can be of any help, do get in touch.' She glanced at her expensive Swiss-made wristwatch. 'Darlings, we simply mustn't miss the cake-cutting ceremony. Have you seen the creation - it's a replica of this place down to the last detail.'

'Complete with nautch girls?' Edith asked with a grin.

'Natch! Could you ever imagine HH without them?' She was gliding out of the room with the grace of a dancer. 'Are you coming?'

'In a moment.' As they made their way back to their escorts Edith said amused, glancing at Hermie out of the corner of her eye,' I half expected her to interest you in her little enterprise and I wasn't disappointed. You know an elliptical remark - the odd hint - that somehow contrives to make its meaning only too clear.'

'What little enterprise?' Hermie interjected puzzled.

'What! You don't know?   She won renown as a gifted classical dancer in the service of the old Maharajah -'

'You mean his concubine?'

'No, no, no, nothing of the kind. Anyway, on her retirement, as a mark of his esteem, he honoured her with a jagir, you know, a grant of valuable real estate, in old Delhi. Parvati told me she realised that her future modest earnings as a dancing teacher, even one with an illustrious pedigree such as hers, wouldn't hit the target of her expensive tastes, so she built a handsome haveli on the land and recruited the best girls as her hostesses.' Edith tucked back a stray lock of hair and her eyes met Hermie's. 'Are you with me?'

There was a pause.

'Oh yes,' Hermie said with a light laugh working it out and reaching the obvious conclusion. 'Absolutely. So she has introduced a touch of class to the oldest profession.   Some women are quite ingenious when it comes to finding ways of earning a living.' She wondered if Edith had been propositioned; somehow she thought not.

'She's very popular among the Indian elite and completely accepted in society. And very discreet.'

The strains of the Walipur Anthem heralded the arrival of THE BIRTHDAY CAKE and they hastened down the marble-tiled corridor.

'Well, as to my being bracketed with her, she has the good sense not to try again,' Hermie said quietly, dampening her outrage and prepared to deal with it if it came. 'She'd be barking up the wrong tree.' She'd sensed that Parvati suspected that, despite her carefully cultivated Englishness, she was AI to the core, for the tawny shadow in the skin above the cuticles gave her away to those who knew about such things. And some AI girls of slender means, like her, were considered to be of easy virtue. But that wasn't her road map to the brilliant future she'd lined up for herself. 'Although she seems to have done rather well.

It's obvious she makes a tidy rake off from that business of hers. Just look at that jewellery.'

Ma very poorly. In hospital. Come at once. Ashley's telegram, the reply prepaid, arrived on a sticky July day, ousting Hermie's vivid memories of HH's birthday party four months earlier. She responded tersely: *Leaving immediately.*

On the pretext that she and her boyfriend wanted time together before he was posted overseas on combat duty Hermie sought time out. She was tempted to confess all to Jennifer. *But once I reopen any discussion of family and Ajeemkot, God knows where it will end.* Edith, in whom she'd have confided, was unreachable as she was learning yoga in an ashram. Hermie steeled herself to bear the burden on her own.

In the second-class carriage, Hermie burst into tears overwhelmed at the thought of losing Ma. But perhaps it wasn't as bad as all that. Or she'd arrive and find her already gone. She gazed unseeingly through the window; the countryside black with rain echoed her thoughts. Hours later, the train chugged into Ajeemkot, and she was sticking her head anxiously out of the window. It was strange to be back, yet there was a comforting familiarity about the sounds, the smells and the feel of it.

There was the usual huggermugger on the platform. Ashley - a much older looking and careworn Ashley - was hurrying towards her with Iris, plumper from childbearing.

He gave her a quick hug and took her suitcase. 'Thank God you've come, sis.'

'I had to. How's Ma?' She decided to tone down the memsahib accent to avoid a jharoing for putting on too much kanni as she caught a guarded exchange between him and Iris, summing up this new, more poised Hermie in a pale blue linen, tightly belted, dress.

'You'll see for yourself, right. Not too good. In fact very, very sick.' Iris said quietly.

Hermie bit her lip. 'Oh God.' she whispered, and her heart jerked in her chest. 'Why didn't you tell me earlier?'

'Ma thought it was just some minor indigestion that would soon right itself,' Iris said. 'Yawl know she's never been one to make a fuss.'

'She's not allowed more than one visitor at a time,' Ashley interjected, 'so we'll drop you off at the hospital first and you can come on home afterwards, right. Iris has told Bishu to have a meal ready.' He hailed a cruising taxi, but two smartly dressed Indian businessmen carrying bulging brief cases who brushed past them quickly usurped it.

'Bloodee swines.' Ashley's face went brick red with sudden anger. ' That was ours,' he said to no one in particular, 'they're getting too big for their boots while we lot are working ourselves into the ground, right. This lousy war has encouraged them to put on airs and graces.' He sensed that coming events were casting their shadows, that with the ebbing of British power, India was a country reaching for its destiny, as an AI colleague sympathetic to Independence had put it. 'And the **bloodee** British will just desert us after all we've done for them. Hostages to fortune - that's what we'll become, right.'

Iris cut in quickly, 'Forget it, Ashley dear.' She squeezed his hand. 'Don't get worked up, it's not good for you. There's no shortage of taxis. Look, here's another.'

This time they were not pre-empted and they got in, Ashley slamming the door hard as if to say behnchote and grumbling all the way to the Civil Hospital, a three storied pink-washed-building.

'Here we are. We'll expect you later, right.'

Iris's hand closed over Hermie's for a brief, reassuring moment. 'I'll direct you to the ward, and then I'll leave you to it and see you back at home, as I'm off duty.'

With its red tiled roof and tree lined compound, the hospital always reminded Hermie of a Portuguese Goan mission house. There was a strong smell of disinfectant and she was conscious of the smack of her sandals on the long stone-surfaced corridors.

In the hospital Hermie noticed how Iris became transformed into a capable woman with authority, a far cry from the Iris she knew. They weaved through areas off-limits to the public and passed a series of wards full of inert grey faces, Hermie feeling shut out as Iris acknowledged junior colleagues with a nod and a smile.

'You're Hermie, Iris's sister-in-law, aren't you?' a nurse asked. 'Pleased to meet you.'

'Ma's upstairs.' Iris said. 'Go through those double doors and take the stairs to the second floor. You'll find the ward sister very helpful. She put an arm round Hermie's shoulders. 'Be brave.'

Half way up the stairs she heard what sounded like Ma's screams. With a stampeding heart, Hermie took the last few steps at full tilt and turned sharply into the ward.

'Ma!' She flew across the room, past a long row of iron bedsteads and stopping at Ma's bed bent to kiss her. That she was ill, very ill she didn't need to be told. The familiar face was emaciated and yellow, the once bright eyes sunken in their sockets. Beads of sweat trickled down Ma's cheeks as she struggled with a nurse and an orderly who were pushing her back onto the thin mattress, trying to hold her down by sitting on her legs.

'Kill me, kill me, I can't stand it anymore,' Ma screamed.

'What are you doing? What's happening?' Hermie cried throwing down the basket of fruit she'd brought with her. 'Ma, sweetie. It's me, Hermie.' She slid her hand into Noreen's and it was like holding a twig. There was an awful lump in her throat; she'd never ever imagined this. But Ma hardly seemed to hear her, the thrashing and raw cries continued unabated, bringing restive moans from other women patients in the crowded public ward.

Eventually the nurse and the orderly succeeded in restraining Ma, whose reserves of strength, Hermie thought, for someone so frail, were almost superhuman. And all the time amidst the uproar, there was a gentle swishing flap, like sea-water lapping against the shore, as the punkah wallah, impervious to the sights and sounds, pulled, with his heel in the loop of a rope, on the wide sheets of heavy canvas that hung from ceiling wires, creating a welcome cross-breeze.

'Take it easy now, Mrs Blake.' A doctor had hurried forward and was administering an injection. Hermie plumped up the pillow and smoothing back Ma's limp hair from her clammy brow felt her tautness ease as the painkiller began to kick in. The contorted face relaxed slowly into something approaching serenity and Ma's eyes flickered in recognition.

'Girlee.' My baby, I've been wishing and longing to see you.' Her voice was a whisper but the tone was excited.

'Ma, get on with you. You knew I'd come.' Hermit said softly and kissed the papery cheek.   They smiled at each other, sadness and love welling up inside Hermie like a clot. 'I'm staying here with you.' The look in Ma's eyes frightened her.

'You look very pretty.' Ma's fingers came up to stroke her hair. 'And you've kept your figure.'

Hermie giggled. 'Not like Iris...'

'Yes, she has filled out, hasn't she? But she's a good wife and mother.' Ma's eyes never left her. 'Have you seen little Delphine yet? Such a spoiled little Miss Muffitt.'

Holding hands they talked about inconsequential things until Ma's voice tailed off and her eyelids drooped.   Stiff and exhausted, Hermie tiptoed away and sought out the over-worked, under-sized Indian doctor. He told her Ma had cancer of the colon; that she'd sat on her illness for far too long so that by the time she was admitted it was too advanced to benefit from surgery; that pain relief was their primary concern; that morphine was expensive and the hospital lacked an adequate quota of free painkillers to administer to her on anything like the scale her condition warranted; that Wilburt and Ashley were already stretched financially paying for the bed and nursing care. He shook his head sadly. 'Unfortunately, we have to strap your Ma down to the bed to protect her from herself - '

'What do mean?' Hermie stared stupidly at him.

'- To stop her from jumping out of the window when the pain becomes intolerable.'

'Oh God.' Hermie put her hand to her mouth.

The doctor placed a hand on her shoulder, his tired eyes fixed on her face. 'I'm very sorry.' His voice was gentle. 'There's nothing more we can do for your Ma, apart from trying to make her comfortable.' He hesitated and looked down at the ground. 'She is terminal - six months at the outside - and the pain will worsen. And we've other considerations, other demands - other patients - among whom our limited stock of free morphine must be shared.'

Hermie's knees were trembling and she reached into her bag for a cigarette. 'How can this be? Our state's one of the major opium poppy growing areas.'

The doctor sighed. 'That's the sad irony. It's not readily available because the war has diverted essential medical supplies to the troops, and that includes painkillers such as morphine. I know this is very hard for you, but we must share our quota between all our needy patients.'

Hermie said quickly. 'I could get opium in its raw form.'

The doctor shook his head. 'We can't administer raw opium. It has to be properly processed.'

Ma will suffer the sort of torment one wouldn't wish on a pet dog. Hermie's thoughts slid to the days when Ma had been homemaker, peacemaker and the most generous and loving mother and friend. She'd shared her dreams, uncomplainingly, unselfishly let her do what she wanted. Hermie couldn't find it in herself to rest until she'd repaid Ma's understanding and all she'd done and sacrificed for her. If she pooled her resources with Wilburt and Ashley surely they'd be able to pay for the morphine Ma so badly needed.

She asked the doctor how much it would cost and he told her. Hermie gasped in disbelief, steadying herself against the wall. It was quite beyond the family's combined resources for a week, let alone several weeks - probably months. They were cash-strapped. They didn't possess that kind of money and never would. Hermie fished hurriedly in her bag and withdrawing a wad of bank notes pressed it into the medic's hand. 'Doctor, please do what you can with this as a starter. I'll have a word with Pa and Ashley and see what else we can arrange.'

Refusing to leave the hospital, Hermie tossed and turned at night on a bedding roll in the hot, humid corridor outside the ward, unable to sleep as pariah dogs bayed at the moon and Ma's harsh screams and those of other cancer sufferers made the air vibrate; helping to tie her down and to sponge her sweat drenched body until a meagre syringeful of the narcotic drove the timorous woman into semi-stillness.

Some days were better than others and then a nurse would ease Ma into a wheelchair and push it on to the verandah. Hermie produced the mahjong set in its inlaid ivory rosewood case that she'd brought from home and they'd play the centuries old traditional game.

'That's what I like to see, **girlee.** Chasing away the evil spirits.' Propped up against pillows Ma watched as Hermie tipped out the tiles and built the enclosed walled square two tiles high. She knew the ancient Chinese superstition.

'They're gone forever.' Hermie said cheerfully, feeling anything but. If only it were as easy to shut out the present, Hermie thought. For a few minutes there was nothing but the familiar click, clack, as they played with fierce concentration.

'Just like old times,' Ma said as she ended an impressive run. Her hand groped for Hermie's and they smiled at each other, the conversation slipping comfortably back to old familiar things, and for a few moments a crazy little hope stirred in Hermie that Ma wasn't going to die. She let Ma talk, hoping she'd lull herself into sleep and put her arms round her holding her closely. She'd never felt closer to any person.

On another day Hermie, following ancient folklore, bought a caged, shiny black crow from the bazaar that Noreen in time-honoured tradition promptly set free in the hope that as it flew away it would carry away her tumour.

At the end of the week something closed round Hermie and she quitted Ma's bedside with a sense of having said the last goodbye. Feeling wretched, she hovered at the ward door, her last glimpse of Ma being that of a wasted figure lying with her eyes closed.

'Here's some cash, Ashley to cover the cost of drugs for the next few days and as soon as I get back to Delhi I'll try and raise some more money.'

The Blakes sat in a worried silence in the small garden on the last morning of her stay. Hermie felt awful leaving Ma but in a sense relieved to be escaping to a more normal atmosphere since family tensions had been mounting. Raiding her savings account she planned to leave all she could. She exuded more confidence than she felt for this would exhaust most of her ready money and wondered how she was going to find more in the weeks ahead.

Ashley rubbed a hand over his face. 'Thanks, sis, we could do with it, right.' He looked haggard from working round the clock, like other AI railwaymen, for the war effort. 'As it is, Pa and I are struggling to meet the hospital bill.'

Wilburt, now somewhat pot-bellied, a sullen flicker in his eyes slumped in a chair under a tree, a knotted handkerchief over his head and let the valves blow. 'Hermie it's all your doing, mind - this wouldn't have happened if you hadn't caused so much trouble, so much anguish to my darling Noreen –'

Hermie crossed the danger zone. 'Yawl baying for my blood again. Ma slaved for you and Ashley and neither of you showed a jot of appreciation. Yawl took her for granted, and now yawl so guilt ridden you have to find someone to blame. Me. Well, I'm not having it. I refuse to be your conscience.'

Wilburt's face went deep purple and the hand with which he lit a cigarette trembled.

'Hermie, shame on you! Don't...' Iris cautioned her sister-in law with a sort of controlled sharp patience.

Delphine, sitting on a cotton dhurry playing with the blue felt elephant Hermie had made for her, sensed the tension and began to snivel.

'Quack, quack, quack. When'll you ever learn to shut your beak, you windbag?' Hermie flew at Iris, her voice very shrill. 'You may have married into us Blakes but that doesn't give you the right to interfere.'

'Pa will have a stroke if you carry on at him like that and as I'll be the one who'll end up nursing him, so yes, I do have rights.' Iris retorted spiritedly, her back very straight. 'Hush, my precious,' she whispered to Delphine and dropped a kiss on her head, looking anxiously at Wilburt out of the corner of her eye.

'Just you leave Pa alone, right,' Ashley, emboldened by Iris, seconded her, glaring at Hermie. 'He has enough to cope with, right - haven't we all - so show some consideration. It's all very well for you.' His mouth twisted. 'You can just take off, go back to your selfish, fancy la- de- dah life and wash your hands of the problem, right.'

'That's not fair,' Hermie said quickly. 'You know I've promised to do what I can for Ma. My staying, jobless, with yawl is hardly going to help her, is it?' Nevertheless, Hermie subsided, on the verge of tears, all too aware that they were still polarised, that time and distance had only suspended hostilities. The gulf between them was quite unbridgeable without dear Ma and her gentle, conciliatory ways.

Iris got up and stooped over Wilburt's chair. 'Don't you go upsetting yourself now, Pa. Don't pay any attention to Hermie - I expect she'll apologise when she comes to her senses. We're all worried and edgy about Ma.' She gave Hermie a hard look.

Wilburt patted Iris's hand, but said nothing. All at once he looked very old.

Hermie glanced down at her watch. 'I'd better be making a move or I'll miss the train,' she mumbled.

Ashley yelled at Bishu, older but no wiser, to fetch a tonga and he carried Hermie's suitcase out to it. Delphine screamed to be allowed to sit on Hermie's lap and Ashley lifted her up as Iris doubled back into the house, re-appearing with a tiffin carrier. 'Here, take this - you'll want something to eat on the journey.'

'Thanks,' Hermie murmured, slightly ashamed at having lashed out at her sister-in-law, and aware that she could now ill afford to waste money on station meals. She stroked Delphine's curly dark hair and kissed her pretty, upturned face. 'Bye, bye, pet-lamb,' and pressed a bag of sweets into her little hand. Hermie looked at Pa for a few moments. 'Bye, Pa.' She smiled at him, a little strained, but there was no answering smile on his face.

Ashley reached across and lifted his daughter down. 'Say bye bye to Aunty Hermie.'

Delphine wiggled chubby fingers as the tonga creaked away. In the train, unable to concentrate on the who-dun-it through her tears Hermie's thoughts scratched at the problem of raising more money. Time was not, she feared, on her side, and for several days after her return, her subdued manner and sad expression had Jennifer and Peter worrying about her.

***

'Buss. Put me down here.' Hermie clambered out of a tonga at the mouth of a rutty lane in old Delhi. Waiting until she reckoned the man and his flea-bitten mare were safely out of sight and sound, she made for a lime washed three-storied balconied haveli at the far end of the lane shrouded from prying eyes by a high surrounding wall.   Flies buzzed but a breeze tempered the heat.

Hermie had taken particular care with her appearance that day, the reflection in the mirror showing a girl of wholesome freshness but even the familiar routine of doing her hair and face didn't stop her heart thudding like a sledgehammer. Just over a week since her return from Ajeemkot, the thought of Ma made her pick at her food and gave her sleepless nights.

Then very suddenly she'd dragged herself out of her indecision, slipped into a pink spotted cotton dress, adjusted the pretty straw hat bought all those years ago from Madam Olga that still came up smiling, and left the bungalow.

At the full-leaved fig tree growing by the gateway the emotional swings returned. *I must be mad. I ought to have asked the Oakleys for help. Even now it's not too late. They're a decent Christian family after all. They'd have wanted to help, considering all you've done for them.* But could Peter have pulled strings to get Ma transferred to the BMH and free medical treatment? She rather thought not since she knew that a similar request from an AI parishioner hadn't met with any success although Peter had tried his utmost. *How can I approach the Oakleys after the tale I told them all those years ago. What will they think of me?* Hermie couldn't bear to go down in their estimation, to unpick the deceit. *Oh, what a tangled web we weave when first we practise to deceive....*

She'd even rejected Edith's offer of a small subvention but Edith, refusing to take no for an answer, told her she'd sent an anonymous donation to the hospital earmarked for Ma. Hermie told herself sternly that she was doing this for Ma and Ma alone. There was nothing more she wanted than to turn and run, but

125

something held her; she took a deep breath to steady her heart-beats then putting her hand on the gate pushed it open.

The freshly painted white shutters seemed to have eyes, for no sooner had she negotiated the manicured lawn and reached the front verandah when her ears caught the sound of shuffling footsteps and an elderly man emerged. Immaculate in a dazzling white dhoti, he imparted an air of respectability.

'Namastae,' he croaked and she returned the greeting. Then, bowing slightly, he beckoned and Hermie, a little hesitantly, followed him into a large drawing room, thick with the fragrance of fresh flowers and elegantly furnished in European style. The old man moved away arthritically to return with a tray bearing what Hermie recognised as a Wedgwood china tea service. He poured out a cup for Hermie and the instant she took a sip, she knew it was finest first flush Darjeeling. She sipped slowly trying to organize her agitated thoughts into something approaching calmness.

'Thank you, Bapa.' Parvati, groomed to a gloss of perfection, appeared at another doorway in a dove-grey Chanderi sari. The women's eyes met and she advanced towards Hermie.

'How nice to see you again, Miss Blake. Hermie, if I may. How long has it been - four, five months?' Parvati said encouragingly, sizing her up. She held out her hand and smiled and waited for Hermie to speak, gesturing her to brocade upholstered armchair of the kind Hermie had seen illustrated in the catalogue of the Army & Navy Stores. This was a shop much patronised by Muriel Ward, a horsey-faced friend of Jennifer, who had her eye on Hermie for her own children in the event of the Oakleys transfer elsewhere.

'I hope I'm not intruding.' Hermie faltered, clearing her throat.

Parvati proffered an elaborately enamelled cigarette case.   Hermie shook her head, and then clasping her hands together blurted out, 'have you a vacancy?'

A little startled, but concealing it, Parvati gazed at Hermie for a moment through the curling smoke of the cigarette.   Her first reaction was that Hermie was under the mistaken impression that she ran some sort of school. ' For what? Are you thinking of leaving your present post?' Her eyes were steady, autocrat's eyes.

'No. I thought of being a hostess.' Hermie blundered on.

Parvati frowned and Hermie fought to remain composed under the appraising eyes. 'My dear,' Parvati began carefully,' you know what my business is -'

'And it's not philanthropy.'

Setting down her cup, Parvati digested this and gave a short laugh. *The girl is not stupid.* Although she wasn't entirely sure how much Hermie knew, she wanted her to be under no illusions. 'Let there be no misunderstandings.' She leaned forward and took Hermie's chin between her fingers. 'Has anyone told you that you possess a certain indefinable allure that no man could resist?' It was a matter of pride to her that her girls spelt quality; they were superior, discreet, and reliable and Parvati with her exacting standards of culture and comfort ran a high-class salon of entertainment that she likened to an exceedingly private, exceedingly select, gentlemen's club.

Hermie plunged on. 'Edith has described what happens here. You'll help me then?'

There was a heart-freezing pause. 'And you'll help me?' Parvati said finally without stirring. It was more of a statement than a question. 'It must be a matter of money - it nearly always is. But it's not in my nature to pry. You have your reasons and I have my business to run.'

The room had grown suddenly very dark. Outside it had clouded over and a thunderclap cracked out.

'What can you offer my business?' Parvati enquired more sharply, her eyes fixed on Hermie's face.

Hermie swallowed, an icy sweat breaking out on her brow. The unsatisfying fumbles with Mervyn could scarcely be described as a sexual experience and although she'd liked Barry, she'd kept him at arm's length.

'I ... know what's... involved,' she said tentatively, deciding to tell it like it was hoping that what she knew so little about wouldn't put paid to her prospects.

Parvati didn't answer then she touched Hermie's arm. 'That's the first step. But if I'm right, your technique is, shall we say, undeveloped?'

'Um, er.' Hermie murmured. 'Correct.'

'Aha.' This troubled Parvati not in the least but she was aware of Hermie watching her anxiously. 'Honesty is a good beginning.'

Hermie was impelled to explain why she was there even if Parvati chose not to listen. 'I need to know that...my services... will be amply rewarded...' Her voice tailed off.

There was a silence as Parvati considered, tapping ash from that ruby studded cigarette holder of hers. *All these questions the girl dares to ask.* Hermie was untried. She was sexually disingenuous and to use her might be a great mistake as far as her business was concerned.   Her clients were from impeccable backgrounds - indeed her charges were so steep only the truly wealthy could afford them.   And Parvati was more accustomed to hiring a girl and then discussing remuneration rather than the girl setting pre-conditions. Across the smoke she stared at Hermie, her eyes boring through her like a red-hot poker through a sheet of paper.

'Not to put too fine a point on it, I can't live in and Wednesdays are my only free days,' Hermie added.

Parvati made a slight dismissive gesture as if that was of no account. 'I'm always on the lookout for a fresh face.' She was blunt. 'My gentlemen clientele like to ring the changes here; it's something that the married can't.' She vetted her clients with the same care as she vetted her girls. 'You're an intelligent girl - it won't be difficult.' She paused, adding huskily, 'and you look as though you'd be a quick learner.'

Why she was prepared to take on someone like Hermie who was certainly attractive, but untried and not quite the type of girl she normally recruited, Parvati simply didn't know.   But some instinct prodded her on.   She knew she was taking a calculated risk and hoped it wouldn't be her undoing.

Hermie drew a deep breath. Anticipation and relief mingled with dread and Parvati said, more gently, 'I know what you're thinking. You don't know if you're relieved that you've passed muster or pained that you've done so. It's understandable. Now, there'll be more than enough money for your purposes,' Parvati continued briskly. She knew her girls well, and their weaknesses; she knew her clientele, their varying tastes and sexual proclivities even better. Knew too, that she held in her hands the ultimate weapon of blackmail.   She measured her words. 'Let me be frank. I have overheads, expenses... I demand, and expect, loyalty. But I'm also fair. Clients, money-'

 She unveiled a range of incentives and benefits – 'everything's fairly shared. That's how envy and jealousy is nipped in the bud.'

'I seem to have known you all my life,' Hermie said.

Parvati gave her sudden warm smile. 'I always knew you'd come. I've been expecting you for some months,' and Hermie found herself smiling back.

Parvati was not, as Edith had once laughingly told her to her face, a tart with a golden heart. She didn't pretend to be, nor did she try to justify herself by claiming that she provided a welfare service for the unloved, the unhappily married, or the dysfunctional. Her motive was profit. And what Edith suspected was that, in spite of all Parvati's pious talk, the person who gained the most was Parvati herself.

'When you join us you'll be known as Malthi. I have a rule, to protect my girls, that real names and identities remain secret.'

Hermie nodded. 'When do you want me to start?'

Like Reverend Mother, Parvati didn't hesitate. 'I'll expect you next Wednesday.' She got up and swung back a picture that concealed a wall safe.' Here's a little something on account. Now run along. I've things to see to.'

Hermie shut her eyes and felt her face fill with sudden colour, unable to speak, unable to believe that it had been so easy. She didn't dare ask Parvati as she'd meant to *Can I rely on you not a word of this to anyone.*

She couldn't remember how she got back to the Oakleys or whether anyone had seen her coming away from Parvati's. All she knew was that the inward battles had evaporated. The deal was done - she did some quick mental arithmetic – it would more than cover Ma's medication and she'd be able to rebuild her depleted savings account. It was just like any other deal. A cold needle of ice pricked her. Or was it?

CHAPTER 11

Over the next couple of Wednesdays Bapa handed Hermie an envelope brimming with crisp rupee notes, but she wasn't assigned any duties. This, she sensed, was somewhat uncharacteristic of Parvati, who was notorious, but not for her generosity. Nevertheless, by talking to the other girls with whom she formed an unexpected alliance, who laughingly dispelled myths of twirling nipple tassels and in animated conversation over cups of tea with Parvati, she learned a great deal about what was expected of her. She found herself warming to Parvati, unaware that to her she was presently no more than another girl whose loyalty could be bought with hard cash and who'd soon be made to earn her keep.

A persistent Ashley questioned, as she knew he would, Hermie's source of funds and she explained that she'd raised a loan from her employer. From Iris there was consoling news that Ma was comfortable, her pain managed. Conscious that Ma was on borrowed time, Hermie wrote her chatty letters and telephoned every Sunday always replacing the receiver with a heavy heart.

Parvati was beset by an over-arching problem, which was to dispel the boredom of one grand and aristocratic client. With an air of challenge, he'd told her that he felt jaded and no amount of new faces and experienced bodies satisfied him anymore. At her wits end, Parvati sensed she was in danger of losing a regular and very valuable source of income.

On Hermie's next visit, Parvati took her aside. 'There's someone I want you to meet; he's one of my best clients. I've told him you're special but first you must come with me.'

'Oh!' Startled, Hermie hadn't envisaged that this was how it would happen. Nervously she followed Parvati to a dressing room where a woman servant transformed her. Standing in front of the full-length mirror, Hermie thought back to how she used to get ready for Mervyn - but this was very different. An ombre pink sari trimmed with a deep border of handcrafted gold thread work now fell to her ankles, a rib-clinging choli revealing the swelling curve of her bosom and creamy expanse of smooth skin. Chains of snow-white jasmine were entwined in flowing hair, her finger and toenails varnished to a deep pink, her feet shod in gold sandals. Amethyst jewellery - dangling earrings and a pretty necklace - completed the attire, lending colour to her cheeks.

Parvati stepped back, head tilted, checking every detail with characteristic thoroughness. She puffed the tasselled spray of a crystal, silver-topped scent bottle. 'The smell of an English country garden on a drowsy summer's day,' she said and quoted with a smile the French poet Valery *A woman with the wrong scent is a woman without a future.*

Hermie's mouth felt dry. She searched her reflection, scarcely recognising herself. As an AI, wearing a sari was something she was unaccustomed to - indeed would have died rather than be seen to have *gone native* - but here was a beautiful stranger she did not know. She shut her eyes tightly for a moment and, as she sought to get her feelings under control, she thought, *I've got something to offer. This is my highway to a new world, and the shape of things to come.* It was as if she was bidding farewell to someone who'd inhabited her body for so long and yet it was not she. Now she felt as if she'd stepped out of a locked room. All these years she suddenly realised she'd been repressed, like a cork in a bottle just waiting for the stopper to be removed. She was wanted – and by someone important - and her worth was high. Her chin went up.

When she opened her eyes, Parvati's eyes snapped, her manner conveying that Hermie now belonged to her world. 'Come with me.' Parvati made for a set of private chambers at the end of the marble floored passage.   'He's in there waiting for you.' She gestured to a hesitantly smiling Hermie to enter.

A casually, yet immaculately dressed Indian man turned round and moved towards Hermie from the window with a broad smile. 'I don't believe I've seen you before. Why have we never met?' He slipped his arm through hers. *Who is this attractive woman, so much fairer skinned than the others?* 'Tell me about yourself.'

'I…I'm…new here,' Hermie stammered softly, 'My name's Malthi.'

He threw back his head and laughed and this immediately relaxed her. 'That sounds like one of Parvati's little jokes. You're no Malthi. Come on, what's your real name?   What would you like me to call you? It'll be our secret.' He laid a finger to his lips. 'I promise not to tell.'

'Hermione.'

'Ah, that's very nice, after Hermes, the messenger of the gods. So classical, so Shakespearean.' He smiled again and it threw up an attractive dimple. 'It suits you.' He rested his hands lightly on her shoulders, her musical, well-modulated voice and perfumed body filling him with longing. 'And you shall call me Sunny.'

Hermie gave no outward sign that she had recognised this well-bred man in the open necked, Prussian blue silk shirt and expensively tailored trousers as HH

Sanjay the Maharajah of Walipur. He was even better looking than she remembered. *Why has Parvati given me, a newcomer, this prominent client?* The thought made her nervous and she was unaware that this unrehearsed diffidence enhanced her charm, rendering her teasingly erotic.

'Will you drink some champagne?' She rallied and remembered what she'd been taught, crossing over to a table where a bottle stood in a silver ice bucket.

'Will I not.' His eyes followed the graceful sway of her hips. 'My favourite drink in my favourite setting with a beautiful lady, who,' he added a little tactlessly, 'will become my favourite.' He patted the sofa. 'Come over here and sit by me.' His soft dark eyes sparkled with keen interest over the flame of a cigarette lighter.

Hermie moved towards him slowly and, handing him a glass, sat down and they talked. HH seemed enchanted by her air of refinement and English accent and laid a caressing hand on her knee. 'There's an aura of mystery about you which intrigues me greatly. Like a breeze on a terrace.'

Hermie hadn't dreamed it could be like this. 'You're too kind,' she murmured. There was nothing coarse, or cheap or furtive. She was not a vice-girl. This was what, this was with whom it was meant to be.

'Had I been a painter I'd have captured you on canvas - the shades of light, your sari, the shades of dark, your hair.'

'You've the heart of a poet,' Hermie said and meant it. Somewhere outside an owl hooted under the full moon. She slipped her hand in his and led him to an adjoining room furnished with Parvati's attention to detail with all the props of a fantasy boudoir.   Filled with apprehension and anticipation Hermie quickly downed the champagne, a drink that she didn't particularly like, and when she'd said as much to Bettina-Lorna her response, like Ma's, was *Like? What's like got to do with it?*

Slipping an arm round her waist, HH gently drew her towards him. 'You know, this moment is fulfilling what was pre-ordained.'

'In what way?' Hermie felt as if an electric current flowed between them.

'My chart forecast a tryst with one who's of my race but whose blood bears the marks of conquest. I couldn't understand the paradox. Now I know it could only have meant you.'

'I will fulfil the promise.' Hermie felt the colour rise in her cheeks. He'd articulated what she'd always believed and clung to - that destiny would change her life.

'You smell as good as you look. So dewy and untouched, like ...an unpicked rose.' HH drew closer, and ran his fingers lightly over her hair and over the lips that beckoned come hither. She breathed in the warm smell of him, every nerve hungering to be pleasured.

'Hermione.' He gave her a look that stripped her naked.

There was no need for words. Hermie gave a soft gasp and tipped back her head and gazed into his face and the gentle expression in his eyes said it all. She ached for him, for his kisses, for his love as she'd never ached for anyone else before. She had no defences against him - no place to hide her need, her want, her desire. 'I'm yours and yours alone.'

It was what he wanted to hear. 'And you're mine, little bulbul,' HH said in a low voice.

As she yielded to the wild thrusting of his hips, Hermie knew she was his completely. *He's not indulging some fleeting lust.*   'I've been waiting for you all my life,' she whispered and realised that she meant it.

***

HH constantly demanded Hermie. 'Parvati, you've no idea what she's done for me. I was like an iron statue and she's renewed me, brought me to life. No one else can compete.'

Parvati pursed her lips and tried to look severe. 'You know HH, I'm violating my own first commandment that there can be no exclusivity.' But she knew that the business risk she'd taken with Hermie was vindicated. He sulked like a little boy until Parvati, simulating a relenting to his wishes, assigned Hermie exclusively to him.

'She's fresh and fun to be with, Parvati, that's what's so different. We chat non-stop about so many things. It's impossible to be bored in her company. I'm wretched without her. '

Parvati's price rose proportionately.

To Hermie he confided as they sipped cognac, 'I'm fascinated by your beautiful body, my bulbul, by your independent and lively conversation.'

It was rapture to see him again. 'I love to hear everything about your life,' Hermie said and meant it.

He needed no further encouragement for she was the best of listeners. With her head against her shoulder, they'd talk about the latest films, his trips to the Bombay race-course where he'd win - and lose - the kind of money she could only dream of, his demon bowling on the palace cricket pitch, his beloved Tinkerbell and Pixie and the Crufts champions he'd owned, his record Cresta run, his carefree days in a punt on the Cam, how he'd bagged a man-eating tiger that was terrorising his subjects.

Holding hands, they strolled in Parvati's secluded garden, where he told her about his pig-sticking exploits - how one year he'd won several coveted trophies, and how the next he'd been thrown from his horse and been charged by a sharp tusked wild boar to within an inch of his life. And then she was his consolation that sad day when his favourite polo pony tripped and broke a leg and had to be put down. He planned to give him a state funeral and bury him beneath the polo ground at Walipur while a bugler played the Last Post. Slowly and gently she'd talked him out of this idiocy.

'You're sensible and sane and sympatisch and you know just how to treat a man. You're my temptress and the prettiest girl I've ever known.' HH stopped by a richly scented, flower-strewn trellis, drew her into his arms and kissed her.

Here are sweet peas
On tip-toe for a flight
With wings of gentle flush
O'er delicate white.

'That so wonderfully captures the essence of these heavenly flowers. You're so gifted.' Hermie didn't recognise the quotation from Keats and he didn't enlighten her but looked rather chuffed.

These were things in his world that he could never discuss with Parvati's other women. Hermie had stepped into his world and shared it. In the padded seat of a canopied swing, they sat side by side like lovers in a Persian miniature and Hermie dreamed her dreams.

HH felt reborn in her company and Hermie, for her part, eagerly anticipated their trysts. He was gentlemanly, courteous, his lovemaking passionate and satisfying. To Hermie it was a date like no other - a date with her lover. And for all this HH rewarded Parvati very handsomely indeed, particularly since Hermie's once weekly visits imparted a scarcity value.

Pleased that her investment in Hermie was paying dividends, Parvati said laconically, 'he's delighted with you.' Hermie's eyes shone, her expression exultant. 'But remember, you're not here to get pleasure but to do your job - to give pleasure - to make sure he enjoys himself and to do that well,' she added dryly.

Hermie took care to cover her tracks knowing that any whiff of scandal would put paid to her days with the Oakleys. Peter and Jennifer didn't pry into how she spent her free time but she'd volunteer that she'd gone with friends to a dance or to the pictures.

***

HH was constantly in Hermie's thoughts when they were apart and her imagination took flight. *Her Highness the Maharani Hermione of Walipur, Chatelaine of Ajeemkot and Sivalik. And there in the Royal Box beside members of the Royal Family sits the gracious Maharani of Walipur, herself no mean player who has flown over specially to Wimbledon to attend today's Gentlemen's Single Finals.*

Every detail about HH beguiled her, and like a happily married couple, they had no secrets from each other.

'That divine smell - what is it?' Hermie wrinkled her nose delicately. Wanting to know about these things, she knew he liked to be asked.

'Trumper's *Eucris*. It's a favourite, and you're looking exceptionally pretty today. That colour suits you.' He always remarked on her appearance.

'Nice of you to say so.' For every rendezvous she wore a new sari and it made her feel different - like an actress of stage or screen and she was the star. Tonight it was the colour of pistachios, her jewellery the finest Chinese jade. Hermie blushed at the compliment. How she loved to hear his brown velvet voice and to share his pleasures. He treated her like a Maharani.

'Shall we dance?' Parvati had supplied a wide selection of records.

As usual, Hermie said 'I'll choose.' She riffled through the pile. 'Just the thing,' she said with a laugh and taking a record from its sleeve placed it on the turntable watching his face break into a broad smile as *He's My Guy* blared out.

As accomplished a dancer as he was a lover they moved in perfect unison, Hermie's head against his chest, feeling the solid beating of his heart. 'And you're my girl - the girl I'll never forget.' The song drew to a close and he made love to her with all the tenderness and consideration of a husband, as she cried out his name when she came. She'd found herself; she'd found passion.

How she hated it when he had to leave. And how empty she felt when, on the verge of tears, after he'd gone, she had to put on her clothes and return to the humdrum world of the Oakleys and the clamour of the children. On one occasion HH left behind a large blue-bordered, white silk, monogrammed handkerchief

135

and she'd purloined it, to have something of him, of his smell, to take to bed at night.

She'd have jumped through blazing hoops to be with him and she savoured the spice of the double life. Never had she been happier. In the entire world he was the one person who made her feel warm and safe. He was paradise - a future without him was unimaginable.

***

'Have I told you, my bulbul, how much you mean to me?' HH had and he never tired of telling her   again and again. He put on a record of Indian classical music. 'It's a song of the night. If you listen carefully you can hear the unbridled passion like the kind I feel for you.'

Hermie didn't like to say that she didn't like Indian music. Suddenly Ma's voice was in her ears. *What's like got to do with it?* But now as she forced herself to listen she could hear the haunting, hypnotic quality of the melodies and soon found herself humming its variations under her breath.

HH handed her the harmonium that always stood on a corner table and gave her that heart-shaking smile of his. 'Here. Try this.'

Cautiously, she picked out the tune on the keyboard, pressing the bellows.

'Wah, wah,' he clapped his hands. 'You certainly have a good ear,' he added, impressed.

Filled with sudden elation as if nothing could ever go wrong for her again, Hermie said, 'I had a few music lessons when I was a youngster, but had to abandon it as my parents couldn't afford to continue paying for private piano tuition.' This wasn't exactly true. Noreen had been happy to scrimp and scrape to pay for a second hand piano and music lessons, but the hard graft of practice was not for Hermie and the tutor had told Ma she was wasting her money.

He picked up the tabla and drummed the beat, singing in Hindi, 'Come to me my love...' and gave her a look that turned her bones to jelly. Hermie set down the harmonium and as she lay in the curve of his arm his kiss seemed to go on forever.

***

'It's as though I'm looking at the world anew. Everything's so different, so radiant. I notice stuff I've never noticed before - the vividness of flowers, the smell of earth after rain, the birdsong at dawn. And food and drink tastes so fresh, so good.'

'Everything has a price; just make sure you can afford it.' Edith sounded a note of caution, not censure. Hermie felt she couldn't conceal her assignations from her, and Edith herself knew that Hermie must have considered, but rejected, other options.

'Every meeting's divine. I don't feel used or a sex slave,' Hermie said breathlessly. 'He's so good to me, so kind and appreciative. And Parvati hasn't forced me to consort with other men.'

'Yet...' Edith murmured under her breath, suspecting that Parvati was planning a new venture that would blur the gender boundaries.

'I feel so happy, so desired, and so bloody marooned when I have to return to the Oakley mayhem. And then there's a ghastly vacuum of a week before I can see him again. I feel like a piece of stretched elastic. How I long to run away with him, to go where no-one would find us.' Hermie's voice rose a semitone and she closed her eyes.

Edith gaped. She'd never seen her like this before. Face glowing - a woman besotted. She tried her best to bring the infatuated Hermie down to earth. 'Don't fool yourself,' she said, 'you'll get nothing at all out of HH.'

***

The year 1945 opened cold with grey skies. Hermie glimpsed a uniformed telegram boy pushing his bike up the drive and throwing down her knitting rushed out. She ripped open the buff envelope that bore her name and with a lurch of horror read: *Ma expired peacefully this morning. Funeral tomorrow.* Her eyes blurred and she closed them tightly, shaken to the core. *I wish I'd been there to the very end holding Ma's hand.* Unable to bring herself to attend the funeral, Hermie telegraphed a sum of money to cover the cost of a wreath and the expenses of the undertaker. Grieving for Ma, Hermie cried herself to sleep every night and felt that if it hadn't been for the interludes with HH she'd have lost it

Not long afterwards came an unexpected condolence letter from Aunty Al whom she hadn't seen in years, and remembering the woman's forthright kindness at a time when she'd been groping to find herself, Hermie felt a twinge of conscience that she'd turned her back on the AI.

Aunty Al brought sad news that some weeks earlier Mervyn's ship had been torpedoed. There was a lump in Hermie's throat. Through Bernadette, who'd set up house with Gerald in Bombay where he was carving a name for himself as a doughty advocate, she conveyed deepest sympathy to Ma Webb who she knew would be devastated by the loss. Thanks to Gerald, who'd happily assumed financial responsibility for the Gannons, Bernadette's family had relocated to a comfortable bungalow near his parents and the Powleys (much to the annoyance of Ma Powley who considered the Gannons social lepers) and the twins were doing well in good schools. Tears of pride and joy were shed when the Gannons and Reids gathered to witness Vincent, who'd spent his final year as a seminarian at the English College in Rome, celebrate his first Mass as an ordained priest at St Columba's, having been assigned to the parish.

The month slipped into March and there was a missed period that she attributed to the trauma of the past few months. But one morning, engulfed by nausea, she knew. Mechanically she dressed and brushed her hair, forty long hard strokes, gradually beginning to feel better, looking forward as usual to her meeting with HH that evening. As she passed the sitting room on her way to supervise the children's breakfast she glimpsed Edith, eyes red-rimmed, slumped on the sofa with Peter and Jennifer hovering solicitously over her.

What's she doing here at this time of day? Hermione flew to her side. Peter whispered that, through the Red Cross, Edith, in Delhi with HH, had received word that morning that Jean-Claude, about whom she'd had no recent news, had been found dead. A member of the French Resistance, he'd been betrayed to the Gestapo, arrested, tortured and shot. It was a cruel double blow coming after the tragic loss of her parents and brother in a British bombing raid on Stuttgart several months earlier.

'Oh God, Edith, I'm so terribly, terribly sorry.' Hermie took Edith's hands in her own.

Edith made a little sound unable to put into words her sense of emptiness, loneliness and desolation. Jean-Claude was all she had. Now he was gone. Love was gone. She turned away from Hermie and the Oakleys and rose to her feet staring out of the window with unseeing eyes, her desire to be alone with her grief palpable.

***

That afternoon Hermie arrived at Parvati's in sombre mood, her thoughts filled with fate's cruel destruction of Edith's hopes and happiness.

'Hermione.' HH said her name and it was the most beautiful sound in the world. 'We're together again; it's never soon enough.' His large eyes with their thick, coal black lashes gazed ardently at her.

Hermione gasped and stopped short, her gloom lifting. He'd transformed the room into the sweetest smelling bower with roses and peonies flown in from Kashmir. Captivated, she struggled for words.

' Come, Hermione.' HH patted the carved sofa and she sat down beside him. Gin rummy was his favourite game and Hermie shuffled the new pack and dealt and they played companionably for some time. As always Hermie won, but HH never seemed to mind that. He revealed gently that he'd stayed in Delhi   for as long as he'd dared all because of her but had now run out of excuses and his ADC was adamant he had to return to state affairs in Walipur.

HH gave a tormented groan. 'The bells of duty summon me and sacrifices must be made. But my bulbul, I'll be back and the glorious prospect of being with you again is the only thing that'll   sustain me when we're apart.'

Hermie tipped her head back and smiled up into his face. *Duty - he doesn't know the meaning of it.* She gripped his hands, her heart heavy. *He's going home.* It was a death knell.

'The flowers are for you as I want this to be an unforgettable occasion.' He saw the gleam of a tear and pulled her towards him and nuzzled her neck. 'Now let's have none of that. Every moment we've shared is memorable.' He kissed her lips, her brow, and her hair.   'True friends are like diamonds precious and rare, false friends are like autumn leaves found everywhere,' he added softly.

He has the knack of saying the most heart-warming things, Hermie thought. 'I hope I'm your true friend.' She'd always wanted his friendship and now, as she listened to the velvety depth of his voice, she wanted more than that - she wanted him to love her like this forever, for better or for worse.

'I think of you day and night. Every hour apart is an hour too long, and you've bewitched me, you sorceress.' He gathered her to him, and they gave themselves to each other in a long, mutual explosion of pleasure. Reason, common sense, today, tomorrow, was lost in the bliss of surrender.

As they lay in each other's arms, HH leaned across and reached into the pocket of his jacket. If Hermie was any judge of the signs, he had a surprise in store. From a satin pouch, with a tasselled drawstring, he shook out a heavy gold bangle overlaid in gold cloisonné enamel and studded with diamonds. 'It's the best of Walipur's workmanship, for only that's good enough for you.' Brushing her fingers with his lips, HH slipped the bangle over her slender wrist, and fastening the clasp crowned with the Walipur crest, kissed her palm. 'You've given me a great deal of fun and pleasure.'

Hermie propped herself up on the bolster. 'Oh my, my, my.' Her eyes widened and she sucked in her breath. She whispered the words of an inscription engraved unobtrusively on the inside. *To Hermione from HH. 1945. Until we meet again.* Hermie was overwhelmed - by his status and now by his gift. He had the manners of a nobleman.   Hermie laid her hand on his arm, heavy with the weight of the bangle, her gaze wandering round the room now such a familiar part of her life. When would she see him again? But she knew she mustn't voice her dreads or speak to him of her fears.

'Yes, Hermione, I feel the same as you. The void's always painful but how sweet will be the reunion.'

She nodded, and felt his hand in hers. 'I want always for us to be together.' She had a right to happiness, too, even if it was a commodity to be bought and sold.

Throwing a silk dressing gown round his shoulders, HH gathered up the harmonium. He pushed the bellows while one hand ran along the keyboard. 'To the one and only Hermione,' he said, and moving his head from side to side and smiling at her, began to sing in a somewhat quavering voice. For a moment she thought it was a raga, so oriental did it sound, as he slithered from note to note, with the harmonium wheezing away, but then she recognised it as *Drink To Mee Only With Thine Eyes* - a traditional English song.

To her, HH was the greatest operatic tenor in the world, although to a trained ear he'd have sounded decidedly off-key. Seldom doing things by halves HH began the second verse and this time, with her head against his chest, they sang together like a love duet.

I sent thee, late, a rosie wreath,
Not so much honoring thee
As giving it a hope, that there
It could not withered bee
But thou thereon did'st only breathe
And sen'st it backe to mee
Since when it growes and smells I sweare,
Not of it selfe but thee.

As they reached the last few bars, HH's voice trailed off and he lowered his head and kissed her. 'Just remember every passing moment brings us closer together. So, you see, it's not as though we've said farewell.'

In his company, Hermie forgot everything - the Oakleys, and the drudgery of looking after the children, herself, the new life inside her. All she knew with him was love and passion, caring and warmth - there was no ugliness, no regrets. And when he had left, Hermie secreted the gift in her handbag away from Parvati's prying eyes.

***

'HH does tend to get somewhat pre-occupied with affairs of state,' Edith said, picking her words carefully. She'd said no more to her friends about her sad loss and was about to return with the court to Walipur. She knew HH only too well to expect that, out of his sight, Hermie was likely to be out of his mind, and she didn't want her to have any unreal expectations.

'I don't imagine he'll write any letters,' Hermie said coolly but nevertheless hoped that she might be proved wrong. None came.

She didn't confide her fears about the pregnancy immediately to Parvati, although now and then, as she awaited instructions about a new assignment - a thought that only made her feel worse - she caught the woman appraising her thoughtfully. Eventually, giving a false name and describing herself as Mrs, Hermie consulted an Indian physician, picked at random, who had a ramshackle surgery in the centre of the vegetable bazaar. He confirmed her suspicions. For the first time in her life, Hermie, who'd always known the course she set - or thought she did - neither knew what to do nor what she wanted.

Edith whom she telephoned in Walipur understood her dilemma; she revealed she'd faced the same quandary years ago in Germany. She'd chosen an abortion. The political situation was precarious and Jean-Claude and she didn't know if there'd be a decent future for them and their child. Sensibly she pointed out to Hermie the impossibility of concealing her condition from Jennifer and Peter as the months passed and although once the news emerged, the Oakleys wouldn't judge her, the Bishop would demand her dismissal.

'Don't I know it. I'll be back where I don't belong and to where I've run from,' Hermie whispered, the ignominious prospect of returning pregnant to Ajeemkot or even to Aunty Al's, too dreadful to contemplate. She knew she'd stumbled steeply. *I can't go back to that. How could I have been so stupid? Should I have a termination?* It was an option, but she knew it wouldn't be easy or legal since a safe abortion, although possible, needed the right connections and a fat purse whereas a messy back-street procedure carried serious health risks.

'Sorry, Edith - I didn't catch that. What did you say?'

'If it's a matter of money, I can help and you must speak to Parvati,' Edith bellowed. 'Immediately. She has contacts.'

'You're right.' Hermie knew she must.

'Do you want to keep it?'

There was a pause. Hermie's nerves tightened. 'Yes. No. Oh, I'm so confused. I'll let you know what Parvati says. Goodbye.' She replaced the receiver feeling shattered.

The following day, warmer but with a breeze and feeling her nerves tightening to breaking point, Hermie found herself at Parvati's. Having disposed of a rat-faced man carrying a sheaf of papers Parvati beckoned her inside. She couldn't see Hermie paying her a purely social visit.

'I've just seen off my accountant.' She threw a friendly arm round Hermie's shoulders.

'I hope he brought tidings of comfort and joy,' Hermie said, tongue in cheek, registering that Parvati had acquired several new works of art.

'Can't grumble,' Parvati said a humorous light in her eyes. *She gives nothing away,* Hermie realised, wishing she didn't have to and slightly disturbed that Parvati was the craw of just one secret too many of her own.

'And how's it with you?'

' Parvati...' Hermie's heart fluttered. 'Er, er, I'm here to give notice. I'm sorry, but I'm not able to continue working.' She felt miserable, as though she was behaving badly and ungratefully after all she'd done for her.

'Indeed.' Parvati arched her eyebrows. 'A somewhat precipitate decision.' It was her business to know why Hermie was giving up and she asked as much. 'Is this just a temporary pause while HH is away, or something of a more permanent nature?' She didn't want Hermie to leave but it was against her code to prevent her.

'For the foreseeable future.' Hermie didn't want to cut herself off entirely from Parvati given the hope in her heart that HH would once again seek her out. She'd planned to say that she'd overcome the personal problems that had drawn her there in the first place, but reading the knowing expression on Parvati's face she realised there was no point in prevaricating. It was obvious Parvati suspected that there were more pressing reasons. Hermie decided to come clean. 'I'm pregnant,' she blurted out. 'Sick as a dog in the mornings, and my boobs hurt. It has come as rather a shock.'

Parvati inclined her head slightly. 'It's as I thought. It happens. But I thought you'd taken care of that side of things.' She refrained from calling Hermie a complete dolt who'd failed to take the precautions Parvati had advised, or to weigh the consequences, but she accepted Hermie's decision and would not mourn the loss of the girl. 'One of my best hostesses going,' she remarked wryly. 'However, I'm glad you're honest with me. Don't expect me to help you ...but I will.' It was a heroic gesture, for Parvati, who was inclined to let those who left her service sink in the mire of their own making, was not in the business of arranging such things without hope of reward. 'And remember you'll always be welcome here. I can do with someone like you.' To her amazement for the first time she'd found herself treating Hermie more as a friend than someone in her pay.

That cheered Hermie up and her spirits rallied. 'You're so good to me.' Her heart was breaking but she didn't pretend that it was not a blessing to have friends like Edith and now Parvati, conveniently pushing to the back of her mind that she didn't have forever to make choices.

'Let me offer you a piece of advice,' Parvati said. Her voice was smiling; her tone chatty but it deceived Hermie not a bit.

'Don't lecture me. I couldn't bear it.' Hermie tucked back a wisp of hair.

'I know these people. I have lived with them in their palaces. I advise you against saying anything to HH. You took the risk and I'm afraid you must bear the consequences, because he won't.'

'That's self-serving. You're only interested in a cover-up to protect your reputation. Don't pretend you want to help me. You've a vested interest in ensuring my discretion because the scandal might ruin your business.' Tears rolled down Hermie's cheeks and she longed for HH. 'I don't want his money. I want him. I want his baby.'

'You're overwrought,' Parvati said calmly. 'Dear child, this is the reality of the situation. If you don't believe me, ask Edith. Discuss it with her. She'll tell you no different. I'm not gagging you. You're free to say and do as you please. What I'm saying is that only fools rush in -' she pulled a face, '- *cliché, cliché* - where angels fear to tread.' She scribbled something on a piece of paper, folded it over and handed it to Hermie. 'This woman will be able to help you in your predicament. She has helped my girls before to...shift their merchandise.'

Hermie took the paper without a word.

***

143

The air was hot and still. The heat of April brought out the red and orange blossoms of the gol mohur tree, and there was universal relief and rejoicing at Germany's surrender after the suicide of Hitler.

'Thank God the war has ended,' Peter said. 'And we must hope and pray for an everlasting peace.'

Almost immediately Jennifer started packing for a long delayed furlough to Wiltshire that had been denied them during the war years, owing to dangerous shipping conditions. 'We're going home for the summer and we'll see to boarding schools for the boys.'

'Must you send them away?' Hermie couldn't understand the English desire to have their children nurtured by strangers. She regarded her own boarding school years as being of necessity rather than choice.

'Oh, yes. If they stay out here much longer, they'll be saddled with that dreadful chee-chee accent that would be just too awful,' Jennifer said thoughtlessly.

Hermie looked away, biting her lip. 'When do you think you'll be back?' Their departure couldn't have been better timed.

'Towards the end of December. There's talk of my being transferred elsewhere in India after that,' Peter said enthusiastically clearly looking forward to a new challenge. Two years previously he'd been battling for his life after being struck down with typhus fever but that hadn't turned him against another spell of duty in the sub-continent. 'We'll learn more about that when we're home.'

Jennifer paused, wondering if she ought to pack their tennis racquets. 'You're coming home with us, of course, Hermie.'

If only things had been different, Hermie thought sadly. Still she supposed there'd be other opportunities, other English families, with whom she could go **home.** 'I'd like to but not just yet,' she smiled at Jennifer intending her to assume that her reluctance to accompany them was due to her boyfriend, who they believed was still serving in the Far East. The Oakleys could have no reason to suspect anything was amiss for although Hermie had experienced nausea and craved tinned sardines she'd been spared the other symptoms of pregnancy such as darker pigment under the eyes and swollen ankles.

'But while you're away, I fancy a change of scene, although the chowkidar will be here to keep an eye on the place.'

'Of course. Don't feel you're tied to the place. Anyway, it won't be vacant for long, since the Bishop's drafting in a locum from a mofussil to keep the parish ticking over.'

***

Hermie steeled herself to visit the address Parvati had given her but when it came to it was too scared to go ahead with the arrangement proposed. She'd casually broached the matter to Bettina-Lorna who told her that throwing oneself down a flight of stairs or the consumption of several stiff gins were stratagems her friend could try, for getting rid of the pregnancy and vehemently denying it when Bettina-Lorna asked *Tell me, is it you, dahling?*

Edith, worried about Hermie, reminded her that she couldn't dither for much longer and that if she intended the pregnancy to continue, plans would have to be made. On a pretext she came to Delhi and, seated in Parvati's sitting room, determined to make Hermie face facts. 'If you'd kept your legs crossed, you wouldn't be in this position.'

Hermie gasped and even Parvati was taken aback at Edith's bluntness but knew her friend too well to believe she was moralising or shaming Hermie. All she was doing was reminding her that a decision had to be made.

'An abortion...' she saw Hermie recoil '...means: one, you'll be free to chase your dreams.' Edith ticked off the pros on her fingers. 'Two, you'll escape a lifetime's financial and caring burden when your own future is so fragile. Three, you'll be able to make a fresh start; you'll meet someone you love, get married and have a child with him when you're ready. Four, you'll be able to go home or face your family with a light heart and not as an unmarried mother of a love child.'

Outside there was a flash of a yellow-wattle lapwing and the deep chirping of a crimson-shouldered Alexander parakeet in a clump of trees broke the silence.

'You'll feel empty and sad. You'll have to learn to deal with your feelings.' Parvati said. 'As I had to.'

'Ma always said a child is a joy.' Hermie burst into tears. 'I can't do it.' But she knew that if she hadn't fallen in love with HH she wouldn't have hesitated.

'That's settled then,' Parvati said briskly,' at least for the time being. But it isn't over. Other issues still have to be considered.'

Hermie blinked.

'To keep it or to give it away'

Hermie's sobs redoubled. Parvati exchanged a glance with Edith and mouthed. 'One step at a time.' To Hermie she said, 'you've got to look after yourself. Baby's on the way.'

Eventually, at Hermie's request, Parvati agreed to look for a house that would respect her desire for anonymity and a few days later telephoned to say that she'd found just the place.

'Not too expensive I hope?' Hermie said in a small voice betokening caution. Parvati might have a bottomless purse but she didn't and she resolved not to be harried into renting something she couldn't afford.

Parvati chuckled. Hermie always believed she had less money than she actually possessed. 'It's a bargain as it's in Gurgaon, a rural area on the outskirts of Delhi. Come and see for yourself. I'll pick you up this afternoon.'

'What a find.' Viewing the house Hermie was captivated by its charm and seclusion and a few days later she moved in with Putch and Suzie and a young, slightly dim-witted woman servant hired by Parvati. 'It's magic,' she told Edith. 'A lovely old place with thick walls, an inner courtyard, and a fresh water well.' And for a while her instincts for home making made her almost forget why she was there.

To the occasional curious neighbour Hermie explained that her husband, she pointed to a framed photograph of a young officer Parvati had purloined for her, was back on duty fighting the Japanese, which drew sympathetic clucking. 'You poor dear thing, all alone at a time when a woman needs her husband most.'

As Japanese hostilities persisted after the war in Europe had ended, Martha wrote: *On a more personal note Greg and I sadly realise that we can't be parents. It's not for want of trying and praying, but God's will be done. We've reconciled ourselves to the pain of it, and after much meditation and prayer we've decided to open our hearts and go the road less travelled. There're many unwanted babies in this country, which we've grown to love as much as our own. Humbly we beseech the Lord to make us a worthy Mom and Dad to a baby who has none.*

Edith's heart went out to her friends who'd borne their childlessness in silence and with dignity. It must have been particularly hard to bear when, at times like the Annual Mission Picnic, colleagues foregathered with boisterous offspring.

***

The novelty of Hermie's new surroundings soon wore off. Monsoon frogs croaked incessantly, the tedium relieved by visits from Edith and Parvati and from jolly Italian Franciscan friars who'd ministered to Italian POWs in India and who lived a simple life ploughing the fields in Gurgaon. In exchange for lessons in conversational English, they taught her Italian and the finer points of Italian opera, and she looked forward to their robust company. A local doctor monitored her condition, and her nearest neighbour was a masterful Sindhi woman who, supervising the building of a large country house for her busy, lawyer husband, was too pre-occupied to pry into Hermie's life, boasting that she'd ensured that not even a thimbleful of cement was unaccounted for by the contractors.

'My dear,' Parvati reminded her on one of her frequent visits, 'it's pointless saying anything to the father about this baby of yours.' She'd a lingering suspicion that Hermie harboured thoughts of a disclosure of sorts to HH.

The endless drip, drip of the monsoon got on Hermie's nerves. Hermie had written countless letters to HH but had torn them all up. 'I'd pretty much reached that conclusion,' she said ruefully. 'This isn't a fairy tale with a happily - ever-after ending.' But she bore HH no grudge and he was always in her thoughts.

As she struggled in the later stages of her pregnancy through August, one of the most disagreeably humid months of the year, Hermie felt abandoned and miserable, resentful of the being growing inside her, and very scared. She refused to think of the child, and made a show of stoically knitting, recalling one of Ma's little economies of re-using unravelled wool by gentle steaming, then hanging it out to dry after which it was just as soft and new as before. All she could think of was being fit for duty again when the Oakleys returned.   The following month newspapers trumpeted *Jap Emperor May Be Tried As War Criminal.* The dropping of the atomic bomb had hastened the surrender of the Japanese and peace was restored to southeast Asia.

Parvati was unforgiving, as she'd lost a nephew in the Burma campaign. She glanced at Hermie who was sitting slumped in a chair. Edith, on a brief visit to Hermie, whispered in Parvati's ear when Hermie lumbered out of the room that she avoided all conversation about her unborn child.

Parvati looked scandalised.   'You must broach the subject,' she said loudly in her no nonsense fashion. 'Ask her about her plans and don't let her fob you off.'

Edith gently re-ignited the debate. 'You've got to think seriously about your baby. You owe it at least that much, now you've decided to have it.'

'It's too early for me to make a decision.' Hermie brushed her off.

'It's almost too late for you to do anything else,' Edith said, inwardly despairing of getting through to her. 'You're being perverse.'

Hermie gave her a frosty look and retreated into her own world. 'I don't want to discuss it any further.'

Edith gave a huge sigh and got up to leave. She could make no more headway with the obdurate Hermie.

 Days later Hermie raised the subject herself with Edith.   She was dispirited; her ungainly figure and the heat were pulling her down. 'I can't keep my baby - you know that as well as I do. I'm penniless and who'll give me a job knowing I have an illegitimate child?' Her dreams had brought her nothing but misery. 'My character's in ruins, I've squandered my future.' Her shoulders shook and burying her head in her hands she burst into tears, howling like a dog that had been kicked. 'I feel like ending it all.'

Edith waited for the convulsion to pass. 'You can always count on me.' She touched her arm.

'I know.' Hermie gave a wan smile. 'But you've got yourself to think of and I couldn't burden you with my dependence.'   They sat in silence listening to the maddening tap-tap of the brain fever bird high up in a monsoon green tree. Hermie rose slowly to her feet, the lump inside her heavy and uncomfortable and closed the inter-communicating door with the kitchen where her maidservant was grinding spices on a stone slab. The pungent smell, peppery and enticing, filled her nostrils.   Her voice was choked. 'I've no choice. I'll never be able to give baby the best. I've no job, no home. I'm disgraced. I can't and won't go back to Loco Quarters. I'm in no position to keep the child. The only alternative is an AI orphanage.' She shuddered, shutting her mind against Bishop Forrester's Home and the clean, nourished but subdued children who lived by its rigid code of discipline. She paused and Edith knew what the decision was costing her friend. 'I know I must think about my baby's future. Please check out adoption in a nice **European** family.'

'Leave it to me,' Edith promised putting an arm round Hermie's shoulders.

***

Edith put out feelers. Parvati booked and paid for a private room for Hermie under an assumed name at a nearby rural hospital. 'It's a first class place with all the latest equipment,' she assured her. 'You'll get the best of care. The hospital was constructed just a few years earlier on land that had once been in the ownership of a Muslim princess who'd wed an Irish adventurer. Her family cast her off for marrying out.'

Hermie with a weight off her mind still possessed a sufficient sense of humour to appreciate that.

'Years later, 'Parvati continued, 'the princess converted to Catholicism, bequeathing the land to the church on her death. American Catholic missionaries acquired the site from the Diocese of Delhi and promptly put up this ultra-modern health centre.'

As Edith made for the door Hermie looking rather petrified stopped her and asked her to be with her when she went into labour.

'Of course I will,' Edith said delightedly,' I'm honoured.'

The contractions started late one afternoon and Edith rushed Hermie to hospital. Throughout, she held her hand and, after an easy labour, the baby emerged with olive skin tone and wisps of dark brown hair.

'6 lbs 12oz. He's a lovely little fellow and altogether perfect,' said the Goan midwife, holding up the bawling infant and claiming that Hermie owed her safe confinement to St. Gerard Magellan whose relics - a tooth and a lock of hair kept in a little leather drawstring pouch - she'd swung over Hermie's tummy during the last stages of labour. She wrapped the baby in a shawl and surrendered him into Hermie's arms.

'He's a mix of you and HH,' Edith said airily, stroking his head.

149

Hermie said nothing. She pillowed her son against her breast allowing herself the luxury of loving the tiny tot, his long, feathery eyelashes sweeping his cheeks. She felt a deep bond with him, and dropped a kiss on his cheek. She'd never thought she could feel so deeply maternal, and if circumstances had been different she could've shared this moment with HH. *But I've no husband with whom I can share the joy of parenthood.* Somehow she'd botched it; she felt cheated.

'Let me do a bit of cuddling.' Rocking him in her arms, Edith hummed a traditional German lullaby under her breath. She glanced across to Hermie and said softly, 'an ode to the little prince. Schlafe bei silbernem Schein... Was wird da künftig erst sein?... schlafe, mein Prinzchen, schlaf ein! *Sleep by the silvery light...But what will the future bring? Sleep my little prince, sleep!*'

She kissed the top of his head and Hermie reached for him.

A knock on the door heralded a beaming Parvati bearing a bottle of champagne and Hermie watched without enthusiasm as she uncorked it. Parvati stroked the baby's cheek and thought to herself that he had HH's nose and eyes.

The Hospital Superintendent, a rangy nun with a Texan accent, privy to the adoption arrangements, was particular that Hermie didn't breastfeed her baby to prevent a maternal bond being established. But Hermie gave her son a bottle, changed his nappy, crooned and bathed and cuddled him and no account seemed to be taken of the bond being established by those things.

***

'There's no hurry but, if you're still absolutely sure, his new parents are all set to take him home.' Edith glanced at Hermie and wondered if she'd change her mind now that she'd held her son, now almost four weeks old, in her arms.

'Who are they?' Hermie sat bolt upright. She felt as though a falling coconut had battered her. A tiny fist curled tightly round her finger and her eyes filled with tears. She wanted to run away with him forever. She'd run and run to Walipur and give him to HH who'd cuddle him as his son and heir and anoint her as his Maharani.

'They're good people who'll bring him up very lovingly as their own flesh and blood. You've given them such joy and hope - and yes, Hermie, they're not Indian.'

'How soon?' Hermie blew her nose, her eyes following her baby as a nurse – the one to whom she'd slipped a wad of cash to take a photo of her son - returned him to his cot in the nursery.

Edith exchanged a glance with Parvati and said quietly, 'you could sign the papers now.' She gave Hermie a hug. 'But you'll need to stay here for a few days until you're fit to manage on your own.'

There was a terrible ache in Hermie's heart. She'd coached herself to face this moment, but nothing had prepared her for the reality of it. All the time she'd thought: *This isn't going to happen.* She propped up the adoption papers against her knee and signed, unread, the consent whereby she relinquished custody of her little boy. She dropped back against the pillows a bleak look lurking in her eyes but relieved that he'd been spared an orphanage. *I'll always love you.*

Edith threw a troubled glance over her shoulder as she and Parvati left the room and saw Hermie's shoulders shaking, her face turned to the wall.

The following day Greg and Martha Addison, looking much as Edith remembered, sat in the hospital parlour holding hands.

'He's gorgeous,' Edith told them cheerfully.   'It's fortunate his colouring's not so different from that of a Native American. He'll fit in very well.' She knew that in parts of the American West, like Nebraska, there were descendants of native tribes who'd inter-married.

Martha burst into tears. 'We don't care what he looks like - to us a child's a blessing.'

The Hospital Superintendent said briskly, 'he's ready and waiting for his Mom and Dad.'

Hermie had given him a bottle and changed his nappy. Now as she held him in her arms for the last time it was too much. Edith gently detached him from Hermie's heaving frame. The baby let out a loud howl and as Edith left the room with him, without a backwards glance, she'd never forget Hermie's shriek, *'he's my son. I'm his mother. She's stolen my son.'*

Martha and Greg loved their precious bundle Louis Dwight, as they were to christen him –Louis after their favourite singer, Louis Armstrong, and Dwight after General Eisenhower - from the very first moment and their adoration of the scrap was so touching that Edith vowed that Hermie would never be allowed to make any mischief in that direction.

For several days afterwards Hermie, somewhat fretful, rested, cosseted by the hospital staff who were kindness and discretion itself. She couldn't quite believe that her baby wasn't there anymore. One day he was there, the next day he'd gone. The Superintendent assured her in her Texan drawl, *he has gone to the very best of homes,* in the tone of voice as if referring to an unwanted kitten and Hermie had a sensation of pride as though she'd done her best by her son.

Edith sat on Hermie's bed just days before she was due to be discharged. 'I want you to know that you gave the greatest of all gifts - your baby - to a wonderful couple whose dream and hope for so long has been a baby to love and cherish.'

Hermie knew she was expected to forget her son but the pain of the separation was like a suppurating wound.

It was obvious to Edith that Hermie couldn't return to Gurgaon minus the baby. 'I'd thought about that too,' Hermie admitted as she applied her make-up, making a face at the dough-like reflection that stared back at her. 'God, I look a freak. And yes, I'm stumped.'

Parvati chipped in cheerfully. 'A friend has told me that in Dagshai there's an AI bandmaster's widow, in dire straits, who takes in paying guests. I've fixed up for you, if you agree, to stay with her until it's time for you to return to Delhi.' She gave a throaty chuckle. 'I've told her you're convalescing from cholera.'

Hermie said stiffly. 'You've thought of everything.' She stared coldly at Parvati for a moment then took a deep breath. 'Sorry, I didn't mean it to sound like that. I'm grateful, truly I am, to you both, for your support.'

'That's quite all right.' Parvati had wondered when she'd be on the receiving end of Hermie's inevitable resentment. 'You know HH is still enquiring after you,' she added untruthfully, knowing it would make her feel less depressed. 'I've told him you've gone *home.*'

Hermie felt oddly gratified. 'I'm glad he still remembers me,' she said quietly. She knew she could never forget him.

***

Hermie found Dagshai a tiny, charming, if somewhat isolated, hill station, with a few Indian families - mostly villagers - and a sprinkling of AIs living quiet lives centred round the village school, the temple and a Redemptorist Retreat House, but it suited her perfectly. She had all the time in the world to see to her looks that she'd neglected during pregnancy and to regain her strength and figure, taking pleasure in wearing her dresses. With simple yet nourishing food and thyme scented, mountain fresh air, Hermie regained a measure of serenity. She'd kept her baby's booties and would wake in the middle of the night thinking she could hear him wailing, that she could smell him.

To Edith and Parvati she wrote: *Could I have news of my little one? It's been a few weeks and I do hope he has settled in with his new parents, and is loved by them. I did the best for my little boy.* There was no reply and she never wrote again. She knew she'd never forget she'd given him up. *I've lost my son; he's gone from me forever.* When she saw babies in prams she felt a sharp, cold pang. She pined for HH and yearned for the happy times they'd shared, but as the weeks passed she slowly began to feel that she was pretty well ready to face the future.

***

Fit, well, with no sign of her recent ordeal, Hermie returned to the Oakleys, mustering the servants for their return. Peter's eyes twinkled with pleasure at seeing her again. Hermie knew she wouldn't be needed in Madras, his new posting, since Vanessa was of kindergarten age and an ayah would suffice for her and although she'd miss Jennifer and Peter, she wasn't overly concerned, for Muriel Ward, Jennifer's friend, had made overtures.

Jennifer, taking in Hermie's trim figure and smooth, clear complexion commented that she looked blooming and that Timmy and Adam sent her big hugs and kisses. She admitted that she missed them dreadfully. They'd been placed as boarders at Peter's old school and had settled in nicely, loving every minute of it and would spend the holidays with doting grandparents who, deprived of the company of the grandchildren during the long years of war, were spoiling them rotten.

'Just plenty of clean, healthy living in the bracing hill air,' Hermie explained sweetly mightily relieved that she'd been spared the embarrassment of any disclosures. 'And you've pink in your cheeks again.'

That Christmas the end of the war was celebrated with gusto and a revitalized Hermie joined in the partying both sides of the Viceroy's Ball.

***

'I've known the shikar to comprise Archie and his male chums or sometimes on more enterprising occasions wives and girlfriends have come along too,' Muriel Ward told Hermie. 'One January we shot partridge in the Kurrum, another snipe in Malabar.' She closed her eyes briefly.   'Ah, the blissful memory of birds at dawn flying across a pinky-blue sky.'

'The perfect setting for adultery,' Hermie murmured wickedly.

A look of horror crossed Muriel's face. 'It's all jolly hard work - there's no time or inclination for hanky panky.' She was so agitated at the thought she almost spilt her drink, her eyes narrowing as her gaze swept across to Archie her amiable husband, a staff officer at Army Headquarters.

'This time we're pulling out all the stops to making this, our last shikar in India, a grand affair,' Archie boomed. The Wards expected to be posted back to England soon and Archie planned to resign his commission to manage the family farm in Hereford. 'The pursuit of the barasingh, the twelve pointed stag of Kashmir. Ah ha! You find that pretty ambitious, eh? Well, in winter he moves down to lower pastures where we'll nab him, with luck.'

A few days later, the small shooting party comprising Archie and Muriel, Peter and Jennifer, Hermie, and an officer in the Royal Engineers stood by chatting and laughing as the two servants accompanying them loaded up the jeeps with stores. The man introduced to Hermie as Major Hartley Hollingberry, commanding a Field Company, tipped his tweed hat, his warm breath curling mistily up into the cold air. 'I've seen you at Sunday services.'

In sensible outdoor clothes and with cheeks deepened to a glow by the wind, Hermie turned to return the Major's greeting with a warm smile. She, too, had noticed him - indeed could scarcely have missed that tall, spare, alert looking man, in his late thirties, so striking in his uniform. She'd sensed that he'd taken a more than a casual interest in her, and had wondered how to stage-manage a meeting with him, unaware that he was trying to wangle an introduction to her. He worshipped alone, sitting by himself a few feet away from Hermie and Jennifer, at the end of a pew.

'And it's my pleasure to meet the owner of that attractive baritone.' Hermie looked at him with fresh interest.   Hartley lustily joined in the congregational hymn singing and she was certain he was single - he didn't have a married look about him.

'That's kind of you to say so. I usually only sing in the bath.'

Hermie was aware of a sort of happy lift of her heart. 'And your Christian name's the same as Coleridge's son. How did that come about?'

'I'm impressed. Father read his poetry to Mother when she was expecting although I hope I'm not the prodigal Hartley was.' He explained the Wards were old friends of his and he was godfather to their youngest child.

The party spent that night sleeping soundly under the stars, camped by the side of a freshwater jheal. The ground beneath the tent was covered with a striped cotton dhurry, laid over a layer of straw, and after a hearty and warming early breakfast, cooked by the servants over a small stove, of porridge, *rumple-tumple* (scrambled egg), and kitcheree, the party started out at first light. Hermie wore woollen trousers that showed off her long legs and slim waist to perfection, and sturdy boots and pulled on an extra jumper to follow the guns, thrilling to the new experience and realising, for the first time, why it had so excited HH. She rubbed her hands to keep the circulation going as Archie checked that the male guests were suitably equipped with guns and ammunition.

'The place will be all the duller without Muriel and Archie. Even in the few weeks of my Delhi posting,' Hartley said, in his rich, deep voice - altogether pukka, Hermie noted approvingly - 'it's obvious they make the most of life here. It's one long party, unlike Assam where conditions were dire.' His voice became suddenly flat, his face paling at the recollection. 'Keeping the Japanese at bay - a litany of atrocities you wouldn't want to hear.' The experience was obviously something he'd rather forget. He added, ' Although I wish I'd been in the thick of it   right to the bitter end, but recurring bouts of malaria grounded me so I'm kicking my heels in Delhi.'

Hermie nodded sympathetically and changed the subject. 'Archie's shikars are such organized yet such relaxed affairs.' She made it sound as though she'd shot with the Wards all her life. 'Muriel says...' Hermie who'd never called the Wards by their first names, indeed had never been invited to, felt it trip off her tongue with ease. Hartley's stride was unhurried and she drew level with him.

'Have Peter and Jennifer said when they'll be leaving for Madras, or do you intend to take a long deserved break at home before settling down into a new routine with them?' Hartley stopped and gazed around him. 'Good old Archie. This is the right approach to the stamping ground of our quarry who invariably returns, you know, year after year, to the same valley. Its steep sides will shield us from the chill wind and screen us from its view.'

'I'm not leaving Delhi just yet.' Hermie swiftly switched him back to the subject of herself and gave him a soft melting smile. She'd resolved that Hartley would be the way in, if not up, for her. 'But they're busy making tracks.' She was panting as they climbed; the path up was twisting and narrow and the going rough and slow, over rocks and boulders.

Hartley smiled at her. The wind had loosened her hair and she was quite the loveliest creature he'd ever seen and for one mad moment he felt like taking her in his arms and kissing her.   'And, if I may say so, you're a first rate walker.' His eyes flitted round her face. If Hermie was in any doubt that she'd morphed from working class AI to pukka Englishwoman, it was laid to rest that January day.

Like a baby king cobra she'd shed her skin, only it had taken her that much longer.

'The boys are boarders now and Vanessa at kindergarten so Jennifer won't need me as a companion.' Hermie hastily upgraded herself. She was conscious of Hartley's admiring gaze as she removed her jumper and tied it round her waist, revealing the outline of a firm, rounded bosom beneath the blouse. The sun was coming up bright and welcoming, banishing the chill of the early morning and bringing out the burnished glints of her hair.

They climbed the rugged terrain; snow fed streams flashing like diamonds tumbled over the rocks making the going slippery and precarious. The sunlight dazzled, the air was scented with wild herbs and small birds fluttered from branch to branch.

'Whoops! Watch your step!' Hartley saw Hermie stumble and she'd have gone dashing down if it hadn't been for his timely steadying grip round her waist, lingering longer than necessary. 'That was a near thing.'

'I'm too young to meet my maker.' Hermie giggled, letting herself droop against his shoulder and feeling suddenly breathless as she gazed into steady blue eyes.

'And I'm here to make sure you don't.' He detached his arm almost reluctantly. ' Hurrah! We're almost there.'

The shikari, with a quick appraising glance around, gave a short sharp whistle and motioned with a hand. The party obediently fell to their knees and hauled themselves along keeping out of sight below the crest. Hermie's heart tumbled against her ribs and she was conscious of Hartley shuffling ahead of her.

Pressing his finger to his lips the shikari commanded complete silence and inched forward to test the wind. 'Wait here, sahib,' he ordered in a whisper as he crept along to pinpoint the location of the stag, and then gestured to Hartley to follow him.

'Here goes,' mouthed Hartley. 'Hope I don't pot a monkey instead for that's said to bring bad luck.'

Almost holding her breath, Hermie watched as he slowly tracked the shikari. She glimpsed the stag, erect and motionless, surveying the valley with his horns flung slightly backwards, a truly superb sight against a backdrop of distant mountain peaks where the snow never melts. Like Landseer's *Monarch of the Glen,* it captured the spirit and drama of India's wilderness. A strange prickling sensation washed over her as Hartley stiffened, adjusted the rifle against his shoulder and aligned the sights.   He took aim and fired and an echoing roar rolled across the ravine.

Hermie gasped, momentarily closing her eyes.   When she opened them, she saw the stag lurch forward heavily and his hindquarters buckle under him. She felt a stab of pity for the animal and glanced at Hartley who was about to re-load his rifle.

Hartley stared at the supine beast. 'That's it, he's done for,' he said quietly, 'no point in a second shot.'

'You're a champ. Well done!' she cried.

The shikari ran forward to where the animal lay and in his excitement Hartley swung Hermie off her feet and gave her an exuberant hug. He was inordinately pleased. 'The antlers are yours.'

'But you made it happen. You shot it,' she protested. 'No. No. You keep them.'

'I want you to have them. You're a good sport.' He paused then added softly. 'I hope you don't think this is awful cheek, but you're good value, too, as Father would have put it.' She seemed to be knowledgeable about shooting and country pursuits, and wasn't a sort who was squeamish. He liked that. 'Tell me, have you yourself ever shot?'

'Not really.' HH used to talk about it at length and she'd picked up the jargon from him. 'But I'm no stranger to shikars.' She blushed and he thought how adorable she looked. 'But if you insist, yes, thank you.'

Hermie liked Hartley's directness; there was nothing devious or underhand about him. He was a military man, not a politician and saw no point in gamesmanship. He liked her, was smitten with her, and he saw no harm in letting her know that. *I've been too long without the company of women.*   Dash it, he'd been through hell on the Burma Front; his widowed mother for whom he'd assumed financial responsibility after the early death of his father, had been killed in the Blitz, and his younger brother blown to bits in the Normandy Landings, and there was something un-heroic about it if you couldn't let a girl know you fancied her.

Hermie was dazed by the way he monopolised her. She told him she'd made no plans for after the Oakleys' departure. 'I expect something will occur to me but I really haven't given it much thought.'

'I can see you're not the worrying type, and that's refreshing, Hermione.' Hartley seemed to prefer that to Hermie, and the timbre of his voice gave her name a music all of its own. He poured out some claret and raised his glass. 'Here's hoping we have many more tomorrows together.'

'I should like that very much.' Hermie dipped her eyelashes, and her heart soared. But would there be sufficient time for their relationship to develop she wondered a little anxiously. She resolved to find out before she wasted any more of her charms on him.

Hartley poked the ground with a stick. 'I'm fascinated by India. I've still got a good few years left in the army, and hopefully I'll be in Delhi for many months yet.' Their glances locked. *This is my Waterloo*, he thought as the moonlight struck Hermie's face and a gentle breeze tugged at her hair. *I can't afford to lose her.*

Archie sharpened a carving knife against a boulder and began carving, more appropriately sawing, Hermie thought, the venison roasted by the servants over a rudimentary spit and they handed round generous portions accompanied by baby potatoes cooked in hot ash and a fresh green salad. 'Dinner's up.'

They huddled round the berry red flames of the campfire. The sound of tent ropes straining in the wind and the chuckoo-chuckoo of the nightjar mingled with the faraway yelps of doe and the rustle and swish of the Indian countryside made it for all of them an unforgettable occasion. For Hermie it was magical, and held a promise of better things to come, not least because of Hartley. She began to think of him as her Hartley – with those honest eyes, square, open face and closely cut light-brown hair. He was no Clark Gable, she admitted, but that was a mere detail. As far as she was concerned, to her he was every bit as desirable. *Hermione Hollingberry, Mrs Hartley Hollingberry. Major and Mrs Hollingberry.* She tried it out in her head. It sounded good.

Packed into the jeeps, Hartley's thigh pressed against hers as they jolted back to Delhi. Back home, Hartley jumped out and handed her out of the jeep. *What lovely soft hands she has.* He went away on fire for Hermie and she waved goodbye to him with a song in her heart.

***

Over the next few weeks, it was all Hermie desired of a courtship. Hartley wooed her in the language of flowers and showered her with gifts and chocolates. He was direct, uncomplicated, considerate and doted on her. Indeed he was the perfect gentleman, little knowing that had he not been, she'd have been putty in his hands. It hadn't escaped Peter and Jennifer that Hermie had caught Hartley's eye and they furthered the friendship as much as they could.

Hermie lost no time introducing Hartley to Edith and they immediately hit it off.

'I'm in love with her, you know,' Hartley confessed, as he packed his rucksack for a summer hiking holiday in the Himalayas with Archie and Peter. 'She's the one woman I thought I'd never find. Do you think she'll have me?' All things being equal he meant to propose to Hermie before he left – the three carat solitaire diamond ring already chosen and paid for.

'She never stops talking about you and if you ask her I'm sure she'll say yes,' Edith said confidently. 'It's obvious to me you're both well suited.' It was also obvious to her that Hermie had found what she was looking for. That Hermie was indeed extremely fond of Hartley, Edith didn't doubt, but at the same time she suspected her affection was tinged with more than a pinch of expediency. Edith shrugged. *Most people have mixed motives for marriage. What does that matter so long as they're happy?*

Edith was pleased for Hermie, the pleasure slightly coloured by an uncharacteristic spurt of envy that Hermie had someone with whom she could share her life and who'd cherish her. Edith shut her eyes tightly. No one quite like Jean-Claude would ever knock at the door of her heart; she missed him more than words could say. Had grieved for him so much that for months after she'd learned of his death, her hurt had been too deep for tears. Her fingers went up to clutch the posthumous medal awarded to him for his bravery which she wore on a chain round her neck, his parents having made it over to her as a keep-sake.

***

'You make me very happy, my darling,' Hartley said in his quiet voice. 'You're the best thing that's happened to me.' He'd no intention of letting the years stretch out ahead of him lonely, unmarried and uneventful.

Hermie responded freely to his ardent embrace, knowing what he was working up to but somehow not quite believing it was happening to her. 'I can't imagine life without you,' she whispered against his lips.

'I love you with all my heart and soul - your beautiful eyes, your smile, the way you listen. You've filled me to the brim.' Hartley closed his fingers over the ring. 'Give me your left hand - that's it. Now shut your peepers and count up to three.'

'One... three!' Hermie looked down at the ring shooting fire and caught her breath. 'Hartley... what can I say?' she said shakily.

'Say yes,' he said huskily.

'That goes without saying.'

'I'm leaving the wedding arrangements to you, Hermione. You girls are so much better than us chaps at these things, but there's one condition,' he paused,' make sure we're spliced as soon as possible as I couldn't bear another Christmas without you as my wife.'

'I want it as much as you.' She was to share his life. She knew with cast-iron certainty that she'd be cherished. And she knew she'd so much to give him. Hermie closed her eyes and snuggled against his chest rubbing her soft cheek against his rougher one, taking in the manly clean scent of him. As far as she was concerned, the sooner they wed the better, for at last, stranded for so long on an empty platform, scanning the horizon for a sign of engine smoke, the good train *home,* long overdue, was clanking round the bend.

Hartley placed his hand on his heart with mock solemnity. 'I promise faithfully to write every day I'm away and I shall get plastered every evening with Peter and Archie.' He gave an infectious laugh as Hermie jumped a little. He'd started as he meant to go on, determined not to let marriage derail his friendship with his chums and knowing that once he took his foot off the pedal, Hermione would, he suspected, never allow him out of her sight.

***

'Congratulations!' Edith was at the summer palace at Sivalik. HH's young cousins had been packed off to England to complete their education. The Royal residences echoed hollowly these days and she felt like a pea in a pod rattling around with just HH, the ADC, the Comptroller and a few other functionaries in the State service for company. 'Hartley will look after you. He won't play away.'

'Oh Edith. He's solid as the rock of Gibraltar and so dependable. And your turn will come.' Hermie believed it was only time before Edith would love again. Her thoughts flew to HH and she longed to ask Edith about him. But she must not - could not. Only Hartley was her concern now and Hermie reminded herself that she must never forget that. 'Parvati has probably already heard the news.'

They laughed and chorused, 'little escapes her.'

'But,' Hermie added a little timorously, 'about Parvati...'

'Like me, she's your friend, remember that.' Edith knew Hermie craved reassurance that her dark secret was safe with them. 'And you can rely on her discretion – that's the secret of her success.'

Hermie couldn't wait to share her news with Bernadette who ventured to ask her about her plans for training college. 'Abandoned.' Hermie was unrepentant. Once it had seemed a way up, if not out, of her narrow life. But now she was to become the wife of Major Hartley Hollingberry and earning her living didn't come into it.

The news of Hermie's engagement had inevitably reached the ears of Aunty Al who'd heard a rumour some time ago that *an Indian had seduced Hermie* but she hadn't managed to get to the bottom of that. In a letter wishing her all the best she reported that Mr Turton Jones had *gone to God* a few weeks earlier and gifted his classical records to Hermie. The convent school was packing them in with year -long waiting lists and the girls swept the board in all the exams.

A crusty bachelor cousin of Aunty Al had bequeathed his nice house down south to the Castons, the only relatives who'd put themselves out for him in his last illness, and they'd given up the Delhi bungalow, conceded to Deepak's entreaties to take him with them and were moving lock, stock and budgies to Bangalore where Aunty Al hoped the more equable climate would work miracles for her arthritis.

Shopping for her trousseau like someone crazed, Hermie bumped into Barry who whisked her off to the *Blue Danube.*

'Spill the beans, my beaut, yours truly wants to hear all.' He gave his late-night smile, taking in her elegance and self-assurance. 'So it's turning out magic for you after all? That's my winning gal!' He'd picked up the rumour from Aunty Al. He still had a reputation as the local Casanova, but contrary to what Hermie had once believed, would never have proposed to her or any girl unless it was to bed them. But marriage was for never.

Hermie grinned. 'You're further back in the field.' Barry was fun company with his brash outlook on life, enhanced by his war experiences, but was he quite the company she should keep once she became Hollingberry memsahib? 'Still on debt row, I suppose?' There was something about him that struck her as different - the boyishness had vanished; there was a lived - in look about him, the body harder and more muscular than she remembered.

He flashed a victory gesture. 'A well-earned reprieve has arrived in the shape of a sound engineer job I conned my way into at All India Radio in Bombay. You've not heard the last of yours truly.'

'Hartley old boy. Come for a parochial chat?'

Hartley laughed and followed Peter into the sitting room. 'Just thought I'd check to see if there's anything wanting doing although it seems Hermione has a flair for this sort of thing and has it all nicely in hand. I've left her in my quarters at the club seeing to the invitations. It seems most of the guests are from my side.'

Peter paused and turned his back as he poured out a couple of glasses of beer. 'I believe,' he said carefully, 'she isn't close to her family. No reason to be, I gather.'

Hartley held up the glass. ' Here's to you and Jennifer for delivering to me the best girl in the world. Yes, parents deceased. She's an only child and estranged from distant relatives.'

The men sat in silence for a while nibbling samosas and pakoras. Peter and Jennifer hadn't been long in India before they'd cottoned on to the various layers, nuances, grades, and deep social divides between the Raj and its sub-strata, domiciled Europeans, which ghettoised AIs. They'd long since realised that Hermie was AI. A flicker of complicity passed between the two men. Hartley had suspected, given his years in India and from his experience of army AI personnel, and he knew that Peter knew he knew, that Hermione was AI.

'You're a lucky man,' Peter said genially. 'Hermie will make a wonderful wife.'

'And a handful.' They laughed and downed more beer. 'But I wouldn't have it any other way, no matter what.' Hartley knew he could never raise the AI issue with Hermione. That he never would. She'd shown herself to be downright touchy, the way she'd change the subject when the subject of AIs innocently arose. Hermione meant everything to him; she was his life. She'd hate him for tackling her about it; hate him for opening the book on her past and all for what? It was enough for him that he knew. Knew by what he'd seen and heard of the AI condition that she'd been driven to turn her back on the community and seek to pass herself off as English. It was all very well for some to belittle or mock her actions. He came from good, solid upper-middle-class English stock and hadn't known the same obstacles. It was all too easy to say that none of that mattered - that the war had changed all that. It mattered dreadfully to those like Hermione who craved acceptance and if that meant doctoring her past, well that wasn't a hanging offence. His crime would be to force it all into the open. She was entitled to her secrets. If one day she wanted to talk, he'd listen. Meanwhile he'd cherish and protect her.

***

On 29 September 1946, Hermie woke to her wedding day. *Today I'll become a wife.* It sounded very grown-up. The weather was still very warm, but they'd had a good monsoon. Hartley had given her carte blanche to spend, as she wanted, on the outfit and the reception. And Hermie wanted it all just so. She'd spent weeks poring over the latest bridal looks in *Vogue* and *Ladies Home Journal,* weeks with pattern books and dress fabrics and earnest consultation with the durzee and endless fractious fittings; weeks when she'd almost come to blows with the caterers, but not daring to with Peter, to whom she'd eventually bowed on the choice of music. She wanted her wedding day to be the perfection she'd longed for and dreamed of ever since she was a little girl.

Iqbal Khan, a kindly engineer friend of Hartley who Hermie had come to know and like, was best man. Peter performed the ceremony, as Jennifer beamed proud encouragement at little Vanessa, who, like the Wards youngest girl, looked fetching in a pink bridesmaid's dress. As the chords of the voluntary thundered out, Hermie walked up the aisle on Archie Ward's arm, entrancing in a sprigged ivory muslin Victorian-style wedding dress and a fine, five-yard train trimmed with lace and pearls, flowing below a coronet of yellow jasmine and carrying a fragrant bouquet of orchids, sweet peas and myrtle.

In full dress uniform Hartley stood at the altar rail, the hilt of his sword glinting in the shafts of sunlight streaming from the church's central dome. His heart swelled at the sight of Hermione. *We're starting a new life together and neither of us has a care in the world.* 'You're so beautiful', he whispered.

' Beautiful for you.' Hermie felt nothing could trouble her now. She'd gone through the furnace, but winning Hartley made it all worthwhile. *I'll never want.* There was a lump in her throat. *If only Ma could see me now.*

Never had St James' witnessed a lovelier bride. A detachment of Royal Engineers formed a regimental guard of honour and pelted with confetti and rice, the Hollingberrys were driven in a beribboned Rolls-Royce to the reception at the stately Maidens Hotel, the setting of many a grand Imperial affair, where they opened the dancing with *Cheek to Cheek.*

Ignoring Bernadette's advice to heal wounds, Hermie hadn't invited the Blakes or kindly Uncle Bruce to the wedding having severed all links with them after

Ma's death. Edith and Parvati in their usual forthright manner hadn't refrained from asking Hermie how she'd stonewalled Hartley's inevitable enquiries about close relatives.

And Hartley had asked.   With tears in her eyes, Hermie reprised the story she'd told the Oakleys all those years ago. She was getting on with her life and saw no reason to explain the truth of her past to Hartley; she'd made her peace with herself and had no questions to answer.

Hartley had put his arms round her and kissed her. 'You have me. We have each other. I'm your family now.'

On a houseboat on the lotus strewn Dal Lake of Kashmir, fringed by mountain peaks, they were very much on honeymoon returning blissfully happy to Delhi to what had been the bungalow of the Wards, who'd sailed home after the wedding, and to Putch and Suzie, inherited from the Oakleys.

'Thank God, bachelor quarters in the club are a thing of the past,' Hartley said with a grin, but no sooner had they settled in than he was posted to Poona, much to Hermie's delight.

'My dears,' she said excitedly to Edith and Parvati, 'I can't tell you how relieved and pleased I am. I'll only feel the past is truly behind me if I can get shot of Delhi for a while and after that Hartley's bound to make tracks for **home.**'

Barry, who she felt could've proved an embarrassment, was neatly consigned to Bombay. She'd heard the Powley brothers had won promotion and been transferred to duties elsewhere in India, and Bernadette, heavily pregnant with her second child, hadn't thought it wise to risk the long journey to Hermie's wedding in her condition.

CHAPTER 13

Violence stalked the country the following year as the Raj began the countdown to the separation of the sub-continent into India and Pakistan. At Partition, cries of *Mussulman Murdabad* - or conversely - *Death to Hindus/ Sikhs* were at full throttle. There was massive population exchange and scenes of unprecedented inter-communal slaughter when morgues were stacked to the ceiling with putrefying corpses, and service people were asked to opt between India and Pakistan. Hartley, who'd been mentioned in dispatches, was promoted to Colonel. The princely states, too, were required to integrate with one or other country.

'I've thought about it long and hard,' HH told Edith, a grave expression on his face.

'You mean for as long as it takes to soft boil an egg?'

He reached over and patted her knee. 'You're a wicked woman. I've said it once and I'll say it again. Anyway, I've plumped for India and in return I'm allowed to retain my title and assets.' He beamed and added hopefully, 'and perhaps our new government will now up-grade my gun salutes.'

The AI and Christian communities were largely spared the religious strife although militant Hindus had forced Wilburt to strip to prove he was un-circumcised and Ashley narrowly managed to avoid a bullet in the head from a Muslim gang by reciting the Lord's Prayer. Nevertheless, the changing political climate triggered an exodus of AIs who reckoned   there was no future for them in India or Pakistan after Independence. The majority chose the United Kingdom, with the fair skinned scraping into Australia, while some families opted for Canada.

 As the Hollingberrys watched the Indian tricolour of saffron, white and green flutter in the scented breeze from the Secretariat Building on the 15th of August 1947, as schoolchildren marched to the tune of *Under Freedom's Flag,* and newspaper headlines declared *India Independent - British Rule Ends*, Hermie was blissfully unaware that Hartley had privately come to a decision that she'd never bargained for.

***

After the troubled birth of the two nations, the year 1948 opened with Hermie brimming with plans for ***home.*** British civil servants and armed forces personnel were disengaging from India and she assumed that any day now Hartley would be ordered back to England.

It was a damp day at the end of January, with a breeze blowing that made it seem colder than it was and Poona was shrouded in a fine mist.

'You know, darling...' Hartley relaxing in a steamer chair concentrated on pressing the tobacco down into the bowl of his pipe. His voice was calm and un-emphatic.

'Yes, dear?' Hermie glanced up from her crossword and at the sight of his expression her heart sank. *What is he going to say? Has he somehow found out about me? That I'm AI or, God forbid, about my liaison with HH and the love child?*

'I must confess I don't really want to go back home.' Hartley was slightly apologetic, knowing how for the past few months Hermione had lived and breathed and longed for it and talked of nothing but. 'I've grown to love it here and I'm exhilarated by the idea of a new India. I want to stay on. **This** is my home now and this is where I want to stay.' He had many Indian friends. 'It'll be hell living in a shoebox in some parochial place like Bromley or Bournemouth, having left one's heart behind in India, scraping along on a pension, reduced to exchanging reminiscences with club bores about Poona in the '40s, or, even worse, catching the 7.36 into the City to time-serve in some thoroughly uninspiring job. I honestly don't think I could face that.'

Hermie opened her mouth and closed it again, then rose to her feet ostensibly to arrange the freshly cut blooms of plumbago, candytuft and white chrysanthemums the mali had brought in, but actually to give herself time to think. Hartley hadn't consulted her or asked her what she wanted, she realised. He'd made the decision for them both and assumed she'd fall in with it. She wasn't ready for such direct dealing. It was as though he'd plunged in a knife or pulled the trigger. A cold wave of fury washed over her and she shivered, drawing her cardigan tightly round her. *I must stay calm.* She couldn't lash out at him as she'd done with Pa and Ashley. That side of her could never be allowed to surface.

'Dear, do you mean to stay here, in Poona?' she said with as much steadiness as she could muster. She knew better than to argue with him. But there were other ways to skin a cat.

'No, no.' He took the pipe out of his mouth. 'I thought we'd go back to Delhi.' He sensed that this would put him on safer ground, since dear Hermione who he realised with affection had the attention span of a gnat, had, after the first flush of enthusiasm, found Poona rather dull and hadn't sought to hide that from him. 'There're some tremendous openings there and I'm convinced it's where we ought to be. I've made some enquiries about some rather nice Lutyens-style bungalows that are under construction - ' He made as though it was only of casual interest but unknown to Hermie, he'd already put a deposit down on one. The houses were, in fact, pricey, but he suspected it was the only way to placate her. He was relieved to see the bright colour subside from her face.

'You have been busy, dear,' Hermie said tartly.

'Didn't want to worry you dear while things were still in the melting pot.'

'So, what's cooking?' She saw a spark of excitement in his eyes.

He squared his jaw a sign she'd come to recognise. 'I'm leaving the army and Iqbal Khan and I are going into business together. My severance will come in useful.' It was providential that she already knew and liked his friend. He hoped to forestall further argument and added a little lamely, 'it'll entail some overseas travel and, as always, I'd be lost without you. Of course, you'll accompany me, won't you dear?'

Hermie stared at him speechless for a moment or so. Dear, mild, unaggressive Hartley had ever so nicely out-manoeuvred her. 'Naturally, dear.... my place is... beside you,' she said summoning all her reserves and dashing the angry tears that had sprung to her eyes.

His pipe had gone out and he pushed it down into a pocket, reaching over to switch on the radio as if to signal that their conversation was at an end.

But Hermie determined to say more. 'I...' she began more calmly. Her face was more disappointed than he'd ever seen or imagined it could be.

'Hush a moment.' Hartley's voice was sharp for him. 'What's that now?' He turned up the volume on the radio and they heard the tail end of a news flash that Gandhi-ji had been gunned down at a prayer meeting that day by a Hindu fanatic, who believed that by trying to reconcile Muslims and Hindus, the Mahatma had betrayed the Hindu cause.

Shocked, Hartley put his hand to his mouth, and said quietly. 'You know, Mr Gandhi once said that the seven great sins are wealth without work, knowledge without character, commerce without morality, science without humanity, pleasure without conscience, politics without principle and worship without sacrifice. I've thought about that a great deal and ... ' His voice tailed off as Prime

Minister Nehru came on the air, his tone solemn and emotional, *'the light has gone out of our lives.'*

'Nothing will be the same again,' Hermie said quietly, her eyes brimming with tears not so much for the dead Patriot as out of disappointment that the bright prospect of *home* had gone out of hers.

Hartley started to say something but Hermie turned on her heel and hurried to their bedroom, so hateful was his presence suddenly to her. If she didn't get out of his sight, she felt she'd square off against him - say what she really thought and felt. *How could he have done that to me? How could he have been so unfair, so insensitive?* She felt like hitting him. He'd robbed her of all she'd lived and breathed for. Snatched her dream from her after all he claimed she meant to him. Rocked their marriage to the core. She couldn't believe he didn't truly appreciate what he'd knowingly done to her. She burst into tears, fury mingled with bitter disappointment. She might as well have married Winston or Marcel and saved herself all the years yearning for *home.* At least she'd have known where she stood, like Bernadette, whereas now...once again a deep void yawned before her.

After the past comfortable months with her worries behind her, her future more or less mapped out and now having to face this... it was too much to ask of her. Hermie blew her nose and moved to the dressing table stool, taking up the tortoiseshell-backed hairbrush. What shall I do, where shall I go? Knowing Hartley as she did, dislodging him from his decision would be as easy as re-arranging the cave reliefs of Ajanta. She chewed her lip. Hartley had been her ticket out. He gave her status, credibility. When she married him she never expected to be placed in a dilemma again.

What would she become if she were to leave him? The straight answer was nothing. Granted, he'd pay her alimony but that wouldn't quite keep her in the style to which she'd become accustomed. She'd acquired no qualifications and if she went *home* under her own steam she would not only have to set to gain some - Hermie shuddered at the prospect - but would be treated as a rather fishy femme sole – someone whose friends wouldn't   let loose in the same room as their husbands. And staying in India as a divorcee, à la Bettina-Lorna, drifting around Delhi as the ex-wife of a successful businessman was hardly a palatable option. Hartley would re-marry, she was sure of that, for he was all for, in the words of the song, getting up and dusting himself down and starting all over again. *But could I?* That night she lay rigid beside him.

The open windows of Edith's private quarters in Walipur let in the serene glory of the day. She opened a letter from the Oakleys, who'd returned home to Wiltshire for good, after Independence. *We felt it only right that the Anglican Church in India is served by its own Indian clergy. Peter is just so glad that he participated in their vocation. He has changed tack and has been appointed Dean of a Theological College.*

The telephone rang and the palace switchboard operator put Hermie through.

'Edith, how are things with you?'

'My dear! HH's wedding on 1st March – and so auspicious according to astrologer Pandit-ji - was a marvellous affair.'

'That was also his birthday, I remember.' Hermie tried to sound disinterested. After all, it was only an arranged marriage. 'And who was the blushing bride?'

'Princess Madhu, a very attractive young woman, the eldest daughter of the Rajah of Bhind. It was frightfully lavish as you can imagine. The festivities extended over several days and exhausted all but the bridal couple.'

A surge of jealousy suddenly ripped through Hermie undoing her composure.

'They're honeymooning in Europe,' Edith continued chattily, unthinkingly rubbing salt into the wounds.

'How nice for them,' Hermie said coldly. 'Now, listen up. Hartley has absolutely no intention of going **home**.'

Edith gasped and nearly dropped the receiver, wondering how she'd taken it.

'I can't get him to budge. I tried everything. Cajoled, threatened...' Hermie had done no such thing although Hartley had told Iqbal that she'd sulked... not a little. 'And did the dance of the seven veils but he's adamant. He says he's heard horror stories about how people like us bitterly regretted the move back. He's done his sums and doubts if his army pension or his earnings in civvy street would stretch to the comforts of life that we take for granted here. So we're making tracks for Delhi. He has gone some way to appeasing me having bought a very nice bungalow indeed, I must admit, in a very select area not far from the club.' She sounded slightly mollified. She told Edith that Hartley had resigned his commission and that he and Iqbal were in the process of acquiring an established engineering company, from the Scottish widow of its previous owner, importing irrigation equipment. 'So there'll be no diminution in our status and not likely to be any as they've forged strong links with a prominent French drilling company to sink tube wells in the Punjab.'

Hartley, you old fox, you've been plotting this for months, Edith thought.

'Isn't it a quirk of fate that after all this I may never go **home**? Hartley's determined not to and I can't see that I shall, unless he's there, by my side.'

That Hermie's hopes had been utterly crushed were evident from the forlorn note in her voice.

'But soon you'll have your own house and I'll have mine.' Edith lowered her voice conspiratorially.

Hermie was diverted from her monologue. 'What do you mean? You already have a place - with the Walipurs.'

'No, no. I wouldn't dream of hanging on there now HH's hitched. It wouldn't be fair to Madhu. I'd cramp her style and she'll only feel resentful and make things uncomfortable for me. Tucked away down a crooked old lane so narrow only a boy and his cow can pass, I stumbled across an airy, flat-roofed, lime-washed stone built little house with lofty ceilings and nicely proportioned rooms centred round a large sun-drenched courtyard. It's in an old quarter of old Delhi - not far from Parvati.' She refrained from saying it needed rather more than a lick of paint and was a complete wreck.

Hermie tried to make sense of what Edith had just said. 'You can't be serious,' she hissed. 'It's not the place for a European. No, I don't want to hear about how Parvati manages - it's quite different for her. And you're bound to miss the creature comforts of the palace. You've gone stark, raving mad.'

The line crackled as Hermie pooh poohed Edith's plans and was later to complain to Hartley that she'd been unable to reason with her. 'There's heaps more you could choose from and we can put you up while you look round properly.' She became managing. 'I'll get Hartley to make enquiries. Hello, Edith, hello, are you still there?' Hermie's voice rose shrilly. 'Operator, oh damn...' The line went dead, conveniently, she suspected, and no amount of jiggling and tapping   restored the connection.

***

Parvati poked gingerly around the rickety stone screened windows wondering if Edith quite grasped the harsh reality of restoring a tumbledown property. But to Edith it was love at first sight. She'd seen the potential and the symmetry beyond. 'I'll convert this dusty yard into a Mediterranean patio with white flagstones, flowering tubs, trailing vines...'

'...And a dog napping in the shade of the old mulberry tree?' Parvati's eyes twinkled. 'My, you've been a closet romantic all these years.'

Hermie wrote off the neighbourhood as a seedy dump but Edith refused to be mentally bullied by her, determined to get the hell out of Walipur. Parvati understood perfectly. Edith was glad someone did. She'd admit it only to herself that life in princely circles had long since palled, and for a long time she'd felt she'd outlived her usefulness there. 'I want a nest of my own now, a sure sign of incipient middle age,' she joked, looking nowhere near it.

Hermie, fingering the triple string of cultured pearls at her throat, Hartley's guilt offering to her, reminded Edith she'd miss the gracious living of the palace and being waited on hand and foot. That Edith had a far too romantic perception of Mother India.

Edith, controlling her impatience at Hermie's denseness, reminded her that she'd earn her living giving private tuition in European languages and philosophy and that she now had an extra language to her bow - Hindi. Unlike Hermie she could speak it like a native, and didn't see why she shouldn't rub that in. 'India has always been a magnet for European businessmen and it won't be long before India and Germany establish full diplomatic relations, so I'm bound to be in demand as an interpreter.' She grinned. 'Don't worry, Hermie, I can earn my keep. I've had enough practice.'

Parvati chortled. Hermie had given a little gasp then smiled, refusing to rise to the bait - a trait she'd learned from Hartley.   It was no secret to Hermie and Parvati that Edith didn't want to go home to Germany; there was nothing there for her. Edith had known love and the pain of its loss.

***

Darting about, a Gitane drooping from her lips and often wondering if she really had bitten off more than she could chew, Edith badgered the workmen with a cunning strategy of carrot and stick, finally taking possession only days before the return from honeymoon of HH and Madhu. Unconventional as ever, the house bore her stamp in the crimson stained woodwork, and on the walls she hung the watercolours she'd painted herself. A Berlin cabinet-maker, a fellow internee who'd remained in India during the war years, had crafted some stylish maple wood furniture and was happy to make it over to Edith on his return to Germany. The house became quite different from those of the clerks amongst whom she lived and with whom she was soon on good terms. Bursting with well-concealed pleasure, she invited Parvati to be her first guest.

'My dear you've done wonders. Only you'd have dreamt of rescuing it. We'd make a fine team and a fine fortune acquiring and refurbishing old houses.'

Parvati's sharp eyes roamed approvingly round the room. 'It has a certain je ne sais quois!' *Edith has made it so charming on a shoestring.*

'One undertaking like this is enough to last a lifetime.' Edith twitched a handloom fabric curtain into place.

'That's what they all say. But it's like childbirth. Mark my words you'll be itching to start all over again.'

Edith quickly changed the subject. Parvati was apt to sweep one up into her schemes unless one was very firm. 'And what have you got there?' she gestured to a large square brown paper parcel propped up against a wall. 'Spending your ill-gotten gains?'

Parvati gave a familiar throaty chuckle and told her it was a house-warming present. Edith tore off the packaging. ' Gott in Himmel! '   In her excitement, she lapsed into German, admiring the fountains of colour in the antique Bokhara rug.

' It's divine.' Edith ran a hand over the soft, smooth surface. 'A rug to make love on in my own slice of paradise.' Parvati's generosity touched her.

On a bubble of laughter Parvati told her she was still an attractive young woman, and in spite of her independent ways, she thought she'd quite like some nice man to look after her. Tolerantly Edith had kissed her on the cheek and riposted that if Parvati didn't have other plans for him, she should let her know. Their conversation turned to Hermie and Parvati seemed to think that Hermie's troubles were well behind her, that her Hartley was a good man, a good provider and perhaps she'd find Edith someone like him given a torrent of suitable men in India.

Edith grinned. 'Men have provided you with a nice little pot of gold, but I give you credit for diverting some of that to good account. All those wonderful musicians and poets you've encouraged and patronised and those intimate recitals you're so good at hosting that everyone fights for an invitation.' Parvati had become a leading benefactor and patron of Indian Performing Arts.

Marvelling at Edith's initiative and bid to cut loose, and pulling rank, the ADC wangled her a telephone, although he warned her that it would be a poisoned chalice. HH would drive her mad with his endless phone calls at all hours of the day and night, he having suffered them himself.

'I can cope with that. But I wasn't going to be doomed forever to the whole Walipur circus.' Edith pulled herself up short, immediately regretting her indiscretion, but the rapid flicker of the ADC's eyes acknowledged that he'd often felt like that himself and he touchingly told Edith he'd miss her.

'And you've another escape route lined up.' His eyes had caught the glint of a polished black motorbike parked unobtrusively in the courtyard. Edith described how she'd bought her vroom-vroom second hand in the bazaar and that a mechanic neighbour had brought it up to scratch.

The next morning, after several cups of black coffee, brewed to Edith's exacting specifications by her maid, Shanthi, a vagrant sixteen year old who'd simply trailed her home from the bazaar and taken possession of the servant's room, Edith settled down to open her post with a sense of one more incident closed. There was an odd flutter in her stomach as she slit open a letter bearing a Nebraska postmark. The Addisons tour of duty having ended, and Greg appointed Senior Pastor of the Baptist Church in Scottsbluff, they'd sailed home for good earlier that year.

My dear, Martha wrote: *It's so long since you heard from me you must have wondered whether you ever would again. The truth is that having such a little precious boy like our darling Louis has meant almost no time for letters. He's a swell little fellow, as you'll see from the enclosed, the apple of our eye and spoiled by four doting grandparents. We continually give thanks to the Lord for His wonderful gift and to you for being His instrument. Louis just adores Goldilocks - his baby sister Lauren, an American orphan that we recently adopted. So the family is complete.*

Edith held the snapshot up to the light. A sturdy little boy with curly dark hair, wielding a child's baseball bat grinned mischievously at the camera. He looked no different from the archetypal, home grown American he'd become. She was sorely tempted to show the photo to Hermie, who'd never spoken to her and Parvati again about her son, but decided it was wiser not to re-open the pages of a closed book. Just then, the telephone rang.

'Edith, Edith, why've you deserted me?' HH's deep voice was tinged with melancholy. She jumped, having almost forgotten about him and Walipur. 'You've gone forever and I'm devastated. Please, please, come back.'

'Grow up,' Edith growled. 'If you and Madhu want to see me, you'll have to come over here and be my guest.' Gone, too, were the days when she felt under a compulsion to do his bidding.

'The very invitation I was angling for. And by the way there's a little something winging its way to you.'

To her delight it was the Bechstein.

***

In the summer of 1950 Hermie accompanied Hartley to England on a business trip. Rationing there had not been lifted and although she found the threadbare and depressed post -war country unpalatable and life for many British returnees not easy, as Hartley had wisely predicted, she still harboured a grudge that she'd not been given the option to settle down at *home*. She resolved not to torment herself by another visit there and to confine future overseas journeys to Continental countries.

Well, if she couldn't go *home*, her resentment was somewhat assuaged by her passport that bore the reassuring words: **British citizen.** She hadn't divulged to Hartley that the applications she'd filed on three separate occasions for a British passport had all been rejected as she was unable to establish, as required by British nationality law, that close male antecedents - a father or grandfather - were born in Britain. In desperation Hermie had turned to Barry, who'd gained a reputation as a fixer and who was then in Delhi attending a sound engineers' conference. Twenty-four hours later a grinning Barry met her at the *Blue Danube* flourishing a stiff, blue-backed British passport bearing Hermie's name. She'd fallen on it gratefully, recalling his motto: *Don't ask.*

***

Beset by a feeling of piety, Parvati decided to do puja and her chauffeur halted the gleaming new Studebaker outside the temple. She climbed the few, shallow steps, mingling inside with other devotees, some men, mostly women, with offerings of money and garlands of flowers that they draped reverently round oleographs of the deities. Parvati sniffed, loving the sweet smell of incense that lingered perpetually in the air. The altar was covered with a crimson cloth and strewn with tinsel and clay miniatures of Hindu saints. Bells rang out and saffron robed priests entered, chanting amidst the flicker of oil lamps. Covering her head with the pallu, Parvati folded her palms together and stood reverently with bowed head, giving thanks and praying for continued health and prosperity. Then reaching for a stick of incense she lit it and placed it in a lump of sacred Ganges mud.

The short service ended and, as the worshippers filed slowly away, Parvati lingered behind, chatting and joking with the priests to whom she was well known as a generous benefactor, the degree of munificence proportional to her mood of religious zeal.

Eventually they exchanged namastaes. 'I must fly or I'll be late for a committee meeting,' Parvati said, patting her immaculately sculptured hairdo.

'Take care of yourself.'   Their gaze followed her graceful walk down the steps. Even after all these years her dancer's gait was unmistakeable. Passers-by milled around, lepers held begging bowls in their stumps, chokras cried out their wares.   Parvati's mind was filled with pleasurable thoughts of the evening ahead, a gossipy dinner with Edith and a glass of chilled Riesling.

'Parvati-ji.' A female voice, a raucous voice using the honorific, a voice she didn't recognise rang out. Parvati turned round. Wearing a blue cotton sari pulled over her head, a woman approached, elbowing her way through a knot of bystanders, a tight hard smile on her face that did not reach her eyes, her hands curved tightly round a jar clutched against her chest.

Parvati returned the smile, sensing there was something odd about the way the pallu was draped across the woman's head as if she sought to avoid recognition; she was clearly not a village girl for there was a whiff of expensive French perfume.

'You she-devil. You've corrupted my husband,' the woman shrieked on a harsh, ugly note, astounding bystanders into a sudden hush. Her puckered face was grey with loathing, deep lines scoring her cheeks. She'd moved to within inches of Parvati who was too astonished to speak or move, but she stiffened at the hate in the woman's eyes. 'You bitch,' the woman hissed and before Parvati could make any sense of it all, she'd hurled the contents of the jar over her. 'You've shamed me.'

'Ai, ai, aiee...' Parvati let out an agonised scream. Her palms splayed in self-defence as a pale, corrosive liquid splashed across her hands, caught her hair and eyes and dribbled down her face, onto her chest. Dimly aware of the commotion around her, Parvati felt herself collapse. In slow motion she heard her own demented howls like that of a trapped animal. Someone wrestled her assailant to the ground; someone, probably her chauffeur carried her, moaning, into a shop doorway. She felt as if a great fire was consuming her; as if she was being burned alive. 'Ram, Ram.'

***

Parvati struggled into waking, to someone holding her hand, and lifting a finger to her face, she had the impression of a bandage round her eyes. Searing pain hovered beneath the surface, temporarily deadened by shots of morphine, just waiting to burst through.

'Who's this?' she muttered, running a tongue over dry lips.

'Edith.' Parvati's ghastly condition sent shivers down her spine.

'My friend...' Parvati heard the faint scrape of a chair being dragged near the bed.

'You're in the American Hospital. Some crazed woman doesn't like the way...you do business but she has been apprehended.'

'Who is she?' She squeezed Edith's hand. 'Why...?'

'Hush, take it easy.' Edith bent her head and whispered a name in her ear. He was one of Parvati's most prominent clients. 'His wife learned of his indiscretions and vowed to avenge herself.'

'I am ruined.'

'No. No,' Edith nearly shouted. 'You'll get out of here to renewed triumphs.' She said it with more confidence than she felt. 'The fiend sent a servant to the bazaar for hydrochloric acid.' The substance was in common use domestically to clean soiled lavatory pans. 'She'd not needed much. She's now in custody awaiting trial.'

Parvati struggled to sit up, but fell back on the pillows, defeated by the effort. 'When can I get out of here?'

'Darling girl. I think they'll want to keep you captive a bit longer. You know what these medics are like once they grab hold of you.' Edith's jocularity hid a terrible ache in her heart, for the specialist had told her that complications could ensue; the burns were so extensive and horrifying that treatment would involve many weeks of intensive care, good nursing, and ultimately skilful plastic surgery. They'd not been able to save Parvati's sight.

Parvati turned her head slightly as someone else come into the room in a rustle of starch.

'I'm afraid you'll have to leave now, Miss Müller', a nurse said gently, 'the patient has had enough for today.'

'Don't go,' Parvati whispered thinly.

'My dear, for the first time in my life I'll have to obey otherwise they won't let me darken your doorstep again.' Edith stroked the black hair lying like a fan across the pillow. 'But I'll be back, with Hermie, if we can manage to wade through this ocean of bouquets, HH's is the most sensational, needless to say, gifts and goodwill messages from your fan club.'

Hermie never saw Parvati again. Her condition rapidly deteriorated and only Edith was permitted to visit. Late one evening, with Edith holding her hand, she lost her fight. Edith hastened to Hermie's and they grieved quietly together. Parvati would always hold a special corner in their hearts. And Hartley, who'd met Parvati briefly at a cultural evening, comforted his wife in a way he knew he couldn't be faulted, with a 22 carat gold and diamond starburst brooch.

***

Edith didn't think she'd ever forget the tumultuous months of 1953. On 5 March of that year, Iqbal's young daughter came home from the Convent of the Holy Martyrs and chatting to her parents about her day told them that Sister Veronica had asked the class to offer up prayers for the Soviet Leader, Marshal Joseph Stalin who was seriously ill.

'You know, children, dear Uncle Joe, as a young man, planned to become a priest. We must all hope that God in His mercy spares him and that he makes a full recovery. Hail Mary full of grace...'

Towards the end of May, mountaineers Edmund Hillary and Sherpa Tensing conquered Mt. Everest. In early June, Queen Elizabeth II was crowned, the young monarch making media history when the solemn and momentous event was televised to the nation and the world for the first time. In Britain it was celebrated with pomp and ceremony, street parties and much rejoicing. In Delhi, Hermie and Hartley were invited to a party hosted by the British Diplomatic Mission where, with other British citizens, they listened to the Coronation service from Westminster Abbey broadcast live over the radio, as TV had not yet been introduced in India, and at a reception enjoyed a slice of Coronation fruit cake washed down with sherry.

A news headline that never failed to chill Edith was that of 20 June - *Rosenbergs Executed* – which harked back to an event in America the day before. Sent to the electric chair in Sing Sing Prison within minutes of each other on what was their fourteenth wedding anniversary, the death of Julius and Ethel Rosenberg came at sundown, as thousands around the world kept vigil and campaigned for a reprieve. They'd been charged and convicted of conspiring to pass atomic secrets to Communist Soviet Russia. President Eisenhower rejected the plea for clemency.

***

One overcast winter's morning two years later a line at the bottom of an inside column of a national newspaper told readers that the Maharajah and Maharani of Walipur had divorced.   Always ahead of the curve, they were the first couple to secure a divorce by mutual consent under newly enacted legislation.

Edith's thoughts flew back to husky-voiced Parvati, and smiled to herself; she wouldn't have needed to hear it from the media. Edith had suspected trouble in paradise when the serpentinely attractive Princess Madhu was escorted out of Walipur back to her parents. It transpired that even before she wed HH she was a heroin addict- a fact hushed up by her family. Admitted to an expensive Swiss rehab by HH, she'd promptly absconded; she'd made sexual advances to the startled ADC, sought to re-arrange HH with one of his bejewelled swords and was caught red-handed feeding ground glass to HH's beloved pets. That was the last straw.

Edith turned the page. There was disturbing news of growing tensions between India and its big neighbour China despite Prime Minister Nehru's efforts with his Chinese counterpart towards *Hindi-Chini bhai bhai*. Martha's recent epistle reported that Senator Joseph McCarthy was denounced by Congress for his redbaiting tactics, censured by the Senate and described by President Eisenhower as a peril to the Republican Party.

Reading the same announcement about HH in the comfort of her home Hermie, ejected from the even tenor of her day, nervously fingered the thin gold chain with its heart-shaped ruby pendant given to her by Hartley last night. She'd made life easy for him and this offering was typical of him - gifts were not confined to special occasions.

Hermie lowered the paper and closed her eyes, feeling for a cigarette. For a long time after her marriage, when she stumbled across HH's photo in some publication or another, the very sight of him could dominate her thoughts for days; she ached to be held in his arms; yearned for those sensual nights of love-making which life on an even domestic keel with Hartley didn't provide. She felt she couldn't tell Hartley that it was that kind of lovemaking that satisfied her sexual appetite. She felt he'd have felt shocked or even worse, disgusted and she couldn't bear him to think badly of her. Surely today of all days she could yield to past memories. Could things could have been different if, disregarding Edith and Parvati, she'd told HH that she was carrying his child... the heir which he craved and which, in the event, his Maharani did not give him? A cold shiver went down her spine. Could she have been his Maharani...would he have overturned custom, risked opprobrium, and defied society, to marry her, an AI?

In a sort of joyous fantasy, Hermie had always clung to the notion that her destiny could have been different had she stood firm against what she characterised as pressure. She was quick   to place the blame elsewhere to salve her conscience or to allow herself to live with it in peace, and occasionally allowed herself to indulge in it. And even now...she wallowed pleasurably in the scenario... the happy family life that could have been hers at the court...the chubby little boy she'd held at her breast...where was he now?

Suddenly she was revisited with feelings she' d not had for years - a most desperate sense of loss - the loss of HH, the loss of the son she'd borne and so coldly rejected. She'd expected to forget him but could not. The loss was utterly acute, exploding in her like a cricket ball fast bowled into her abdomen. Meeting babies and small children had always reminded her of her son. He'd be crawling, learning to walk, to sit, and to talk. How was he getting on? Where was he? These were things that always haunted her on his birthday. To her he was always her little prince. She slid the baby's photo from her purse and stared at it choked with tears. A sense of grieving, of death, devoured her.

She'd clung to the thought that she'd made the right decision giving him up but often she felt it was the worse decision she'd ever made. She tensed her hands till she could feel her fingernails digging into the soft flesh of her palm. Then, with a supreme effort of will, she became mistress of herself again, wiping her eyes on a scented, lace-edged hanky, and resolved to consign to limbo these thoughts that could only lead to madness.

Hermie's gaze alighted on the silver -framed photograph of her and Hartley on their wedding day cutting the pretty three-tiered cake, and a sense of serenity crept over her.   She wanted Hartley there beside her. He was never to know that through him the pain of her loss had gradually eased. With him she could, in the words of the song, smile *though my heart is aching, smile though my heart is breaking.* Yet they'd no children. God knows he tried hard enough...

But unknown to Hartley, Hermie, still haunted by the tragedy of June/Juanita and petrified she would produce a dark throwback to Wilburt or Ashley, had used a Dutch cap or douched to prevent conception. The fear had mounted in her until she felt she could endure it no longer and when Hartley was unexpectedly called away overseas on business one year, she promptly booked into an expensive New Delhi clinic and had herself sterilized, explaining to Hartley on his return that the scar he saw was the result of urgent surgery to remove an ovarian cyst. Theirs was a civilised relationship...never a cross word...often a dull moment...there were no ripples to disturb them...it was made in Heaven.

Hermie stooped to tickle Putch and Suzie, descendants of their namesakes, then leaned back in her armchair and thought with satisfaction of her marriage. It had brought, perhaps not the long-envisaged settling down at *home* (but that was neutralised by urban myths trickling back to her via Bernadette about AIs who felt like fish out of water in an alien land and longed to return to India) - nor the excitement and passion she craved - but that was a small price to pay - but much happiness, peace of mind, status in society, considerable financial stability, a beautiful home and a posse of servants. Hartley himself was deeply content and was always concerned for her well being.

The years had marked off the steady expansion and prosperity of Hartley and Iqbal's business, helped in so small measure by its reputation for integrity and reliability. Their social circle centred round the club and the Indian and foreign business community, and if Hartley missed having a family, he said nothing to Hermie about it, not wishing to upset her. This was amply compensated for by her devotion to him. She considered his every wish, indulged his every whim, and was the perfect hostess and shrewd business confidante, accompanying him on almost all his trips away from home. To Edith, Hermie said sombrely, *'I've already lost one child and one man and I don't want to lose another.'*

A stranger looking at Hartley would see a much-loved 'uncle' to Iqbal's three children and a hardworking and much respected person who never regretted his decision to remain in India. His life was full and varied. A keen photographer and ornithologist, he also enjoyed shooting, trekking and casting a fly in the company of good friends, and contributed the occasional feature article on wildlife and country pursuits to English and Indian periodicals.

The years had closed over Ajeemkot and, from the security of her life as Mrs Hollingberry, and known to be charming and gracious, Hermie was drawn into a round of social activities. But occasionally there were times when the nagging feeling, which never really left her, of being exposed as AI, of the revelation of past indiscretions and the existence of the Blakes, became almost unbearable and in those troubled moments she'd summon a taxi and wander by the Jumna river at Okla, hurling sticks and stones into its treacherous swirling currents, as bronze-winged Jacanas and painted storks kept her company.

***

Edith's optimism of a bright future wasn't misplaced. Independent India soon exchanged diplomatic relations with West Germany. Technology co-operation and trade agreements between the two countries flourished, bringing Edith, whose skills as a translator/interpreter were unparalleled and much in demand, a valuable source of income. She parked her motorbike and going into her white-washed courtyard evocative of Moorish Spain paused for a moment under the mulberry tree, sniffing the fresh air and looking with pleasure around her, experiencing as always her delight in returning home after a particularly difficult assignment.

Indoors, she'd just kicked off her shoes and was enjoying a cup of black coffee when Shanthi announced HH. He'd become a regular, if somewhat unannounced, visitor, as Edith wasn't easily persuaded into leaving her little house for Walipur. Now in his early forties his waistline had thickened with the passing years and there were flecks of silver in the dark hair, but he was still a handsome man. The moment he strode in, Edith guessed he was pursuing a new interest.

'I'm going into politics.'

Edith stared at him. 'Politics? You've never shown the slightest interest in politics. What makes you think any Party will have you?' It had to be said, she resolved, and said bluntly. 'Why, for God's sake, this sudden urge to stand for Parliament? If Pandit-ji has told you it's in your stars, he ought to be pensioned off.'

HH lit a cigarette. 'It's not a sudden decision. I've been making discreet enquiries over a period of time.   I wouldn't have put my name forward as a candidate if I thought I'd be turned down.' He gave her that film star smile which had made many a girl's heart beat furiously and which he fondly hoped would dazzle voters.

'Then why ask me?' Edith said crossly, pouring out another cup of coffee. She was sure that this was only another of his fads. She could do little to help HH settle as she'd carved out her own happy routine earning a living.

'For the simple and completely illogical reason that I want your approval.'

'Are you trying to change your image? Why? Doesn't the playboy prince get what he wants anymore?' She looked at him sourly.

'You're a hard woman. Times are a-changing and so am I.'

'There wouldn't be a woman somewhere out there in these changing times, would there?' She raised her eyebrows.

He looked affronted. 'Going into politics is a very high price to pay for any woman if one wasn't interested in government. And listen, wasn't my beloved Walipur one of the first princely states to cede to the Union?'

'But if the woman was to be won, it would be a price you'd be prepared to pay?'

'A price I'd gladly pay. Besides, politics and princes have always gone hand in hand. I'm making that discovery late, but not too late.'

'Oh, wake up.' Edith stabbed at the floor with the heel of her foot. 'You can't shake off a constituency as easily as getting a divorce,' she said with a savagery that surprised even her.

HH's face paled and the smile went out of his eyes, but he bowed his head slightly and said without rancour, 'you're right to say these things. But believe me, I'm serious about standing, although I won't let it interfere with my enjoyment of life. There's no reason why politics and play can't be bedfellows.'

'No reason at all,' she said softly, 'but the trouble will come when one becomes mistress and the other wife.'

'I shall make it work.' Hands on his thighs he leaned forward and confided. 'And at last I've found my own true love.'

'Not again.'

'She's the gorgeous Princess Amrita, the only daughter of the Rajah of Gwat. He's a connoisseur of the works of Amrita Sher-gil, the noted Indo-Hungarian artist.'

'Oh, yes.' Edith had inherited Parvati's eclectic art collection that included several Sher-gils. 'It's a shame she died so young - in her late twenties wasn't it? One wonders how her talent would have developed. But I digress. Yes, I've heard of Gwat.' Edith knew him by reputation as a notorious ascetic and penny pincher who'd been a devotee of Gandhi-ji. Now himself a prominent member of the Congress Party, he doted on Amrita, his only child, and after the death of his beloved wife, relied heavily on her as his social hostess. He'd shown no urgency to find her a husband and had seen off a number of, it was said, highly suitable suitors anxious to make a dynastic connection with the powerful house of Gwat, characterising them as stupid, weak, lazy, unworthy and extravagant.

'No man's apparently good enough for her,' Edith continued with a sniff, 'and so you've concluded that the way to his heart and the hand of his daughter is by embracing politics. I must say I've heard strange things in my life but this is a new slant. You must be smitten. And wasn't it Robert Louis Stevenson who said that politics is the only profession for which no preparation is thought necessary?'

'I'm serious.' HH leaned forward and took her hand. 'Please help me.'

'How? I've no influence with the Party bosses.'

'The Princess is keen to learn a European language. That's where you come in.'

'I'm not running half way across Delhi teaching French and German to some spoiled Rajkumari.' *It's not going to be a replay of Walipur*, Edith promised herself, her memories of her life there still sharp. 'You seem to have taken a great deal for granted.'

'Please, listen to me. There's no question of your running anywhere.' HH tapped the arm of the chair, 'she will come here, to your home, for private tuition. It will be an honour and a privilege.' He refused to be defeated.

'Of course...' Edith smiled, knowing what was coming next.

'And I'll simply drop by on you, quite casually, on the days that she's with you... and we'll talk.'

'Just that? Talk? You are a reformed character! And meanwhile you'll show her father what a dedicated, honourable, political animal you are, far removed from the corrupt riff-raff. And such a deserving man and worthy husband to be. Are we speaking about the same HH?' She was gently mocking.

'We are. And you'll do it, Edith? Thank you.'

Sniffing and scenting biscuits, Andy, a golden cocker spaniel she'd acquired from a pedigree litter bred by Reverend Mother, circled lazily. The nun was busy as ever hatching new business schemes, of which this was one, to augment the Holy Martyrs ever-rising income. 'Let me know when.' Edith indulged Andy with his favourite ginger nuts and he crunched contentedly.

'Next week. Her father's Parliamentary Aide confirms that the Maharajah grudgingly admits his daughter's education needs to be broadened. And Edith,' he waggled his finger at her, ' he has heard and approves of you. That I might say clinched it.'

'With all that blarney, I could hardly say no. How old did you say this paragon, this maiden most perfect, lady of light is?'

'Twenty and so beautiful.'

'Well, she's almost on the shelf,' Edith teased, 'only there's prince charming on a white charger galloping to the rescue.'

'You're so cruel, so unromantic.' HH was smiling with a kind of delighted satisfaction. 'However, you're my truest friend. I know you'll be hers.' He got up and kissed her hand. 'You're as lovely as ever.'

'Nonsense.' Edith tried not to sound pleased. 'I'm but a husk. The Indian sun has played havoc with my skin and spicy Indian food has rotted my guts.' She'd cheated death when cancer kicked in and was still convalescing after major abdominal surgery.

But he'd have nothing of it. Always ready with a quote from the Romantics, he gazed deep into her eyes.

Edith expected something along the lines of *For she was beautiful - her beauty made the bright world seem dim, and everything beside seemed like a fleeting image of a shade.*

'The Italians have a saying - the older bird makes the tastiest dish.'

***

Enchanting, bright, and self-willed, the Princess Amrita had swept HH off his feet and her father made sure that HH's feet never touched the ground. There were gruelling times grooming him for a seat when Edith wondered if he'd stay the course. Opportunity knocked only weeks later when the MP for Walipur, a marginal constituency, died from cerebral malaria and HH was adopted as the Congress Party's parliamentary candidate.

A bitterly contested by-election ensued, but, inspired by Nehru's leadership, HH routed the opposition, substantially increasing his party's slender majority. Jubilant supporters broke through police cordons, feting him with pink rose petals and garlands of marigolds.

HH was a man who'd always been used to power, but by degrees the campaign had transformed him from a man whose power had been used for his own selfish ends to a man who said soberly to Edith, 'Now I see how my influence can be put to the good of the entire country.' She could have wept at his idealism.

HH and the Rajkumari Amrita were married in a ceremony that was the highlight of the social calendar.

'My dear Hermie, her trousseau.' Edith, not usually given to hyperbole, and who was a wedding guest, waxed lyrical. 'Footwear and bags from Florence, glamorous lingerie from Paris, bed linen from Ireland, towels - best Egyptian cotton - from the Nile,' she told her friend who'd been dying to hear every last detail, 'plus so much jewellery that it warranted a vehicle of its own. And literally reams of saris - in every colour, pattern and fabric under the sun, all so different you'd never have believed possible. And her bridal sari! IT WAS OUT OF THIS WORLD. Scarlet and gold in heavy Benares shot silk. She was a picture!'

Hermie, leafing through the many photographs of the happy couple looked up. She'd never heard Edith sound so rhapsodic. 'I wish them well,' and to her surprise she meant it, for all manner of things were well with her and Hartley. He was the most important thing in her life. HH now seemed a distant stranger, a part of her past now firmly behind her, with no power at all to hurt her and at this, his second marriage, she felt neither pain nor regret.

***

Ten months later their Highnesses first child, a daughter, was stillborn. A year later Amrita miscarried; it was another female. Then a third, premature daughter survived just three days. Not long after that an ectopic pregnancy ended at nine weeks. Tragedy stalked them yet again when another little girl suffering from cystic fibrosis died just after her first birthday. It seemed Amrita was incapable of bearing a healthy baby. But she was determined to do her duty - to bear her husband a strong male child.

'The future holds nothing for me without our son and heir,' Amrita cried, an ancient Vedic prayer floating in her mind: *The birth of a girl grant it elsewhere, here grant a son.* She felt disgraced. Over the next few years the couple spent a fortune on top gynaecologists in Switzerland and America and Amrita underwent more tests than she had saris.

Then, after a pregnancy spent largely prone in bed, a longed-for boy was delivered by Caesarean section, his lusty cries echoing strongly through the marble corridors of the ancient sandstone fortress, as had the cries of all new born heirs down the centuries.

'Now my son can aspire to be Prime Minister of India,' HH said proudly as he pressed the infant Rahul to his shoulder, while outside drum beats celebrating the birth reverberated throughout Walipur until sunset and village girls, following tradition, upturned pails of freshly drawn cow's milk over the palace steps to herald the birth.

185

***

At the time when Rahul's life was beginning, Edith, too, had reason to celebrate. The West German government had agreed to pay compensation to victims of Nazi persecution, so she'd filed an application at the appropriate German Ministry and not long afterwards was awarded a lump sum and a sizeable monthly pension. But, ever practical, she didn't squander it. She was shrewd, engaging Herr Friedrich, a fellow internee who'd made a name for himself in India as an architect after he'd left the Aliens Internment Centre, to design her a house in a smart neighbourhood. This she let to members of the Diplomatic Corps or foreign business families while she remained in her old Delhi home.

With her new-found prosperity, she traded in the ancient motorbike for a brand new Indian manufactured car that purred happily to the hills, the occasional trip to Walipur and around Delhi, where only that evening at a German embassy do – *How can you consort with those Germans after what happened to you?* Hermie had once asked to which Edith responded: *they're not the same people* - she'd glimpsed Bettina-Lorna. Edith made a mental note to ask Hermie for news of her.

Had Edith known it, Hermie itched to tell her about the echo from her past that resounded in her life that very day. On a visit home to Bareilly from Bombay, Barry Maddox made a stopover in Delhi and dropped in unannounced on the Hollingberrys, much to the chagrin of Hermie, who lived in dread that a ghost from the past would let slip that she was AI. Unknown to her, Hartley had long suspected it, although had said nothing for in spite of her carefully cultivated Bettina-Lorna drawl, Hermie's vowel sounds and occasional singsong betrayed her in moments of stress.

'It's good to meet yours truly,' Hartley said with a warm handshake, 'and you've hit the drinks hour. What do you say to whisky and soda?'

'I won't say no, but I like mine neat. Any thoughts on the programme?' Barry cast his eye around. There was a groomed look about Hermie's place, which was what he'd have expected. It was spacious and light with a tree-shaded compound back and front, deep verandahs and a tranquil atmosphere; the comfortable deep sofas and cushions were covered in restrained colours, there was a smell of furniture polish and fresh flowers, and servants moved with well-trained efficiency.

Hermie was flawlessly made up, wearing a becoming navy blue outfit and a discreetly clanging charm bracelet. And Hartley was a solid, pipe and slippers sort of man.

'It's unique,' Hermie said, studying Barry's spruce, freshly shaved appearance and on whose face unless one scrutinised it carefully one could not see the march of time etched. With a Tony Curtis quiff, he was debonair as always. 'Your very own programme, and we're you're number one fans.'

'That's what I want to hear.' Barry swallowed a large mouthful of whisky. 'My own show - you can say that again, and you should just see the bulging postbags.' With a couple of lucky breaks, Barry told them, with uncharacteristic modesty, he'd swapped the technical section for the studio, eventually rushed in as Presenter, when the compére of a sagging light programme went down with typhoid. Barry had turned round the lack lustre slot and there was no looking back.

A Date With Yours Truly was an ingenious hybrid of record requests and the airing of the latest chart toppers, interspersed with Barry's unique style of patter and wisecracks. It had listeners of all ages, judging from some of the golden oldies that were played, and the written requests, which Barry insisted be authenticated with name and address, otherwise he'd consign them to oblivion, were invariably signed off yours truly and were of the kind: *Please play Vic Damone singing On The Street Where You Live, for Dilip, on his birthday, from his sister's friend, Kusum.* Then Barry would quip *'let's give Dilip a filip from Kusum, his friend of the bosom...'*

Introduced by its signature tune *In The Mood*, the programme was beamed out for two hours every Friday night and from its inception several years earlier had struck a chord with its audience and proved immensely popular. It was Barry's brainchild; he devised the programme, edited it, presented it and he loved his baby. 'Often I'm called upon to arbitrate between the Pat Boone and Elvis fans.' Impartial as always he didn't state his own preference merely grinning, 'but by gum, the talking section of *Love Letters In The Sand* drives me nuts.'

Hermie laughed. She'd rocked and rolled with zest and her large record collection included Bill Haley and the Comets, Fats Domino, Little Richard, the Everley Brothers (she was partial to them) and all the Presley and Boone albums.

'So, what's next?' Hartley asked, topping up Barry's glass. He'd taken to this roistering character that treated life like a joke. He suspected Barry and Hermie's friendship went way back as did her links with Bernadette and Gerald, now very comfortably off in Bombay and parents of four children.

'There's only one other way and that's up.'

Hermie could tell he was nursing a secret by the light in his eyes. 'You've got something up your sleeve.'

Barry latched onto the pun and smiled. 'I'm going to make it big overseas. I'm winding up the programme at year's end and taking off. Anything Cliff can do,' he referred to Cliff Richard, the hugely talented, young AI vocalist whose hit *Living Doll* had given him a lucky break in Britain, 'I can do better.'

'India not big enough for you, then?' Hartley offered him a cigar and began to fill his pipe.

'England's where it's all happening, and that's where I see myself. Up there with the Beatles. Y'know they were in the wilderness for years honing their craft. *Please, Please Me* propelled them to stardom.'

Hermie felt a twinge of envy that he was going **home.**

'You'll miss your family,' she said, mouthing platitudes. She ignored his sharp look that shouted loudly she had not; how could she assume he would?

'Ma and Pa feel they're too old to up sticks and Sis has no problems with India. Her husband has a well paid as Head of Science in an elite boys boarding school and with two great kids and a nice house, they've no intention of going anywhere.'

That he was AI had never bothered Barry. He hadn't pined for **home** in the same way as Hermie and others, although he was aware, as was Hermie, that after Independence and again in 1964, after the death of Nehru that year, another huge tranche of AIs had migrated to Britain, Australia and Canada, fearing that future Indian governments would undermine their constitutional rights. 'But I'm a restless beast and a big-hitter.'

'You'll make for London?' Hermie said, almost knowing the answer.

Barry nodded. 'Where else? It's the entertainment and musical Mecca.' He locked himself in his fantasy, picturing himself mobbed left and right by teenage idols.

'Radio will be all the poorer without you,' Hartley said.

He beamed. 'Thanks. I'll let you know when I'm leaving. Hermie, you've struck lucky. How long have you two been married? I forget now.'

'Not long enough,' Hartley said quickly, reaching over and patting Hermie's hand. 'And I hope you find what you're looking for. Now, old boy, you'll stay with us for a few days before you make the big leap won't you?' he said comfortably, ignoring Hermie twitching edgily beside him.

'Done.' Barry was absurdly happy. 'Now I must buzz or I'll miss that ruddy train. Bye.' He blew Hermie a kiss and waved as he negotiated the semi-circular drive.

'Nice chap, although I hope he isn't disappointed,' Hartley said thoughtfully, as he stood on the verandah, puffing away. He slipped his arm round Hermie's waist and her heart gave a little somersault.

***

'Edith won't let on, but dear I'm sure she has a lover,' Hermie said, dressed to kill in the latest fashionable tennis togs, as she bobbed alongside Hartley to the club's grass courts. There was a welcome fresh breeze.

Hartley gave a little sigh. *Dear Hermione was inclined to come out with inconsequential remarks.*

'There they are.' Hermie's face shone with pleasure and she waved to the English couple waiting for them at the net. Unbidden, the Devonshire Club and Mr Armitage that repulsive old soak, probably long since six feet under by now, things she hadn't given a thought to for donkeys years suddenly flashed into mind. Hermie resolutely set her mind to the present. The past was a distant place that froze her insides.

Hartley quickened his pace. *Speculation, speculation, how Hermione revelled in it.* But for once she could be right, and although he didn't like to say so, he'd reached much the same conclusion himself some time ago, for Edith had put a bit of information about the markets his way. He hadn't asked her sources; that wasn't how he did things, but it had proved entirely reliable. Granted Edith was not over-generous with her tips, but if she said that such and such was a good buy, or you ought to think of selling that now, he listened. 'Who do you think it is?'

'I don't know and I've not been able to find out.' It was not for want of trying, but Edith had always managed to dodge the issue.

But they were wrong. Edith, still loyal to the memory of Jean-Claude, couldn't find it in herself to commit her affections again. But being far from home, she had a feeling for her own people and had had torrid affairs with some

189

rather well placed German expatriates that came to nothing. And as she'd reminded HH who'd pressed her on the subject, 'you know I treasure my sovereignty.'

Amongst her language pupils, however, was a wealthy Parsi (she was yet to meet a Parsi who was not) who, in defiance of India's foreign exchange regulations, maintained several fat, secret, numbered bank accounts in Switzerland and who, out of prudence, had resolved to learn German and French. With the passage of time, Edith's Communist sympathies had become somewhat diluted and she wasn't averse to a flutter on the stock exchange. A serious player himself, her Parsi friend - there was never anything romantic between them - gave her sound advice most of which was blatant insider dealing.

***

The last broadcast of *A Date With Yours Truly* was preceded by a jammed radio station switchboard and sacksful of protest letters but ended nevertheless just before Christmas. Barry without so much as a backward glance immediately boarded the train to Delhi and the Holllingberrys.

I badly need advice about Sinbad.' There was a worried expression on Barry's face as he gestured to a cardboard box standing on the bedroom floor. He'd accepted Hartley's invitation to stay with them prior to his departure to London and the Pan-Am flight was less than forty-eight hours away.

Hartley, who when he'd first met Barry had wondered if he'd been Hermione's lover, had since roundly dismissed that notion. He raised an eyebrow and flung up the lid of the box, only to shut it quickly with a sharp intake of breath. 'It's a snake.'

Over the top of his head, Barry corrected him gently, 'It's my pet snake. A friend in Bareilly has offered to look after him for me, but I'm not sure how I'm going to get him there.' He tapped on the box and made the choo-choo sort of noises one would make to a much-loved infant. 'Who's a lovely boy, then?'

Astounded, but with considerable presence of mind, Hartley pulled himself together and applied himself to the problem. 'Here's what we'll do...'

They drove to the bazaar and bought a boiling fowl, then settled the reptile comfortably in a covered basket with choice pieces of chicken. Then making a stout brown paper parcel of the consignment that they labelled GLASS. FRAGILE. HANDLE WITH CARE they despatched it by rail to the safekeeping of Barry's friend.

'I'm eternally grateful to you,' Barry said with considerable relief. 'He's a cheeky chap and if I miss anyone it'll be him.'

***

So pre-occupied was Hermie with her life as a burra memsahib and Hartley's perfect helpmeet, she scarcely gave a thought to anything else, until one day, tidying out her dressing-table drawer she chanced upon the carved, ivory bangle that Barry had left her as a farewell present. She slipped it on remembering the times they'd spent together when she'd first set foot in Delhi. *God, that's in the deep and distant past, and two years ago Hartley and I made a grand affair of our silver wedding anniversary.* There'd been no hard news from Barry apart from an occasional greetings card at Christmas *with love from yours truly,* scrawled in untidy handwriting.

The routine of life in a fast moving world absorbed them both. Hermie played a good hand of bridge and a good game of golf, was known to be a superb dancer and travelled overseas with Hartley on his business trips to return with several smart Continental outfits. They'd not moved from the bungalow - there'd been no need to. And they'd extended generous hospitality to the Oakleys and the Wards who'd made several return visits to the India they'd known and loved.

The Hollingberrys had lived through momentous times in a world that had changed rapidly both politically and technologically: the Independence of many African countries, the assassination of President Kennedy, and the death of Nehru, the birth of Bangladesh in 1971, a vicious border conflict between India and China, repeated wars with Pakistan, the My Lai massacre, the first heart transplant, the American moon landing, the introduction of CT scanners.

Hartley's engineering business prospered but success took its toll on him who often returned home speechless with exhaustion. He'd lost most of his hair, needed reading glasses and his forehead was furrowed, but he was still lean.

Hermie watched his diet- and hers- like a hawk. Time had treated her more kindly and as she moved into middle age she was still very attractive with a shapely, supple figure, good legs, a smooth, unlined skin and could have passed for at least ten years younger, a state engendered by weekly beauty treatments, exercise and regular body massage. She could honestly say that Hartley had denied her nothing. Holidays, thoughtful presents, bills paid promptly, a generous housekeeping allowance, a nice home - all these and more were as much an integral part of her married life as they were remote from her youth. The security he provided gave her the confidence to involve herself actively in charitable causes. She was elected on to the Board of the local Red Cross, proving herself a dab hand at fund raising. She launched a thriving cottage industry on the back of her charming knitwear and soft toys - her lady Golliwog being a hot perennial – that raised record sums for a slum colony. She paid for a nephew of Gopi, their long serving bearer, to train as an aircraft technician; defrayed the cost of the servants' medical bills and was the lifeblood of the Delhi Flower Show.

CHAPTER 14

From Bernadette, Hermie learned that Winston Powley, married to Thelma Lord, was Indian Ambassador to a Latin American country. His brother Marcel wielded immense influence in the corridors of power occupying the highest echelons of Indian government service, his long bachelorhood ending when he surprised everyone, not least himself, by marrying a Gannon twin, now a physiotherapist, many years his junior. The other twin, a gold medallist in dentistry, had moved to Toronto for postgraduate studies where he'd settled after his wedding to an AI of the diaspora.

After many comfortable   years of retirement in Bangalore, Aunty Al and Mr Caston had passed away within months of each other, although Reverend Mother, sharp as ever, still defied the grim reaper. Madam Olga was found grilled amid the ashes of the flat that had gone up in flames caused by a short circuit in the ancient hair dryer. The Misses Casey, Hermie's erstwhile colleagues at the Holy Martyrs had, tiring of slaving for the convent school for little reward, raised a loan and opened their own kindergarten in Delhi that was making money hand over fist, but not before Reverend Mother had extracted the last merciless ounce from them. As for Bettina-Lorna she'd long before wooed and won a tonsured Bhutanese nobleman, twenty years younger, and had whisked herself and her intriguing off to his Himalayan fastness.

As the hours ticked down to President Nixon's last day at the White House, Hermie stood with a bag of knitting by the open window of the sitting room observing with mounting curiosity a brand-new sports coupe, chrome gleaming, chassis polished to the nines, cruising up to the front verandah. Its driver flung open the door and jumped out, snappy in cream suit and blue tinted sunglasses.

'It's Barry.'

Hartley bounded from his chair and like two children they rushed out. Only yours truly would arrive thus precipitously.

'Do you own that?' Hermie asked bluntly.   Barry presented as a man who'd kept it together - not exactly youthful then again not exactly ageing, with a firm jaw line, nimble body, a sleek ponytail and perfect teeth.

'All mine and legal.' He gave the thumbs up, pecked Hermie on the cheek, taking in her crisp and fresh appearance, and slapping Hartley on the shoulder, shouted to Gopi to unload the crate of Scotch whisky. 'And honey, I'm home - for good.'

The two men resumed their friendship as if Barry had never left, Hartley insisting that he should be their houseguest for as long as he liked. It was an odd alliance, Hermie reflected, for on the face of it, there was nothing in common between the under-educated, cocky Barry and her own cultured husband. During Barry's absence, they'd heard virtually nothing of him, although gossip suggested that, despite his talent, he'd been compelled to take a number of low paid, if not exactly menial, jobs and the nearest he'd got to showbiz was as a bouncer in a Soho clip joint.

The situation was little better for many other AIs who'd migrated to Britain. Professionals found work but were placed on the lowest rung of salary scales; non-professionals had to take what was available, which was generally the jobs the British themselves would not do. Many AIs bitterly regretted the move overseas but having burned their boats could not return. In England, despite their English sounding names and Christian faith, they were viewed as immigrants and discriminated against. Few first generation migrants truly integrated there. On the other hand, those who'd gone farther afield – to Canada, Australia and the USA and those who'd chosen to throw in their lot with India - fared much better.

It was plain to Hartley that his friend wasn't short of the readies - indeed he appeared so flush that Hartley wasn't persuaded that it represented modest earnings carefully squirreled away.

'What's it with the dough, I hear you say.' Barry was not one to mince his words.

Hermie eyed him a little warily and took up her knitting.

Barry poured himself another Scotch and topped up Hartley's glass.

Hartley coughed. 'Well, er, yes, now that you ask.' He sensed Barry was on the brink of a disclosure. 'This mysterious accretion of funds.'

'Just a little game that yielded big dividends.' Barry flicked open a vintage art deco Ronson lighter and lit a Cuban cigar.

Hartley frowned and set down his glass. 'You've lost me, old boy.'

'It's like this...' As an attendant at a Chelsea petrol filling station used by a number of groovy young society chicks driving the latest models, Barry perfected a winning formula. 'Take wealthy, over-protective parents, versus me - a coloured Adonis , hashish-smoking nobody - then add besotted daughter wanting to live and love dangerously. I reckoned it was a crime not to share myself with womankind so I concocted a scam. I became engaged. The first father asked me what I'd take to leave Daddy's girl alone. My number one rule is never suggest a figure. He then asked if £X would be acceptable. Rule two is feign shock, horror and disgust at what's on offer. That loosened the purse strings considerably and I racked up another 75%.'

Hartley sucked thoughtfully on his pipe. Barry was the sort of person Edgar Allan Poe must have known when he wrote the essay *Diddling* that listed the key features of a typical swindler: perseverance, interest, audacity, ingenuity originality, impertinence, nonchalance and grin. 'Were there any you actually managed to avoid marrying?'

'No problem. The profits poured in on the back of one engagement after another. I had no scruples - why would I - until the night I dreamed I was ambushed by gun-toting hitmen who resembled the irate Dads. That brought me out in a cold sweat so I decided to pack it in before I ended up swinging from a meat hook. And here I am. And best of all they forked out for a suitcase of sharp clothes and a first class air ticket into the bargain. Yeah. It took me time to suss that England wasn't freedom.' He patted his back pocket. 'Freedom's in the wallet.'

'If there's anything in it, I'll have fifty per cent,' Hartley shot back.

'And here's what I'm going to do...'

The next day after Hartley had left for the office, Hermie showed Barry round the landscaped garden.

'Yawl has designed it to perfection.' Barry sensed her stiffen beside him but went blithely on. 'What news of your folks, then?'

Hermie hesitated then feeling the weight of his bright eyes, tilted her chin and muttered somewhat sulkily that Bernadette had wanted to keep her in the loop, but years ago she'd very firmly discouraged it. Barry clipped a flower and inserted it into his buttonhole pointing out that she was cutting herself off from a lot of fun with her niece, Delphine, and the younger generation.

Hermie covered her ears with her hands. 'Barry, PLEASE. I don't want to hear talk like that. I don't need them. I've got Hartley. He's all I want and need.'

***

A gambler by nature, Barry sank his ill-gotten gains into a small disco club in New Delhi that he brazenly named CHEE- CHEE. Within days of opening, its shabby-chic, sweet, hot fun proved extremely popular with the younger Indian

195

set. Even the twenty-one months Emergency between 1975 and 1977 imposed by the administration of Indira Gandhi that strangled Indian democracy, scarcely dampened the partying. Within months CHEE -CHEE was followed by YOURS TRULY and SOLAR TOPI and a chain was spawned that spread like an epidemic throughout the country. Driven by a single-minded hunger for wealth and success and blest with native cunning, Barry was well on the way to establishing a fiefdom of his own.

***

Edith's journal recorded that the Emergency witnessed a dark period of widespread police brutality, detention without trial, and crackdown on civil liberties. The free press was muzzled, oppressive laws were passed, homes bulldozed; people disappeared - presumed state sponsored murdered.

HH was horrified. 'Indira's insane,' he said to Edith over post-prandial brandies at the palace where she was a guest at a private dinner party to celebrate the Maharani Amrita's birthday. He'd waited until the other guests had retired for the night. 'She's a totalitarian despot who's doing untold harm to the country. But you know she has the backing of a bunch of sycophants - all those bullshitting industrialists.'

Amrita bejewelled in impeccable taste entered and exchanged a goodnight smile with Edith. Despite the age gap they'd become firm friends. 'Sunny on his hobbyhorse? Well, I'll you leave you two to ride together.'

HH threw her a loving glance. 'Dearest, I shan't be long. Oh, and that rascal son of ours has demanded more pocket money to buy some fripperies. Would you call the school in the morning and find out what that's all about?'

He turned gloomily to Edith. 'I 'm a staunch supporter of the Party but I never imagined it would descend to this.'

HH had more than justified his constituents' trust in him. After years as a playboy, he'd found politics hard going but with the devotion and support of Amrita and the birth of his son that seemed to put new meaning into his life, he'd worked tirelessly and gained a reputation for being a straight talking, compassionate, incorruptible man who always put the interests of his Walipur constituents first. Not quite in the same league as his illustrious father, he had, nevertheless, done his best to respond to local concerns. His marriage to Amrita had brought him great joy; Rahul, their only child, was much doted on and was a boarder at one of India's elite schools.

Rahul led a charmed life, Edith thought. He'd inherited the best of his parents looks, was wealthy, healthy and clever and didn't he know it.

HH sighed. 'My dear Edith, I'm confusion personified. What do you advise?'

Edith threw back her head and laughed. 'HH, you're incorrigible. But seriously, for once I don't know what to say. Maybe it's a question of wait and see. You've been a Congress wallah your entire political life. Besides, you didn't impose the Emergency.'

'I think I shouldn't show my face in the capital. I don't want to be complicit or dragged into our leader's nasty little schemes. And that crooked son of hers who unfortunately bears my name. I'm bound to say or do something that wouldn't be in the interests of Walipur. That woman and her gang of thugs wouldn't hesitate to make my people pay dearly for my folly. She can't touch me, but she'll get to me in other ways. Yes, I'll keep a low profile and make sure things tick along here.'

Edith said softly,' That's just what I hoped you'd decide.'

***

HH protested vociferously when a lorry load of his constituents, humble farm hands, on their way to work one morning, were herded off at gunpoint and forcibly vasectomised. For his pains, HH was arrested and thrown into a Delhi jail for two nights. After his release, his constituents, fearing for his safety, refused to allow him to venture out of Walipur.

The Emergency ended in March 1977 when Indira Gandhi called a general election when she could no longer resist mounting pressure by western governments to restore democracy. The Congress Party was trounced at the polls, swept from power by a coalition of opposition interests, and she lost her Parliamentary seat. HH was amongst only a handful of Congress Party MPs who retained theirs.

When writing to Martha about the tumultuous events, Edith finished tongue in cheek: *The new administration has banned the Coca Cola Company from India. It's reckoned it'll be many years before it's on sale again here.*

Martha's response was coloured by sad news. Greg, who some years earlier had proudly attended Louis's graduation from the University of Nebraska at Lincoln where he'd majored in history, had died after a brave fight against prostate cancer. Photos showed Louis as a rangy man with a cheerful expression and a sweet disposition, according to Martha. Having won a scholarship to Yale, he subsequently joined the Foreign Service and had been in an African diplomatic post when his father, to whom he was devoted, passed away. Louis' sister Lauren had undertaken fashion shoots even whilst chemistry major and, married to a college classmate, now modelled full-time.

***

For several more years and despite failing eyesight and the onset of osteoporosis, Martha's epistles to Edith never faltered. But when in the late 1980s as a monsoon wind got up and Shanthi handed her a bulky package postmarked Scottsbluff, addressed to her in unfamiliar handwriting, she just knew. Louis and Lauren reporting Martha's death included a memento, a pair of handsome antique ivory bookends the Addisons had acquired during their very first tour of duty in the sub-continent. *We know how much you meant to Mom and Dad. They looked forward to your penetrating and trenchant insights of life in India complete with those whimsical sketches and when we became older we, too, devoured your letters. They never stopped talking about you, and we kids sure got to know and like you.* Edith buried her head in her hands. With Parvati gone she'd no one with whom to share this loss. She crossed to the sideboard and mixed herself a stiff bloody Mary.

***

Rahul threw off adolescence and became a man. And in the very room where he'd drawn his first breath, Amrita, stony-faced, cut a forlorn figure in a white sari with the pallu pulled over her head. By her side, Edith, shadows under her eyes, grieved silently. HH was piloting his plane on a flight to Delhi with the long-suffering ADC on board when an engine failed on descent. There were no survivors. That afternoon, as HH's body was helicoptered back to Walipur to lie in state overnight, rows of ravens hunched motionless and silent on the palace boundary walls.

Edith paid her last visit to HH. Beyond the bier small lamps burned. His face – uncovered - looked so vital and at ease. Jasmine and marigolds lay strewn across his body. 'HH,' she whispered and burst into tears. 'My dearest, dearest friend, how I'll miss you.' All the fun they'd shared together crowded her thoughts. The parties they shared, his tomfoolery, his irrepressible good nature, lack of stuffiness, how she'd scolded him about this and that, his comforting words to her when Jean-Claude died. Laying her bouquet at the foot of the bier she bent to kiss his forehead. *'Goodbye until I bid you good morrow in some other place,'* she quoted softly.

The next day a 17 gun salute – HH had never succeeded in getting it upgraded - reverberated throughout Walipur as the gun carriage bearing his remains, covered in rice and garlands, was led by a solitary foot soldier carrying aloft the pinky-mauve Royal banner fluttering against a louring sky. Caparisoned camels and elephants lumbered in its wake escorted by full military guard and sombre-faced torchbearers. The cortege slowly wound its way down the six -mile route, deeply lined with mourners, to the Royal Cremation Ground. Behind it shuffled sobbing and praying constituents, many having journeyed non-stop through the night from far-flung villages on bullock-cart or bicycle to pay their last respects. Even more thronged rooftops, verandahs, windowsills and crumbling balconies - anywhere, everywhere - shinning up utility poles and trees - to gain a vantage point.

Eventually the procession reached its destination. Attired in white, the traditional Indian colour of mourning, and standing behind Rahul and Amrita, Edith watched with a heavy heart as HH's body was shifted gently onto its final resting place. Orange-robed priests chanting from sacred Sanskrit texts performed the last rites. Then, against the muted booming of distant cannon, Rahul stepped forward and set light to the pyre.

'Ma-Baap!' An anguished wail escaped the crowd. HH had been their protector, their guardian, their mother, their father.

Hermie dabbed her eyes when she heard of HH's death, but she found she wasn't, as once she could have been when memories were still bright, heartbroken. She stole a glance at Hartley sitting by the window immersed in *The Times of India.* He was her life, her reason for living. And just a few years earlier had seen the sweet fulfilment of another of Hermie's long cherished dreams. Fleeing, as usual, the cruel summer heat, that year they'd chosen Sivalik, a hill station 6,000feet up in the Himalayas. Almost from the start of their married life Hartley had resisted his wife's plea to acquire a holiday home. One property was quite enough, he maintained, and he wasn't going to tie himself down with another, or commit himself to the same hill station year after year.

But unexpectedly *Bonnie Brae*, a cottage hidden high up in a rhapsodic setting within a knot of birch and pine, came on the market, and whereas Hermie's wiles had previously fallen on deaf ears, this time her persistence paid off; Hartley, semi-retired, in a momentary lapse weakened, and she snapped it up. Long neglected, it was in need of a complete overhaul to satisfy Hermie's love of creature comforts, but she revelled in the challenge, and soon it was ready to receive them without the loss of its rustic charm.

Bonnie Brae, whatever the season, eased them after the pace of Delhi, and Hartley, like the first English settlers of Sivalik in the 1820s, fell under its spell. Here in the pure mountain air Hermie and Hartley unwound with tranquil rural pursuits - walking the scented hillsides, reading, bird-watching, picnicking at Hardy Falls, riding the sturdy hill ponies, and when Barry, now honoured with the Padma Vibhushan, the second highest civilian award in India, joined them for ten days every year, he and Hartley went trout fishing in the mountain-fed streams.

Yes, Hermie mused, *Barry has done all right for himself.* Unencumbered by marriage, children, lovers - straight or gay (Hermie had wondered), he lived in some panache in a rambling tree-screened farmhouse in Mehrauli, on the outskirts of Delhi, where he kept his finger on the pulse of his diverse and ever burgeoning high-worth business empire and unobtrusively undertook significant charitable works, surrounded by a retinue of servants culled from Bareilly, a poodle, a Rotweiler, a yellow beaked mynah bird with a colourful vocabulary and, ever the reptile fancier, two snakes, not to mention his unique antique collection of vintage smoking accessories.

***

They'd owned *Bonnie Brae* for about six summers when quite suddenly the day before they were due to descend to the plains, Hartley, while roaming the hillside photographing wildflowers for a book he was authoring, suffered a massive stroke. He did not survive the night. Hermie discovered afterwards that Hartley, not wanting to worry her, had forbidden his physician - unlike Hermie he lacked faith in homeopathy - from disclosing to his wife that he was on medication for high blood pressure. Hermie was devastated; for a long time she blamed herself for his death believing that she'd contributed to it by dragging him up to Sivalik.

Iqbal couldn't find it in himself to carry on the business without his old friend, and with Hermie's approval it was sold for a handsome profit. Hartley had arranged his affairs so that Hermie would lack for nothing. The Delhi house and *Bonnie Brae* were mortgage-free; there was a huge portfolio of valuable blue chip shares, a large life policy, even larger savings accounts, liquid assets and a generous widow's pension.

Iqbal's son Yusuf, a lawyer in private practice, lifted the burden of probate off Hermie's shoulders and swiftly concluded the administration of the estate outmanoeuvring the usual bureaucratic hurdles.

Hardly knowing what day it was, Hermie was inconsolable and moped for months, shouting at the servants for the least thing. As she told Edith, 'my bed's like a grave. I've never felt so alone.' *Could I have loved him more?* she asked herself.

As Edith, Barry and Bernadette helped her through the slough of her loss Hermie's mood gradually improved; she took renewed pleasure in everyday activities and the following summer Bernadette yielded to her invitation to visit *Bonnie Brae.* Gerald, now a retired Supreme Court Judge but much tied up chairing this Committee or that Public Enquiry, made his excuses because he hated the hills.

Unlike her friend, Bernadette didn't mind getting dirt under her fingernails and had brought some cuttings from her home, hoping they'd take in the cottage garden. Wincing a little as an arthritic joint played up, Hermie sank back in a cane chair watching as her friend, a motherly little pumpkin in a shapeless brown smock, iron-grey hair escaping from an untidy bun, kneeled on the warm, springy grass happily tackling weeds.

The air was full of the scent of geraniums and there was a bracing breeze but the sunlight was bright, so Hermie donned designer sunglasses. *It's nice to have company,* she thought. *I'm so lonely - miss Hartley so much. I know I wasn't really in love with him when I married him but now I realise just how much he meant to me.*

'You've missed a bit...look, right there, under your nose.'

Bernadette grunted and beavered away and for some minutes the only sound was the faint braying of a donkey against the whirring of cicadas.

'Am I going to hear how Pa, Ashley and Iris fared? And Delphine - she'd be a mature woman now. Vincent must have kept you posted.' Hermie hitched her pearl buttoned, meringue coloured Cashmere jacket closer to her.

For some time now Vincent had been Archbishop of the Diocese that included Ajeemkot and was tipped to be the next Cardinal.

Bernadette jerked round, her jaw dropping.

'Yes, go on tell me. You've always wanted to.'

'You always wanted me not to,' Bernadette said roundly, getting slowly to her feet.

'Well, you have my permission now.'

Bernadette bent her head. 'Yes, memsahib,' she mocked gently. 'Where do you want me to start?'

'Just get on with it. The way you're acting you'd think you weren't burning to.'

Emptying the watering can over giant spikes of maroon and white hollyhocks, Bernadette sat down heavily in the chair facing Hermie and wiped stained hands on her smock. Then drawing on all her remembrances of fact, rumour, gossip and hearsay, began:

Wilburt, who never stopped grieving for Noreen, lived in retirement with Ashley, Iris and Delphine in Loco Quarters. An only child, Delphine was spoiled by her family, her honey-gold skin set off by almond eyes and glossy black hair. After she'd left school with her Senior Cambridge Certificate, like her mother Iris, she took a nurse's training at the hospital and struck up a friendship with Leslie, a good looking, young AI in the police force, of whom her parents approved. They'd met through the family connection with Bishop Forrester's Home. Abandoned as a baby, Leslie was found, wrapped in a cotton sari inside a tea picker's basket, on the steps of the Home in Darjeeling. It was suspected he was an illegitimate son of a failed AI tea planter who, in the loneliness of his empty hillside bungalow, had his wicked way with a local tea picker, only to pay her off when she inevitably became pregnant. When, during World War II, the army requisitioned the Home, Leslie and other inmates were transferred to its counterpart in Ajeemkot.

Life wasn't easy for Delphine. In the 1960s catastrophic monsoon floods caused the Ajeemkot sewage system to pollute the water supply and in the cholera epidemic that swept over hundreds died, including Ashley and Iris. Distraught, Delphine sought comfort in Leslie and they became engaged, marrying one hot summer's day at St. George's. Police accommodation came with Leslie's job but they swapped that in order to remain in 22 Loco Quarters, which Wilburt would've had to vacate after Ashley's death, believing that uprooting Wilburt would only worsen his dementia. He was often found wandering the streets of Ajeemkot clad only in a pyjama top, confused Delphine with Noreen and demanded his conjugal rights, and was once nearly run over by a car.

*Like her aunt Hermie before her, Delphine longed to go **home**. Leslie didn't need much persuading to emigrate, and after Wilburt's death and many years of*

*scrimping and scraping to save for the fare, Delphine and Leslie boarded a flight
to Heathrow.*

*Delphine and Leslie were overwhelmed by life in England. Those AI families
who'd settled there after Independence were scattered and there was no back up
of a solid AI community life. Leslie, who'd much enjoyed the police service in
India, was unable to get a job as a policeman in London and had to take a lowly
post first as a bus conductor and then as a ticket clerk with London
Underground. They missed the sunshine and colour of Ajeemkot, the socialising
at the Inster and the cosy bungalow in Loco Quarters so close to all their friends.
Accustomed to having a chokra, however inefficient, Delphine was un-used to the
sheer grind of juggling a nursing job with shopping, cleaning, cooking and child-
care. It was all new to her and hard work; she became querulous and took to the
bottle.*

*Everything was a tremendous disappointment to them; they realised they'd
made a mistake in coming to England, where they were just another unwelcome
pair of "bleeding immigrants" and where they felt misfits. For Delphine home
was not Utopia – in fact it was a place where, with her skin tone and dark
brown eyes - she once had stones thrown at her - she was just another Indian
economic migrant to whom the notices 'no dogs and coloured's seemed to apply.
Had either suggested a return to India, the other would have leaped at it.*

*Then one day Leslie dropped a bombshell.   That he was leaving Delphine. That
he was fed up with married life and was clearing out. That life together had been
a sham for the last few years.   Delphine burst into tears. Leslie said his bag was
packed, his passage to Canada booked. He felt he had a better future there
where he wouldn't be discriminated against. He paused, shaking off Delphine's
vice-like grip. 'You've only your perpetual **ruddee** drinking to blame for this,' he
added heartlessly. Rubbing in her faults was something he rarely shrank from,
unwilling to admit that for Delphine, and no less for him, England had been a
complete culture shock, quite the reverse of the rosy picture of **home** that had
been painted in India. This was to be a well-worn scenario over the next few
months. One evening Leslie said he was going out to buy a packet of cigarettes
and was never seen again.*

'I want to find my Delphine.' Hermie, who'd listened without a trace of
emotion, said abruptly when Bernadette had finished. She got up and wandering
over to the helichrysum examined the large pastel heads shimmering in the sun
that would be the mainstay of her dried flower arrangements.

Bernadette's bespectacled eyes were alert. 'You can't be serious. You haven't shown the slightest interest or inclination up to now.' *What the hell's she up to?*

Hermie sighed. 'What's past is past and life's not the same without Hartley. We shared so many lovely moments and memories.' Befriending long lost family (long lost being Hermie's gloss for rejected) won't matter now, she thought. *My position is secure and can't be undermined. I'm self made, retooled.*

'Well, I can understand that. The thought of losing Gerald makes me go cold. But...' Bernadette's thoughts were spinning. *Memsahibs didn't have the same status any more. Hermie was a memsahib in a country where memsahibs no longer mattered.*

'There's no harm in looking, surely?' What she'd do if she actually found them, Hermie hadn't the foggiest. 'I want you to do some digging for me.'

There was a long, uncomfortable silence. 'Oh...well, all right then,' Bernadette said reluctantly, 'I'll do what I can.' Hermie was not, she realised, prepared to put herself out. *And it doesn't seem to occur to her that she could be messing up someone else's life.*

They did not speak of it again for the rest of the holiday.

After a discussion with Gerald, who was less charitable about Hermie than Bernadette would ever have imagined of her fair-minded husband, they enlisted Vincent's help. Weeks later, as twilight deepened into darkness and the smell of night scented stock drifted in through an open window, the phone rang at Bonnie Brae.

'What we've gleaned is that after Delphine and Leslie split up, their daughter (we're not sure of her name or whether they had more than one child) remained with Delphine. Then it seems Delphine went completely to pieces and no one's seen or heard of her or Leslie, for that matter, in years.'

For a moment Hermie was at a loss to say anything, not knowing if she felt relieved or disappointed. She shrugged. 'I suppose that's that and now don't you go saying I didn't try.' Her mind was already elsewhere.

It was a pretty half-hearted effort, Bernadette thought, suppressing a spurt of anger. *You could've hired a private investigator or written to the last known address.* But what was the point of saying so? As far as Hermie was concerned her conscience was clear.

This page is intentionally left blank

205

For Kay Forrester the worst thing was that she was left to cope with Delphine on her own. The night Leslie walked out, Kay, then nudging fourteen, found a scrap of paper nestling in a pocket of her pyjamas:

TO DADDY'S GIRL
When land and sea divide us
And you're no more in view,
Remember it was I
Who wrote these few lines to you.

Delphine hit the streets like a soul condemned clutching photos of Leslie and, seeking clues to his whereabouts, thrust them under the noses of passers-by and plastered them to lamp posts.

Drowning her sorrows in a cocktail of gin and meths, Delphine was put on suicide watch. Neither she nor Kay heard from Leslie again, until the day when an envelope addressed to Kay in Leslie's scrawl and postmarked Winnipeg dropped on the doormat. Inside was an eighteenth birthday card and the scrawled verse:

Memories drift to scenes long past,
Time goes on but memories last.
Sunshine passes, shadows fall,
But sweet remembrance outlasts all.
Love always, Dad

They were sustained by state welfare benefits as Delphine was incapable of holding down a job. Kay went on to excel academically, winning a scholarship to a girls private school and graduated from University with a good honours degree in Catering and Hospitality Management. A junior post in a high-end London hotel led to two years in Paris at an equally prestigious one where she learned to flirt and dance in high heels and thrilled and spilled in love. More happy years followed, spent organising the household of a wealthy diamond broker in Antwerp where she was treated like one of the family. They were heartbroken when four summers later she returned to London, a move prompted by Delphine's continuing slide. Friends warned against it, but she argued *how can I just wash my hands of Mum? She's my flesh and blood.* Her alma mater, recognising her talents, assigned her to a clutch of young grunts with celebrity chef aspirations.

Delphine rallied, but not for long, becoming a terminal no-hoper. Always on tenterhooks not knowing what mood Delphine might be in when she came home from work- or even if she would be there at all - Kay endured another few exhausting years of Delphine, a debt-ridden habitual shoplifter with a string of prosecutions who screamed at her for the slightest thing. One morning, by then a chronic alcoholic - it was a wonder Delphine hadn't become one sooner – she tripped down the stairs that led from their small flat to the street, fatally fracturing her skull. Grief, tinged in no small measure with relief, came to Kay with the realisation that she, an only child, was on her own.

***

*This is **not** a good start.* Puzzled there was no one to meet her at New Delhi's International Airport, Kay at 5'5", a good few inches taller than petite Delphine, and wearing blue jeans, cotton tee shirt and trainers, elbowed her way out of the terminal building, enveloped by the warm late September air, through a crowd of smiling brown faces, to the taxi rank. Importunate taxi wallahs converged on her and a portly man seized her suitcase and hustled her to a somewhat senile black and yellow cab.

'Where to madam?'

Kay gave him the only address she knew. If she'd been less anxious she'd have seen the funny side of it. She'd landed in India, driven by a primitive instinct to search for roots, and already was sabotaged. Hemmed in by cars, scooters, lumbering oxen and battalions of bell ringing cyclists, the driver nudged his way, horn permanently hooting, a faded garland dangling from the interior mirror, through the press of traffic. Kay wound down the window, donning sunspecs as brilliant sunshine danced across the passing scene. There was a profusion and colour of life not seen in the West - sadhus with black, matted hair and saffron robes, maxi-skirted, smooth-skinned village women labouring on grimy building sites, gaudy posters plugging the latest action-packed Bollywood movie. The air was full of floating dust and the heady scent of incense and marigolds. Kay took a deep breath determined to savour every glorious moment of it to the utmost, yet... she fought down a sense that something had gone dreadfully wrong.

The strong tea suddenly tasted of ashes. The cup and saucer clattered as Kay set it down sharply on a brass, mother-of-pearl ebony inlaid table. 'You're saying

207

the position you offered me as Senior Lecturer in Modern British and European Cuisine has been withdrawn owing to lack of funding?' Her voice rose as she stared disbelieving at Mrs Bhatia, Principal of the Catering and Hospitality Industry Academy. 'And flown me all of 6,712 km to tell me that?'

Now Kay realised why there'd been no welcoming garlands, no one to meet her flight. She wasn't expected. Her heart dropped to her knees.

Mrs Bhatia gave an unhappy shrug of her plump, sari-clad shoulders, a contrite expression in her large, kohl-rimmed, black eyes. 'Ms Forrester. I'm so sorry, so very sorry. What can I say?' Her gold bangles jangled as she moved towards a tall, authoritative man on the far side of the room who she introduced as Rahul Ratan Singh, Chairman of the Academy's Board of Governors.

 Kay saw a lean and offensively fit person with skin the colour of teak and sable black hair, apparently urgently summoned from other business by an agitated Mrs Bhatia and, from his compressed lips, clearly resentful of the awkward situation.

All pumped up, Kay vented her frustration on him. 'I'm asking you to explain. You made no effort to contact me. Why not? I would then, at least, have known not to waste precious funds on an airline ticket the cost of which you agreed to defray.' Beside this immaculate looking man in polished handmade black shoes and elegant, sharply creased dark trousers and bund jacket, Kay felt dishevelled after the long flight. What impression he was getting of her she didn't care.

'Any misunderstanding is entirely of your own making.' Rahul Ratan Singh's perfect command of English was spoken with an east coast American accent. 'Mrs Bhatia despatched a letter to you six weeks ago rescinding the appointment and backed it up with an email. I can't accept you didn't know.' He gazed at her genuinely perplexed, his black hooded eyes seeming to register her travel-creased trousers and crumpled tee shirt, and coming to rest on her face. Her photograph had not lied; she was pleasing to the eye with that wavy chestnut dark hair, large Kashmir grey eyes and roses and milk complexion. And had a cute ass.

Had she known how incensed he was, but not with her, Kay might have been more favourably disposed towards him. She was later to learn that the Education Minister had gone over Rahul's head and appointed his own Manchester - returned nephew to the post. It was not lack of funds but downright nepotism that had cost Kay the job. Rahul didn't blame Mrs Bhatia, who was powerless to intervene, but he was determined not to let the matter drop. He'd table a question in the Lok Sabha and force the Minister to explain his chicanery; he'd name and shame.

'I hope that's not meant as a criticism.' Kay leaned forward, resting her elbows on her knees. He'd put her on the defensive. It was autumn in London but here, in Mrs Bhatia's office, she was perspiring in spite of the efficiently whirring ceiling fans. 'I received damn all from you. You're responsible and I mean to get to the bottom of this.' She gave the chair arm several hard thumps. *What am I to do? These two beauties appear to have washed their hands of things.*

There was a short silence then Rahul stepped forward slightly, his hands thrust in his pockets, his aristocratic, seamed face holding hers. His voice was deep and incisive, his manner cool and firm.   'Could there be any reason why you didn't get our communication that you and only you know, Ms Forrester?'

'I sublet my flat and went on holiday to Italy before flying here from Rome,' Kay said stiffly. 'And I asked my tenant and Royal Mail to forward my post to a friend.' She refused to accept that she could be involved in the shambles, her gaze wandering from the man to the carved stone elephant on the centre table and the jute mats dotted about the floor.

'So!' Rahul said with soft triumph. 'Now that little muddle's hardly our fault - and I suppose you also scratched your ISP subscription because our email bounced back.'

'Anyway, even if your wretched message had reached me there wouldn't have been adequate time to reverse my arrangements. Just what am I to think? I'm going to sue you for botching it. It's crunch time.' She closed her eyes briefly, her mind racing, sifting the options, debating if she ought to consult a lawyer and wondering if it would be throwing good money after bad, then opened them to see Rahul observing her intently.

'This is India - you don't stand a string of chances of winning a lawsuit.' His tone was dry. 'Mrs Bhatia, a word if I may...' They went into a huddle, Mrs Bhatia's contribution being limited to several rapid nods of her head and a nervous glance over her shoulder in Kay's direction.

'Good.' Rahul crossed back to Kay. 'You've come a helluva distance and you probably won't want to see the inside of another plane for a while so,' his voice softened a little,' what I suggest is that you chill out, enjoy Delhi and I'll re-book your return flight for say, ten days hence. And as a five star hotel is expensive and a budget hotel's likely to be somewhat of a culture shock –'

Kay jumped up, her eyes still only just level with his unsmiling mouth. 'Do go on, I'm fascinated to hear your plans for me. Only this time I hope they're fool proof.'

He was impervious to the gibe. ' – I'll arrange for you to stay temporarily at our expense at a women's guesthouse. You'll find it extremely comfortable.'

'And it's being very safe. Oh yes, I'm personally inspecting,' Mrs Bhatia chipped in and, in spite of herself, Kay was amused at her obvious relief that at least she didn't have to extend the hospitality of her home to Kay.

Kay's eyes met Rahul's realising he'd no intention of letting her drift indefinitely round India. She mentally reviewed the situation. Once she got in touch with the British High Commission she could more easily be able to assess what chances she had of getting compensation from the Academy. Then she'd take a day at a time, see if she couldn't find a job that would enable her to extend her stay if there was really no hope of forcing the Academy to employ her.

The prospect of a reprieve buoyed her up considerably. 'Well, all right,' she heard herself agreeing somewhat meekly, 'I've obviously got to lay my head somewhere in the meantime.' The upset and anger had left her quite drained and she wasn't sorry to have the uncertainty removed for the next few days.

Mrs Bhatia rang a small hand bell. A uniformed servant materialised and scurried away with Kay's suitcase. Rahul gestured to Kay to follow him and nodded briefly at Mrs Bhatia who clasped Kay's hand apologetically. 'It's not our fault,' she said lamely, giving Rahul a timid glance as he waited, impassive. She's a frightened rabbit Kay thought, sympathy welling up for her. She couldn't have been more mistaken, for she was yet to learn that Indian women were manipulative of their men folk, while being outwardly submissive.

Outside the building a chauffeur - a towering, white-uniformed Sikh, sporting a pinky-mauve turban, lolling by a silver Mercedes - sprang to attention, saluted and held open the passenger door.

Kay was conscious of her own rumpled and travel-worn state against the pristine leather upholstery. She glanced at Rahul seated beside her, suddenly overwhelmed by his compelling personality. There was something about his sensual and uncompromising mouth, his bearing and features that were so like those of the Rajput princes in the Indian miniatures collection of the Victoria & Albert Museum. Then he turned his head and looked away across to where an emerald green lawn was being mowed by a bullock pulling a grass-cutter.

While seeming not to, Kay concentrated on his profile; the firm jaw line with a beaky nose below curving black brows; the wide forehead, only now it was creased in a frown. She knew what had brought that about but **who** exactly was he? All that deference she'd just witnessed - that was for no ordinary man. She pondered on this for a few moments feeling herself relax as the air-conditioned interior and tinted windows brought welcome relief from the sun's glare and glancing out idly watched a ragged band of demonstrators picketing the radio station.

And soon the chauffeur was drawing up outside a pleasing, freshly whitewashed two-storied building with a satellite dish roosting on the roof.

'Would you take a seat on the verandah Ms Forrester whilst I sort this out?' Rahul said crisply as he headed into the guesthouse. Before Kay could summon up the riposte that she wanted to check for herself exactly what he was proposing to sort out, he'd vanished. Her anger had dissolved and feeling very near to tears she flung herself down in a deep bottomed, feather- cushioned white cane chair and gazed around, slowly unwinding in the beguiling tranquillity of shady ashupal trees and the masses of red clay pots containing vivid flowering plants.

A quarter of an hour later Kay heard Rahul's footsteps rounding the corner of the building. He was holding a key swinging from the end of a circular marker. 'You'll have to share a twin bedded room for the time being, I'm afraid, but if a single becomes vacant, you'll be given priority for a transfer. I've arranged for your luggage to be taken to your room.' He glanced at his watch. 'I have to leave you to your own devices as I've an appointment with some constituents at Parliament House, but if you need anything, you'll find the reception desk very helpful.' Without altering the even tone of his voice, Rahul got in a slight dig at her. 'Not that I see you taking any advice that's offered.' Then he was gone, lifting his hand in an oddly final gesture and striding without haste to his car. Out of my life she thought, biting her lip and feeling suddenly oddly panicky at being abandoned to fend for herself.

Kay mentally squared her shoulders. Here goes. She glanced at the room number on the key that indicated that it was on the ground floor and headed along wide, ochre walled, terracotta tiled corridor to a door at the end.   She pushed open the door and dropped her handbag on a chair. Not knowing just what to expect her spirits lifted; the room was simply appointed but spotless, enormous and airy, the terrazzo floor scrubbed to an inch of its life and covered with cheerful cotton dhurries. The handloom orange and red checked curtains matched the bedspreads on two plump single beds, and the whiteness of the lime

washed walls was relieved by bright colour prints of the coral strands of Kovalam
and the lions of the Gir Forest.

Unlocking her case, Kay glanced round; there was a sturdy almirah decorated
with a traditional vine motif along one wall where she'd hang her clothes. But
she felt herself weakening and decided the unpacking could wait. Texting her
friend Yvonne in London letting her know she'd arrived, she stretched out on the
bed, her thoughts scrolling back to the events that had conspired to bring her to
India.

It was a dismal afternoon those nine months ago the day after Delphine's funeral.
The wind, filled with the stomach-turning smell of diesel from the adjacent bus
garage, rattled the ill-fitting windows of the shabby little flat. Kay sank to her
knees on the threadbare sitting room carpet and fished in the pockets of her jeans
for the rusty key she'd found in Mum's handbag. She fitted it into a battered
leather trunk and lifted the lid. There was mustiness, a suggestion of damp, and
the sickly odour of a crushed beetle. Kay shuddered slightly and pinched her
nose. This search through the relics of someone else's life was strangely
unsettling; she felt it was like prying, as though she were opening a letter
addressed to someone else. Something she couldn't identify frayed
uncomfortably at the corners of her mind. With quickened heartbeats she slowly
took out and laid to one side a yellowing, crocheted christening shawl, several
china ornaments - badly chipped - a few silver-plated trophies wrapped in
discoloured tissue paper, a moth-eaten fan of peacock feathers. A pair of worn,
scarlet velvet, Turkish type slippers with turn up toes lay on top of an inlaid
rosewood box containing, she recognised, mahjong pieces. Kay paused and ran
her fingers through her hair. She'd never known Mum to play - never knew she
was interested.   Lifting out a dog-eared copy of Palgrave's Golden Treasury
inscribed *To dear Delphine from Leslie*, Kay had a sudden vivid picture of them
in happier days. Dad, where are you now?

And here were two very tarnished, brass candlesticks, a little dented, but with
a spot of Brasso they'd gleam like old gold and look quite presentable on the
sideboard.

Dusk was closing in and from the road came the clatter and grind of the
municipal refuse collection vehicle. Kay got up and made herself a cup of coffee
then resumed her exploration of the trunk. A moth eaten, blue felt elephant
emerged that must have been Mum's childhood comfort toy, some baffling bric-

a-brac that had taken Mum's fancy and a few old receipts. Kay reached for a tissue and wiped her grimy hands. Nearly done she thought with a feeling of satisfaction - and no skeletons - and laughed at her earlier prick of premonition.

What's this...? Something crackled at the bottom of a small, rust-coloured earthenware jar. Kay shook out the contents, several folded sheets of coarse, unbleached paper and some faded black and white snapshots. She gasped. She'd never ever seen these. Here was Mum and Dad on their wedding day, smiling broadly. Dad handsome in a lounge suit and bow tie, sporting a pink carnation in his buttonhole and Mum in a cloud-like confection of silk and lace holding a pretty bouquet.

And these other photos, of nobody that she knew. She turned them over. Ajeemkot. The name sprang at her like a stone from a catapult. On the reverse, stamped in smudged violet ink was Kumar Foto Studio, 5B Kingsway, Ajeemkot. Kay could hear the wild thumping of her heart. It struck her that Mum hadn't meant her to see this. But why? She dropped into an armchair and pored over the snapshots. What held her eye was a clean featured man in his mid twenties with a mass of thick, dark hair flanked by two slender young women standing beside a middle aged couple, narrowing their eyes against bright sunshine, on the steps of a white-washed building called Railway Institute. On the back in faded blue ink were the initials – W, N, A, I and H.

Who are they? And another photo of the young couple in the earlier picture holding a baby wrapped in a christening shawl identical to the one in the trunk. On the reverse were the words 'and D makes three.' It must be Mum and her parents. There was a marked family resemblance even though some looked swarthier than others. Kay's mouth felt dry. It didn't make sense. Perhaps these other bits of paper might. Turning away from her contemplation of the photos, she smoothed the sheets out on her lap.

True Extract From Register of Births in the Municipal Limits of Ajeemkot.

Father's name and occupation: Ashley Blake, Engine Driver.

Address: Number 22 Loco Quarters, Ajeemkot.

Mother's Name: Iris (née Quinn).

Child's name: Delphine Delicia Blake

Sex: Female

Caste: Anglo-Indian

And the date and time of Delphine's birth.

Kay felt very tense. And very bewildered. Not daring to imagine what else might transpire, Kay unfolded the other sheet, registering with some considerable shock that it was Delphine and Leslie's marriage certificate and that they'd wed at St. George's Anglican Church, Ajeemkot.

Kay's thoughts slid to a certain day when she was seven years old and she heard Mum's whining voice: 'Your Dad was having gallstones removed at Guy's Hospital, that's the other side of London, where I worked as a nurse. That's how we met. It was love at first sight so as soon as we could we got married in the hospital chapel and made our home here in this flat where you were born.'

'This flat' was in Ealing, west London, near a commuter underground station and comprised two cramped bedrooms and a sitting room that led off what was only a kitchenette. With its avaricious landlord, leaking roof, curling wallpaper, scruffy furnishings and dodgy guttering, they'd been unable to afford to move elsewhere.

Why had Mum and Dad packaged the past? Why had they lied? What secret did they want to hide? Kay felt poleaxed and utterly let down especially by Mum who'd become so dependent on her.

Then the doorbell was ringing, and Kay went into the narrow hall. 'Hello, Yvonne.' She hugged her friend. 'God, am I glad to see you.'

Yvonne's eyes widened and she knew at once that something was wrong, just by the way Kay sounded.   'Suppose you tell me what's happened?'

'Take a look at this, and tell me what you make of it.' Kay moved to the kitchenette uncorked a bottle of Australian Shiraz and emerged with two wineglasses.

Yvonne sank into the sagging sofa, and for several minutes there was no sound but the patter of rain against the windowpanes. 'Well, well.' Yvonne raised her dark head from the photos and paperwork and her round black eyes met Kay's. 'They're a good-looking lot. I always assumed from their singsong lilt that Leslie and Delphine were from the Rhondda Valley. And her looks - that ink-black hair and those dark eyes seemed Welsh enough.'

'That's what Mum said. Well, near enough. Actually, she maintained she was Maltese but raised in Wales.' Kay's voice rose and her face had gone pale. 'And Dad claimed he was a Welsh orphan and had never known family. I tried to coax more out of him but he'd just clam up.'

Yvonne studied her friend's face. Kay was so obviously hurt and angry that she, who'd done so much for Delphine since Leslie's disappearance, had had a secret kept from her.   'But it's illogical to lie about being Welsh, and even worse, no rhyme or reason to conceal what's plainly an Indian background.' Yvonne's tone was disapproving. In her vast, tentacled Jamaican-born family, with relatives going back to the nth remove, reticence had no hiding place.

' I wonder if...perhaps... I have any relatives – any connections - out in India, I mean.' Kay's voice was a little unsteady.

'Would that be a reason for celebration or commiseration?' Yvonne had despised Delphine – a once pretty woman whose looks had been marred by bitterness, discontent and alcohol, a woman with no inner strength whose constant moralising and uncertain temper had frozen out her few friends and destroyed Kay's chances of happiness with the gentle son of the Belgian diamond broker. Kay had been a saint with her boozy, petulant Mum, who'd mooned unkempt around the flat in a grubby housecoat until well into the afternoon, emerging only to blow her welfare benefit on drink and bingo and incurring ever mounting credit card debts.

Kay folded her slender hands behind her head. 'I've always thought a sibling would be nice. Cousins, uncles, aunts will do nicely.'

Yvonne gave her slow smile. She knew Kay only too well to believe she would just let the matter rest.

Kay pushed back her shoulder-length hair from her forehead and reached up to the bookshelf for the atlas. ' Call it sixth sense but I've always had this odd feeling that something, somewhere was not quite what it seemed - was kind of missing. I've got to fill in the gaps. Got it.' She pointed excitedly. 'Look. There it is...   That dot's Ajeemkot and the large black circle not so far away – probably a major town - is called Walipur. So now we have the co-ordinates.'

Yvonne glanced at the topography and back to Kay's flushed face. She wasn't classically beautiful - her slightly retroussé nose and a chin with the hint of a cleft too determined for that - but her charm lay in her wide, curving mouth, the soft darkness of her hair and deeply lashed eyes.

'It looks rather arid and it'll be helluva of a task.' Yvonne sounded a note of caution. 'And you'll need time, a helluva lot of savings that you don't have.' She suspected that Delphine had died penniless.

Kay turned down a corner of the page and glanced out of the window to the gaunt leafless trees and louring sky. 'I just know what I'm meant to do. It's as if I'm walking down a corridor and someone I don't know is standing at the end of it and is beckoning to me. I have to find out who it is, what that person wants. I can't stand still. I can't ignore it. You've a large, warm family and I want to be able to think that at least I tried to find mine.' She smiled wryly. 'Sorry, that must sound insane.'

'No. But are you sure you're up for it? India's enormous and just where would you start?'

' Where Mum did. Ajeemkot.'

Yvonne gave an infectious laugh. 'And you'll be texting me to say you've found a clutch of relations who've taken you to their bosom…'

'Do you think they would?' Kay put in anxiously.

Yvonne gave her a reassuring hug. 'How could they not?'

And although a family history website where Kay posted a message hoping for clues to relatives drew a blank, Lady Luck was on her side. Not long afterwards she spotted the advertisement for the Delhi post, was short-listed and was counting the days to her departure.

Kay drowsily glanced at her watch, which still showed Rome time. She must have fallen asleep and stayed in that happy state for several hours for it had gone dark. The clack of sandals stopped at the door and Kay propped herself up against the bed head. There was a token knock; the door was flung open and a woman with a head of glossy black curls bounced in. If ever Kay had felt in need of a friend it was now. The newcomer was, she supposed, her own age, with smooth bronze-gold skin, and dancing dark eyes. She wore jeans and a loose over-shirt and grinned, showing pearly teeth.

'Hello there!' Her tone was friendly, its lilt a strong echo of Mum's, Kay realised with a start. 'I'm Renee Merriton. The management said I had a new roommate. And what brings you here?' Obviously bursting to know all, she sank into a cane chair and was slipping off her chappals.

Kay immediately warmed to her, not least because Renee didn't appear at all put out at having to share her room with a complete stranger. 'The saga so far...' Kay began, paring it down to the essentials - the death of her mother earlier that year which brought sympathetic clucks from Renee, and how, feeling she was amply qualified, she'd answered an advertisement for a two-year contract at the Academy. Kay's natural impulse to go into specifics, Mum's sad mementoes, the real reason visiting India wavered, and she held that back. 'So here I am, blooded but unbowed.'

'Did you say Singh? Rahul Ratan Singh?' Renee's eyes widened.

'Arrogant so and so but,' Kay added grudgingly, 'hot.'

'Very. And very important.' Renee lifted well- shaped eyebrows. 'You mean you don't know?' She steepled her fingers and by the pressure of them, Kay guessed she had a surprise in store. 'One of the mags featured a riveting canter through his life.'

'And what emerged was a moneyed womaniser?'

Renee giggled. 'I like your take on life. He was voted India's sexiest bachelor. And not such a geek. He's Member of Parliament for Walipur. Why, what's wrong?' Renee's brows knitted.

Walipur. Ajeemkot. Kay felt a sudden jolt. 'No... It's nothing.'

'With a string of business interests and a finger in every pulao and, that's not all.' Renee took a deep, dramatic breath. 'He's got a very grand bloodline. He's the Maharajah of Walipur.' She must have detected, Kay thought, the slight change in her expression that was brought about by her very determination not to react. 'Aha, I knew that would make you sit up. Princely titles are irrelevant nowadays as the government abolished those and privy purses decades ago and in theory he's plain Rahul Ratan Singh, but that does not undo his lineage.'

'So that explains all the deference. I must admit I did wonder.'

Renee wriggled her toes. 'He's rather a cold fish.'

Smiling, Kay sensed that Renee revelled in a weekly fix that chronicled celebrity lives.

'And girls have downloaded a wallpaper of him to their mobile.'

'Naked and unashamed?' Kay asked impishly.

Renee grinned. 'If only! But where was I? Oh yes, he was educated at one of our leading schools - one only the elite and nouveaus can afford - and then at Harvard.'

'The best of all finishing schools. So that explains the accent.' Kay heard again those transatlantic tones and tried to work out what it was about him that made her feel uneasy.

Renee waggled a finger at her. 'Don't try and make it uncomfortable for him.'

Kay gave a disparaging sniff and pushed back a strand of hair thinking it would test Rahul's ego to find she was capable of squaring off with him. The thought was oddly comforting. 'As far as I'm concerned he has a great deal to answer for and I'm not inclined to let the matter drop.'

Renee hesitated just a moment too long. 'You can't be serious. Few people pick a fight with Rahul and come up on top.   Let sleeping cheetahs lie.'

Kay waited for her to enlarge on this but she didn't and Kay felt silent for a minute trying to make some sense of the warning. 'I'm a novice in the ways of the East, but I'll take your word for it.' She steered the conversation in a different direction. 'But enough about me. I come out here only to find I'm sharing with a girl who has an English name. I'm intrigued.'

'The eternal mystery of India. I'm that ethnic cocktail - an Anglo-Indian.' She didn't seem to register the sudden jolt of Kay's hands. 'India born and bred like all my family for generations back. When I'm not doing gigs I live with Mum and Dad in Jalandhar –it's a five-hour train journey from Delhi. We've never set foot in England – no, I tell a lie- we took a fortnight's package holiday there some years ago, but that's about the size of it. In bygone days my parents say the British and Indians looked down on AIs and inter-marriage was pretty much taboo. Many of us migrated after Independence. At the last count, it's reckoned we're down to about 200,000 strong here. Some of us do well, others less so. Frankly, I'm all for a dual heritage as it's the best brew.' Renee glanced at her watch and crossed the room to the almirah, lifting out black leggings and a swallow tailed evening shirt, the colour of her eyes, frothing with beads and sequins.

'That's a rather smart variation on the salwar kameez theme.' Kay reached forward and touched the silky material wishing that her life, her odyssey, could be explained as simply as Renee's. 'You do dress up, don't you?'

Renee laughed as she made for the bathroom. 'For work, always! I'm a singer/ songwriter and am premiering some new pieces tonight at The Nawab, one of Delhi's luxury five star hotels so a certain glitz is expected. You're welcome to come along and catch some of the after-dark action.'

'Just the antidote I need.' Kay raised her voice to make herself audible over the gush of the shower. 'I wasn't exactly relishing the evening on my own and you could almost say I'd got my second wind, so I'm ready to be persuaded.' The sagging feeling she'd had when Rahul had taken himself off had been banished by Renee's warmth.

There was a small fridge in one corner and Kay decided to investigate. It was alarmingly well stocked with an array of soft drinks and she opened a can of fizzy orange.

'And you'll meet Tony, my fiancé. As our work schedules differ - I'm a night owl just when his shift is starting - we have to do a fair amount of juggling if we're to see anything of each other.' Renee emerged, wrapped in a thick towelling robe. 'He's Manager of a busy Call Centre operated by a British company. Usually he collects me and gives me a lift out to The Nawab on his motorbike - it's better than a car for navigating Delhi's crazy traffic - but I'll text him to meet us there.'

'Oh, please don't change your plans for me...' Kay began, fearing she might be intruding. 'Some other day would work just as well. I honestly don't mind.' *Am I so obviously in need of rescuing?*

Renee was blow-drying her hair. 'No problem. I want to print off some stuff so you don't need to bust a gut. I'll be in the cyber cafe that's just off the verandah.' She made up her face, shrugged on her outfit, pirouetted in front of the long mirror to check the effect and humming a tune from a popular musical, sashayed out of the room.

CHAPTER 16

The sun dropped behind the trees. Rahul's day generally moved like clockwork, oiled with efficiency by his Parliamentary Aide, Steve Powley - Winston and Thelma's grandson - an Economics graduate from Delhi University and fluent Hindi speaker, who headed Rahul's team of staffers that shared the MP's passion for sparing no effort. Except that today was marred by a flapping Mrs Bhatia. Today there'd been Kay Forrester who, until this moment he'd dismissed from his thoughts. He leaned back against the upholstered car head-rest and rubbed his eyes. *I must get her to cut her losses and head home. What with the Vimla ruse and the fancy footwork that'll entail, the last thing I want or need is a situation with Kay. I've had a taste of her perverseness that almost rivals that of Hermie's.*

 Lost in contemplation, Rahul scarcely registered he'd arrived home, a town house constructed some years previously to replace Walipur House that had been made over to the nation for a Fine Arts Museum. He made straight for his rooms, showering quickly, donning black jeans and a tee shirt emblazoned with the logo of the World Wide Fund For Nature. Gertrude, his Great Dane, licked him silly.

There was the ring of voices. Might as well meet and greet and be done with it, he thought sourly, taking a heartening swallow of Scotch and soda that a servant had ready and waiting for him. *God that tastes good.* He walked slowly, his trainers noiseless on Persian carpets laid across marble floors.

'Good evening, ladies.' He assumed a cheerful expression smiling at the four women crouched over a green baize bridge table in a smoke filled room.   The Rajmata Amrita was dealing, her face absorbed, but she raised her thin eyebrows and her pale eyes flickered a greeting. From her mood of suppressed excitement, he could tell the game was going her way.   She always bid more than her hand was worth and invariably partnered by Hermie, whom she'd met through Edith after the death of their respective spouses, they made a formidable pair.

Rahul felt Hermie's eyes on him. 'You look tired. You ought to learn the art of stress- busting something I'm sure wasn't on the syllabus at Harvard Business School. Why don't you take up bridge?'

Elderly she might be, but she still played a mean hand. It wasn't the first time Hermie had suggested that and it certainly wasn't going to be the last, but Rahul was prepared and the usual answer was waiting.   'You know, I really must do something about that kind of detox.' He'd no intention whatsoever.

'Vimla is being delighted in partnering you,' chipped in Mrs Vohra archly. He saw her exchange a conspiratorial look with Amrita and his heart would've sunk had it not been for the little deceit, of which he was justly proud, he'd hatched that day. They'd been matchmaking again. He was in their sights. He and the charming Vimla who was Mrs Vohra's elder daughter. Dr (Miss) Vimla Vohra M.B.B.S. (Delhi) as Mrs Vohra boasted to anyone who came within earshot. Rahul smothered a yawn. And if fate decreed otherwise Mrs Vohra was sufficiently flexible to switch him to Vimla's younger sister.

Melon-shaped Mrs Vohra was a Punjabi lady with a light laugh and a bunch of household keys that clanked at her waist who had herself made an excellent, sensible marriage.   She was determined not to fail her daughters. They would marry - that was axiomatic - but more importantly they would marry well. No, she corrected herself, not just well, but brilliantly. That was her duty as a wife and mother and no dowry was too large, no amount of scheming too troublesome, to discharge it.

'Vimla prefers playing the sitar to playing cards, doesn't she? But thanks all the same.'

Undaunted, Mrs Vohra pressed on, her homely face lit by a big smile. 'Vimla is saying you are having sense of humour and I am agreeing with her.   Oh, by the way, my husband is wanting picking your brains. He's liking that you come by for drink next week. You are calling and fixing ?'

'Of course.' The ploy was all too obvious. Rahul knew that Mr Vohra, a well-to-do, self-made businessman who'd managed things pretty well for himself, had no need of his advice. But he could hardly decline - indeed he felt he'd be well advised not to - with four pairs of stiletto female eyes stabbing him.

'I am hearing that new American Ambassador, Mr - oh dear, his name is escaping from me, is in the town,' Mrs Vohra, who had a highly developed line in cocktail party chatter, observed merrily, determined at all cost to keep open the lines of communication with her future son-in-law.

Rahul downed his Scotch. 'You mean Addison. Yes, the press ran the usual profile on him. I expect I'll meet him someplace soon. Now, you look as if you're itching to finish the rubber. Sorry I barged in.' His broad smile belied the relief he felt at being able to slip away so easily. He glanced at Edith whose eye he could be guaranteed to catch in circumstances such as this but she was staring out of the window, a flush on her cheeks.

'Rahul, before I forget,' Amrita laid her hand face down on the table. 'I promised Hermie I'd have a word with you. She'd like you to help her - '

' - at your convenience, of course,' Hermie put in hastily, evidently reading the irritated expression on his face.

'- interview the applicants who're responding to her advertisement.'

Rahul was fed up with hearing about Hermie's plans for a companion and was convinced she was more than capable of weeding out the phonies and loonies on her own.

' I'm really rather tied up. And hadn't you plumped for that nice Goan woman?' He could hear the faint note of interrogation in his tone.

' No, not entirely,' Hermie said quickly, giving Rahul the impression that she was really rather enjoying all the interviewing, the fleeting power of control it gave her, and the evident sense of regret that the process would soon be concluded. 'She has a place of her own and so there's a big question mark over her living in.'

' I'm not sure I could add anything useful. Try Edith.' In a sort of quiet desperation, Rahul appealed to her. ' You're good at sorting out humbugs.'

But Edith, who didn't care for card games but was reluctantly dragged into it that day as Mrs Vohra's regular partner was laid low with flu, was having none of it. 'I've a timeline to meet for a German power company. I've already told Hermie she can't rely on me.'

'Please Rahul, it won't take long and I'd value your opinion,' Hermie said, a slight quaver in her voice.

 He hesitated, perfectly aware that Hermie was trying it on. 'Oh, very well.' He relented. ' I'll do what I can. Let me know when.' He knew he sounded grudging but was unrepentant. Women! Could he ever call his life his own?

'Thank you. I knew I could bank on you.' Delighted at the easy victory, Hermie returned to the more serious business of evaluating her hand for yet another. 'Two no trumps.'

' I must move on. I've some material to review before I head out.'

'And where might that be taking you?' Mrs Vohra's inquisition was shameless.

Rahul paused at the door and dispatched a superb shot. 'Vimla and I have a date at The Nawab tonight.'

Edith fixed him with a sharp look that he pretended not to notice and even as he sensed the ripple his announcement made on the others, he considered if he should have invited Kay to join him on her first, lonely night in Delhi. With a slight ill-defined unease, verging on a pricking of conscience, he wondered what she was doing at that moment.

***

A hot, scented shower, the familiar routine of doing her face and hair and Kay felt a new woman. She donned her favourite outfit - a strapless, ballet length frock in Thai silk, the colour of claret, with its collarless, tapestry shrug, humming as she inserted the silver hoop earrings Mum had given her on her eighteenth birthday, the only piece of good jewellery she possessed. A generous spray of duty-free perfume and the face that smiled back at her looked terrific. No girl can face a crisis unless she's properly dressed Kay thought, wondering what the ensuing weeks would bring or whether she should just hightail it out of Delhi. As she gathered up her evening bag her thoughts slid to Rahul, the cause of her predicament, she reminded herself sharply.

'Will I pass muster?' Kay asked as she joined Renee on the verandah. The scented, tropical night had descended, without warning, like a velvet curtain, and from the distance came the faint drumming of a Hindu wedding celebration.

'You're a chilli-cracker, as Dad would say.' Renee fingered the hem of the dress. 'Quality material and such a lovely texture. I wouldn't have thought you could look so different - almost regal - with your hair swept up. And that little throw-on will come in handy. It's hard to believe, but the temperature drops like a stone when the sun's gone down.' She pushed back her chair. 'Chullo.'

As the taxi turned the corner, The Nawab, once the town mansion of a wealthy nineteenth century merchant, was revealed - illuminated, stately as a liner. They cruised down a curving drive and spluttered to a stop outside the imposing arched entrance. Kay followed Renee through revolving doors into a pink-veined marble floored lobby. There was a buzz of conversation, of laughter, of people enjoying a good evening out, the smell of flowers and of expensive perfume and as the sound of mood music came closer, Renee swept into a large room where, on the raised platform, a four-piece band calling itself *The Shakers* was playing some bluesy electronics.

'Tony shouldn't be long.' Renee mimed a hello to the drummer and shepherded Kay to a table, catching a waiter's eye and ordering some drinks. Kay glanced round the softly lit, semi-circular salon taking in the damask covered, carved

club chairs, the potted palms, the gleam of rich silk and the bosomed and
bejewelled sari- clad women shimmering beautifully in every shade from
delphinium to silver, escorted by shining examples of the modern Indian male.

'Moneyed Delhi-ites, nouveau riche and the urban middle-class,' murmured
Kay, 'out for a night on the town. And don't they look fabulous?' She was not
unaware that she, too, was winning a few hearts.

Renee grinned impishly. 'Every man in the room's mad about you. You won't
be a wallflower and thankfully, neither will I. There he comes,' she said with
obvious pleasure giving a little wave as a stocky man, on the brink of thirty-five,
Kay guessed, with a toothbrush moustache forged his way to them.

'Kay, this is my fiancé, Tony Braganza.' Renee gave him a peck on the cheek.

'How very nice to meet you, Kay,' Tony said cheerfully, holding out his hand,
his teeth very white in his round, tobacco-brown face. 'Welcome to India. She
has been waiting for you for five thousand years.'

They're very much together, Kay thought. Tony was a homely person who'd
make Renee a dependable, loving husband. She felt a sudden pang, then
reminded herself sharply that she'd better things to do than pine for a man.

'You're wondering about Tony aren't you?' Renee said with a broad smile.
'Well, he's one more of India's many surprises. His Portuguese surname
signifies he's from Goa, that oceanside paradise on our west coast, once
colonised by the Portuguese, and it was St. Francis Xavier no less, that well-
known travel-aholic, who converted those beachcombers to Catholicism.'

A turbaned, red-sashed waiter set down a Pepsi for Renee and a vodka shot for
Kay and over a dish of mixed nuts they chatted easily or rather Renee, small-
talked nineteen to the dozen while Tony, a beer drinker and obviously the strong,
silent type and Kay, listened.

The place was heaving. Kay glanced casually about her unable to reconcile the
affluence with the starving beggars at the traffic lights. The effort of working this
out was too much and she took another sip, amusing herself trying to lip-read
conversations. That hip Indian foursome at the table by the door - what sort of
group dynamics were they into?

And then she glimpsed Rahul. In an Armani jacket over a gunmetal grey polo
neck, he greeted people with a traditional namastae, threading his way with
panther like grace between the tables.

'The man himself,' murmured Renee nudging Kay. 'I suppose that's
understandable if one's got a financial stake in the place.'

Tony blew a thin cloud of cigarette smoke into the air. ' I suppose it's to keep the staff on their toes or make sure my Renee isn't corrupting the cream of Delhi society... although that would be rather like locking the stable door after the horse has bolted.'

Kay stifled a giggle but his face was a model of bland innocence.

'Look over there. ' Renee had Rahul in her sights. 'Do you see the elderly gent he's chatting to?'

Kay shifted her chair a little and craning her neck observed Rahul joking with someone in a black velvet jacket worn over a ribbed turtleneck. 'The guy with the silver haired ponytail chomping on a cigar?'

Tony nodded sagely. 'That's The Nawab's owner - well, more correctly, its majority shareholder. That's Mr Maddox - '

'The legendary Barry Maddox,' Renee broke in reverently. 'One of us. I'm signed to his label,' she added proudly.'

'Old scoundrel Maddox,' Tony said with a grin. 'Bad boy supreme. Mr eighty per cent - the balance of The Nawab's split between Rahul and a shadowy Parsi nominee company.'

'What's the legend?' Kay asked curiously. 'You make it sound like some fantastic slum to glitz story.'

Renee's eyes sparkled at the prospect of broadcasting rumour much embellished by the passing years.   'Once upon a time... Look, even better - come and say hi to him. He's partial to pretty girls of marriageable age. Tony, you stay put and keep our seats warm.'

They crossed the floor as Rahul moved away from Barry.

'Hi, Barry. No, no, please stay put.'

'Renee! My beaut, so nice to see you. Finessed that new album yet? And who's the stranger in our midst?'

'I'm airing my new tunes in the second half. This is Kay Forrester who's just stepped off a plane.'

Kay beamed and returned Barry's handshake. The backs of his hands were dotted with brown age marks but the grip was firm and the bright eyes fixed her with keen attention.

'You know Kay, Renee's the hottest ticket in town. Now what will you two lovelies have to drink?' He smiled, his teeth so perfect that he must have a damn good dentist, thought Kay.

'Can't really stop, Barry. Just thought you'd like to meet Kay.'

'You thought right. You'll share some champagne with me, young woman? It's the cure for all ills and jet lag.'

Renee giggled and sketched a wave at Tony across the room. Kay exchanged the usual pleasantries with Barry and sat down.

'The diva was about to tell me all about you but I'd rather hear it first hand.' Barry waved his cigar. 'Question number one. Answer this and you're mine forever. Great men have many disciples, but it's always Judas who writes the biography.'

Renee groaned. 'Pass. I'm not in the mood for *Who Wants to be a Millionaire.*'

Kay tilted her head and said, 'Give me ten seconds. Ooh, that   sounds a lot like Oscar Wilde.'

'Mmm, I'm impressed. Now what can I do for you, Kay?' The girl had a lovely speaking voice, and she was easily one of the most attractive he'd seen in a long time with those breasts like peaches and a hidden sensuality.

Kay hesitated. Barry looked the sort who'd know what buttons to press. If she got stuck in her quest, he'd be someone she could see herself turning to. 'I'll take a rain check on that.'

Barry had folded his arms across his chest and looked searchingly at her. 'Sure thing.' That soft mouth simply invited kisses and he was suddenly reminded of Hermie at much the same age. Someone tapped him on the shoulder and he turned momentarily away.

Renee pushed back her chair on hearing her signature tune. 'That's my cue. Barry, we'll have to buzz.   Listen, I've got just the song for you to guest on.'

Barry smiled. 'As Kay says, I'll take a rain check.' He winked at them, his eyes following Kay as the girls drifted away.

Renee gulped down her drink. Tony stood up and gave her hand an affectionate squeeze as the lead guitarist of *The Shakers* bounced up to the mike. 'And here's the luverlee R-e-n-e-e M-e-r-r-i-t-o-n'. His voice had that familiar lilt. There was a spontaneous burst of applause and, as the lights dimmed, Renee hollered, 'tonight I'll sing my new ones but first here's some old familiar ones.'

'And how's the hyper Ms Forrester?' Rahul stopped by their table, a hand in his trouser pocket. He smiled. 'Evening, Braganza. May I join you?'

Tony nodded and mumbled absently, his attention fixed to the stage and Kay saw that he only had eyes for his girl.

'I've every intention of calling you Rahul, so call me Kay.' Kay said breezily. 'Ms Forrester's rather formal.'

'And you're not a lover of formality, I gather. Hence you're here tonight with a complete stranger like Braganza?'

'Renee's my roommate at the guesthouse and surely you know she's Tony's fiancée? You seem to know most things. And she's earning a living like the rest of us and doing a darn good job of it,' Kay continued as the singer's throaty voice belted out *Smoke Gets in Your Eyes*. 'They were kind enough to ask me along. Remember the guest house?' Kay was gripped by a sudden belligerence. 'Cast your mind back - you deposited me there earlier today before rushing off as though I had an infectious disease.'

So it still rankled, but to be met by this pugnacity was rather more than Rahul had expected. He raised his eyebrows. 'Indeed.' We're like two dogs snarling over a bone, Rahul thought, and sighed in some exasperation. He supposed Kay was suffering from jet lag, from the shock news of the non-existent job - but that was hardly his fault - and he was prepared to be sympathetic - up to a point. But he refused to feel guilty.

As Renee switched the tempo to *As If We'd Never Said Goodbye*, Rahul took Kay's hand and pulled her onto the floor. 'Shall we dance to the music of the sultry chanteuse?'

Slightly ungraciously Kay submitted, and he drew her close and they moved in perfect unison, his palm firm, almost caressing, against her spine. He was a divine dancer, and, despite herself, she felt herself melting into him, unaware that more than one glance was thrown in their direction.

'Try and forget your problems,' he murmured.

'They're yours, not mine,' she flashed back looking away at a point beyond his ear.

'Are you settling in all right?' It seemed safer to stick to neutral things.

'It's comfortable, but that's not really what you're asking, is it?'

'What am I asking?'

'When I intend to turn round and go home.'

'Since you mention it, yes. I'll firm up the return flight for say, ten days hence?'

'Now I've arrived I might as well make the most of it. I may not ever get the chance again.'

Rahul caught the evasion behind Kay's tone and glanced at her sharply.

This time she met his gaze. Her eyes were an astonishingly warm grey and at this moment held an expression of pure innocence. He was deceived not a bit.

'Listen, Renee's crooning another golden oldie.'

My Way was pounding out straight from the diaphragm, with diamond-hard clarity.

'That could almost be said of you.' And he swung her out of range of the other shimmying couples.

'Almost? You underestimate me and however awkward and embarrassing you might find it, I shall do as I please.'

'I wouldn't bank on that if I were you.'

'You brought me out to India on a crazy game so you can damn well lump it if I choose to stay as long as it suits me,' Kay returned incautiously.

Rahul considered this. She was intransigent but he was in no mood to be challenged, and by a woman at that. A strange, troublesome woman that he didn't really have the time to fuss round. He braced himself for another spat. 'I can't allow that.'

'Can't or won't?'

'Let me spell it out. You're redundant.'

'And expendable, is that what you mean?' She was goading him on but he sidestepped .

'Since you're ready to implicate me in this debacle then, very well, I shall be involved in every aspect of it and that includes arrangements for your future.'

'This is just....' Kay almost uttered a four-letter word but bit it back. ' ...unreasonable and perverse.'

'Kay, for Chrissake, lighten up.'

Her arms slid to her side and she moved away, furious with herself for having mismanaged the situation and allowing him to stalemate her.

Rahul watched her wend her way back to Tony's table and after a moment's hesitation as the key- board player wove nifty patterns, decided he ought to follow.

The band had stopped on a roll of drums. Renee and Tony were crouched over the table, their heads touching, whispering sweet nothings. They sketched an invitation, but there was wistfulness in their smiles.

 Realising that they had so little free time together Kay said quickly, 'great vocals - that was real cool, Renee. And now Rahul has offered to show me the grounds. I hope you don't mind if he whisks me off.'

 'Not a bit,' they chorused, trying without much success to conceal their pleasure at being left to their own devices.

 Kay saw Rahul look momentarily disconcerted and then he took her elbow. 'What was all that about?' he said softly as he piloted her away. Through double doors and along an airy terrace, they descended shallow steps into romantically lit lawns of close-cropped, sweet-smelling grass and curving flowerbeds of crimson cannas and bronze chrysanthemums. Couples strolled about laughing and chattering, enjoying the air and the rustle of the breeze through the trees and in the distance could be heard the homely sound of barking dogs. The moon silvering the tree branches sailed across the tropical indigo sky studded with a train of stars that reminded Kay of a sequinned shawl.

 She told him and he nodded. 'That was thoughtful of you.'

 Kay wandered over to a patch of glossy foliage and bent her head 'Heavenly fragrance - what is it?'

 Rahul moved to her side and plucking several creamy blossoms, tucked them into her hair. 'Jasmine, but we call it *rath ki rani* - queen of the night', he said and as his fingers adjusted the sprigs for a moment their eyes met and held and there was something in his eyes that nearly swamped her senses. Her heart began thudding violently. Then he had looked away and his voice continued with its customary crispness that Kay was certain it could only have been a trick of the light. 'I expect the lovebirds will want to eat together and perhaps we could dine, too, at a discreet distance, so that they don't feel guilty about leaving you to do battle on your own.'

 He's softening you up. 'That sounds very nice.' Kay's tone was as neutral as his own.

 'Success at last.' A woman's voice floated across. 'There you are, Rahul! Nothing like seeking and finding. Sorry I got delayed but such are the demands of the labour ward. Am I too late for dinner?'

'Hi Vimla.' Rahul greeted the glamorous, smooth-skinned woman with considerable warmth. 'Kay and I were just debating the merits of that. Kay, this is Dr Vimla Vohra.'

She was, Kay guessed, in her mid to late twenties with stylishly cut, thick black hair swinging below a perfect jaw line and a smile that was out of an ad for toothpaste.

Vimla eyed Kay with lively interest. 'Thank heavens for a new face. I haven't seen you before, have I?'

'You haven't. I arrived today to a job that doesn't exist,' Kay said airily making it sound as if she'd just caught the wrong bus. She caught a spark in the amused exchange of glances between Vimla and Rahul and wondered how serious the friendship was.

Vimla giggled. 'That sounds familiar. I'm dying to hear all about that little accident - every little detail, mind you. I can see you're a mistress of understatement.'

'Vimla is,' Rahul cut in with a broad grin, 'one of those dreadful exponents of psychobabble, so beware. She'll whittle your darkest secrets out of you.'

She's really the most exotic creature, Kay thought feeling suddenly very nondescript by comparison. The midnight blue sari deeply bordered in an unusual hand stitched folk motif was nothing ordinary, the snugly fitting choli exposing a silky expanse of gleaming brown skin.

'You must visit Rahul's ancestral seat,' Vimla said chattily as they strolled across the lawn. 'Walipur Mahal, that's the palace, is in his constituency. It's been painted and photographed; men have written and sung about it, fought over, loved and died for it. Where you can catch the most romantic sunsets. And although it morphed into a deluxe heritage hotel some time back, the family still retains a mere twenty roomed private wing. I'm sure he'll be only too delighted to give you a conducted tour.'

Kay glanced at Rahul's face that looked as if it was carved in granite, so she took a perverse delight in egging on Vimla. 'And what else can I expect him to reveal to me?'

Vimla threw back her head and laughed 'And –'

'- hold the commercial, Vimla,' Rahul swiftly interjected.

But she blundered on. 'You ain't heard nothing yet. The most breath taking winter snowscapes and the loveliest wild flowers are at his country pad in

Sivalik, a hill station in the foothills of the Himalayas. That's strictly off-limits to the public though, where the emphasis is on fun,' Vimla rhapsodised, darting a teasing glance at Rahul that drew from him a sudden smile.

Quite suddenly, Kay felt a victim of her emotions - irritation that Rahul was maintaining a cold and polite distance, curiosity about his relationship with Vimla and an odd sort of twinge that she refused to recognise as the irrational stirrings of jealousy. Well, although there was nothing she could do about that, there was, she thought with considerable satisfaction, everything she could do about exploring dynastic dwellings - his or anyone else's for that matter - as a free agent. She wondered too, how she could quiz him about Ajeemkot without risking the inevitable inquisition, for she was less minded now, given his attitude, to share her quest with him.

'Ten rupees for them.' Rahul's voice pierced her thoughts and Kay blinked, suddenly recalled to the present.

'You were somewhere else,' Vimla remarked.

'Yes, Ajeemkot.' She heard herself blurt out. 'Where's it in relation to Walipur?'

'Not far - '

Rahul's broad shoulders lifted briefly and he cut Vimla short with a little impatient gesture of his hand.   'Why do you want to know?'

'You make it sound like a no-go area,' Kay said lightly with considerable presence of mind. There was a short silence and she met his gaze unflinchingly.

'I can recommend its website.'

'Oh, of course.' Kay gave a wry smile. She could've kicked herself for not having considered the obvious.

Just then Vimla's mobile chirruped.   'Here we go, a text from the hospital. The inevitable 90 hour week'. To her credit, Kay thought, Vimla didn't look at all dismayed at being deprived of a cosy evening with Rahul. 'Sorry Rahul, but I have to head back. I'll call you.' She smiled again at Kay. 'Meanwhile, you have this English rose to keep you company so get her to sample The Nawab's finest cuisine.' And on that note Vimla disappeared in the same sort of flourish with which she'd materialised, the faint perfume smell of her hair oil drifting after her.

'Wise words and my feelings exactly. You must be famished.'

Kay stifled a yawn. 'Forgive me, you must think me very rude.'

'That's nothing new,' Rahul said a tinge of mockery in his tone. 'But you're more tired than you're hungry.'

'Yes, I think I am.'

'Do you want to wait for the song thrush to finish?' He pushed back his cuff and glanced at his watch. 'She's got a titanic night ahead but I could run you back now if you prefer.'

Renee had embarked on a *will they won't they* song from her new repertoire that had the audience swaying. Kay felt absolutely ragged. 'If you're going my way.'

'No problem.' Rahul slipped the shrug round her shoulders and steered her to the waiting Mercedes and soon the steady motion of the car made her feel drowsy.

'You nearly nodded off then,' Rahul said.

He'd disarmed her and she was annoyed with herself for having let down her guard. 'And I'll say it again. You botched it.' She'd no intention of letting him forget.

'Not a bit. It was sheer bad management on your part.'

'You're Chairman of the Governors. You can do, in fact I've seen you do, pretty much what you like.' She took a deep breath and added, 'you have authority, influence. You could re-create that job or offer me something else if you're minded to.'

'I'm not,' Rahul said evenly, the amusement in his eyes deepening.

With an irritated click of her tongue Kay turned her face to the window. A wind had risen and they were sliding down through a darkness lit by bright stars along a wide tree-lined boulevard, bordered by ponds that shimmered in the pale moonlight, past glowing sandstone buildings. The beauty of it made Kay catch her breath.

'The symmetry of Lutyens,' Rahul said softly. 'That domed building behind those ornate railings is Rashtrapati Bhavan, the President's House.' He pointed out some other historic landmarks with the enthusiasm of one who loved his city, whetting Kay's appetite to see the grandeur of the capital.

'Sweet dreams, Kay.' They'd reached the guesthouse.

'Goodnight, sweet prince.' Her legs might feel too weak to hold her but the quotation was ready and waiting.

Exhausted, Kay threw herself down on the bed; all her carefully mapped plans seemed to have unravelled hopelessly. She was even too tired to think but she was annoyed with herself at her clumsy handling of Rahul. Much later, her ears caught the growl of a motorbike, the door opened quietly and Renee crept in, shoes in hand.

'I hope I haven't woken you. How did you get back?' Renee creamed off her make-up. 'I saw you with Vimla earlier - three's a crowd, I thought. What do you think of her?'

Kay sat up. 'Oh, she's nice enough although the encounter was somewhat short-lived as duty called.'

Renee began to brush her hair. 'It's assumed she and Rahul will get hitched, although the big question is when?' She wiggled the brush at Kay. 'Do you know when he went off to Harvard they say the dragon Rajmata – that means Queen Mother- gave him strict orders not to return with a foreign wife.'

Kay got up and helped herself to a Pepsi. She was beginning to feel better; Renee restored her sense of proportion. 'I can't imagine he hasn't been up close and personal with a bevy of foreign beauties.'

Renee hung up her clothes. 'It's a complete mystery why they haven't tied the knot yet.   It's not as if they're cash-strapped and need to put by a nest egg like Tony and me. Vimla's well connected, well heeled, and astrologically compatible.'

Kay rubbed her eyes. 'I expect Vimla's so sure of him she can afford to spin it out. She's probably making the most of her freedom.' She reached for her nightie.

'You're very cynical.' Besides you're never sure of a man unless you have him hooked, booked and cooked and even then, like black labradors, they'll stray.'

***

Kay woke late to bright sunshine and the harsh cawing of purplish-black crows. Renee had left her a note to say she'd gone shopping, modestly adding that reviews in the papers described last night's performance as a *supercharged, moody stadium shaker and that a new sound was born.* 'It's lonely at the top!' she'd quipped.

Kay showered and donned white trousers and a V-necked turquoise tee shirt. After an ample self-service breakfast in the spacious dining room she settled herself in a cane chair on the shady verandah, watching the colourful antics of the parakeets and mynah birds. Would she see more of Delhi on her own or should she join one of the many guided coach tours, she wondered. Engrossed in her thoughts, she didn't register a figure standing on the verandah steps who cleared his throat to attract her attention.

'Oh!' Kay gave a slight start. For a moment her mind was a complete blank then recognition dawned. It was Rahul's driver.

'Rajah-ji is instructing me to deliver this.' He held out an envelope addressed to Ms K. Forrester.

Kay took it from him, frowning slightly. The man waited, patience etched on his face and it occurred to her that he expected a reply. She slit open the envelope with her thumbnail. The handwritten note was in rather flowery English, Rahul's epistolary style quite different from his usual, everyday speech and invited her to come sightseeing with him that day. It ended, *I wouldn't want you to leave with a poor impression of India or Indians.*

Leave? Huh! I've no intention of leaving yet. 'Yes, that sounds interesting.' Kay decided it was an offer she couldn't pass on and picking up her shoulder bag she followed him to the car where Rahul waited behind the wheel. He dismissed the driver.

'Morning,' he said cheerfully. Kay looked rested and fresh. She was nicely proportioned with killer curves and he wasn't averse to being seen with an attractive woman. 'Sleep well?'

'Never better.' She smiled showing dimples. With the new day, she felt herself again.

Rahul's thoughts flew back to the dilemma, wondering if he really could help to retrieve the situation. If he hammered away at the Minister it was possible that he might shame him into his nephew relinquishing the appointment and eventually making it available for Kay. Equally he might not. He decided to say nothing to Kay. It wasn't fair to get her hopes up. 'We're heading for old Delhi now - the ancient part of the city, a fascinating mix of alleys, gateways and bazaars enclosed by a seventeenth century wall.'

Soon he'd nosed the car under a large leaved tree and helped her out. 'Do a bit of time travel, back to the seventh city of Delhi - the Delhi of the Mughal Emperor Shah Jehan. Over there ' he pointed,' is the Red Fort.'

'How regal and aloof it is, like a haughty dowager.' Kay drew a breath. 'And so different from our stately homes and castles.' Unaccustomed to being eyeballed by passers-by, Kay tried not to let it irritate her. 'None of the background reading quite prepared me for this.'

They wandered through the ancient building's airy chambers. 'I feel as though I'm spirited away to a romantic, heroic past.' In the subdued indoor light, it drew her into its magic. 'Do those gold squiggles over that archway mean anything?'

'It's a Persian couplet. *If there be a paradise on earth, it is this, it is this, it is this.'* Rahul quoted softly, and the poetry of it made her heart miss a beat.

They emerged into the sunlight and skirted a coach-load of tourists toting cameras. A majestic building with tapering minarets and an onion shaped dome caught Kay's eye.

Rahul, anticipating her, said, 'That's the ancient Friday Mosque, the Jama Masjid.'

'How fresh it looks and what a landmark.' Kay shaded her eyes with a hand. 'Can one climb to the top?' He'd escorted her into its courtyard and she was caught up in its tranquillity.

'Yes. For a small fee.' Rahul paused and gazed at her, adding mischievously, 'but a woman has to be accompanied by a responsible male.'

Kay opened her mouth to denounce him then saw the joke and laughed.

'And now if you're not too footsore, we could stroll through Chandni Chowk - ' he broke off to chase away importuning street urchins. 'Jao. Get lost.' Unexpectedly he added, 'do you know, I'm enjoying this.'

Kay surrendered herself to the raffishness of the Chowk, to the gaudy craftwork in the open-fronted stalls, to the aroma of sandalwood soap and grilled lamb kebabs.

'Stick with me or you'll lose your bearings,' Rahul warned and taking her elbow dived with considerable economy of effort down the labyrinth of alleyways, fighting off hawkers and fortune- tellers, deftly dodging tail-swishing cows cropping vegetables from open stalls. A colourful wedding procession, with bridegroom nervously astride a grey, caparisoned horse meandered along to the accompaniment of a tinny band.

There was more junk than Kay had ever believed possible. And brass candlesticks bolder than those she'd left behind. But here was a jade hand-carved figure that she absolutely craved and a papier-mâché bowl finely painted with flowers that simply glowed. She simply couldn't resist that satin shirt, the colour of an aubergine, although would she ever wear it?

'Honestly, I'd just like to browse,' Kay said a little mournfully. Rahul was going at a fair clip and all she wanted to do was savour the allure of the bazaar and hunt for mementoes.

'Of course. How thoughtless of me. 'Look, you'll want - or if you don't, you ought to - the crème de la crème so let's go over there, just past that sweetmeat shop which once boasted a rather unusual customer.' Rahul weaved through the throng with Kay almost moulded to his side as bargains were shouted out and caged birds squawked at dancing monkeys.

'And that was?' Kay pressed her handkerchief to her nose as the smell of open drains hit her.

'Shah Jehan's favourite elephant.'

She giggled. 'You can't be serious.'

'A cunning beast. It halted outside the shop and refused to budge till it had consumed a belly-full of choicest sweetmeats. And from that day onwards - well you know jumbo never forgets....'

'So the shop has lived off the tale ever since?'

'Oh, it's well patronised by two legged mammals. Come and have a look if you can drag yourself away from all this fairground stuff.'

He ducked inside and Kay followed him, and amidst much salaam-ing, chairs were dusted off and cold drinks produced.

'Here, sample this.' Rahul offered her a pale green lozenge.

Kay nibbled cautiously. 'Do you want my professional opinion? Very sweet, definitely pistachios and quite simply delicious.'

'And there's more.'

She bit into sunflower yellow laddoos, the size of golf balls, sticky orange swirls of jellaybies, and milky-white slices flecked with dark almonds. Rahul laughed as she licked her fingers.

'At this rate, **I'll** morph into an elephant.'

'And this is for you.' He'd had a box of assorted burfee and halva made up for her.

'How kind.' By now Kay had begun to feel friendlier towards him. He'd shed that arrogance and become less brooding and she found herself enjoying his company.

He ushered her out and after browsing for another hour Kay found herself facing a small glass-fronted shop.

'I think this is what you have in mind.'

'Yes...' Kay said but she was a little doubtful. It looked very superior and probably had prices to match. Nevertheless, it would provide a sort of benchmark. And her feet hurt.

It was cool and shady inside and beginning to think that it wasn't such a bad idea after all, Kay deposited her bag on the polished wood counter and wandered round. She marvelled at the intricate silver workmanship, fingered embroidered velvet bags and bejewelled belts; marvelled, too, at the price tags.

Graciously attentive, the shopkeeper motioned her to a seat and Kay feeling like a minor potentate, lowered herself onto a low, amply bolstered divan. A well-dressed man of average height and Kay's age, materialised with a tall glass of ice-cold nimboo pani.

'Enjoy.' He introduced himself as Suresh, the shopkeeper's son.

'He's taking good care of me.' She glanced across to Rahul and could have sworn he'd muttered asshole under his breath.

Rahul had arranged himself, with some grace on a soft wine-coloured rug, his long legs folded under him, smoking a bubbling hookah prepared for him by the shopkeeper. 'They're just superb salesmen.'

'Such exquisite designs. They're out of this world and so, I'm afraid, are your prices.' They were too dear for Kay even to be tempted. 'But,' she was suddenly inspired, 'perhaps you has some smaller pieces?'

'Certainly.' The shopkeeper pulled out a drawer and brought it across.

'Yes, this is my budget,' Kay confided to Rahul who was looking on in amused tolerance. 'May I try this on?' She held up a silver filigree bracelet. Its little charms are so unusual.'

'Come here, Kay.'

Kay crossed over, and knelt beside Rahul resting her arm lightly across his thighs. As he took her wrist his fingers brushed against her skin and instantly the same treacherous flicker she'd felt last night in the hotel garden fluttered inside her.

There was the sound of a sharp click as he fastened the clasp, but he didn't immediately release her hand, his touch lingering on her wrist for seemingly endless moments. Kay was almost incapable of movement, her heart beating like a drum. For a moment nothing else existed, nothing else mattered. Rahul had driven out of her head her reasons for being here. With an effort of will, she slipped her hand out of his own and held it away from her to admire the effect, surprised at the steadiness of it.

'I'll take that, and perhaps that, no, I think not... yes, on second thoughts... '

'Making up one's mind's seldom easy,' Rahul said, his eyes probing hers.

She stared at him. He was so able to discomfit her. 'Well, there is the small matter of money...'

'Is that what you thought I meant?'

'Isn't it?'

'Yes.'

'You're a lousy liar.'

He laughed, then got up and pulled her to her feet. 'Come on, we can't stay here all day.'

'I'll wrap them for you.' The shopkeeper whisked away the bracelet along with some other pieces - keepsakes for friends, and dangling, cobwebby earrings for herself.

Kay looked round for her bag but it wasn't where she'd left it. 'Did you move it?'

The shopkeeper shook his head and the most complete comprehension hit her. 'Oh God, don't say it's been pinched. I couldn't bear it.' Kay felt utterly numb, all the fun of the day draining from her.

'You should've known better than to have left it unattended.' Rahul's eyes had darkened and his voice had an edge she didn't like. Roughly addressing the shopkeeper, who was deeply apologetic, he reached into his wallet and slammed down his bankcard.

'I thought it would be quite safe here, and I can't let you do that,' Kay said as levelly as she could, feeling close to tears.

'I can and shall do as I choose,' he remarked grimly.

She might have known he'd say that. Scooping up her little parcels, he hurried her out of the shop and through the chaos of the Chowk to the car.

'You can reimburse me, if and when you get your bag back, although I rather think you've seen the last of it.'

'Thank heavens my passport's in the guest house safe deposit.' Kay's wry smile belied the sick feeling sweeping over her.

'Praise the gods for small mercies...'

'Please don't...' Kay objected reproachfully.

Rahul shot her a look from under his brows but said nothing. They sat in silence as he negotiated his way through the congested knot of old Delhi and then he was cutting through a leafy residential area. The sound of traffic blurred as he decelerated through a walled gateway manned by a saluting khaki-clad sentry. There was a swish of tyres on red-gravelled drive and beyond it, in a landscaped setting of velvet grass, well shaded by trees of peepul, banyan and gol mohur stood a large cream-coloured town house. It shouted wealth, taste.

'A silly question but where are we?' Kay asked.

'This is my home,' Rahul said simply. 'Let's see what I can do from here that divine intervention cannot, about re-uniting you with your bag.'

Even as he stopped, a uniformed servant, a pinky-mauve sash round his knee-length white coat matching the colour of his turban, was padding out and opening the car door.

Kay hung back. A Great Dane bounded up, sniffing and circling her.

'That's quite enough, Gertrude. Come on in, Kay.' Rahul's face had softened a little, and he touched her arm. Another saluting servant relieved her of her parcels, though that was scarcely necessary.

Rahul led her through to a sitting room filled with huge bowls of fresh flowers and furnished with panache. Kay glanced round - only the Mughal miniatures, contemporary Indian art, Persian and Kashmiri rugs, and bronze deities yielded clues to its locale.

'Look, you can freshen up in there,' he pointed, 'and you'll want some coffee. Meanwhile I'll see what can be done to sort out this... self-inflicted mess of yours,' he added, reaching for his mobile as much as to say he didn't intend firing blanks.

Behind the door lay an ultra modern bathroom and, slipping off her sandals, Kay washed her soles and hands, slapping cold water on her cheeks. A generous squirt of a rather heady perfume from a large bottle on a glass shelf and she emerged altogether a new woman. Who was she to object if Rahul chose to shoulder the responsibility for her?

Kay sat down, still a little shaken and although not comprehending his conversation in Hindi with the local police, getting the impression that he was giving them the chilling benefit of his tongue. She sighed and closed her eyes - her ready cash gone ditto credit cards, mobile phone and camera and, back home, a busted bank balance. What a f-k up. Thus engaged she didn't immediately notice a tall, slim woman with aquiline features pause briefly in the doorway, gliding into the room in a swish of silk.

Half reclining in a comfy chair, Kay hazily turned her head. There was something innately patrician about the woman's demeanour that impelled her to spring to her feet. She was intimidatingly assured, wearing her years lightly, her coal black hair with a dramatic white streak, knotted at the nape of her neck. Her pastel sari, its lavender threads catching the light, was striking in its sheer simplicity. Yet there was nothing remotely simple about her bearing - the symmetry of the pale brown face, the emerald-flecked hazel eyes - a throwback to some northern Indian ancestor. Her aura proclaimed wealth, power, breeding. Even before Rahul had introduced her as the Rajmata Amrita, Kay knew. She looked every inch the archetypal Queen Mother.

'Mother.' He killed his mobile. 'This is Kay Forrester who's vacationing in Delhi.'

'How do you do.' Amrita's handshake was brief, disinterested, at odds with the sudden flare in those eyes, a lioness protecting her cub. Kay swallowed.

'Before I forget, Vimla phoned to say she's off duty tomorrow night, Rahul, and wants to take in that new Brad Pitt movie. Would you to call her?' Amrita settled herself in an easy chair facing Kay. 'Tell me, how you come to know my son?' she probed without preamble her gaze travelling lightly over Kay and coming to rest on her ring less fingers.

A bearer appeared with a heavy silver coffee pot and poured out smoking hot coffee that smelled as good as it would probably taste. But that one swift glance of Amrita's told Kay more clearly than words that, for all her apparent indifference to her, she meant her to understand *Rahul is not for you.*

Kay was momentarily rendered speechless but recovered herself quickly, unwilling to let Amrita rattle her. 'It's a long story. I'll start at the beginning. I flew from London via Rome recently and Rahul will tell you the rest...'

The Rajmata gave a slight start, although she concealed it well, at what she plainly regarded as Kay's familiarity at the use of her son's first name. 'You're from England?' Amrita raised shapely, enquiring eyebrows watching Kay over the tip of her cigarette.

She put it rather oddly, Kay thought. 'Yes, I'm English,' she said firmly.

There was a short silence and Kay could feel Amrita's eyes on her face. They conveyed an odd suspicion, and she seemed to bite back something a remark. Then her lips curved in a little half-smile. *That's what you might well say,* Amrita told herself. *You're no more English than my old platinum blonde AI assistant under-nanny. That tawny shadow above the cuticles betrays you.*

'Kay's arrival in Delhi is the stuff of sagas, Mother. At the moment, she's trying to track down her handbag that disappeared, surprise, surprise, in the bazaar.'

Amrita withdrew another cigarette from a flat, silver cigarette case and he leaned across and lighted it for her with a solid gold table lighter. 'How very unfortunate,' Amrita acknowledged. 'You've probably seen the last of it.' She didn't sound particularly sorry. 'But I suggest you try and put it to the back of your mind and leave the worrying to Rahul.' She stared at the cigarette between her fingers and gave a dry chuckle. 'There's nothing he likes better than a thorny problem.'

With every heavenly mouthful of coffee Kay felt better, even to the extent of feeling somewhat amused as Rahul resumed his mauling of her.

'I can't think what possessed you to leave it lying around. You wouldn't have dreamed of doing that in London. Anybody would think you'd never travelled before.'

The bearer re-filled Kay's cup. 'This tastes and smells wonderful.' She was determined not to let Rahul suspect that he niggled her.

'It's from Mysore, in the south,' Amrita looked at her reflectively. 'Won't you have some something to eat?' She passed a plate of samosas and pakoras accompanied by a tangy, coriander and coconut dip. Kay, suddenly conscious that breakfast had been hours ago, fell on it.

'I'm being fatalistic about my loss, why can't you?' Kay said lightly. 'The way you keep hammering at me you'd think I was in trouble with the law. I'll just have to email my bank for more funds.' *That's if they haven't blacklisted me already. And scrounge off Yvonne.*

He cut across her thoughts. 'Don't be flippant.' He spoke without emphasis but he wasn't going to let her off. 'Have you any idea of the value of money?'

She crushed the impulse to be equally provocative. ' A little.'

To her amazement, he gave her a broad smile and she smiled back.

Amrita had been watching the exchange in silence and said languidly, as Rahul stepped out of the room to take a mobile call, 'you know when Rahul was at Harvard I told him he didn't have to marry every girl he dated.'

Before Kay could think of a suitable riposte, Amrita was ringing a small hand bell and another flunkey appeared bearing a polished silver box, intricately incised, which he placed on the carved coffee table.

'Paan-daan', Rahul said, 'Mother's paan box.'

Amrita lifted the lid and Kay glimpsed several tiny compartments filled with various, curious things. From one, Amrita extracted a glossy, green betel leaf; from another, using a miniature silver spatula, a white substance the consistency of thick cream that she smeared over the leaf. 'Lime paste,' she said. 'And now this is betel nut, or more properly, areca nut and then...' She scooped out some catechu-scented tobacco and it occurred to Kay that she was witnessing something of a ritual. 'Sometimes we also add coconut.' Then, wrapping the leaf neatly round all the ingredients so that it became a perfect little triangular parcel, Amrita secured it with a clove and handed it to her. ' For you,' she said bestowing a thin smile on her. 'I don't know if you will like my paan, but do try.'

Kay didn't like to refuse, sensing that it was an honour to be offered something personally prepared by the lady of the household, particularly when she happened to be a Rajmata. Hesitantly she took a nibble, and to her surprise, liked the fresh flavour that spilled from it. 'It's like nothing I've ever tried.'

'Well, you've endeared yourself to Mother.'

Amrita looked at Kay her eyes instantly blank and cold. She was the sort, Kay sensed, who could squeeze blood from a stone. 'It's invariably offered after meals, as a digestive and a palate cleanser. Rahul, can I tempt you?'

'With all due respect, you know I prefer Benarasi paan.'

Amrita didn't seem at all offended. 'Hark, Kay. There speaks a true connoisseur.'

He's the gin in her tonic and Kay wondered if Rahul was a mind reader when she caught him giving her a trenchant glance.

'Would you excuse me, I have some charitable business to attend to,' Amrita said eventually, rising to her feet obviously sensing the strained atmosphere between Kay and her son and unwilling, thought Kay, not without a certain perverse satisfaction, to become embroiled in what her expression clearly regarded, even if her words did not, as their contemptible squabble. She smiled vaguely at Rahul her eyes sharpening as they rested briefly on Kay's face. ' I hope you find what you're looking for.'

What the hell does she mean by that?

'More coffee?' Rahul glanced pointedly at his watch and Kay supposed he was fed up with having wasted an afternoon in trivia, but had felt duty bound as a gentleman.

'No thanks.'

'Go home to London, Kay. Now. You're not capable of looking after yourself and I'm damned if I'm going to.'

'I didn't ask you to,' she retorted cheerfully. 'If you recall, you volunteered your services.' To her surprise he grinned. She was glad to be able to turn the tables on him. She gathered up her parcels. 'Now lend me the money for a taxi or as I'm obviously so helpless, would you organise one for me?'

He was still smiling. 'I'm heading back to the office. My driver will drop you off.'

The return journey was made in silence, the scents of the city blowing in through the open windows. Rahul busied himself with official papers and Kay gazed out watching with fascination as an armoured black limousine flying the Stars and Stripes on the right fender and the Ambassadorial flag on the left fender accompanied by a police escort roared round a loin-clothed yogi standing on his head in the middle of the road.

Rahul glanced across. 'That's the new American Ambassador on his way to present his Letters of Credence to the President. Let's hope he's as approachable as the previous incumbent.'

Deposited at the guest house and mumbling a thank you, Kay hurried inside, one half of her slightly dismayed that Rahul hadn't mentioned that he'd see her again, and the other telling her he was best forgotten.   Most of the occupants were out, and there was a beautiful stillness   about the place. Her head throbbed and she sank thankfully into a chair after emailing Yvonne from the cyber cafe and forced herself to consider that other crucial poser - how to remain in India. For a brief moment in Rahul's house, fed up with the turmoil, she'd wanted to head home but something held her and now she knew that she couldn't until she'd exhausted her personal crusade.

Kay sat for a long time watching the antics of a pair of crimson crested black and white hoopoes, and the chirping of a bulbul. Then she crossed to the notice board crammed with advertisements. *For Sale; To Let; Music Lessons; Cook Wanted; Bridegroom (sober habits) wanted for wheaten skinned, very beautiful, convent educated, sweet, homely girl, BSc (Home Economics). Age 36 (but looks 10 years younger). Father and brothers holding government positions. Divorced and disabled need not apply. Green Cardholder preferred.* If only it were that easy, Kay thought wryly.

COMPANION REQUIRED. A sheet of blue paper tacked with a brass drawing pin to the top left hand side of the board caught her by the scruff of the neck. Moving closer, Kay read: *Colonel's widow seeks English-speaking companion, 25- 47 years. Dog lover. No nursing or domestic duties. Pleasant New Delhi residence. Summer in the hills. Remuneration by arrangement. Apply Mrs H. Hollingberry.* And it gave a telephone number.

Intrigued, Kay jotted it down on a page torn from her diary. It could be just what she was looking for, always assuming Mrs Hollingberry wasn't a tyrant. Perhaps they'd been one of those British couples that had stayed on after Independence? The temptation to ring her immediately was almost overwhelming but Kay checked the impulse concluding it was wiser to discuss it with Renee first. But already she felt more cheerful.

As she strolled to her room, the receptionist waylaid her to say she had visitors waiting in the TV lounge. *Who can that be?* It was the shopkeeper with Suresh who, brandishing her handbag, smirked as he peered down her tee shirt.

Kay fell on the bag in delight and learned that Suresh had apparently retrieved it from a street kid and punished the *unworthy perpetrator*. He urged her to check the contents and Kay did so assuring him that everything was intact. 'I can't thank you enough.'

'My Suresh is being very pleased to showing you round Delhi. He's UK returned and is liking London very much.'

'Well,' Kay smiled at Suresh, 'I second that.'

'I am noticing you are very charming virgin.'

Kay giggled.

'Suresh is being a very fine boy and is making good husband and giving you many, very nice babies. The wedding is happening in Delhi. I am guaranteeing it will be best occasion and you are receiving from us big cash, many priceless jewellery pieces and latest model BMW. Suresh is then entering UK as your husband. I am very rich and you are not regretting. Suresh is being very happy about this.'

Kay was speechless and although she hadn't been long in India she sensed one didn't say no outright. Recovering herself she said graciously. 'I'm honoured by your offer. But you must give me time to consider.'

'It is being straightforward,' the shopkeeper said a little peevishly. 'What's there to consider? Surely you are not requiring I discuss with Ratan Singh-ji? '

Suresh chimed in, a note of urgency in his voice. 'Ji is busy and he will be saying yes, so no reason for asking permission.'

Kay smiled. 'I don't need Rahul's consent or approval to anything I choose to do.' She wondered how to get rid of them. Suresh had sidled up to her and put his arm round her waist and she politely disengaged it. 'We're not on *Strictly Come Dancing*. Now, I'm going to be in India a while yet so that'll give me time to get to know you, Suresh and to sort things out.'

The shopkeeper rapidly tilted his head from side to side. 'Accha. But anything you want you ask me.' To Kay's relief they exited, Suresh leering at her. No sooner had they left the room than Suresh texted her to say she was *byootiful* and promised many champagne fuelled nights together.

***

Jolted about in the auto rickshaw that she wondered if she'd any sound bones left in her body, the following day Kay wearing a crisp, yellow cotton dress with a wide black hide belt that emphasised her slim waist, reached Hermie's. Renee had said she'd nothing to lose by sussing it out. It was six o'clock by her watch and still very warm and hundreds of feet up, in the cloudless expanse of blue, multi-coloured kites skimmed and glided.

Kay made her way up a semi-circular drive towards the house. It couldn't, she realised, be compared with the contemporary chic of Rahul's, but it had a settled, cared look about it, a flat-roofed bungalow constructed, she suspected, in traditional Lutyens-style, standing in a well tended compound, surrounding a round, shallow pond lit from inside among lotuses and goldfish. She stopped, a brief moment of indecision that brought two dachshunds racing out from some private hide-out, circling and sniffing up her dress and barking as though she were a midnight prowler. Kay stood her ground, refusing to be bullied, pinning a foolish smile on her face as one does when one's escape route has been cut off.

She was rescued by an attractive drawl. 'Putch, Suzie, STAY!' Hermie's expression was one of uncomplicated welcome. She advanced slowly leaning on a carved walking stick. Shrewd brown eyes sought Kay with frank appraisal. 'You must be the girl who rang me yesterday.'

' I am. Hello!' Almost before Kay noticed anything else about Hermie, she saw the rock of a solitaire and the host of fine, gold bangles jangling at her wrists. She was not as Kay had supposed. She wasn't fat, rheumy-eyed, or toothless. She was well preserved from her professionally manicured shell pink fingernails to her coiffured hair, subtly tinted with a dark rinse, and pearl ear-studs. Her face was expertly made up drawing the eye away from the few lines, her clear, creamy complexion giving no hint that she'd ever lived in the tropics. There wasn't a whiff of incontinence but of L'air du Temps and her eye shadow harmonised with the expensive pale lilac trouser suit. *In fact,* Kay thought, *she looks less in need of a companion than I do.*

'I didn't quite catch your surname, Miss... It was a bad line.'

Kay realised the woman was peering at her. In the school holidays she'd often helped out as a volunteer in an old people's home and knew the tendency of some old dears to affect visual or other handicaps knowing that people would be more inclined to rally. 'It's Forrester. Kay Forrester.' Kay smiled and shook hands.

'Well don't,' Hermie said briskly, 'just stand there like a stuffed doll, come in. NO, Putch, NO, not you.' The dogs licked her hand and obediently loped away. 'I'm particularly fond of dachshunds – they're the descendants of the very first pair I had, way back in the forties.'

Kay took hold of Hermie's arm but she twitched it off. 'I believe you said you
like dogs, dear?'

'Yes, and cats. Now this is quite something.' Kay stopped and stared,
absolutely riveted. In a corner of the verandah stood a massive, age-blackened
temple gong hung on an elephant's tusk.

'Ah. That's always a talking point.' Hermie didn't bother to conceal her
satisfaction. 'Everyone's fascinated by it. Listen!' She picked up the hammer
and struck the gong; the reverberation, pulsating, throbbing, vibrating, went on
and on and on and on, well after it was sounded, making the hairs on the back of
Kay's neck stand on end.

'It's astounding. How on earth did you come by it?'

'My husband acquired it in Rangoon but goodness knows how he managed to
ship it over here. But then, he was a very resourceful man.' She smiled at Kay
again and Kay noticed that her gait seemed miraculously to have improved.

They went into the sitting room that was immediately reassuring. It was
flooded with light; fresh flowers scented the air, and the sun glanced off bowls of
copper and brass set against pale pink walls. Invitation cards requesting the
pleasure of the company of Shrimati H. Hollingberry to this, that and the other
lined the mantelpiece. Large pastel sofas and chairs with silk cushions were
arranged on charming old rugs laid across well-scrubbed terrazzo, and a glass
panelled showcase held a set of blue and white Copenhagen porcelain. There
were some pictures, amongst them two landscapes - one an Indian scene with
reds and browns and yellows, sun bleached and strong - the other unmistakeably
English, moss green and greys, cool and limpid. Kay looked enquiringly at
Hermie.

'That's a corner of Wiltshire where I was brought up,' Hermie said fumbling for
the cigarette box on a carved, side table which held a cluster of silver framed
photographs showing a tall, wiry man striking huntin', shootin' and fishin' poses.
There was the suspicion of a tear. 'That's the Colonel, my dear, late husband,
Hartley,' she added as if an explanation was called for, Kay thought amused.

Kay looked about her. Those ashtrays! She'd never seen anything like it
before, held as they were in the outstretched hands of two feet high, orangey-
scarlet shouldered and blue legged, wooden figures depicting Afro-Caribbeans in
tailcoats and knee breeches. Kay reached out and touched the bright uniform.

' Stop. You mustn't do that. 'Hermie said forcibly. 'I'll tell you why in a minute,' and Kay withdrew her hand as if scalded. 'Gopi, the bearer, takes a duster to them but he has strict instructions to be very careful not to over-handle.'

Kay felt uncomfortable. If the woman was this house-proud she wasn't going to be easy to live with.

Hermie's bright gaze roamed thoughtfully over Kay. 'I was told by someone who knows about these things that they were made in Germany in the 1930s by a man called Goldscheider, and if you were to run a Geiger counter over them, it would crackle like something gone berserk.' She laughed heartily at her own joke. 'That paint contains uranium oxide, which has a life of four billion years.'

Kay smiled at the unexpectedness of it. 'Well, thanks for the salutary warning, although it makes one wonder about the longevity of the craftsmen.' What other surprises did the woman have in store?

'Now won't you sit down? No, dear, **not** there. That's my chair.'

'And I'll sit here.' Without warning, Rahul had swung from out of nowhere. He stood at the door for a moment, surveying them, his hands in his pockets then crossed the room and stooped to kiss Hermie. 'Sorry I got delayed, Hermie. Well, well, Kay what a surprise.' His glance, more curious than hostile, touched her briefly. 'Hello again.'

'All the better to judge me,' Kay murmured, drawing a swift breath wondering what he was doing there. 'It's a small world. We simply must stop meeting like this.'

'So you two know each other?' Hermie's eyes flickered between Rahul and Kay. 'How very fortunate.'

'I wouldn't go as far as to claim we know each other,' Kay said sweetly. 'Let's just say we've met.'

Hermie's eyes snapped, demanding to know all. Intervening smoothly before Kay could give her own version, Rahul launched into a somewhat understated account of her arrival in Delhi. He looked decidedly pleased with himself.

'May I offer you a glass of sherry?' Hermie broke in.

'Thank you, I'd love that.'

Gopi, eyeing Kay with a very grumpy expression, poured a parsimonious measure from a crystal decanter and dumped the sherry glass beside her on a circular brass table. Hermie didn't seem to notice.

Kay put out a feeler. 'You and Rahul must be old friends.'

'Well,' said Hermie placidly, 'since Hartley's sad passing some years ago, Rahul has been kind enough to help me with all those tiresome business details which my husband invariably attended to.' She smiled. *Hermione dear, Hartley would say, don't you worry your head about a thing. It's a man's job.* And so I'm confident that Rahul is well equipped to sort out your little muddle.'

So that's why he's present - to help vet the applicants. Kay stirred in her chair but pushed aside her unease. 'Can you tell me something about the vacancy?' she heard herself asking conscious of Rahul sitting there in judgment, his fingers laced behind his head.

'Of course. How very remiss of me. That's surely why you're here.'

Question and answer ran its course. Kay talked about her qualifications and experience, and Hermie got onto the subject of pay that seemed adequate rather than generous, and other terms while they drank sherry and nibbled pakoras.

Hermie said genially. 'It's a live-in position and since I can't abide chopping and changing, the successful applicant must commit to at least a year after the initial three months trial period.'

'That's only what I'd have expected. After all it's a gamble taking in a complete stranger and you'll want to have some idea if it'll work out in the long term. And the successful applicant must be satisfied, too.'

The interview seemed to be going rather well, and Kay found herself warming to the older woman who was considerably less doddery and shrewder than she'd imagined. She prayed she'd be offered the post, and if it were as much Hermie's decision as she liked to make out, she was sure it was hers for the asking. Yet there was Rahul to contend with. She looked at him sideways. Rahul who sat there like a sheathed knife. She shut her eyes briefly against that look of him, nursing the hope that Hermie would trust her instincts and hire her.

'And how do you think your parents will view your going into service?' Hermie picked up some knitting from a basket by her chair.

There was an uncomfortable silence then Kay said brightly. 'I don't regard it as that. Mum has died although I looked after her for a number of years when she was an... invalid and Dad...'

'Yes, yes.' *Very conveniently dead,* Hermie thought, still quite unperturbed at the way she'd decimated her entire family to Hartley. 'Now, as you can imagine, there's a flotilla of excellent candidates, so cultivate patience. I'll get in touch when I've made a decision.' She took a perverse delight in concealing her approval of Kay's aura of calm efficiency, her fresh appearance and well-spoken, nicely mannered, educated ways and her own sense that here was the companion corresponding to her ideal.

'May I assume it won't be long before you notify me? I do have other plans.' Undaunted, Kay intended that Hermie should know that she couldn't be trifled with.

'Indeed.' She seemed stung by this gutsy display. 'Well, for your sake, I should certainly hope you've got other options lined up.'

Kay didn't shrink from Hermie's sharp gaze and stuck to her air of smiling independence.

'That will be all for the time being.' Hermie said abruptly.

Kay picked up her bag and glanced out of the window realising how rapidly the daylight had faded. 'Goodbye and thanks for seeing me. I look forward to hearing from you.' They shook hands but she ought to have remembered how fast Rahul could move.

'You stay put, Hermie. I'll see Kay out.'

As Kay preceded him onto the verandah, he said quietly, 'what the hell are you playing at?'

'I'm not playing.' They were now in the garden, walking towards the wide gate. She felt suddenly exhausted by the endless routine to justify herself. 'I'm deadly serious. I can't stay on in India unless I have a job.'

'I thought you'd just decided to make it a flying visit?'

'No,' she said sweetly, 'you decided that.'

He looked thoughtfully at her. 'The question is why the compulsion to remain here?'

'It's a beautiful country. I'm fascinated by it, and don't forget I was originally contracted to work here for two years. My life's planned round that timeline. So that's my reason for persevering.'

He stopped. 'Listen, ' he said more gently. 'Hermie is...inclined to be...difficult. Believe me, I know.'

'You mean she's a gorgon?'

'You said that. I'm just cautioning you that you won't find it easy caring for an old woman fixed in her ways.'

Kay felt the situation beginning to slip away from here. 'I don't expect I shall but I really do want to stay on. Just put my madness, if you want to call it that, down to the fact that I've fallen in love with India. I can't be the first person to, and I certainly won't be the last.'

'You will, at least, think about it carefully?'

'At the moment there's nothing to think about. Hermie hasn't offered me the post.'

'That's correct. She has made no promises, but if she asks for my advice, I will give it.'

Kay stared at him a little unhappily. 'I suppose you will.' She began to walk away from him.

What sounded like a bellow of rage from Gopi, who'd come running out, stopped her in her tracks.

'And another thing, Kay. You forget to ensure the auto-rickshaw wallah shut the gate behind him. Look at **that!**'

That was a plump cow lumbering through the flowerbeds cheerfully decapitating the mali's lovingly nurtured blossoms. Throwing Kay a dirty look, Gopi roared again and another servant bounded out and as Rahul and Kay watched, the two men, sweating and swearing, pulled, whacked and shoved the beast out onto the road before banging shut the gate.

'Much help you're going to be to a frail old lady,' Rahul remarked.

'I'm not psychic. How was I supposed to know that would happen?'

'It happens all the time.'

'Not in London, it doesn't.'

'Perhaps that's where you ought to be.'

Kay marched over to the mangled beds. 'It isn't a complete disaster. Once first aid's administered it'll be burgeoning again - a riot of colour.' She sketched a goodbye and hurried through the gate shutting it carefully behind her. She was in need of a good cry she told herself.

'You never know your luck.' Renee was encouraging as she heard all about it from Kay later that day.

A natural optimist, Kay brightened as a quotation from the great divine, Julian of Norwich, drifted into her mind. *And all will be well; all manner of things will be well.* She'd simply to believe that it would.

Rahul walked slowly back indoors reflecting on something that had suddenly occurred to him that here was his Kay problem neatly solved. But like any man he soft-pedalled his inclination.

'What do you think?' Hermie asked eagerly. She'd already made up her mind.

'Well,' Rahul began carefully, 'Kay's by far the most suitable. The testimonials I've seen for her are excellent, but when all's said and done, it's up to you.'

Hermie said nothing for a while, smoothing Putch's coat with a gentle hand then spoke in a rush. 'Since Hartley died I've really missed someone to talk to round the house. It has felt so dreary after the years of paradise.' She felt as though she'd been cast adrift. 'I'm not good at being on my own and I'm sure I could get on with that young woman. I'll call her tomorrow and sort out when we can rendezvous.'

'Call me Hermie.' She was Hermione to Hartley and HH and no one else. Mrs Hollingberry was a mouthful, she'd decided or rather Edith had told her roundly that she could hardly expect Kay to address her as that, or madam. After Hartley's death, Hermie told Kay, she'd sold the Jaguar and now took taxis everywhere as she didn't herself drive. And she'd resisted joining the mass exodus of the moneyed to south Delhi with its tedious shopping malls and unexceptional high-rise apartment complexes complete with private gyms and leisure facilities.

Hermie's staff, although it was nothing like the retinue Kay had seen wafting about Rahul's place, was introduced to her. At the top of the pecking order was Gopi, the stubby-nosed cook-bearer who'd been in the Hollingberrys service as long as Hermie could remember. Sweeper and part-time mali had joined the household a mere twenty-five years ago.

'Keep this safe.' As if they were the Crown Jewels, Hermie, with a flourish, entrusted to Kay the keys to the stores and drinks cupboard. 'You're custodian now. As to your other duties, they're really quite simple. Word processing my letters, supervising the servants, accompanying me to the shops and various social engagements, helping entertain my friends, this and that, and, let me think, anything else, oh yes, walking the sausages.'

Mod cons like a washing machine and dryer meant that Hermie had reluctantly dispensed with the dhobi with whom she'd secretly relished the weekly verbal shoot-outs, but then she'd re-hired him to load and run the machines and do the ironing so the clashes continued.

Kay's large bedroom with its own adjoining bathroom and verandah at the back of the bungalow had a view of a gnarled fig tree, which Hermie told her had never borne fruit.

Fanned by a milk-warm breeze, that evening they sipped drinks on the springy lawn beneath the diamond moon, in the glow of a blue shade, tasselled standard lamp, its long stem an old rifle barrel. Crickets rasped moths and winged insects danced thickly round the bulb.

'Here's what we do with the perishers.' Hermie said, jangling a hand bell and Gopi who had a lugubrious air and a permanent yellow duster over one shoulder, appeared with a brass bowl of water that he positioned beneath the light. Soon it was crammed with dead insects.

Kay's eyes widened and Hermie chuckled. 'An old trick and it never fails to work. They sense the light reflected in the water and dive down to investigate only to meet their doom.'

It suddenly occurred to Kay that she mightn't have made a wise move; the guesthouse had been a safe little haven that she'd been sorry to leave.

As if reading her thoughts, Hermie reached out a hand and patted her arm. 'I'm glad you're here.' Her face looked tired in the subdued light. 'I was becoming so bored with my own company and one simply cannot expect one's friends to dance attendance. They have their own lives to lead.'

The cobweb of foolish fears suddenly dissolved in Hermie's unexpected warmth and Kay gave a little inward laugh, slightly ashamed at her wild imaginings. 'Nothing has quite turned out as I expected, but I'm pleased we're both satisfied.'

Some day she knew she'd look back on this time and it would seem like an episode from a novel or even almost another life - one of those re-incarnations that Hindus believe in - and she wondered if the startling quality of India had that effect on all foreigners.

Kay's thoughts drifted to Rahul. *Is he with Vimla?* Until that moment she hadn't given him another thought. Careful, she reminded herself, you're on dangerous ground.

***

So this was the girl Hermie enthused about. Edith took in Kay's pleasing air of confidence, her casual yet well-pressed clothes and attractive face. She simply oozed wholesomeness - not unlike Hermie herself at much the same age - and seemed just the person to cheer Hermie up. And, with bags of attitude, to stand up to her – not seeming the sort to be easily browbeaten. That gave her an advantage for Edith knew Hermie well enough to realise that once she sensed your over-eagerness to please, there was no pleasing her.

Kay's impression of Edith was that of a silver-haired, tall, bony, sun freckled but still fresh complexioned woman, with a strong but not unattractive German accent, and piercing blue eyes. In black trousers and tunic, a Pashmina shawl thrown loosely round her shoulders, she seemed completely at ease with herself.

Edith herself had news – news that she couldn't share with Hermie. That day there'd been **that** telephone call. Shanthi, Edith's maid, knew the mem only too well not to disturb her when she was working. Yet the voice on the line was male, authoritative, the accent foreign. And not one she recognised, although possibly, *Umricun,* Shanthi's way of saying American. She tossed her oiled grey head. No way would she interrupt Edith mem for that dead loss, no-hoper neighbour of hers from down the lane, although he had his uses, she grudgingly admitted, like doing a spot of decorating or servicing the car, so she, Shanthi, couldn't be too rude to him.

'Phone mem,' Shanthi began in a wheedling tone from the doorway, which Edith had long since recognised as equivalent to *don't shoot me, I'm only the messenger.* 'Not knowing. New man.'

Edith knew her well enough to know that if it didn't sound important, Shanthi would never intrude. 'All right then, put him through.' Edith straightened up, still a supple figure, and reached for the telephone.

'Ms Müller? Edith Müller? Louis Addison here. You remember we wrote each other.'

Edith's right hand flew to her mouth, but she quickly composed herself. 'Of course. Greg and Martha's boy. How very nice of you to call.' She cast her mind back to the unexpected letter he'd written to her from Scottsbluff some months previously. He'd been non-committal, reminding her he was the son of the Addisons and that his next diplomatic posting was Delhi. Her response had been cordial and if he'd care to get in touch with her when he'd settled in, she'd be pleased to see him. It left the initiative entirely to him. Louis liked that. And now, it was common knowledge that he was the new American Ambassador to India and Edith sensed he'd expect her to know that. 'I hope you're enjoying your new assignment.'

'It's swell. I've got a great team, and everyone has gone out of their way to befriend me. Carolyn, my wife, will love it when she joins me in a few weeks time. She's gotten held up at home sorting out care arrangements for her Dad.'

Seldom an observer of protocol, Edith said, 'will you come to dinner? What day would suit you best?'

'I don't want to put you to any trouble. Tell me when it would suit you.'

Edith flipped through her diary. 'How does Friday sound?' She sensed a hesitation in his voice that suggested he wasn't prepared for anything so immediate.

'Uh huh...'

'If you'd rather we put it off for a while...'

After a moment his deep voice flooded back down the line. 'No, no. Thank you, that's really mighty kind.'

'I look forward to seeing you. We'll talk then and you can tell me all about yourself.' It was surprising how un-involved she could make herself sound.

'I'll bring the latest family pictures,' he promised.

'Goodbye for now.' Edith's hands were sticky on the receiver. It had been more of a shock than she'd ever thought possible. The past catching up with the present. She gazed unseeingly across the courtyard hardly aware of the outer stillness and the subdued light of late afternoon. Then catching sight of Shanthi peering curiously round the door, she said briskly. 'Don't just stand there young woman - there's work for you to do. Some serious bazaar-ing.'

Shanthi, well into middle age, tittered behind her hand, repeating parrot fashion, the shopping list Edith reeled off. She'd no need to jot it down - couldn't - she was illiterate, although Edith had tried her best to teach her. But there was nothing wrong with her mental arithmetic and that, and the fact that no one in the bazaar dared cheat her, was what mattered.

Shanthi stumped off and the translation abandoned, Edith poured herself a glass of Riesling. After decades the memories were as vivid as ever. A pregnant, sobbing, confused Hermie; the Addisons joy as they held the baby in their arms. And here he was now, as American as pecan pie, a husband and father himself. That mystical human cycle. Edith's thoughts wound back to Martha's newsy letters from rugged Scottsbluff on the route of the old wagon trails. They'd never hidden Louis' origins from him. He was the centre of their lives, as they were pivotal to his, the most loving, and loved, of parents.

Edith decided she wouldn't have Louis to dinner on his own, since she wasn't sure she trusted herself sufficiently to keep the past buried. And to invite Hermie was out of the question, although that malicious notion had entered Edith's head and hadn't been easily dispelled. Her urbane Parsi pupil who still came to her twice a week to maintain his fluency in conversational French and German was away in Zurich, practising what he preached: that money was a precious egg and should be placed in a warm nest. Amrita and Rahul? She rationalised that in the circles in which Rahul moved it was inevitable he'd get to meet the Ambassador. *Ah well.* She reached for the phone.

Amrita had a prior engagement, so that left Rahul.

'Addison was guest of honour at an inter-party Parliamentary function the other night. We conversed - not that it was a meaningful discussion - just the usual small talk, but I guess he's trained to remember a face. Thanks, I'd be pleased to join you.' It did cross his mind to ask Edith how she'd made Louis' acquaintance but he pegged back. That wasn't the sort of question he could put to her, who informal though she was, drew an invisible line between genuine interest and prying; one was never too sure where one was with her - she was continually shifting the goalposts.

Towards early evening that Friday, Edith riffled through her wardrobe, her heart beating furiously, wondering what the next few hours would bring. Her train of thought led to Parvati. Dear Parvati! How she'd have revelled in the secrecy and intrigue. They'd have sat up to the small hours in a lively post-mortem, Parvati gesturing dramatically with her trade mark bejewelled cigarette holder of hers and laughing that throaty, roguish laugh. Edith gave a deep sigh. How she missed her sparky friend. She sighed again, eventually deciding on a pair of grey silk palazzo pants with a co-ordinating silky knit V necked tunic top; she piled up her hair securing it with twin tortoiseshell combs, then checked the table setting, buried her nose in the vases frothing with pink roses and fern, saw to it that the white aperitif wine was chilling and the red was chambray-ing. And sent up a prayer that her rumpled, shambling neighbour wouldn't do a materialising act.

It was a starry night with a cool breeze, the moonlight turning the earthenware flowerpots into crocks of silver as a faint smell from distant cow-dung braziers floated across. There was a rumble of voices and Edith flew to the door, just in time to take over from Shanthi ushering in Louis bearing an enormous box of chocolates.

'Welcome!' Grasping his hand as if she was meeting an old friend after many years, Edith took in the well-cut clothes and the smooth, neat-featured face. 'Is this for me?'

'Indeed!' The grip of his big hand was strong. 'Who else?' His friendly brown eyes crinkled in a smile. His voice was pleasantly deep, the accent easy on the ears.

Edith controlled the urge to burst out and reveal all, so sympatisch did she find Louis even in those first minutes. 'I only ask, as once, with the presumption of youth, I was foolish enough to assume, wrongly so, that the gift borne, very much like your own, was intended for me. It wasn't and I don't know who was the more embarrassed - I or the poor gift bearer.'

'Allow me to put you out of your misery. It is yours to have and to hold.' His voice was pleasantly deep, the accent easy on the ears. 'And it's a privilege to be here.' He unbuttoned his brass-buttoned navy blue blazer worn with a pale blue shirt, silk tie, and dark trousers. He was strongly built and wider shouldered than Edith expected and taller than what she could recall of HH, with short, grey-flecked dark hair, a tanned square face that could pass for that of a Latino American, and a hard body that told of a liking for the outdoors and a striving for physical excellence. Something in the shape of his face reminded her of Hermie, and when he smiled it was though an electric shock jolted her for it was HH all over again.

But for all that Edith realised that no one who wasn't aware of Louis' true parentage could possibly make fresh threads of connection. His mannerisms, his outlook, were all his own, or rather she supposed the product of the Addisons who'd nurtured him, and the country he was raised in.

'What will you drink?' Edith asked.

'If you have it, Scotch on the rocks,' he said just like HH who'd been partial to it.

'Coming up, and make yourself comfortable.'.

He bent down to pat Andy, like his namesake, a golden cocker, taking in Edith and her surroundings with a practised glance, the genial expression never leaving his eyes. The Embassy security guys had checked her out before he'd called her. An unconventional past, a Communist sympathiser in her mis-spent youth but harmless enough now, with a surprising lack of skeletons. Clean, no known affiliations. But she was far from bland, he decided.

'This is a nice place.' Louis registered with some amusement the atypical colour scheme, the colonial roll-top walnut wood writing desk covered by a knoll of papers, and several clocks all telling different times.

'Off the beaten track, you mean. I like surprising people.' She felt comfortable with Louis who seemed to have inherited HH's easy manner.

He pointed. 'Those are rather striking pieces of contemporary art.'

'How clever of you to notice. This rather earthy pair is by the famous woman painter Sher-gil, who committed suicide in the early 1940s. But she'd already made her mark and now fetches dizzying sums. And over here's a Jamini Roy - easily recognisable by those elongated eyes. Those and that seventeenth century miniature of Lord Krishna and the milkmaids over on that wall and lots more were bequeathed to me by a dear friend who tragically died of burns.'

'And that charming little watercolour in that corner?' He went and stood in front of it for some minutes, examining a view of mountains towering over a rowing boat on a lake. 'Pastoral delights and so nicely done.'

Edith laughed. 'That's an early work by an obscure German.'

Louis bent forward to scrutinise the signature. 'You're too modest, Edith.' He was amazed at the dancing light, the quality of the brushwork.

'My bedroom's simply crammed with pictures. Now if I guess rightly, you're wondering how I can afford it!'

'No, not at all - ' he interjected lamely.

'Fear not, I'm no Matahari. When I started getting my German pension and my parlous monetary situation eased somewhat, I decided that occasionally I would ask the people for whom I did business to pay me by purchasing a painting of my choice. And no, I haven't lived to regret it. All of them are now household names, like...She reeled off a list. 'The contemporary ones are into installations and conceptual art now and I'm trying to get my head round that.'

'You don't say.' Louis was impressed by her shrewd eye and willingness to gamble. 'You and Mom exchanged letters for years. You know she kept everything. Yours to her and copies of hers to you. Lauren and I thought that published they'd make great reading. *Letters of a Scottsbluff Missionary to a German....*'

'Hausfrau? That I was never.'

He laughed. 'Come to think of it though there weren't all that many from you'.

'I couldn't compete with Martha's pace. Her accounts of life on the Mission were riveting and I longed for the next instalment. When she and Greg took you home they were just as exciting. Full of zeitgeist and happenings in America and on the range.'

He looked pleased and helped himself to a pakora as Edith checked on Shanthi.

She returned and Louis flipped open his smart phone 'My family,' he said with a smile, scrolling through the pictures.

'This is your wife, Carolyn, of course. She's very pretty,' Edith said honestly, staring at the lanky, rosy-cheeked blue-eyed blonde standing on the porch of a large ranch-style house. 'Was this taken at home?'

He leaned over her shoulder. 'Sure. That's upper Willana. Every window has a swell view of the ponderosa pine-clad Wildcats.'

Edith refilled his glass. 'And here are your boys, or rather your grown sons. Goodness, they take after your wife.'

'That's Bobby. He's a biochemist and Tyler - the terminator we used to call him – followed in his grandpa's footsteps and is a Pastor. They're pretty hot sportsmen.   Bobby's a fine high board diver - you should see him jack-knife - and Tyler yearns to win the Men's Singles at Wimbledon. And here's my sister Lauren who still models - now it's fashions for the mature woman- with her husband and their two daughters and son. All medics in Nebraska. Folks say we lacked Mom and Dad's sense of adventure.'

Edith laughed. 'India was a big adventure in those days. Did you get to visit it before this posting?' She wondered if like many adoptees Louis had sought to find his birth parents.

He gave her a long hard look. 'I vacationed here for about four weeks with the family about seven ago. The Union Church and Mission bungalow was much as Mom described. It was kinda strange seeing where I spent the first year of my life. Then we blitzed through the usual tourists spots and Rajasthan ending up in Walipur where we stayed in a heritage hotel that's part of an ancient palace. Of course, now I remember why it sounded familiar. Mom mentioned you had links with it.'

Edith's voice sounded strange to her. 'Oh, not for long. I just happened to do a bit of casual tutoring there.'

 Louis said slowly, 'Mom told me how you introduced Dad and her to me.'

Edith nodded, wondering what was coming next.

'I've never had the slightest urge to look beyond Mom and Dad. Lauren and I worshipped them. I've never wanted to trace my natural parents.' He paused. 'Who never sat by my bedside when I had gotten chickenpox. Who never swung me in their arms when I swam fifty yards for the first time.   As far as I'm concerned, Mom and Dad were my flesh and blood and I couldn't have asked for better.'

Edith, who'd half thought of showing him the letter written by Hermie to her and Parvati all those years ago, if he'd been at all interested, knew she must not. Louis hadn't chosen to open a closed book and it wasn't for her to do so. 'You were Greg and Martha's baby joy. They thought the world of you.'

Her sharp ears had picked up the sound of footsteps. 'Will you excuse me for a moment, Louis?   I think I hear my other guest.'

Smart casual in a preppy outfit not unlike Louis's own, Rahul's lips brushed Edith's cheek. 'You look sensational.' *She's certainly made an effort.*

He shook Louis's outstretched hand. 'Your Excellency, we met the other day. It's good to see you again.' He'd dismissed with contempt rumours circulating that the Ambassador was C.I.A.

Rahul was being very formal, Edith observed, a shade uneasily, but both men were smiling although very alert.

I might have guessed Edith would know the Leader of the Alliance For Progress Party (AFPP) Louis told himself, half listening to the small talk. She lives unpretentiously but knows movers and shakers. He couldn't make Rahul out. He was a cool customer, aloof, and Louis hadn't decided whether he liked him or not. He reckoned he wasn't the sort of man who'd be easy to get to know, or indeed if he wanted to. Louis turned to smile at Edith unaware of her inner tension. 'How do you know each other?'

Edith took a sip of white wine and said lightly, 'It's a long shaggy dog story...' The two men are so unlike, she thought greatly relieved yet even that did nothing to melt the uncomfortable feeling that rested like an iceberg in her stomach.

'...But a fascinating one,' Rahul put in. 'Edith joined the State service of Walipur and became a close friend of the Maharajah, my father.'

Louis wondered if friend was a euphemism for mistress but on reflection, decided it wasn't. *But why not?* He probed himself. Edith's Nordic looks would surely have attracted many an Indian man, princely or otherwise, yet he couldn't quite see her as arm candy. He searched his mind for the right word - sensible was not quite the right description. Free- spirited – yes, that's what militated against her being cast as mistress.

'What sort of man was he?' Louis remembered the lurid accounts he'd read of the dark and decadent lives of Indian princes.

Edith beckoned to Shanthi ostensibly to refill their glasses, but in reality to enable her to gather her wits together. Rahul's reference to HH nearly made her *say your father,* Louis, but she'd managed to check herself in the nick of time. And now here he was, innocent and unsuspecting, waiting expectantly to hear about the man who'd sired him. She nearly choked on her drink and wondered at her recklessness at having brought the two together.

'Are you all right?' Louis asked solicitously.

'Just a frog in my throat.' Edith quickly recovered herself and said with a smile, 'HH loved life. It was a great game to him, even when he matured and developed with the passing years. And he had a way with people - a special knack you might say. So like the two men beside me,' she couldn't resist adding slyly.

Shanthi announced dinner and in the old fashioned, courteous way of HH, Louis took Edith's arm and escorted her through an archway into the inter-communicating dining room. Shanthi had her faults but they didn't lie in her cooking, and Louis who disliked spicy and chilli hot food was pleasantly surprised, for it was neither, being deliciously tasty and aromatic, and the Mughlai chicken butter-soft in his mouth.

Steered by Edith, the conversation moved on to more general matters.

'Walipur's blessed with a splendid new foreign-owned chemical plant that has created a new era of employment and prosperity,' Louis observed.

Rahul frowned and rapped the table with his knuckles, and Edith stiffened. 'Do you know what you're saying?' He sharply set down his knife and fork. 'It's environmentally questionable, potentially lethal and one day it'll cause a humanitarian disaster. I've been campaigning for years to have it shut down but to no avail.' He was jabbing his forefinger at Louis who suddenly realised he'd lit a fuse. 'But as it's quite impossible to say anything about the management without risking a defamation suit, I shall say no more.'

'But if the facility is as unsafe as you claim surely the government would de-licence it?'

Rahul snorted. 'The government either doesn't care or it has been bribed or bamboozled. The company that runs it said it was introducing superior technology that why it's allowed to continue operating.'

Both men fell silent. 'And you also oppose the Party - the Congress Party - that your father joined and represented?' Louis leaned forward interested to know what had driven the son in a different direction from HH.

Rahul shrugged as if the answer was obvious. 'Oh,' he said dismissively, 'the Congress with its moribund ideas, its mediocre henchmen and tottering economics. Do you know that in fifty years, its policies made twenty million people homeless? And its dubious, profligate and grandiose schemes at the expense of education, health care, human rights and civil liberties. But I'm glad to say that the voice of my party- the AFPP- is being heard in the land.'

He sees himself as the saviour and redeemer of India, Louis thought.

'That was quite a little speech. I could almost have written it myself,' Edith said lightly knowing that, at least, in part, she had as Rahul's occasional unofficial speechwriter. She'd lived her thwarted political ambitions through HH and now through his son.

They moved on to talk about jazz as Shanthi served mango ice cream and eventually Edith asked 'anyone for coffee?'

Louis glanced at his watch and rose to his feet. 'I'm afraid I must head home. There's an official delegation arriving in the morning that calls for me to be up early, bright and bushytailed. But I've had a very enjoyable evening, Edith, thank you very much. We're sure to meet again, Rahul. I look forward to that. '

Rahul was helpless against Louis' good-heartedness. 'Yes, so should I.' He suddenly realised that he meant it.

'By the way, Edith,' Louis turned at the door. 'I meant to ask. On the way over, I passed a rather imposing mansion - I think it was called *Parvati Niwas* - where a cultural function was in full swing. What do you know about it?'

So he'd noticed. Edith gave him full marks. If only he knew. 'Its literal meaning is abode of Parvati - quite simply Parvati's House - and she was the friend who left me those pictures.' She told Louis as much as was necessary. 'Even in retirement she maintained her interest in music and dancing.' *Not untrue,* Edith told herself. 'And bequeathed the bulk of her not inconsiderable fortune to establish a Foundation For The Performing Arts. One of these days you shall be my guest. I'm a trustee and on the receiving end of more tickets than I can possibly use.'

'I'd like that,' Louis said promptly, meaning to participate fully in India's rich cultural heritage.

Edith and Rahul walked Louis up to the mouth of the lane where his official limousine, which had drawn the usual crowd of gawkers, was parked. 'Goodbye and thanks again.'

A strong desire to be by herself with a very stiff drink suddenly possessed Edith and bundling Rahul off with scant ceremony, she acknowledged to herself that the evening had been more of an ordeal than she'd anticipated. Two men so different from each other she could never have imagined.

***

The cane chair creaked as Kay settled herself in it beneath a neem tree and she found herself glancing across to a few yards away where a trap had been laid with a large wedge of cheese. For the last few days it hadn't lured a single mouse but now, as Kay lazed with eyes half-closed, a bushy tailed, grey striped squirrel scampered down the tree and minueted round the trap, occasionally pausing to glance about for predators. Its antics made her laugh out loud.

'Grinning like that, talking to yourself, is a sign of incipient madness,' Hermie called out from the verandah.

'You've scared him off. And don't be so hasty- I'm not ready for the funny farm - yet. Give me a few more weeks here though and I might qualify.'

Hermie chuckled. Servile her companion was not. Nor, in those orange-splashed trousers and aubergine shirt, was she a woman that let colour frighten her .

There was the noisy sound of a gear change. 'Hark, my wheels. Now grab hold of Putch and Suzie. I've known them to chase me as far as Connaught Place.' Hermie got into the taxi and the driver battled to Edith's.

Kay hung onto the dogs till she judged that Hermie was well on her way, then watched as they bounded across the lawn like rabbits. They looked set to carry down the road and she breathed a sigh of relief when they suddenly pulled up at the gate.

She took stock of the last few weeks as companion to Hermie who'd revealed herself as someone accustomed to getting her own way, a meticulous observer of out dated standards of etiquette, very domineering and inclined to be testy and obsessive in the way she filled her life with various diversions.

Life fell into a loose routine - bridge mornings, beauty salon, the garden (where mali was Hermie's proxy), the ladies' weekly luncheon circle, her knitting and soft toys, the club - *oh how she went on about the club* - a round of golf - a sport Kay heartily detested but was constrained to learn to keep Hermie company- a few sets of tennis, the endless feuds with committee members, all these and more kept her permanently on the go like an electronic toy.

Kay wondered if Hermie's energy levels were cultivated to fill the void left by Hartley but came to the conclusion that she must always have been like that. And, try as she might, she'd not succeeded in penetrating Hermie's reticence about the pre-marriage years. Kay hadn't known any elderly people, who'd needed much persuasion to reminisce fondly about their youth, but Hermie was different and she suspected that somehow her chance of a college education had got derailed. But there was a canny seam running through Hermie who didn't miss a beat.

Having spent the last few weeks observing the servants domestic routine, Kay considered that more than a few matters had slid that wouldn't have passed

Hermie's eagle eyes had Hartley been alive. It wasn't entirely surprising- grief had given way to indifference when there was no Hartley to enjoy life with her. The staff was indolent, careless and unpunctual. It was high time the domestic arrangements were reviewed and she, Kay, resolved to introduce a new regime. She asked Gopi to assemble the servants in the sitting room and took a seat on the sofa facing them. She knew no Hindi but was aware that Gopi, if not the others, sweeper, dhobi, and mali had an adequate understanding of the English language.

She smiled . 'As you know, memsahib (she used Gopi's form of address to Hermie as he'd never got around to calling her by the more modern madam) has put me in charge of the household.' Her gaze flickered to Gopi whose face was wooden. Mali gazed into the garden, sweeper and dhobi exchanged glances. 'I want to make it clear that this will be a well-managed house that memsahib can be proud of. All expenditure will be accounted for and good reasons will be expected for any deficiencies.' She made it clear she was running the show. 'Now let me remind each and every one of you of the precise nature and extent of your duties that you all appear to have forgotten, and the standard to which you're expected to perform them.

She spoke to each of them in turn. 'You're well paid so I expect you to make memsahib's money work for her. For instance...' Kay got up and went over to the mantelpiece and ran a finger along the top of it. 'This hasn't seen a duster in days and that mirror should sparkle and doesn't. And why hasn't the water in these vases been changed?' She was well into her stride. 'Then there's the lawn that should have been mowed last week and the table napkins haven't been properly ironed and folded. It won't do.' She tapped her foot with annoyance.

Gopi stepped forward, his face now brick red under his dark complexion. 'I'll see to it.'

'Yes. Do that.' Her confidence was growing. 'Anyone who isn't happy to do better is free to go.'

There was a faint collective gasp and Gopi shot her a malevolent look. Kay was determined to end the run of bad habits, and it would take more than an ancient retainer to stop her. 'And for several days running, breakfast tea has been stewed and dinner plates unheated. Be assured that this will stop.'

There was a pause then Gopi said, 'Will that be all, madam?' in a tone that bordered on the insolent.

Kay kept a grip on herself. 'For the time being, yes. Would you fetch me the hisaab book and a pot of coffee.' She dismissed the staff crisply and congratulated herself on having made such an excellent start. There'd be no more slacking; there'd be a time and motion study; there'd be sound stewardship - there'd be an accounting for every packet of tea and coffee; every bag of daal, of sugar, of flour, of rice, every tin of ghee, every kilo of lamb, every bottle of sherry that was emptying at an alarming pace. It would be the best-run household in Delhi.

***

The weeks passed and there was a chilly nip to the nights. Kay's frustration in tracking kin mounted steadily. Exploring Ajeemkot meant taking time out to which she was as yet scarcely entitled and she hesitated to approach Hermie for any special favours, knowing she would only freak out and demand, and expect, an explanation, or conclude that Kay was neglecting her duties. It was difficult to keep secret anything, however trivial, from Hermie who wasn't averse to asking direct questions yet Kay resolved that, for the time being at any rate, she'd keep her own counsel.

She'd logged on to www.Ajeemkot.in only to be confronted with a line of men toting tools and a cheery message dated several years earlier: WELCOME! SITE UNDER CONSTRUCTION! PAY US A VISIT AGAIN VERY SOON! Rahul must have known about that she concluded sourly.

***

Kay had told Renee about Suresh and they'd had a good laugh. 'His Dad's a rich but stingy fellow,' Renee declared. 'I'm surprised **he** didn't ask for your hand - he was widowed a few years ago. Perhaps he reckoned he'd fork out less for that idiot Suresh. Son in England married to British citizen and he'd spin some sob story and apply to settle down there as a dependant relative pleading compassionate circumstances. That's his idea, the old rogue.' She added, 'Make sure your price is high.'

Kay leaned forward. 'Suresh is bombarding me with texts and emails. From messages of undying love he's regressed to hard porn.'

'Aha, cyber bullying. Are you going to tell Rahul?'

Kay did, out of a sense of mischief, and Rahul nearly lost it. 'That behnchote. Do you want me to hit him with a restraining order? I reckon he concocted the missing handbag scenario. Do you know, he was engaged to be married but was spotted in the red light district so the girl's parents called it off. Not surprisingly, since then he has been on the marriage circuit with no takers and now preys on unsuspecting European targets. He had enrolled as a student on some bogus two-

266

year business administration diploma course in London, worked in breach of visa conditions and overstayed. UK Immigration Officers nabbed him working illegally in an Indian takeaway and he was ordered to leave England. He jumped bail and went to ground until he was arrested a year later when he claimed asylum, pleading that as he was gay he was at risk of persecution in India.'

Kay laughed. 'He's nothing if not determined. What happened then?'

'Well, that didn't get him very far. He's such a plonker he couldn't remember the tale he'd bought off the peg and when he was interviewed his account was so riddled with discrepancies, inconsistencies and contradictions that he was found not to be credible. But he played the system. Exercising appeal rights gave him a further eighteen months in England but eventually even this was exhausted and he was deported at British taxpayers' expense. He has been denied a visa ever since.' He paused. 'You aren't serious about the offer are you?'

'Perhaps he has reformed. It does happen, you know.' Kay's tone was teasing.

'He's semi- criminal,' Rahul said derisively.

***

'Amrita has invited me to their Divali shindig,' Hermie announced one evening as they watched a rowdy game-show on TV, or rather Hermie did, for not only did she never relinquish possession of the remote but she was an addict of such things, brought to them courtesy of the consumer liberalism that gripped the country. She gestured negligently at the expensively designed invitation addressed to Shrimati H. Hollingberry propped up prominently on the mantelpiece. 'And she has graciously consented to your accompanying me.' Hermie made it sound both like a Royal Command and as though Kay would be there on sufferance.

The truth was that Hermie's social life, which had nose-dived since Hartley's death owing to her reluctance to go anywhere on her own, had, since Kay's arrival, resumed its manic pace. She now socialised non-stop, and enjoyed it all the more with that token someone by her side. Not that she actually needed Kay there - Kay was quick to recognise that - indeed, she invariably ignored her. And Kay can scarcely, Hermie told herself, be compared with Hartley's staunch, chivalrous company but, nevertheless, Kay's presence, seen but not heard, was decidedly preferable to enduring on one's own. She was a useful and decorative trophy, a credit to Hermie's good sense in choosing quality.

'How kind of her.'

Hermie flashed Kay a sharp look. She couldn't make the girl out at all. Kay was polite but didn't seem at all grateful. She sighed. Well, she supposed society was not easy on single females, whereas single men... Her thoughts flew to Rahul and Vimla. Pity about that...young Kay would be a better match, but Amrita would go ballistic. Even now she could almost hear the Rajmata's rant. *My boy marrying out? Over my dead body!* Besides, men like her precious Rahul didn't marry penniless girls, however pretty. Hermie pulled herself up short. *No, wiser not to meddle in that. Remember what happened to me and HH? Stop it. Looking back is the one luxury I've never been able to afford.*

'Sorry, dear...what did you say?' Hermie was suddenly aware that Kay had addressed a remark to her.

'Tell me about Divali.' Kay rubbed a shod foot against Suzie's rump and she wagged her tail with pleasure.

'The festival of lights. Light triumphing over darkness, good over evil. Rama's return from exile after vanquishing the demon Ravana. It's quite an occasion and if ever there's an excuse to pull out the stops this is it.'

Kay fell silent, wondering how she could live up to it. She had nothing grander than the cocktail dress she'd worn on that first night. But she did possess a sleeveless black silk dress with a cleavage-skimming neckline that she'd run up herself and it looked wonderful against her flawless skin and shining silken hair that fell in soft tendrils to her shoulders. Inserting the dangling silver filigree earrings bought in Chandni Chowk, Kay's reflection told her she looked divine.

It was the night of the new moon, a wedge of melon high in the sky. From the garden, as far as the eye could see, Delhi was ablaze with trees strung with golden necklaces of light. Every rooftop was adorned with myriads of little clay diyas illuminating the paths of departed souls re-visiting old homes. The still air pulsed with the flash and boom of fireworks.

'It's amazing how Divali almost coincides with Halloween.' Kay, balancing on her knees a large gift-box of sweetmeats, sat beside Hermie in a taxi en-route to the Ratan Singhs.

Delicately perfumed, elegant in a pale gold brocade two-piece, all at once, Hermie suddenly felt very old and vulnerable. *What does the future hold?* She'd never felt so alone in years. HH had been her sun, but like Icarus she'd flown too near and got burnt. But always there'd been Hartley - wonderful, precious moments with dear Hartley who'd wrapped her in care and comfort. Hartley who was the moon and the stars. And before that it was Ma who let her dream her fairy tale dreams. She saw Ma's face again, dreadfully hurt by Hermie's going, but determined to be brave. *If only I could hold Ma's hand again and hear her voice.* Hermie felt her eyes pricking with tears and she fumbled in her bag for her lace handkerchief. *Keep it together and stop wallowing in self-pity*, she told herself sternly. Then, quite unexpectedly, she found herself reaching for Kay's hand and gave it a quick squeeze.

'Isn't it a sensational? And you'll soon witness for yourself what always makes the Ratan Singhs bash such a sparkler...'

Kay gave a good-humoured groan.

'When all's said and done, I'm bound to confess that I honestly prefer Divali. You don't get all the terrorism of trick and treat.'

Kay's appearance had unleashed in Hermie a sense of magnanimity and she'd surprised herself by lending Kay her Tibetan silver choker for the occasion. 'This is one of those nights when women raid their jewel boxes so I can't have you looking like a poor servant,' she'd told her rather dismissively.

Long before they'd reached the Ratan Singhs stylish house it shimmered a welcome. The taxi turned into the driveway; every inch of the verge was lined with tiny twinkling diyas, the shrubbery glowed like a burning bush, lighted by strategically hidden miniature candles.

Looking very regal, Amrita and Rahul stood on the lawn greeting guests. Hermie, who'd seemed to Kay a little weepy earlier, had overcome whatever had precipitated her tears for she was out of the taxi in a trice, arthritis forgotten, and was sailing past Kay to vanish into a circle of cronies.

'Good evening,' Rahul said coolly, inclining his head. 'I hope our Divali party will be a new experience for you.'

His formality rather surprised Kay who'd hoped for a little more warmth from him.

'I'm sure it will be,' she replied just as coolly and without haste strolled in the direction of a softly lit shamiana drawn by the ring of laugher and the buzz of conversation.

Guests eddied around like flocks of beautiful birds, making and savouring, the latest social and political gossip. Drinking, joking, flirting. The clink of crystal. The scent of roses. The gleam of fluted silver dishes. The silkiness of napery. A uniformed servant filled her glass, heaping her plate with a variety of Indian and international delicacies from a damask covered buffet table. It was, she realised, the sort of swanky do that came naturally to the Ratan Singhs.

But it was the music that intrigued her most - the rhythms of another cultural heritage that sent strange shivers down her spine. Intrigued, Kay made for a section of the shamiana set aside for the instrumentalists, seated cross-legged on a thickly carpeted dais, wearing traditional dress.

'They're playing a raga, which is a special kind of melodic pattern of descending and ascending movements based on variations of scales,' a familiar voice whispered in her ear and looking over her shoulder she met Rahul's faintly ironic smile. 'I thought you might need a code-breaker.'

For some time after she'd left him, he'd stayed where he was, wondering if he could have been a little more cordial, then had slowly followed her and was caught up in the partying, but still very conscious of her and the natural charm of her ways.

'Then you've a flair for mind reading, so I wait to be enlightened.'

'It would take a lifetime to explain.'

I haven't got as long as that,' Kay laughed. 'I'm only here until next year.'

'There're literally thousands of ragas, all associated with different times of the day and night, the seasons and ceremonial occasions. You wouldn't play a morning raga at nightfall or an evening raga at dawn. It would be, and sound, utterly inappropriate.'

Kay stood for a few minutes listening to the poetry of the plaintive notes, and Rahul found himself moved by the delight on her face.

'It's extremely potent,' Kay said at last. 'Am I hearing things or is that a droning sound of sorts?'

Their eyes met, the music swelling gently round them below the silver swathe of the moon. The scented night sharpened by the whiff of cordite mingled with the sound of the cicadas and the whisper of the breeze. Rahul leaned towards her and she felt his breath on her neck.

'You're not hearing things. He's plucking the tamboura - that five stringed guitar - that emits the characteristic drone which underlies our music.'

'It takes getting used to,' Kay said faintly when the raga came to an end.

'It's an acquired taste, yes. As are the sound of bagpipes.' His eyes were teasing. 'So for once we're in agreement.'

Other music lovers trickled towards them and a friend caught up with him. Kay slipped away, yet his presence lingered as she mixed with other guests. The men attentive, the women parading new clothes - all bombarded Kay with some intense questions about her personal life which she deftly dodged, but which she realised were only kindly meant. *Are you married...? When are you going to settle down...? How much do you earn...? How many children will you have? ...Do you like Rahul...?* Amused, Kay took it all in good heart, yet inexplicably as she listened to the chatter and gazed at the circle of foreign faces, in spite of the warmth and goodwill, she was beset by a sudden wave of homesickness.

Have I really done the right thing attaching myself to Hermie? That Kay herself was prone to impulses she knew and it was not the first time, and possibly not the last, she told herself ruefully that sudden inclination had got her into situations that cool reflection could have avoided. At that moment she'd have given anything to have Yvonne beside her.

'Enjoying yourself?'

Kay's melancholy lifted at the sound of Rahul's deep voice. 'You're the expert, so tell me about Divali.'

' You really want to know?'

'I do - I'm interested in all your customs. I want to know about your country, and its people. It isn't, I would have thought, particularly surprising.'

Rahul's face lit up. 'Divali's a time to start afresh; a time of hope, renewal and optimism for all, especially traders and businessmen. Books are balanced, farmers weigh their harvest and people make a reckoning of how much they've made - or lost- during the year.' He lit a cigar and encouraged by Kay's rapt expression went on. 'That's why Lakshmi, the goddess of wealth, is special at this time. We leave on lights in the hope that she'll visit every home, but we also remember to thank her for past help and pray to her for a prosperous new year.'

'I could certainly do with a few favours from Lakshmi,' Kay said softly.

Rahul raised his eyebrows. 'Like what? '

Kay smiled and he didn't press it.

He pointed. 'Watch that! Isn't that just one amazing Catherine wheel? You know, I've watched some of the most sophisticated firework displays all over the world, but none compares with a Divali show put on by even the most humble of Indian homes.'

She'd not realised that whilst they'd been talking, he'd taken her arm and led her to a quiet corner of the house by the verandah.

'The display's getting into its stride. This is the best vantage point – something to do with the angle of configuration. I discovered that quite by chance just after the house was built and I've kept the secret to myself ever since.'

'And I'm the repository of the secret?' Kay's eyes followed a rocket streaking electric blue. 'Goodness, I'm honoured.' She wondered what had prompted the disclosure.

Looking down at his shoes, Rahul said quietly. 'I really wanted to tell you this before, but I haven't had the opportunity -'

'Oh?' Kay wondered what was coming.

'I've known Hermie for ages but she seems so much more cheerful since you joined her. Mother and I had been worried about her.'

'Hermie has always seemed a very positive person to me - '

' -well, in fact Hermie has told Mother how surprised and delighted she is that the bunderbust's working out so well.'

'You'll have to translate. My Hindi's non-existent.'

'Arrangement.'

In the dim light, Kay couldn't read his expression. 'I'm glad of that,' she said slowly feeling oddly at a loss for words. 'I've been trying hard. Thanks for letting me know'.

There was a sudden lull in the eye-dazzling swooshing and spinning that lashed the dark sky and it seemed to magnify that strange rustle Hermie had detected earlier from the trailing bougainvillea overhead. She sensed, rather than saw, a furtive movement.

Suddenly Rahul gripped her arm and said in a rapid undertone. 'Snake.' He placed a hand on her shoulder. 'Freeze.' Then he'd turned and bounded into the house.

Kay felt her veins turn to ice, her throat tightening. After what seemed a lifetime but was probably no more than a minute, Rahul emerged grim-faced, with a shotgun. He steadied the butt against his shoulder, took aim and fired. A thin black snake slid to the ground and while it was still writhing, he fired again, the crack of the shot muffled by a crescendo of fireworks.

Kay's stomach twisted inside her and then hot tears were streaming down her cheeks.

'That's the end of the killer krait,' Rahul said calmly. He put his arm round her shoulders. 'You're okay now.'

Kay felt herself gently piloted inside. She sank into a chair, and he was pressing a glass to her lips. She was shaking so much that her teeth chattered against it.

'Drink up,' he urged. 'It's brandy. You'll feel a lot better.'

His face was a blur. She took a large gulp and the fiery liquid made her gasp, and she burst into tears again.

'Hush Kay, it's all over now.' Rahul passed her his handkerchief. 'Here. Mop up and we'll re-join the party or they'll be getting ideas.' He tried to sound light hearted.

Things gradually steadied round her. 'I wasn't prepared for that kind of snake charmer. I t-t-t t-thought they came quietly, curled up in baskets, not dangling from roofs.'

'It's seldom they make it into town, but it does happen. They sneak in from the countryside but they're normally spotted and killed before they get this far.'

'If you hadn't been there...' Kay's voice trailed off.

'You'd have been carted away in a coffin. It can kill a horse in thirty minutes flat.' Rahul was holding her hand. 'But I was and you're very much alive and it's dead. Cold, stone dead.'

In that moment of terror, he'd made her feel safe and secure.

'Kay...' he began, then as Hermie burst in he quickly slipped his hand from hers but the gesture hadn't escaped Hermie.

'My dear, where've you been hiding yourself? You simply mustn't go charging off when I may need you.' Belligerence changed to consternation when she observed Kay's pallor. 'Has something happened? You look distrait.'

Rahul explained and Hermie's mouth dropped open. 'If anything had happened to you, I could never have forgiven myself.'

'I'm fine now.' Kay mumbled. 'But if you don't mind, I think I'll go home.'

'Yes, you do that and don't you worry about me. I'm having the time of my life, but you must go straight to bed. Make sure Gopi brings you a hot milk and turmeric drink. That'll get the shock out of your system and don't wait up for me.'

Hermie ambled off to rejoin friends. *Rahul seems to have everything under control and poor Kay has had the fright of her life but mercifully she's unhurt, so there's no point in fussing.*

Hermie didn't surface until after noon the following day, complaining she was suffering from migraine. Edith, who'd had enough of Ratan Singh Divali parties to last a lifetime, had made her excuses and stayed away. She'd dropped in on Hermie on her way to a meeting and looked sceptical when Kay told her of Hermie's condition but said nothing. It wasn't migraine, Edith suspected, although Hermie dignified it as such, but pure and simple hangover.

As they waited for Hermie to appear Kay told her about the krait.

'I'm surprised you didn't pass out. After all these years in this country I still can't abide the slimy beasts. Once, under protest, I went on shikar with Hermie and Hartley and woke to find some sort of snake curled up beside me. Not quite the pillow talk one's used to. I was literally struck dumb with shock and didn't regain my voice for 24 hours.' Edith shuddered at the memory of it. 'You're made of sterner stuff.'

Kay giggled. 'You must have dined out on that for weeks.' Edith didn't strike her as the hysterical sort. Very likely she'd have given her un-invited bedfellow a thorough whacking and tossed it out of her tent before settling down again for the night.

'Have you got over it?'

Kay nodded. 'Although I still feel jumpy.'

Gopi entered with a pot of tea and one of coffee. 'I'll pour,' Kay said ignoring the black look he gave her for he didn't like what he considered her usurping of Hermie's prerogative.

Hermie eventually emerged and tottered into a chair. She leaned back, head against the crocheted chair-back. She picked up her knitting and could choose or not, as she pleased, always a distinct advantage, to look at Edith. For a moment there was no sound but the rapid clicking of needles.

'I gather you've met the American Ambassador, whatshisname... Edith,' Hermie said coolly, her meaning needing no explanation. News of the supper had reached her from Amrita and she was determined to find out why Edith had excluded her. Granted she wasn't invited to all Edith's dos, but she hadn't even known about this one until Amrita had casually let slip.

Edith took a sip of coffee before answering that one. She was a consummate practitioner of the half-truth. 'I'd heard he's a keen sportsman - ' she'd heard no such thing but improvised madly ' - and hoped to interest him in that street kids club.'

'Oh, so that's what it's all about,' Hermie had lost interest. 'Your pet charity. And do you suppose he'll dip into his pocket?'

'He will,' Edith said firmly, meaning to mention it to Louis and wondering if he'd inherited Hermie's tight fistedness.

'Thumbscrews or the rack?' Hermie said innocently and Edith laughed, rather more heartily than usual, and more out of relief than amusement. It was testing her resolve not to blurt it all out to her friend.

'That reminds me,' Hermie sat up in her chair. 'Do you remember that middle-aged American couple who helped themselves to those much prized, rare first editions from our library and jetted off with them?'

The books were part of a valuable bequest by an Englishman to Sivalik Library who, coming up to the hill station in 1915, had been bewitched by it and spent the rest of his life there.

'The husband and wife who called themselves vacationing tree huggers but were actually rapacious antiquarian book dealers?' Edith nodded, fear clutching her heart. She knew what was coming. 'How could I forget?' The incident had sparked outrage in Sivalik.

'Well, you know I'd been writing chasers to them to no avail and in the end had to involve the American Embassy? The last Ambassador promised faithfully to do all he could to recover our precious property, but he was recalled before he could make much headway.'

'Yes, that was a pity.'

'So, as the new man has probably inherited his predecessor's in-tray, I shall remind him in no uncertain terms to honour the undertaking.'

With a little sound that Kay could make nothing of, Edith said coolly. 'I'm sure he'll do his best but shouldn't you leave it awhile - till he's got his feet under the desk?'

Hermie didn't like being told what to do. 'That's a matter for my discretion.'

Kay with her head buried in a book hadn't missed the exchange or the slight drop in temperature between the two women, who were obviously good friends, and Edith, glancing across caught her little puzzled frown. What would she make of it?

CHAPTER 19

Bundled up in a thick cardigan, Kay walked Putch and Suzie along stony ground at the rear of the bungalow to the clump of banana trees that screened it from the servants' quarters.

'Coo-ee, coo-ee!' Hermie's strong voice wafted across the compound.

'Coming.' Kay waved and strolled back indoors with the dogs.

'Chop chop!' Hermie was, as always, rushing madly at things. 'We'll use a new pack of cards, and make sure the pencil's sharpened. The score pads are in that bottom drawer.' Gopi had set up the bridge table in a corner of the sitting room allowing a pleasing view of fragrant evergreen shrubs and creepers trailing harmoniously along the garden wall.

Amrita and Renee arrived separately, heading with almost religious zeal for the table. Kay was sufficiently attuned to Hermie's ways to realise that this wouldn't be a desultory game interspersed with salacious gossip but a serious match, played for high stakes. Hermie and Amrita, familiar with each other's tactics, were well armed for the fight, Kay thought ruefully, whereas Renee was an unknown quantity.

'Let's take a break.' Hermie suggested when after a few games, Renee had laid waste to the older women.

'I was hoping you'd say that.' Kay pushed back her chair and went into the kitchen, still unable to bring herself to summon Gopi with the hand bell. He was inclined to be, she thought with some bitterness, rather like Hermie, much given to moods, especially as she'd demonstrated herself equal to the challenge of tackling the servants' sloppiness and restoring efficiency. Yet, only a few days ago she'd again had occasion to reprimand sweeper for failing to hose down Putch and Suzie regularly and Gopi for the tarnished silverware and leaving cooked food out overnight on a kitchen shelf rather than in the fridge.

He listened to her crisply conveyed instructions in complete silence, pointedly turning his back on her, then after a while came into the room carrying a brass and enamel-ware tray, laden with freshly brewed coffee, a Madeira cake and assorted European style pastries that Kay had baked herself. His face bore a sullen expression and Kay knew why. Set in his ways, wedded to the ritual of the usual Indian savoury snacks for memsahib's bridge mornings and the cocktail hour, Sunday roast, and cake confined strictly to teatime, to add insult to injury, he was now expected to serve Forrester madam's creations that she'd personally prepared in her increasingly frequent incursions into his territory. His eyes spewed acid.

'Utterly delicious,' Amrita said, her fingers contemplatively poised between another meringue and a Danish pastry. 'It's fun to have something different for a change and I shan't count the calories.'

She probably never needs to, Kay thought. Her svelte form comes naturally, like her wealth and breeding.

'All Kay's doing.' Hermie usurped the compliment as a reflection on her own unerring choice of companion. 'And Gopi's delighted to make it his business to pick up a few more gourmet tips from her. Last weekend she simply shone with partridge partnered with couscous and mushrooms. And her pears with sesame seed nougat cream just have to be tasted to be believed. Who'd have thought that an uninteresting fruit like that could be transformed?' She bit into a chocolate éclair and the cream shot out. 'Go on, Renee, spoil yourself,' Hermie urged, delicately dabbing her mouth with a napkin that bore faint stains, Kay observed uncomfortably. She sighed inwardly. Yet another thing to raise with dhobi.

Renee tucked into a large slice of cake. 'You must give me the recipe Kay, if it's not a family secret.'

Kay laughed as she lifted the coffee pot. 'With pleasure. If that were the only family secret, I daresay I wouldn't be here today.'

The cryptic note hadn't escaped Renee whose thin, plucked eyebrows rose fractionally but at a sharp glance from Kay she bit back a comment.

'Shall we resume?' Hermie was keen to trounce the advantage held by Renee and Kay. They played on for a few minutes, the silence punctuated at intervals by Amrita's deep sighs.

'Come on, out with it. There's something on your mind and it's not this game,' Hermie prompted.

Amrita absently played a card. 'I've got to talk or I'll burst. To tell you the truth, I'm at a loss why my Rahul and his Vimla don't get married soon. Oh, how I long to hold my grandson in my arms.'

Amrita wasn't indifferent to Rahul's recent enhanced interest in Hermie's business affairs that seemed, after Kay's arrival in the household, to necessitate rather more visits to her than Amrita thought was strictly warranted. Up to that moment, he'd had to be cajoled, indeed almost bullied, by her into helping Hermie out. 'She's the girl for my Rahul, would make an ideal wife and mother and comes from a well-placed, well-off family. Rahul agrees she has all the right attributes yet...'

Hermie pursed her lips, 'he who hesitates is lost.'

Kay exchanged an amused glance with Renee; they were both agog, seeming not to listen, murmuring to each other.

'My sentiments exactly but you try telling my boy that. He says he's quite happy to wait until she has completed a post-graduate gynaecology course in the States and accepts she wants to be professionally fulfilled.'

'Well, I can't see that a couple of years would make a great deal of difference. She'll still be young enough.' Hermie said briskly. 'And surely marriage wouldn't thwart her plans? Lots of girls these days combine that with studies and motherhood.'

Amrita gazed unhappily into the middle distance.

It had become too exciting for Renee. 'They've been an item for ages, haven't they?' she chipped in.

Amrita froze her off with a long, cutting look, and then resumed her monologue as if she hadn't heard what she plainly regarded as Renee's flagrantly insensitive remark.

'Vimla is entirely suitable and to bring the two of them together took considerable time and effort on my part and on the part of Mrs Vohra, not least because my boy is so cynical and hard to please in these matters. I often wonder if we did the right thing by indulging his desire for a Western education.' Tapping her fingers together she leaned forward and Kay could see a gleam in her eyes. 'And Vimla comes with a very acceptable dowry indeed.' Amrita tempered the mercenary remark with a careless shrug. 'Not, of course, that that colours the situation since it's only a flea-bite compared to our assets...still, a good dowry is always a matter of the bride's family honour.' Her gaze of steely implacability flickering towards Kay told her she was out of the running.

A sharp snap sounded as Hermie broke an almond biscuit in half. 'The arrangement sounds entirely reasonable to me. I'm sure there're many girls who wish they'd had the same opportunities as Vimla.' She, Hermie, hadn't done at all badly for herself through dint of her own efforts. Self-made, although she'd die rather than admit as much. Didn't quite correspond to the memsahib image.

Amrita rummaged for her cigarette case and lit up. 'What's reassuring though is that they're comfortable with each other. She has the makings of an excellent daughter-in law so why don't the two of them get on with it?' Her back became ramrod straight and she expelled smoke fiercely. 'I'm sick and tired of reminding my boy that he has duties - a duty not only to himself but to the regal bloodline of Walipur to marry and beget - '

'- An heir and a spare - ' Renee met Amrita's hard gaze with a careless twinkle across the sudden charged silence.

'- a duty to me, his mother,' Amrita said in a tight voice drumming her fingers on the table, 'to accept that in such matters I know what's right for him. When I recall some of the females...' the word was uttered with contempt, '...that my Rahul has dated...' She shuddered slightly, her eyes lingering briefly on Kay who felt her cheeks flame.

Bitch! thought Kay cheerfully and said impishly, 'you could always acquire a kitten to curb your broodiness.'

Amrita was speechless. Hermie, her cup halfway to her mouth, gazed round-eyed at the girls. Eventually she said, 'don't let Vimla and Rahul sense your anxiety. You know how perverse the young can be. They'll find that they miss each other when Vimla goes abroad, that'll clinch it and you'll wonder why you spent all those nights, tossing and turning.'

The young! Kay muffled a giggle. Rahul and Vimla were hardly Romeo and Juliet.

'That's very consoling.' Amrita's harassed expression was seeping away. 'And you're right - nagging will only make Rahul even more wilful.' She reached for her hand.

They played on in semi-silence for some time, the bidding getting somewhat reckless as Amrita and Hermie sought to make up lost ground. But Renee and Kay powered to victory and Kay somewhat cheered by this, exchanged gloating glances with Renee as the older women, somewhat reluctantly, delved into handbags and paid their dues, Hermie obviously very miffed at having lost to a chit of a girl.

Bridge over, Hermie excused herself returning almost immediately with a board marked with letters of the alphabet, which she set down on the table. Kay had no idea what it was.

'Planchette,' Hermie enlightened her. 'Amrita and I are anxious to make contact.'

'I'm not sure I should. It's a sin to have truck with the spirits in this way,' Renee said uncomfortably, rising to her feet. 'The Catholic Church forbids it.' But it was obvious she was torn.

'Don't spoil it for us,' Hermie cried. 'I'll tell you straight. I've not known it to harm anyone. Ma...' She hastily corrected herself. 'My other friends are practitioners and we've gained some very comforting insights.'

Thus over-ruled, Renee sat down.

'We've got to get ourselves in the right receptive mood,' Hermie said. 'What hymn do we all know? Let me think...Yes. *Abide With Me.* You know Kay, it was invariably sung at Mahatma Gandhi's prayer meetings.'

'I'll do my best,' Amrita said as eager as Hermie to embrace the spirit world.

They all held hands round the table. Hermie nodded at Kay who started, hoping she'd pitched the right key, and the others joined in. When they got to *fast falls the eventide,* Kay saw the incongruity of it as they were singing in the noonday sun and started to giggle. Renee gave her a sharp kick under the table and they composed their faces and finished the verse, Hermie's voice quavering, Amrita half a syllable behind the others as she'd forgotten the words.

> *The darkness deepens, Lord with me Abide*
> *When other helpers fail and comforts flee*
> *Help of the Helpless, Abide with Me.*

Kay had launched into:

> *Swift to its close ebbs out life's little day*
> *Earth's joys grow dim; its glories pass away*
> *Change and decay in ...*

when Hermie held up a peremptory finger. 'Buss. That's enough. No need to over-egg the pudding. Now, I'll ask the questions,' she added firmly. 'Is there anybody there?'

The pencil slowly moved to the word YES.

Hermie shot a look of triumph at Kay. 'Who is it? Please give your name.'

Jerkily the pencil spelled out PARVATI.

'Oh my God!' Kay heard Hermie mutter under her breath. 'I know her.'

Amrita strained forward. 'Ask her what she wants.'

'Do you want to say something Parvati?'

The words HULLO HERMIE were spelled out.

'Well!' Hermie and Amrita nodded with satisfaction as if to say they were getting somewhere. 'Now is there anyone with you?'

A FRIEND.

Hermie whispered encouragingly, 'would you identify who it is?'

The initials HH appeared, rather wobbly.

'Oh!' Hermie and Amrita gasped in unison. Hermie put a hand to her mouth, and Amrita, a little overwhelmed, fumbled for a cigarette.

'No, no, you mustn't smoke,' Hermie said quickly. 'It disturbs the aura.'

There was, however, a slight problem. It wasn't clear exactly to whom HH was intended to refer. It could be Hartley; equally it could be HH. Both women obviously hoped it was for her.

'Is there a message for us?' Amrita's hands were trembling.

Hermie put the question with tightly closed eyes, praying the answer would mean more to her.

I AM NOT FAR AWAY.

Amrita and Hermie turned to each other.

'So heartening,' Amrita said, putting up a hand to brush away tears.

'A great comfort, I swear I heard his voice,' Hermie said overcome with emotion 'See girls, how happy it's made us.

Kay didn't like to say that she thought it was all tosh and utterly inconclusive. Feeling a little sorry for the other women who she'd never have dreamt could be so gullible, she shot a glance at Renee, who'd stuffed a hanky into her mouth, for inspiration.

'Look, it hasn't finished. There's more to come, ' Amrita said in a voice that masked excitement.

The letters KF and RRS were described.

Hermie frowned in bewilderment. 'What do you think that signifies?' She and Amrita stared at it for several moments.

'Someone's initials, obviously,' Renee piped up.

'Or a code of sorts. Hmm...' Suddenly Amrita's eyes narrowed and her breath came a little faster.

'What do you think it could be?' Hermie said quickly.

There was a pause then Amrita shook her head. 'I don't know, it's rather vague.' Her tone was flat.

'I'll ask. The spirit's bound to know.' Hermie's voice was excited. She shut her eyes again and kept them shut for several moments while she questioned the being.

IT IS PLAIN FOR ALL TO SEE. IT IS UNDER YOUR NOSE.

Amrita was rattled. 'We must know for certain.'

'Indeed.' Hermie probed the being but there was no further response. 'Our loved one seems to have gone now; such a pity but perhaps we'll learn more on the next occasion.' She was jotting something down in a notebook.

'What are you doing?' Kay said curiously.

'I like to keep statistics of these occasions.' What she didn't reveal to Kay and which Kay was only to discover much later was that the success rate was far from persuasive, the misses, abstentions and maybes outnumbering the hits. But Hermie always put a gloss on it.

Amrita had collected herself and pushing back her chair laid a hand on Hermie's shoulder. 'Take care. I'll be in touch and we'll get to the bottom of this.'

'Don't say anything to Edith,' Hermie reminded her sternly. 'You know how contemptuous she is.'

Amrita looked askance. 'Of course not. It's as well she wasn't here today, otherwise we may not have made contact.'

Kay gathered from the exchange that Edith was a rank sceptic and considered to be a disruptive influence at the séances, which was why she was no longer invited.

Renee accompanied Amrita to the door and Amrita swept away in her BMW.

Renee cocked an eye at Kay. 'Communing with the other world, my foot. Oh God, it was certainly High Noon for the Rajmata. Did you see her face when KF and RRS popped up?'

There was a little pause and then Kay burst out laughing.

'A-h-h. You miserable wretch! You fraudster!'

Renee grinned, unrepentant. 'There she was being utterly boring about Rahul and Vimla and when I saw the chance to shake her up I took it.'

' You're a creative thinker.' Kay needn't have worried that Renee would pursue the subject. She was already running gloss over her lips and hardly heard her, leaving the house in a sense of purpose as the séance had inspired a new song.

'I'm off to put my feet,' Hermie announced when their guests had departed. 'Tell Gopi to bring me some orange juice.'

With a pile of picture postcards bought from the bazaar, Kay went onto the verandah, penning messages for an hour, the only sound the sweet call of a bulbul in the trees. She leaned back and reflected on the unsubtle warning-off, Amrita had delivered, deciding, with a flash of her independent spirit, that she could keep her son. Vimla was welcome to him.

'Scribble, scribble, scribble...'

There was a voice at her elbow and she looked up. Rahul's hands were thrust into the pockets of black jeans worn under a black cashmere sweater. The mix of sophistication and virility was devastating and, Kay realised, formidable.

'This is a surprise. What brings you here?' Kay's fingers tightened round the biro.

Rahul pulled out a cane chair. 'I thought I might catch Mother and see if Hermie needed any help with the tax return.'

'Amrita has been gone for some time and Hermie's resting.'

'Well, I'm glad I found you alone. It makes what I have to say to you much easier.'

'And that is?' Kay capped the biro, drawing on all her reserves to keep her voice and face neutral.

Rahul's dark brows slanted. 'Hermie's servants have been chatting to mine and they asked me to intervene.'

'You've lost me.' Kay was bewildered. 'Would you care to explain?'

'They resent your meddling and say that if you don't leave them alone, they'll hand in their notice.'

She felt her cheeks go bright red. 'The rotten little mischief-makers. But I can't see what business it is of yours,' she said acidly. 'I hope you told them to address their grievances to me.'

Rahul went on as if she'd not spoken which made her crosser than ever.

'I'm a family friend. That's why they approached me, or perhaps it's because they consider me more approachable?' He gave her a long stare. 'Gopi has been with Hermie boy and man and the others only a step behind. They're reluctant to do anything drastic but if needs must they will, and believe me, it's no idle threat.'

'Just what am I supposed to have done?' Kay cried.

'You've been provoking them by interfering with their working ways. Ways they insist have suited Hermie perfectly.'

Her precarious control snapped and she was on the attack. 'In case you hadn't noticed I'm the new broom here and I intend to sweep clean. When I agreed to take on this engagement it was on the unqualified understanding that I was free to organize the household as I thought fit. I've always kept Hermie's interests paramount and-'

'-Spare me the homilies and listen to me-'

'- let me finish and stop lecturing me. I may not speak their language but I do know how to handle people.'

Rahul leaned back in his chair. 'You must mean mishandling, surely. As far as I can judge you've let in a force 6 gale.

'Be specific then,' Kay said impatiently. 'I'll have you know Hermie particularly wanted me to supervise things and turned over the keys to me. I'm running things here and making life much easier for her.'

'Running's the operative word. She meant running it smoothly, not running it down hill. Until you appeared there weren't any ruptures.,' Rahul said with infuriating calm.

'They're a thieving, indolent lot, making a rake off at the bazaar, profiteering in other ways and helping themselves to stores.' Kay exploded and stood up and pacing the verandah expected him to retreat when he heard that.

'Oh, that's nothing new,' he said dryly, the black eyes mocking her. 'Hermie knows exactly what goes on. They fiddle an acceptable percentage. Just so long as they don't abscond with her jewellery or kick the dogs, their petty pilfering is okay by her. And that goes for us all.'

Kay tried a different tack. 'I discovered cockroaches had taken over the kitchen.' *That'll make you sit up.* She closed her eyes against the memory of those pesky two- inches long, shiny, brown bodies and long, waving antennae. 'I had to order a blitz. The servants were very put out at being made to scrub everything thoroughly from top to bottom, so no wonder they feel hard done by.' She shot him a quick look testing his reaction and added boldly. 'If they want to leave, let them. I can manage perfectly without them and to be honest it's really simpler, and far less frustrating, to do things oneself than to be endlessly chasing and nagging. I'm accustomed to managing without all this domestic help; in fact I'd much rather.'

Rahul reached over and his hand closed over her wrist. 'They don't need your permission to go; they're a pretty independent bunch and only loyalty to Hermie keeps them here. They know full well they can pack their bags and triple their wages tomorrow with a diplomatic family.'

'So what?' Kay shook herself free and hardly heeding what he'd said swept on, 'there's no shortage of labour in this country. I can find others to train, others who're more than willing to do the same job, any job, so long as they can earn a crust. They can go, with my blessing.'

'Ye gods. Don't play the domestic goddess with me. Hell, you're damned naive.' His smile was without warmth. 'You think you can do without? All right, just you wait and see. The weather's cold now. Everything's new. Shopping's different, picturesque. The smells and colour of the bazaar - it's all a novelty. It's fun wandering round, poking about and haggling. Just you wait when the servants have departed and you have to venture out with a heavy bag, in the swirling dust, the mercury at 40C with the sweat pouring off you. Just you wait till the banias see the Angrezi coming and you're fleeced right and left.' He crashed his fist down on the table. 'How can I make you understand?'

Kay stole a glance at his stormy face that told her that he thought she was independent to the point of obstinacy. It was easy enough to spit defiance but quite another thing to live with its consequences. The implications were certain. *I'd better wrap it up or the servants will conspire to get rid of me before I've had a chance to dig into family history. That's scary.* Suddenly panic stricken, she made a sharp little movement.

'Well?'

Kay said shakily, 'I'm sorry.' She bit her under lip. 'I've handled it badly. Put it all down to inexperience.'

Rahul's eyes were hard as they searched her averted face and she sensed that he was wondering about the sudden meekness because she'd shown herself to be something of a firebrand. 'Please make my peace with the servants.' She reached out and touched his hand urgently, unaware that a bleak look had settled on her face.

He seemed as if about to say something then checked himself and started indoors and Kay followed him more slowly, waiting apprehensively in the sitting room. There came snatches of conversation. She heard him lecturing the servants; there was a wheedling rejoinder from Gopi whom she'd long suspected of being the ringleader.

'Right.' He was back. 'I've made a start but things are still finely balanced so tread carefully.'

'Thanks,' Kay said as steadily as she could manage, relieved the landmines had been negotiated. 'I'm –'

'Is that Rahul I hear?' Hermie appeared in a good tweed suit, perky from the nap. She threw them a monitoring look. 'Bernadette phoned a few minutes ago and persuaded me I need a change of scene.'

'That sounds fun. Where exactly and when?' Kay asked a little more eagerly than she'd intended, and meaning to profit by Hermie's absence.

Hermie was too wrapped up in her forthcoming travel plans to notice Kay's mood of elation. 'Bernadette and Gerald live comfortably in Bombay' – she still referred to the city by its former name –'where he ran a flourishing private practice before elevation to the Bench. I'll join them towards the end of January. It'll be so nice to see old friends again.' It was a continuing source of pique to her that Bernadette had done so well for herself. Very well indeed and with so little effort, for someone who'd come from such a humble background. Whilst she, Hermie, had had to scratch her way up. At times such as this Hermie felt a martyr. What Hermie refused, however, to acknowledge was that Bernadette had never pretended to be anything other than she was. Her eyes flickered between Rahul and Kay. 'Now, I don't want to come back and find the place in a mess, so you must keep the servants up to snuff when I'm away.'

***

Christmas was celebrated in style. Kay, in brooding truce with Gopi, helped Hermie host a buffet luncheon for twelve and a fund-raiser for thirty. Learning that Kay's birthday fell in the middle of the month, Hermie presented her with a green jade brooch depicting Ganesh, the pot bellied elephant god, who overcomes all obstacles she'd told her with a smile, pinning it to Kay's scarlet woollen dress, that she'd hurriedly had made up by the durzee for she'd not thought to bring any warm clothes with her, unaware that Delhi winters could be quite so cold.

'What'll you do now you're off the leash?' Rahul tore past a coughing car on their return from the airport one morning having seen Hermie off on the Mumbai flight, delayed for an hour by dense fog engulfing Delhi.

Kay hesitated. She'd eventually intimated to Renee and Tony as much as they needed to know about her quest. Intrigued, they'd offered to help, persuading her that she should include Rahul in her confidences for if anyone could navigate bureaucracy, it was he.

'Come on, the look in your eyes suggests you're up to something.' The constraints between them had melted.

She smiled, fighting against the attraction she felt for him. 'See the Taj Mahal, go here and there, visit Ajeemkot,' she murmured. Wait for it, she told herself.

'Ajeemkot!' Rahul stared at her, mystified. ' Christ, whatever for? It's a dull, untidy little place of no particular resonance. During the Raj it was an undistinguished railway town and it's no different now. In fact, probably worse.'

'All I know is that Mum was born and raised there,' Kay said softly. 'I want to trace links with Mum and Dad's family.'

He looked astounded and Kay was glad of the chance to explain how it seemed that her parents had grown up in India. 'I feel so sad that their life, their family, their milieu are a complete mystery to me. And I think Mum's family worked on the railways. I must have some relatives, even distant ones, still living here, or at any rate, people who might have known of them. I want... to meet them, to ...pick up... the threads.' Kay was seized with a sudden diffidence.

Rahul rubbed his ear, saying nothing.

'I do have clues - family photos and Mum's birth and marriage certificates. It can't be that impossible to pick up leads."

They'd reached the house and Rahul cut the engine but remained where he was studying her for an instant with an impenetrable expression on his face. Rain lashed against the windscreen. 'I don't want to sound a killjoy but have you thought about it carefully? You might not like... what you unearth. Another's life, another's history.' His voice was quietly cryptic. 'Searching for roots can be very unsettling when it turns out one isn't related to princes, rich nabobs, or galloping generals, but rather something quite else. And people hate to face up to the fact that their family had spun fairy tales and given exaggerated accounts of their Indian lifestyle to impress English neighbours.'

'If only.'

His eyes searched hers and he realised that she'd need tactful handling. 'You don't have to rush into anything.'

Kay's fingers tightened over her bag. 'I don't have the luxury of not rushing.' *Dammit,* she thought, *I should have kept my own counsel.* She meant to go and nothing would dissuade her. 'Put it like this, I've a gambler's instinct.'

'You're very obstinate,' he said at last.

'And you're Napoleon,' she retorted pleasantly.

Rahul threw back his head and laughed. 'All right, I have a proposition to make –'

'– like Suresh's?' she shot back.

He snorted. 'That jerk.' He paused to punch a text message into his Blackberry. 'Now, I'm heading for my constituency soon. If you like, you can ride with me and use Walipur as your base for...' adding mischievously, '...exploring the delights of Ajeemkot.'

Having resigned herself to a long and dusty train journey and a cheap, bed bug ridden room in a budget hotel, Kay was delighted. 'How can I turn down an offer like that?' She laid a hand on his arm.

'That's just what I knew you'd say.'

'Very funny,' Kay said crisply, her colour rising.

He opened the car door and taking her elbow they squelched in the driving rain to the house under a large, black umbrella.

'I'm soaked through.' Squeezing the soggy hem of her dress, Kay hurried to change.

That same day, after Rahul had left, Kay called Renee. 'So that's the first hurdle overcome,' Kay said gleefully.

'Well done. But does Hermie know you'll be absent from home?' Bernadette asked pointedly. 'You'd better clear it with her first just to be on the safe side.'

Kay felt a sickening stab of dismay and closed her eyes for a moment. 'Do you think she'd object? Surely not. It isn't as if I'm leaving the bungalow unattended. The servants will be here, making hay as usual, but nevertheless a physical deterrent.'

'The elderly can be... well...perverse, and you don't want that sneaky Gopi making any more trouble.'

What Renee said made good sense. Hermie had a sharp tongue and was not averse to identifying what she perceived as Kay's inadequacies.

'And you won't put all your money on the Ajeemkot horse, will you?' Renee cautioned. 'Railway families moved about a lot in the course of work.'

'Oh.' Kay felt a little glum after the initial euphoria. *First Rahul and now Renee.*

'Mind, don't misunderstand me. I know how you feel. You've got to get it out of your system, only don't let it become a grand obsession.'

Hermie mauled Kay with a few sulky stand-offs before grudgingly conceding her time out.

'For once I'm looking forward to travelling by car to Walipur.' Rahul jumped out from behind the wheel, bestowed a quick kiss on her cheek and loaded her small case into the boot. 'All set? Camera, notebook, unmentionables?'

'Like a good girl guide I've come prepared.' Kay returned his smile, conscious of the current flowing between them and wondering what exactly he was hinting at and concluding that he was master of the ambivalent. That she found him alarmingly attractive she freely admitted but suspected that to have an affair with him would not only be the launching pad for a heady sensual experience but also propel her into danger. It was doomed from the start. Too much divided them. Wealth, culture, status, customs, religion, Vimla, Amrita. Kay reminded herself that a tight rein on her head, if not her heart, was called for.   Yet ...she recalled Edith's quote from Goethe: *Live dangerously and you live right.*

Past the city's urban sprawl, the enfolding rural scene struck Kay. 'There's a sort of timeless exoticism about this.' Dhoti clad villagers sat on charpoys chewing lengths of sugar-cane watching lurching convoys of scruffy camels. 'So different from the English countryside.'

Rahul snorted. 'This is just bloody primitive.'

'You're very scathing.   But I refuse to let you spoil it for me. Oh how sweet, do stop. That'll make a lovely memory.'

He pulled a face as Kay got out and snapped a herd of goats being driven by ragged, bare-foot children.

The Mercedes sliced through golden desert broken here and there by tangled thorn, mud villages and scarred forts.   The few trees were charcoal black against contours of yellow ochre; there was the heavy creak of a bullock cart as the car flashed by. Often they were enveloped in thick clouds of dust raked up as a rickety lorry thundered past and after more than one such moment, Rahul swore lamentably under his breath.

As the road twisted and climbed Kay caught a glimpse of curling blue smoke from distant cooking fires and the smells grew stronger, the sense of open-ness infinite.

'This is the heart of Rajasthan, where relentless warfare spawned heroic fighters, men and women.'

'Tell me about the women,' Kay said quickly.

'Not the men?' Rahul chuckled. 'You disappoint me. All right, let's see now.... Seven hundred years ago, the fortress of Chittor was besieged by a Muslim King, Allaudin Khilji, determined to capture the Rajput Queen Padmini and make her his own, having fleetingly glimpsed her beauty reflected in a silver mirror.' Rahul's eyes surveyed Kay. 'His army razed Chittor to the ground but, rather than surrender, the Queen and her ladies-in- waiting donned their finest saris and jewellery and committed jauhar...'

Kay raised querying brows.

'... Ritual suicide by throwing themselves onto a fire. Allauddin's victory was a handful of cold, grey ash.'

Kay shivered. 'I've never heard anything so gruesome in all my life. What a drastic solution. Was that heroism or cowardice, I wonder?'

'Now you tell me.' Rahul was smiling at her.

'She reckoned that being Allaudin's wife - '

'- One of his wives or maybe one of his many concubines -'

'-was a fate worse than death but I look at it like this. Since he was besotted with her she could probably have twisted him round her little finger, so I think she made a very hasty, very bad decision. She ought to have given marriage with him a go. I know I would've.'

'I hope your brand of pragmatism doesn't extend to that perv Suresh.'

On the crest of a hill, Rahul's ancestral home rose in a feudal silhouette cutting the sky, rose pink by day, violet by night, a fairy tale symbol of the proud Ratan Singh dynasty.

'I'd no idea it was so enchanting,' Kay burst out. 'Photographs don't do justice to it and it's really like something in a dream.'

'Perish the thought. I don't want a mirage. I want my home solid as the pyramids right here before me. It has been in the family, confronting the desert, for six hundred years and you must approach it in time honoured fashion.'

Rahul pulled up and, as if on cue, a caparisoned, tail swaying elephant lumbered across, flapping flies with its cabbage leaf ears. 'Up you get, Kay,' Rahul said snapping his fingers.

The mahout tapped the animal lightly with a stick and the beast sagged slowly to its knees.

'Jumbo's inviting you to ride. Don't jilt him or he'll never forget.'

With a hand up from the mahout, Kay gingerly mounted the bamboo ladder placed against the elephant's side and heaved herself into the howdah. The mahout shouted commands and the elephant, trumpeting bad temperedly, rose somewhat groggily to its feet. Kay grabbed hold of the beaded wooden rail as the motion flung her to one side.

'What a view from a very unusual perch.' Kay gazed around and then grinned down at Rahul who was beaming broadly at her, his thumbs hooked into the waistband of his trousers. 'If the stones could sing, what would they say?'

'That symphony's something you'll have to compose yourself. I'll meet and greet you at the top,' and plunging ahead along the winding ribbon of road he was soon lost to sight.

Jumbo ambled uphill, the howdah gently swinging to the rhythm of its richly decorated body that was hung with strings of tiny silver bells that tinkled in the breeze. The mahout followed occasionally administering a friendly smack and addressing it in colourful monosyllables.

A view probably unchanged for centuries, Kay caught her breath. Walipur slumbered under a hazy sun beneath the soaring towers of temples. Screeching kite birds wheeled and swooped as women in mirror embroidered skirts with firewood bundles on their heads and infants on their backs filed through the fields.

'How was that?' Rahul asked as Kay dismounted in a shaded forecourt.

'A ride I wouldn't have missed for the world.' Servants lassoed her with garlands of tuber roses and she buried her nose in the scent. 'Thank you, they're fabulous. It won't take me long to adjust to a style to which I've never been accustomed.'

'Let's go inside. You're probably travel weary and want to freshen up.' Rahul pointed. 'Just so you know, the hotel entrance is on the far side across there by those cannons –'

'All the better to fire at the hotel guests?'

He laughed, 'and this archway leads to the private wing.'

His hand closed over hers and, to the sound of water bursting into colour from fountains, he walked her on paths by clipped topiary, lotus ponds and erotic statuary to a parquet entrance hall bathed in light.

Glancing down, Kay noticed the Walipur coat of arms inlaid in different shades of polished timber and glancing around couldn't contain herself. 'Wow,' she burst out, ' a window to the Arabian nights, the French Empire and Bollywood.'

Rahul grinned. 'This is nothing to what it was like during Father's day. In the interests of sanity, I've pensioned off the worst excesses to the hotel, like the antelope covered suite of which this chair is a part, the red lacquer furniture and silver urns and all, bar one, of that.' He pointed to a Venetian crystal chandelier that tinkled in the breeze from an open window.

A young woman materialised and he instructed her to show Kay to her suite and to look after her. 'Ji ha.' The maid respectfully bowed her head.

'Goodbye for now, Kay. In Walipur we've a saying a guest is God.' Their glances met and his expression was searching, and for a moment in that vast hall which had once echoed with the leitmotif of the courtly round, they were all alone, all that mattered. He watched her retreating back and then walked swiftly away in the opposite direction, the muffled thud of his trainers along the marble floored corridor, lined with pot plants, fading away as he rounded a corner.

The maid halted and swinging open a heavy brass-studded door ushered Kay into her quarters. Her mouth dropped. Softly lit by glass lanterns, it was like something out of Scherazade. Painted trompe-l'oeil columns framed a four-poster rosewood bed mounted in silver under a brocade canopy, strung with thousands of glass beads. And what a rug!   A leopard skin complete with snarling head and snapping, tawny eyes lay on a floor marbled with different shades of blue that echoed the colour of the ceiling. Drifts of hand-made ivory lace separated the bedroom from the sitting area.

Kay turned and met the smiling gaze of the maid who relieved her of her garlands and draped them round wall-mounted hand coloured vintage photographs, explaining to her that she'd already unpacked Kay's case and hung up her clothes.

'You are liking?'

Kay caught the woman's anxious gaze and grinned. ' It's gorgeous.'

The maid poured out a large freshly brewed cup of coffee from a silver coffeepot. 'Anything madam-ji wants, anytime, I am bringing.' She bowed and floated away promising to let her know when dinner was ready.

Kay crossed to the window and pushed open the teak shutters and the colour and scent of frangipani swept up. It was almost impossible to visualise that this tranquil oasis had been endlessly fought over, impossible to imagine bitter tribal enmities, the clash of cold steel, the whiff of gunpowder.

As the day waned and Kay had showered in a bathroom with aggressive modern plumbing, decorated with Chinese glazed tiles, that would have accommodated her entire London flat, and accessorised by an array of organic bath products that rivalled the beauty counters of many an upscale western department store, a gentle knock heralded the maid.

'Rajah-ji is presenting compliments and informing that meal is being ready when you are wishing it.' She insisted on helping Kay to put up her hair and to zip up a cream calf-length dress.

The rare Burma teak dining table, laid with two silver thali settings, could easily seat fifty guests. 'Father used to plan the seating like a military campaign.' Rahul pulled out a chair for Kay. 'But I usually eat on the hoof. How things have changed.'

'Living like this must make it difficult for you to understand other people's concerns.' Kay felt she was getting to know him in his own environment and little by little it was helping her to understand him better, to realise the source of that arrogance.

'On the contrary, I'm only too aware of the privileges and ...pitfalls and how badly off people are,' he said roundly. 'That's why I chose politics, to do something about that.'

'And do you think you're making out?' He wasn't a big eater she noticed. Picking at a portion of chicken washed down with mineral water.

He shrugged his shoulders. 'Sometimes yes, more often, no. It's a never-ending task.   But I can't be a complete dud at it. Despite the fact that an election in this constituency has always been hotly contested, I've always won a comfortable majority.'

It struck her that Rahul was probably an assiduous constituency MP, campaigning tirelessly for more schools and rural clinics, roads, utilities, power lines, water wells and tabling awkward motions in the House. 'You've been in Parliament for some time?'

He counted off the years on his fingers. 'It doesn't seem long enough to accomplish the things I set out to do.' He was lit with the enthusiasm of a TV evangelist.   'Father was MP here, a dyed in the wool Congress wallah. When he perished in an air crash - '

'I'm sorry.' Kay put in quietly. 'That must've been hard. I felt bereft when Dad....disappeared.'

His hands sketched a tiny gesture. ' - That triggered a by-election which I won, then at the general election I stood again and retained my seat.' He grinned. 'Folk are traditional here and believe the first-born should inherit. Well I did, but on the AFPP ticket.'

'No gerrymandering, hanging chads, elector intimidation, gunning down your opponent or stuffing the ballot boxes?' Kay asked lightly.

There was a pause and then to the tune of *Gimme That Ole Time Religion,* Rahul broke into song. 'That ole time d'mocracy, ole US time d'mocracy, ole US style d'mocracy is just a mockery, don't gimme me no affliction, it ain't good enough for me. Look, I'd resign if the ballot was rigged and believe you me, I'd know,' he added in a tone of voice that could only be characterised as calm reproach.

Kay dipped a dessertspoon into a dish of mango fool.

'I wonder... I mean...' Kay was floundering.

'Yes?' This diffidence wasn't Kay.

'I'd like to make that foray to Ajeemkot as soon as possible,' she said tentatively, hoping he'd not forgotten his promise.

'No problem. That's the object of the exercise isn't it? Will tomorrow suit you?'

'Yesterday would have been better.'

'I'll come.'

It wasn't so much an offer as a statement of intent, his expression considering the matter settled.

Troubled, Kay looked away. He'd been so nice to her, putting himself out for her and it was bliss in his company but she shrank at arriving in chauffeur-driven ostentation.

'I'd hoped to go solo,' she confessed, still not meeting his eye but sensing that he was puzzled and probably a little hurt.

He raised his eyebrows. 'Why?'

She hesitated then felt their friendship was sufficiently consecrated for her to be candid.

'Who said anything about the Merc?' He grinned. 'OK, Kay, me and my Merc - a potent symbol of the moneyed Indian. How corny can I get?'

She smiled at that and finished her coffee, and he took the decision out of her hands. 'And you'll need a tail wind. You don't know the language and having a man in tow will make all the difference.'

Kay heard herself make an inarticulate sound.

'All right, all right, I retract. But you want results so how about this. We'll take the jeep.'

'Oh...' Kay was still a little uncertain and then nodded. 'Okay, that sounds a reasonable enough compromise.'

'And as I'm the local MP my name can open some pretty heavy doors.'

He leaned back as if pleased with himself and she watched him slide a portion of paan into his mouth, shaking her head as he offered some to her.

'Of course.' She smothered a yawn. 'I can scarcely keep my eyes open. It's been a long day and I'm practically dead on my feet. I think I'll turn in.'

'A wise move. You'll need all the beauty sleep you can get as it'll be an early start.' He rose. 'I'll see you to your room; guests find this place spooky at night.'

'Glitzy yes, spooky, surely not.' But as they made their way down low-lit corridors raked with shadows and smelling of incense Kay began to understand what he meant. It **was** spooky and it made her shiver slightly.

They'd reached her room and turning the doorknob Rahul switched on the light. 'Until tomorrow, then.' Her face must have changed for he added quickly, 'don't give it another thought. As they say - what will be, will be.'

***

They set out at daybreak, Rahul easing the 4x4 along a single- track dirt road to skirt fields of winter millet and opium poppies bucking through dust-powdered villages where the slow pace of life hadn't changed for centuries.

Kay looked round enjoying the air and the light, a jazzy patterned Fairisle jumper pulled over blue jeans. Sissoo trees she recognised and was that juniper? But most of the silver-green shrubs were unfamiliar. Ajeemkot. She thought of the Blakes who'd lived and loved in its scorching heat. Her spine tingled. She was on her way and couldn't wait to get there quickly enough. It was as though someone was impatient for her to open a long-locked door. *Wait. I'm coming, I'm coming.*

'Are you okay?' Rahul broke across her thoughts. He was in kurta pyjama that did nothing to disguise his strong-limbed body. 'This thing's like a ruddy great tank.'

Kay drew a long breath, 'I hate being a back-seat driver but you've spotted that herd of oxen, haven't you?' It looked as if he'd every intention of mowing it down.

'It's monopolised the centre of the road so I can scarcely overlook it,' Rahul said drily.

He didn't even brake, just bore down on it keeping his hand on the ear-splitting horn. Kay hung on grimly. The herd slowly moved a few inches to the right and they lunged round it on the wrong side.

A dangerous road she thought and then, after a companionable exchange - he'd laughed when she'd told him she'd happily settle to a cloistered palace existence of intrigue and gossip and he'd joked that he'd make a traditional Indian girl of her yet - in a very short time, they'd shaken off the last of the countryside and reached the untidy sprawl of Ajeemkot.

'Oh God, it's ghastly.' Kay could have wept. It was arid, noisy, ramshackle, down-at heel, swarming with flies and smelt of sewage, rotting garbage and exhaust fumes. There was a queer feeling in the pit of her stomach and all the earlier anticipation had evaporated

Rahul reached out a hand and touched her arm. 'It's a bit of a Cinderella - a small town with few resources - which is why I didn't want you to get your hopes up.'

'You did say, and I oughtn't to have expected otherwise.' She didn't think she could bear it if she were disappointed. Traffic closed in on them; crowds thronged the uneven pavements. Muttering under his breath, Rahul jerked his way behind a line of mangy camels and slid to a stop under the shade of a gnarled banyan tree, its roots spreading like trip wires across the ground.

They sat for a few moments in silence. 'Right.' Rahul reached across and opened the door for her. 'First stop, the church.'

Kay said slowly as she got out, 'do you think it's still standing?' Looking about at some of the crumbling buildings, she had her doubts.

'Open your eyes, woman.'

She followed Rahul's pointing finger and amidst a jumble of electricity poles, hoardings and TV aerials glimpsed the grey finger of a spire etched against the blue sky. 'Sorry, I must be losing my nerve.'

The glance he gave her was measuring. 'You really are scared.'

'Now I'm actually here…' she stopped.

'I really shouldn't worry.'

Kay looked across to where scrawny hens scratched the ground. 'Yes. I know.' She gave a little shrug. 'I'm being silly.'

'A glass of sherbet before we press on?'

'No,' Kay protested quickly. 'Let's get on with it.' The Blakes retreated in every minute that was lost. 'But hadn't we decided to visit the records office?'

'That too, but later. St. George's is more important.' Rahul must have seen a query in her face because he said, 'Oh Kay, don't be so dim. You don't want to waste the entire day wandering aimlessly through the cemetery if the church registers can give the burial locations, assuming your family was interred there.'

'Yes... of course. I see. It's horrible...' there was a lump in her throat '...to be... meeting relatives like this. If,' she blinked away the tears that threatened, 'I find them.'

Rahul touched her hand lightly and his eyes held an expression of great warmth.

They picked their way round potholes and eventually reached the church. He put a hand under her elbow and they started up the steps. The big wooden door swung open easily on a large iron ring and Rahul held it back for Kay to precede him inside.

Kay swallowed hard and looking about her walked slowly up the centre aisle. In this place Blakes had been christened, married and buried. It was cool and dark with stained glass windows, polished pews, old hymn-books and jars of cannas and could almost have been in an English village if it weren't for the distant howling of pi-dogs, the frantic shrill of bicycle bells, and the smell of frying chillies.

Kay knelt down and said a prayer, her gaze lingering on memorial tablets poignantly recording early deaths of those in the service of the Raj then started to retrace her steps.

'Won't you stay a little longer?' Rahul asked.

Kay turned quickly aside her hair swinging down to hide her face. 'I've seen as much as I want to.'

Rahul regarded her averted head for a moment and she sensed he was about to say something but checked himself.

But they'd been seen and heard and as they emerged onto the sun-drenched porch, a plump young man wearing a clerical collar caught up with them from somewhere within, introduced himself as the Reverend John Ali Shah and explained that he served a number of scattered Church of England congregations.

'I wonder if I might ask you something.' Kay gave a bare recital of the facts.

'We are maintaining registers from many, many years back and I am being happy assisting your research,' the Reverend said obligingly, obviously eager to interrupt the even tenor of his day in that dusty backwater. 'So, it is standing to reason that if family is being buried here, then plot register will be elucidating exact locations. You are anxious that I am checking?'

'What do you want to do, Kay?'

She hesitated then said slowly. 'I've thought about it - thought about what you and the Reverend say but I'd really much rather just wander round the cemetery. If I draw a blank, I can come back and consult the registers.'   In a strange sort of way, now that the moment was almost upon her, Kay wanted to take her time, to get the feel of the place.

The men listened in silence, and when she'd finished neither spoke for some moments.

'Most welcome,' said the Reverend recovering himself. If he thought it wasn't a clever idea, his polite expression gave no hint of it. He pointed. 'Old graves are starting just beyond those trees and new graves well, it is being obvious where those are lying.'

'Thank you. Coming Kay?'

A rough curving path to the cemetery, just wide enough for them to walk abreast, ended at a high wooden gate. Rahul had to struggle with the rusty bolt but then with a loud creak, the gate swung free and they stepped through.

It was very still with a faint breeze; round-eyed baboons perching on the white cemetery wall scratched themselves, fixing them with an unblinking gaze.

'Shall we start over there?' Rahul asked.

Kay nodded, but didn't look at him and he took her arm and steered her across coarse, long grass. 'Watch out for snakes,' he warned.

It's very sad, Kay thought, looking past him at the pathetic symbols of the Raj - rows of unkempt headstones dwarfed by Regency and Victorian monuments. Babies, fresh-faced young wives, doughty brigadiers slain by forgotten battles, pestilence and disease; innocent victims laid waste far from the gentle green hills and wooded glades of home.

Here was washday - a fallen tablet being used by a dhobi for pounding clothes, surrounded by many hued garments drying on the grass. And over there another slab, expropriated by a crouching old woman, as a base on which she was busily crushing spices.

A simple stone glimpsed through nettles of a woman attached to the American Baptist Mission brought tears to Kay's eyes. *Born Los Angeles 1838. Died Ajeemkot 1916. She Loved India.*

'In the mid 1800s the journey from America to India lasted more than four months and missionaries were told, quite candidly, that their appointments were for life,' Rahul said softly. 'Few entertained any hopes of going home.' And then he was heading on.

'Kay! The pitch of his voice made her rush across. With bare hands he'd torn aside a thicket of orange creeper exposing a tilted headstone, chipped and weather-beaten.

'Blake.' Kay's heart kicked painfully. 'Mum's grandparents,' she whispered. In death as in life they lay together.

Slowly tracing a finger over the faded inscription she could just make out:

Noreen Delicia Blake
Beloved wife and mother
Not gone from memory
Nor from love, But to prepare
A home for us above.
Sadly missed.

Wilburt Blake
He cannot return to us
But we will go to him.
Reunited with Mum.

Kay didn't think she'd ever forget this moment. She sank to her knees and burst into tears.

She heard Rahul's voice but hardly took in what he said, and then he was sitting beside her on the cracked stone with a comforting arm round her heaving shoulders.

'Sorry, silly me,' Kay managed to say, wiping her eyes. She blew her nose and after a while he helped her to her feet. 'I truly hadn't expected to feel like this.'

'It's only natural. You've been so involved in it for so long.' He looked at her doubtfully, 'do you want to go on?'

'Yes,' Kay said slowly, 'I must. It can't get any worse.'

It seemed natural for him to take her hand and they weaved through several more grave-humped rows. Kay began to lose all track of time; her head ached and she was just about to say she'd had enough when his tightening grip held discovery.

Ashley and Iris Blake (née Quinn)
Cruelly taken in cholera epidemic
How dearly I loved you and prayed you might live
But Jesus just beckoned, and I had to give.
Deeply mourned by daughter Delphine.

Kay didn't know how long she stood there beneath the narrow leafed tree, her eyes stinging. *This is my family; the family Mum and Dad rubbed out. They robbed me of knowing, of belonging.* She wondered if she'd ever understand them, ever forgive them, and then was fumbling in her bag for her camera, but she ought to have remembered how fast Rahul could move.

'Here, I'll do that.' He'd relieved her of it and Kay knew, in those choking moments, that these photos he'd taken, like those a little earlier, would always be the most poignant reminder of her visit to India.

Rahul stroked her cheek and Kay knew what he was thinking: that he was deeply sorry for her and for the sad manner in which she'd been compelled to meet her family. 'We could leave it for another day if you like.'

They'd trawled round for another thirty minutes but found nothing more.

The old neglected monuments and the somewhat oppressive atmosphere of the cemetery had got to Kay, and all she wanted now was to be gone. 'I'm done here. I've had enough. Let's go back to the Reverend and check the registers.'

They retraced their steps, carefully side-stepping the rat holes that led down into the graves and, as Kay cast a backward look, somewhere from behind the cemetery wall, a clock chimed the hour.

The Reverend assumed a suitably mournful expression when Kay told him what they'd found. And no, there were no Blakes, Quinns or Forresters in his congregation. He invited them into his small two-roomed house and gave them strong cups of tea sweetened with condensed milk while they leafed through the registers. There were no records of any more family burials. 'But look-see, Miss Forrester.'

Kay peered over his shoulder. 'Look, Rahul. Grandpa Ashley and Granny Iris were also married at St. George's.' Kay felt she was getting somewhere. 'Reverend I expect you'd know the answer to something else that's puzzled me -'

'- Please to be firing away.' The clergyman was delighted to be of help.

'On my parents marriage certificate under the heading Groom's Father, there's just a black diagonal line.'

'Miss Forrester. Oh, dearie, dearie me. It is being that Forrester. Oh dear, you are asking question that I am finding problem answering.' His Adam's apple bobbed up and down like a cork. 'But I will not be shirking my duty.' He explained that it was customary at the time for illegitimate children, like Leslie, cared for by Bishop Forrester Home, to be assigned the surname Forrester.

Kay was astounded, but mostly filled with anger at her parents for having bamboozled her and perpetrated this deceit. *Even worse, are the lies and the rejection of their AI heritage.* A heritage that Kay now knew for certain that she shared. Only timing, deliberately calculated, made her London, rather than Ajeemkot, born. 'I suppose that means no traceable relatives on Dad's side. But would it be possible to be visit the Home?'

Rahul looked at the clergyman. 'Correct me if I'm wrong, but I believe it was demolished some fifteen years ago to make way for a new primary school?'

'Oh yes, that is being absolutely true.'

They chatted a little while longer then Kay glanced at her watch. 'Thanks very much for your help, Reverend.' She rose to her feet.

'It is always fine to see relatives paying their respects to the departed,' the Reverend said, his small hands clasping hers.

'I'm decades too late,' Kay said a little morosely. She unzipped her bag. 'Would you accept this as a donation to the church restoration fund? And I wonder may I leave a little something for flowers to be placed on the graves?'

'I am personally putting.'

'My aide, Powley, will be in touch. Wonderful job you're doing here. We could do with more like you.' Rahul was impressed with the Reverend's simplicity, strong sense of duty and deep faith.

'God bless and may you be having a safe journey.' The Reverend showed them out.

'I'm starving,' Rahul confessed when they'd walked a few hundred yards or so. He'd seen and was diving into a thatched roadside shack. 'Are you all right?' He registered Kay's pallor as he consumed a large portion of lentils and chappatis. 'You know you really ought to try and eat something.'

'It's been more of a shock than I imagined, though why I should have expected otherwise is a mystery.' Kay tinkered with the food, gazing across outside to where a woman crouched under a tree with a metal pail pulling the udders of a buffalo.

'One thinks one's prepared- that one's defences are up - but it's seldom like that. The reality's nearly always different.' Rahul paused and gave her a speculative look. Kay had hinted at the prospect of a warm re-union with friendly cousins. 'Would you'd rather leave the records office for another day?' That would let her review whether she honestly felt like pursuing the matter

'No. Now we're here we might as well do the job properly. Lead on.'

Rahul felt in his pocket and weighed down some bank notes on the rickety table with a large stone then dodging the traffic swept her across to a rotting municipal building, its once handsome Gothic exterior, a visible monument to Empire, ravaged by sun, desert winds and rain.

'Hope for the best, expect the worst,' Rahul said lightly, pushing open a decrepit door labelled ROOM 164 GENERAL ENQUIRIES. It creaked a loud protest as if they'd no business to be there.

From the expression on Kay's face he judged she could do without his well-meant advice to brace herself.

Behind a wooden counter alongside, Rahul guessed, a crippled data processor, sat a grizzled baboo writing somewhat laboriously in a ledger with the blunt stump of a purple, indelible pencil that he licked at intervals. A withered garland drooped from an askew photo of Gandhi-ji hanging on a flaking bilious-green wall, whilst at the back a tiny window afforded a glimpse of clouds and trees.

'Please to completing five copies Form No. A/379/008K available Room No.258 in Annexe Building C opposite Birla Temple off Magistrates Court Marg near Clock Tower between 11am and 12 noon, Tuesdays only,' the man intoned without looking up. 'Next...'

'Knickers.' Bitterly disappointed, now that she'd psyched herself up for it, Kay looked up at Rahul. 'This means another ruddy trip.' She'd have made for the door had he not taken firm control of the situation.

'I think not,' he said crisply. 'If I may have your attention.' Rahul addressed the baboo in his own language.

The man reluctantly raised his head and peered petulantly over his specs, then, recognising Rahul for whom he was, said respectfully, 'Salaam, Rajah-ji.' He hastily tucked the pencil behind one ear and hopping off his stool flicked ineffectively with a dusty rag at a couple of rickety chairs.

After a lengthy exchange during which the baboo nodded, shook his head and gesticulated rapidly, Rahul turned to Kay. 'He says all records are in store.'

Kay groaned and shut her eyes briefly. 'That sounds like the kiss of death.'

The old man fingered his wispy moustache. Then grinning toothily, he waggled a gnarled finger at her proceeding to unhitch a heavy jumble of keys of varying sizes from a rusty hook on the wall.

'Apparently not,' Rahul said as the other man launched into a rambling account. 'Come on, he wants us to go with him.'

In the wake of the remarkably nippy old boy, Rahul took Kay's hand in his as they stumbled across an overgrown compound that doubled as a rubbish dump, Kay realised, holding a hanky to her nose, to the rotting hulk of a corrugated iron-roofed godown.

With a flourish, the baboo turned a key in the heavy padlock and shoulder-butted the swollen door. He felt for the light switch and the naked electric bulb flickering at first uncertainly, rallied, dispensing a cruel, cold blue light through the musty gloom. Giant shadows leapt against grubby walls; it reeked of mould and smelt sour and fetid. As something scurried across the floor, Rahul felt Kay shrink against him with a little gasp.

'Mice,' Rahul remarked cheerfully as if referring to a household pet. 'We've disturbed their play.'

Kay stared around her and then straight at Rahul. 'I wouldn't want to be the filing clerk here. What an abysmal system and just where do we start?'

Dusty shelves sagged with yellowing ledgers; official papers engrained with dust and cobwebs spiralled higgledy-piggledy; court transcripts spilled convulsively from sodden gunnysacks. Rahul dislodged a ledger at random and Kay stared at it in horror. It was stained and mildewed, its pages riddled with holes, the work of some pillaging insect. He could sense Kay was close to tears.

'I might just as well have not bothered.' The hotchpotch of papers was anarchical in its chaos. 'It'll take weeks of sifting, if not months.' Her voice was edged with panic.

'Hang on ' Rahul said calmly. 'We know most of the relevant dates so it's just a matter of doing a systematic search.'

'How?' Kay gestured miserably. 'This is a shambles.'

'Easy peasy,' Rahul said briskly. 'We just get cracking on finding birth, marriage and death entries for Noreen and Wilburt, Ashley and any siblings, and Iris.'

'If any of the stuff's in chronological order...' Kay grumbled uncharitably.

Rahul gave an irritated grunt and ran his hands through his hair, firing a few questions at the baboo who beamed. 'Believe it or not, there's method in this madness. The disarray's only superficial - it's all sorted and dated apparently, beginning with this little lot.' He prodded with a shoe at a precarious heap disturbing a large black spider that scuttled away into the shadows. 'The baboo says he wants to get back to the office but apparently we're favoured - he has agreed that we can excavate here on our own, provided we promise faithfully to lock up when we've finished.'

'An example of V.I.P. treatment?' Kay said, obviously feeling a little better about it.

'If you like.'

The baboo made himself scarce, clearly glad to be shot of the gloomy godown that he unlocked no more than once a year to hurl in the latest set of records.

It was hot, dirty, eye straining work. Rahul straightened his back. 'Whew! I thought I was on to something just now but my eyes deceived me. It turned out to be Blakiston.'

Kay gave a rueful laugh. 'I've had a few close calls myself.'

'Eureka.' Half an hour later, Rahul whistled. 'Take a look.' He shone his torch on the page.

Kay moved to his side and craned over, staring down at the limp folio. Within the circle of light was an entry in neat black copperplate, faded but still legible, of the birth of Ashley Blake, son of Wilburt and Noreen Blake.

Rahul dropped a kiss on her head. 'We've struck gold. Forward march.'

Eventually, they located entries for Noreen, Wilburt and for Iris.

' I'm getting somewhere.'

'We'll get the baboo to make copies,' Rahul said. Triggered by the success he was embarking with relish on the next stage. 'Let's press on – we've got to find Ashley's siblings.' They'd already agreed on the futility of going beyond that.

But a search ten years plus and minus Ashley's birth date yielded nothing.

'Just one more lead to try and that's Forrester. Okay, I know it's a wild card.'

Kay was dubious. 'Well, Dad was illegitimate and could've been born anywhere in India according to the Reverend. And I'm an only child and wasn't even born here.'

'Look, it's worth a shot while we're still here, although we needn't spend long over it,' Rahul pointed out reasonably.

Kay, suddenly feeling queasy, dashed outside. Rahul watched her go, tempted to follow and comfort her, but aware of time running out he turned back to the ledgers, flicking back and forth for another twenty minutes. *There's nothing here. I'd better call it a day.* He idly turned a few more pages when his eye was caught and held by an entry.

On 15 December at Ajeemkot Civil Hospital to Leslie Forrester, Policeman and Delphine Delicia Forrester (née Blake) Nurse - a daughter - Kay Forrester. Caste: Anglo-Indian.

For Chrissake! Rahul gave a long whistle. *Should I or shouldn't I tell Kay? I must.* His thoughts whirred. *She's been lied to enough; she has the right to know. This is the one time when lies go out of the window.* He picked his way outside over the jumble of paper and picked her out at the far end of the compound leaning against a tree, a soft drink can in her hand. 'Kay! There's an interesting development.' He kept his tone neutral.

She hurried across and he thought she looked rather forlorn. He showed her what he'd found. Her face tensed then something broke in her and sobs tore the air. 'That's me. But how? I've already got an English birth certificate that records me as being London born.' Her eyes strayed from the ledger to his face.

'We can sort this out at home.' Rahul's tone implied deep sympathy. Scooping up the ledgers and putting an arm round her shoulders he propelled her gently to the baboo's office where a menial made several photocopies of the entries on coarse, unbleached paper.

More out of interest than hope, Rahul asked about the gazetteers for that period, which would have listed the occupants of households, only to be told that they'd been accidentally tipped onto a bonfire some years ago. 'Never mind.' Rahul felt in his pocket and tipped the baboo and his menial generously, Kay imagined, judging from the delighted gleam in their eyes. 'You've done a great job and I'll make sure your boss gets to hear of it.'

'I never expected this twist. It's come as rather a shock.' They were in the jeep and Kay's voice was thin and ragged. 'But I couldn't have navigated the minefield without you.' She buried her head in his chest. He'd been an unexpected ally.

'Oh, that's quite all right,' Rahul muttered gruffly, clearly a little surprised.

The jeep was gathering speed. Kay hesitated - it seemed a bit of a cheek to ask considering how helpful he'd been. 'Do you think we could possibly make a detour to Loco Quarters?' she asked a little tentatively.

'No problem.'

Something in his tone made Kay tingle. He made a U- turn and was nosing through a crowded bazaar, horn blaring.

' You know,' he said thoughtfully,' the outcome's even better than I'd dared to hope. And perhaps train records kept at Railways HQ in Delhi will provide a few more leads.' He was executing a series of left and rights. 'Or you may even consider placing an advertisement in the newspapers.'

'In the style of COMPANION REQUIRED?'

Rahul laughed. 'And there's always social media.' At a roundabout he took the second exit. 'It's half way down on the right.'

Kay had noticed the street sign. 'But this is Martin Luther King Marg.'

'We have overcome,' Rahul remarked drily, drawing into the kerb. 'Loco Quarters that was.'

Jumping down, Kay found herself facing dilapidated, water-stained, laundry-strewn, unforgiving concrete blocks of flats occupying the entire site of Loco Quarters surrounded by mounds of cow dung, rubbish and dog dirt. 'Oh my God, there's nothing left - no sign of it,' she managed eventually on a shaky note. It was as if a tree - the family tree - had been brutally chopped down.

Without another word, Kay climbed back into the jeep her eyes filling with tears. They plunged homewards, neither saying much, she silently berating Leslie and Delphine for whitewashing the past but conscious of Rahul's concerned sidelong glances.

The sun had set in a burst of fire and the last traces of crimson and gold stained the sky. As they rounded a bend in the road Kay said in a small voice. 'You did warn me.'

Rahul reached for her hand and raised it to his lips as the palace came in sight.

'What's all the excitement?' Still in a state of mental confusion Kay gaped as the jeep halted in the courtyard. The place was humming; orders bellowed.

'A reception. Expect an eclectic mix of local worthies, bigwigs and my constituency workers. You'll come of course.' He made it sound like an order and noticing the firm line of his mouth she saw that it was.

Kay was horrified. 'I can't. I hadn't bargained for this. From past experience I know all the ladies will be dressed to the nines.' She could avoid his gaze but couldn't avoid the agitation in her voice.

'Why not?' Rahul sounded a little exasperated, his hand tightening on her upper arm.

She sighed. How could he be so obtuse? 'For the very reason that I've nothing to wear.' But that wasn't all. She didn't feel in the mood after the melancholy pilgrimage.

Rahul grinned. 'Oh, that old hoary excuse. Mother's dresser's bound to be able to find something for you. Your maid will have a word with her.'

Kay hesitated, very dubious indeed about borrowing Amrita's clothes. But she was drained, too tired and too filthy to argue with him and they parted, she to shift the strongest shots of vodka that had ever crossed her lips and to wallow in scented luxury in that deep, deep rose-onyx bath; he to shower and change.

***

Adjoining Amrita's private puja room was her suite comprising her own spacious set of rooms, in addition to her sewing room, personal drawing room and one room for her wardrobe and another solely for her saris.

Much rejuvenated after a penetrating Ayurvedic massage, Kay shuffled off the bruising past hours and tackled the matter in hand. Colours and textures dazzled her. There were saris and matching cholis for every conceivable occasion; scented drawers of delicate lingerie, slinky nighties, and fashion accessories. Eventually she homed in on an aquamarine silver-bordered silk sari that shimmered like frost as she moved and had every appearance of never having been worn. Durzee adjusted the petticoat and, at Kay's request, rendered the prosaic choli rather more decadent.

'Urray madam-ji!' Her maid had helped her dress and now sucked in her lips with an admiring gasp, her little head bobbing up and down with astonishment. Coiling Kay's hair into a knot, she entwined a chain of scented yellow magnolia in her hair. 'Dekhiay, madam-ji.' She drew Kay over to the full-length Venetian mirror and Kay was scarcely able to believe that the glamorous vision with eyes smoked into a vampish gaze was herself.

Rahul turned round from the window as Kay entered the reception room. 'Wow!' He set down his glass. 'Excuse me,' he said a little huskily and striding from the room returned with a blue tinged pearl necklace, perfectly strung on silver thread, and matching teardrop earrings.

'Blue pearls. I thought they only existed in flights of fancy.'

'They are unusual in that they hail from Tahiti.' Rahul was rather nonchalant about their obvious rarity slipping the necklace round Kay's neck and fastening the only modern part of it, the diamond studded clasp. She felt herself trembling not so much from the cool touch of the stones as the feel of his fingers against her throat.

'Rajkumari Kay,' Rahul said softly and tilting her chin kissed her gently on the cheek.

The thought struck Kay that Amrita might object to her wearing her jewellery and she said as much.

'It's not Mother's personal property,' Rahul corrected quietly. 'It belongs to the family; it's from the Treasury and they're heirlooms.'

'You don't look so bad yourself.' Kay grinned, her knuckles playfully nudging his cheek. From the jewelled mandarin collar of his white sharkskin bund jacket with its glittering diamond buttons to the black evening trousers, he looked every inch a Maharajah.

'I believe I can hear our guests.' From below there was a faint rev of engines as cars swept through the palace gateway. There was a clamour of voices and Rahul moved to the door in welcome.

Who's that English girl...?

I'm old hand at palace parties and those gems are not her own...

And that sari – it is top notch...

She looks very much at home...

Rahul and she are like steel pins to a magnet...

More than one eyebrow was raised in their direction but Kay didn't care. Rahul huddled with men guests several rooms away, seemed to have the faculty of hearing the ladies' whispers and grinned impishly at Kay as he circulated, still keeping her in his sights.

It was a glittering evening, the floodlit grounds mirroring the jewels of the women moving gracefully in their saris from one chamber to another – chambers specially opened up for the occasion - and in the long corridors deferential omnipresent servants moved around with trays of drinks and snacks.

And as the first streaks of dawn lit the sky, multi-coloured balloons were released and the last car rumbled down the hillside.

Kay kicked off the silver sandals and subsided on to a sofa.

'That was so cool and just the antidote to the earlier part of the day. How clever of you to have persuaded me.'

'There's something I've been meaning to show you,' Rahul said in her ear. 'A slice of yesterday.' He slipped a hand into his trouser pocket and unclenched his fist to reveal an enormous ruby, shooting arrows of fire.

'Where's yours?' Kay quipped and he laughed. She traced a finger lightly over it. 'I feel as though I'm shaking hands with history.'

Rahul weighed the stone in the palm of his hand. 'A priceless heirloom - and uninsurable - we call the jewel of Walipur. It was forfeited by my ancestors from a Mogul Emperor in the sixteenth century in return for a guarantee of safe passage.' He re-filled their champagne glasses with sparkling mineral water. 'It's said that as long as it remains in the family, it'll ensure good luck. So our fortunes literally depend on it.' He paused and Kay drew in her breath as he flung it up into the air, catching it as it planed down, blazing like a comet. 'It's been in the family ever since and passes to every new Maharani on marriage. My woman, my bride, who is above rubies, will wear it on her wedding day.'

Vimla. The spell was broken. Kay felt a sudden, sharp pain. Vimla who would be his wife, his lover and bear his children. It was odd how deeply the thought could wound her.

CHAPTER 21

'Do you know any AIs?' It was the day after the reception and Rahul was putting the finishing touches to a keynote address that would open an agrarian reform meeting.

'Mmm?' He glanced across from his laptop. 'Of course. Supremo Barry Maddox; my excellent aide, Powley; then there's my dentist Dr Boileau and the new Headmaster of my old school ; not to mention my optician, once a lonely Brahmin widower who re-discovered marital bliss with a delightful AI widow who he met through an internet dating site. And there're some big hitters in government service and Parliament...shall I go on? Oh, and those luscious beauties, Kitty Kirkpatrick and Catherine Worlee.'

'Were they at the party? I don't recollect being introduced,' Kay asked a little coldly.

Rahul chortled. 'The divine Kitty stormed in as Blumine in Carlyle's *Sartor Resartus* and as for Catherine - well, she wrapped up things pretty well for herself by marrying Napoleon's Foreign Minister and becoming Princess Talleyrand.'

'Fancy that!' Kay could only laugh at herself. 'Well they've set the gold standard for us. Now I wonder could I monopolise your library? Make some overseas calls and Google?'

'You're welcome.' He hit the SAVE key. 'By the way, I'm heading back to Delhi in a couple of days but you're welcome to stay on here for a while.' He sounded as though he meant it.

'Thanks that's kind but I'd rather go back. I just want to get my head round this business.'

'Fine.' There was a smile in Rahul's voice and he shot her a quizzical look as if inviting a confidence.

Kay was only too aware that she hadn't channelled to him what she really thought about her newfound heritage, and that he must be wondering if she would. What he must have sensed though from the expression on her face was that it had come as a bombshell to her that nothing was as it seemed.

'By the way, you'll have to squeeze in that visit to the Taj Mahal since Hermie's bound to quiz you.'

Kay groaned. 'Oh God, that completely slipped my mind. Can't I just do a virtual tour on the web?'

He laughed. 'You're the first person I know who has ever felt like that about it.'

The library was a vast panelled room overlooking the palace motor museum that housed an eclectic collection of vintage cars - a 1909 Silver Ghost Rolls Royce and a 1938 Phantom 3 among them. Kay punched in Yvonne's number and, glancing at the ormolu clock, realised it was early morning in London.

Yvonne's sleepy tones sharpened when she heard Kay's voice.

'How do you think Mum and Dad registered me as English born?' The mystery of her birth haunted Kay.

'No problem pulling that off.' Yvonne yawned. 'Say you accompanied them to London when you were just a few weeks old. In those days babies didn't need their own passports; the majority weren't even listed on parents travel documents and, at the time, UK immigration control was pretty lax and haphazard . Delphine was a nurse and it couldn't have been difficult to pretend she'd had a home confinement at the Ealing flat. All she and Leslie had to do was to register you in England within forty-two days of birth. Nobody would be any the wiser. What could be easier?'

The scam tripped off her lips with such conviction that Kay wondered if members of Yvonne's Jamaican born community had employed the same ruse.

Kay set about exhuming worthy sociological surveys and earnest doctoral dissertations on the AI that dated from the early 1950s to the present day. Identity, socio-economic status, social exclusion, customs, culture and traditions, inter-marriage - all these features and more and every nuance of them were minutely examined and dissected, and incomprehensible, illogical, unreasoned and. often barmy, findings reached.

It was obvious that the AI despised the 1950s novel *Bhowani Junction* by John Masters and its 1965 adaptation as a movie melodrama starring Ava Gardner and Stewart Granger. And in *Hostages to Fortune* by Frank Anthony, a deceased but much lamented and highly regarded former AI Leader, the British were denounced and an AI template set out.

There were sobering contemporary stories of impoverished remnants in enclaves up and down India who eked out a subsistence existence. There were lively AI websites and chat-rooms in India, the USA, Canada and Australia that united the diaspora. And several un-redeemably awful contemporary films, rather tedious and cliché ridden re-treads Kay thought as she fast-forwarded through the DVDs that perpetuated the tired stereotype and caricatured the AI.

Stumbling across *Letters to the Editor* in a newsletter circulating in the AI community a disgruntled AI in a major Indian city demanded to know what the country had done for them. He was roundly criticised in the next issue by a fellow AI who reminded him about the line in JFK's famous 1961 Inauguration Address: *Ask not what your country can do for you - ask what you can do for your country.*

***

Renee greeted her with 'welcome to the club,' when Kay telephoned with the revelation. She admitted she'd suspected Kay was of AI descent given the Blakes historical connection with the railways during the Raj. Brimming with excitement she told Kay that Tony had been busy in her absence. Paying a visit to a railway veterans home in old Delhi he'd got into conversation with a doddery signalman who'd been stationed in Ajeemkot and formed the impression that the wilful sister of Ashley Blake had turned her back on home after a family row, never to be seen again. Wild rumours suggested that either she was in a mental home or enclosed Order or had sailed to Australia, her fair skin making her eligible for settlement there under the all white policy of its post-war government.

Rahul sped Kay back to Delhi and Hermie had watched their arrival from the sitting room window. Her eyes were dark pouches in a paper-white face and she seemed to have dipped physically and to be rather more dependent on Kay. 'You look as though you enjoyed yourself in Walipur.'

'It was fabulous. I had a wonderful tour of the palace and its treasures, learned a lot about its history and saw something of the rural landscape. Rahul was...well... so kind and attentive,' Kay said, blushing a little at the memory of his face as he lifted the pearls to her throat.

Hermie suddenly caught herself remembering every contour of HH's body. 'Don't allow yourself to be seduc...carried away.' She leaned forward and waggled a finger at her. 'Dwell on the pleasures of the palace and you're on your way to the devil. Just you remember that.'

'You've a fertile imagination.' Kay noticed that Hermie had put down her knitting and her hands lay clasped tightly in her lap.

'What else did you do? What did you talk about, eh? So I was right - while the cat was away the mouse played.'

Kay's eyes widened at the unwarranted interference but said nothing, turning away to pour out another cup of tea.

But Hermie wasn't to be stopped. 'Those kind of men - they're all playboys and stick to their own kind,' she said in a hard, sharp voice. 'A threat to your peace of mind and much else besides.' But she had a feeling her advice fell on deaf ears. 'Does Amrita know you were a house-guest?'

'I haven't the faintest idea,' Kay said stiffly. 'I suspect, however, she was the first to know.'

Sensing the turmoil she'd sparked in Kay, Hermie got in a few grumbles about the sorry and neglected state of the bungalow that was, as always, in pristine condition. 'And I don't hear you asking about me.'

Kay was about to say she hadn't had the chance what with Hermie's inquisition, when Hermie swept on. She tapped her heart.' I suffered severe angina pains and Bernadette summoned the doctor. Mind you, he was first-rate even though he does practise conventional medicine,' she added grudgingly, 'and put me through a battery of tests.' She sounded a little peeved that he'd diagnosed a complaint overlooked by her hakim. 'American trained, at John Hopkins, no less, and ordered me to undergo angioplasty, but I refused. So in lieu he prescribed the latest drugs, and with a bit of luck I'm on the mend.'

Kay wondered if she'd switch allegiance from the hakim.

That same morning, Amrita had buttonholed Rahul at the breakfast table. 'Just a moment before you go. There's something I have to talk to you about.'

Rahul sighed and stared pointedly at his watch. 'Do be quick, Mother, I've a helluva lot on. '

She pre-empted him. 'It's **not** about Vimla. It has been reported to me that you took that woman, Kay, home to Walipur where you put her up for some days; that she helped you host an important event dressed in a sari.'

He turned on his heel. 'What of it?'

'What of it?' Amrita's self control snapped. 'You ask me that?   That woman in one of my saris and wearing my jewellery.'

'I've never seen you in that sari. Indeed, I believe it was still in its original wrapping, a sure sign you've never touched it.'

'And never ever likely to after she has defiled it. Besides, when did you become an expert on saris? What do you know or remember of what I wear or don't wear, and when?'

'And not your jewellery. It was from Treasury stock.'

'Don't split hairs with me. You know exactly what I mean.'

'I don't. Be more specific.'

She raised her voice. 'The whole of Walipur is buzzing. What are your intentions?' She wondered if they'd slept together but didn't dare ask.

Hearing raised voices a servant came running, and Amrita told him sharply to go about his business.

'I don't have any intentions.'

Amrita hadn't finished. 'You forget you're no longer in the States where you can do what you like, when you like, with any woman you like. I'm truly concerned about you. You're playing games with Vimla and how can I explain your entertainment of Kay, so compromising, to Mrs Vohra? All you want is fun and no commitment. I feel completely let down.'

'To hell with Mrs Vohra –'

'No! You're too self-willed,' she said heatedly. 'The world is full of Mrs Vohras. You're getting to be like your father. My father had to warn me against him.'

'Now this is getting irrelevant. I'm not interested in ancient history.' Rahul saw his chance and disappeared.

Amrita felt she'd made her point, but where had that got her? As she brooded on it all day, she admitted to herself that she could have made less of a lecture of it or chosen her moment better when Rahul was less obviously in a hurry.

***

Kay didn't like to leave Hermie on her own that Sunday when Renee and Tony invited her to lunch with a relative. 'I'm sure they won't mind if you join us,' Kay said.

'No,' Hermie said rather more firmly, Kay thought, than was necessary. 'I don't want to get mixed up with that lot...but don't let me stop you. Run along now and enjoy yourself. Edith has promised to drop by.'

That lot! Indeed! Soon she'd learn that Kay herself was now part of that lot. She went to her room to change, feeling insulted. What gave Hermie the right to speak so contemptuously, or even to think like that? Who did she think she was?

Kay took the metro as far as she could and made her way to St. Barbara's Haven, a residential institution in old Delhi founded some 125 years earlier for elderly Christian ladies without a place of their own. Renee, Tony, and Darryl - Renee's brother who ran a thriving travel agency and whom Kay had met before – had already arrived laden with tiffin carriers.

'Is Jyoti ill?' Kay asked referring to Darryl's pretty, shy fiancée, for they were inseparable, and immediately wished she hadn't since it was obviously a sensitive issue.

'She's unable to make it,' he mumbled, and it was clear to Kay that for some reason it was he who'd decided that his fiancée shouldn't come.

'I wish you'd told me about contributions to the commissariat,' Kay said a little testily, eyeing the tiffin carriers and comparing it with her small box of sweetmeats. 'My offering looks rather meagre.'

'Don't sweat,' Darryl said wearily passing a hand over his brow. 'You're our guest.' He seemed oddly tense, and Kay wondered if he'd quarrelled with Jyoti.

They were a little early and sat in a flower-filled courtyard, enjoying the sunshine and fresh air, while waiting for Miss Merriton, their elderly relative, to surface.

Renee told Kay that they'd stopped off at the *Bareilly Deli* en route and loaded the tiffin carriers with a selection of up-scale take-away dishes.

'Yet another brainwave of tycoon Barry Maddox,' Tony said. 'Just when yawl thinks he has exhausted his repertoire, he surprises you. He's a ruddy genius.'

'Mind, he invariably pilots new enterprises in Bareilly, right.' Renee put in.

'Bareilly? You've lost me.' Kay raised her eyebrows.

'That's Barry's hometown and he has a soft spot for it, man. I think it's some private joke. It's a decidedly average sort of place where absolutely nothing ever happens, but he's its local zero to hero.' Darryl offered a cigarette to Kay but she passed. 'Most of his gastronomic win-wins are named after it.'

'Like those three doshas. *Chez Bareilly*, the swanky French restaurant patronised by the smart set or *Mamma Bareilly*, his shining Italian joint, and *Bareilly Bamboo*, the best Chinese in Delhi - '

Renee chimed in, 'and now he's trialling *Bareilly Equator* which is Ethiopian and pan-African food.'

'It's a play on Barry, right?' Darryl said heavily.

A sound made them look round. A hatchet-faced woman with thick eyebrows comfortably into her nineties whom Kay took to be Miss Merriton beckoned imperiously from a doorway that gave onto the courtyard. A distant cousin of Renee and Darryl's father, Miss Merriton possessed a tiny occupational pension but was otherwise without means and occupied a spacious room. Apart from a few residents like her who contributed a little themselves and who occupied privileged rooms with a view of the garden, at the rear of the building was a twelve-bed dormitory where elderly indigents were accommodated for free.

Renee had told Kay that St. Barbara's was entirely dependent on voluntary hand-outs. With the *The Shakers* she gave a benefit performance for it once a year and it featured high on Barry's list of charities. 'The destitute are simply heart breaking but they're lucky not to be living in the gutters, like some of our AIs in Kolkata.'

'Why so? ' Kay was shocked.

'Mind you, it's not their fault. After a lifetime of raising family and living in a close family circle, they've been abandoned by sons and daughters, grandchildren, siblings, nephews and nieces who took a punt on the West, shedding themselves of all moral and financial responsibility for their ageing, ill and impoverished elders, generally dark-skinned, I might add, back in India. All the poor dears receive from them at Christmas time is a cheap, tawdry card, if that. Not a rupee is sent from one year's end to the next. It's a bloody disgrace.'

'This is Kay Forrester from England, Aunty Gloria,' Darryl bellowed the introduction above the radio pounding away from the depths of an ancient hinged, drop-front case.

What struck Kay was that Miss Merriton was not, and could never have been, attractive. Almost everything about her was khaki; her skin, her eyes, her wrinkled stockings peeking out of strappy open-toed brown sandals. Her hair was a resolute shade of strawberry blonde. Over a patterned yellow-brown dress she wore a badly knitted cardigan in combat green.

They lined up to give her a dutiful peck on the cheek, and Kay found herself doing likewise, recoiling slightly from the mildewed smell, and forming the distinct impression that theirs was very much a duty visit.

She glanced round the room. There was a manually operated Singer sewing machine in one corner, hand embroidered silk pictures, and a carrom board perched on a rickety, dark cane table. A triangular dark wooden frame was nailed to the wall from which hung a black umbrella, a shapeless old coat and a crocheted red beret with orange pompoms.

'Don't shout.' Miss Merriton snapped, her harpy manner as a former hospital Matron still undiminished. Her chee-chee tones were harsh and strident. 'I may be a little hard of hearing but I'm not stupid, or soppy, unlike yawl.' She was squaring up for a fight and Kay wondered if she'd been asked along to divert the inevitable, but dismissed it as an uncharitable thought.

'Put those flowers in that vase, child, at once,' she told Kay 'and arrange it nicely, mind.' She went into rigmarole about adding aspirin, testing the water temperature and cutting the stems at an acute angle three inches from the bottom, advice that Kay ignored.

It wasn't long before she'd landed another right. 'The devil has work for idle hands,' she accused Tony who was sitting placidly in a cracked Rexene chair, content to leave Renee, who seemed to know where Miss Merriton kept things, to arrange a brown plastic tablecloth on the folding table and decant the contents of the tiffin carriers.

Tony sprang to his feet, tripping over a moulting black cat that, like its owner hissed and spat, before it disappeared out of the open window. 'Ouch, that damned beast savaged me.' He was nursing a bleeding hand.

'Go and run it under the tap, dear,' Renee whispered. 'I'm nearly done here so we can eat when you're ready.'

They drew up hard backed chairs to the table; the cat, sensing food, re-appeared and leapt into Miss Merriton's lap, its eyes focused coldly on Tony.

Miss Merriton peered and lowered her face to sniff the array of dishes. 'Proper nosh, I trust. Not that Indian rubbish.' Her mouth was pinched and disapproving.

'The best of the *Deli.*' Darryl said immodestly.

'It had better be. Only the best's good enough for me,' snapped Miss Merriton. 'That's why I spurned that Maddox. The only reason I'd go to his funeral is to make sure he's dead.'

Renee rolled her eyes and was later to tell Kay that Miss Merriton was very much the woman scorned when, at rather more than sixty, having nursed Barry through an emergency appendectomy she had, like a host of others, fallen hard for him, a love that was unsolicited, unrequited.

'Wait for it,' Tony mouthed to Kay, behind his hand.

'Where are the condiments?' Miss Merriton was querulous. 'Don't say they're factory bottled; I won't touch it. In my day we got them from a Chutney Mary.' She dug a spoon into a dish with the determination of someone undertaking a ram-raid. 'What's this? Yawl know I can't stand that mushy mucky bhindi bhaji...and I don't like...' The litany of moans was never ending yet there was no stopping her as she heaped her plate with the Indian food, and with egg cutlets, spicy kebabs, mince stuffed aubergine cutlets, puchkas, tomato kasaundi and cucumber pickle, all of which Kay reckoned were AI specialities. Looking at the mountain on Miss Merriton's plate you'd think she was breaking a hunger strike.

'Delicious.' Kay mumbled with her mouth full. 'Tell me, I've always wondered, what's a Chutney Mary?'

Renee laughed. 'Oh everyone thinks she's one of us, but that's a popular misconception. She'd be a hard-up Indian Christian who makes home-made pickle, preserves, jam and yes, chutneys, that she flogs in the bazaar to make ends meet.'

Miss Merriton was a noisy eater. Kay wondered if they'd think her greedy if she helped herself to seconds. She was pre-empted by Miss Merriton who, leaning across with boarding house arms, scraped the dishes clear.

'Next time,' the old woman growled, 'yawl must bring me something I can eat.' She gave a thin smile. 'Now I've got a special treat for yawl. Made with my own fair hands. Over there on the window ledge, Renee.'

Tony shuddered a little for it was just where the cat had jumped in and out. Pushing back her chair Renee went over, bearing back to the table a deep glass dish of chalk-white blancmange snug in an apron of wobbly, yellow jelly. Kay stared at it, stunned and not a little repelled, and Renee went a curious shade of purple.

'Very... er, nice,' Kay said falteringly, wondering how she could offer round the sweetmeats without hurting Miss Merriton's feelings.

'Tuck in,' Miss Merriton ordered.

Kay carved out a large portion for Miss Merriton and she protested. 'Not, so much – it's to be shared between the five us, child. Do you know, it's my favourite and as a little girl, I was addicted to it?' She closed her eyes, 'Sunday lunch with the family, way back all those years ago, used to be roast meat followed by a pudding like this. Not any of this greasy stuff *these Indians* and that conniving Jyoti eat,' she muttered disagreeably.

Provoked, Darryl reached over for the box of sweetmeats, untied the narrow strip of ribbon and snapped back the cardboard lid. Miss Merriton's eyes glinted, and shoving aside her own much vaunted dessert, swooped down like a marauding kite and helped herself to several choice chunks sprinkled with silver vark. She guzzled away, giving every impression of considerable enjoyment, while the others pushed the offending pudding round on their plates, Tony surreptitiously slipping his to the cat that, tiring of Miss Merriton's bony lap, was staring up at him balefully from the floor.

'I'm glad that girl saw fit to absent herself. Have you broken off the engagement?' Miss Merriton pinned Darryl to his seat like a mongoose watching a snake. 'Is this your new lady friend, then?' She jerked her head at Kay.

'Of course not,' Darryl said indignantly adding, Kay thought, with some courage, 'Jyoti won't be visiting you again because I want to spare her the sort of scene she had to endure last time. She was very upset, and I can't say that I blame her.' He took a deep breath. 'You were and continue to be bloody rude.'

'Good!' Miss Merriton said with relish and turned to Kay. 'Listen to the way that boy talks to his elders. And it's always Jyoti this and Jyoti that.'

'Well, Aunty Gloria,' Renee pointed out reasonably as she cleared away the meal, 'they are engaged.'

'Shut your gob, young woman, I'm addressing your brother.' Miss Merriton was actually talking to Kay. 'You know, Darryl gave that scheming Jyoti a pricey engagement ring. It practically cleaned him out. Have you seen it?

'It's very pretty - the diamonds are like stars,' Kay said truthfully.

It was obvious Miss Merriton didn't care for the truth. She scowled at Kay and went on. 'Stars, my foot. It cost him the earth and that's not all -'

They stared transfixed. Miss Merriton was enjoying her captive audience. 'Already they maintain a joint bank account -'

' Who told you that?' Darryl cut in. Aunty Gloria was right but who, he wondered, was the source of her information and he resented his personal affairs being bandied about.

'You don't deny it then?' Miss Merriton's face broke into a nasty smile of satisfaction at her own shrewd guess. 'That Jyoti is *gamaal*- a mischief-maker. You know why Kay she's still on the highest, dustiest shelf without a Hindu husband? She's the youngest of three sisters and her parents having beggared themselves marrying off the others, can't find her a bridegroom because they can't afford the dowry and the older she gets, the more difficult it is for her, because the older you are,' Miss Merriton embellished cattily, 'the plainer you are (not me, of course) and that means you're even less likely to find a suitable boy, so an even heftier dowry is required. So,' she reached for the jug of freshly squeezed orange juice, ' that Jyoti gets her cat's claws into our Darryl, knowing that a dowry is not usual in our community and bewildered and bewitched him, no doubt with those magic Hindu love potions from the bazaar. Spiked his tea with it and date raped him.'

Startled, they exchanged glances.

' Pah! And he can't see what's happening right under his nose.' Aunty Gloria slurped noisily. 'Without him she wouldn't have a hope of marriage. Darryl marrying a Hindu? Over my dead body! Couldn't he have chosen a nice Christian girl from our community or from down south? No. He has to go and choose that one.' Tears filled her eyes. 'And look at her background - her command of English is poor because she has been educated in a Hindi medium school.'

'She's a very nice girl,' Kay ventured.

Miss Merriton hadn't finished her rant. 'You know nothing! I predicted this sorry state of affairs when yawl started learning Hindi - that was the thin end of the wedge. I'll never receive her here, never.' She dealt another blow. 'And I've no intention of coming to the wedding –'

'Oh, Aunty Gloria!' Renee cried, beside herself, 'don't be like that.' No Merriton had ever boycotted a family wedding.

Kay detected a gleam in the old woman's eyes positively gloating over the way she'd wound up her young relatives. 'And I suppose Darryl, you'll do that mumbo jumbo circling seven times round the scared fire?'

Darryl took a deep breath and, to his credit, Kay saw that he didn't lash out. 'Of course', he said evenly, 'plus a hocus pocus Nuptial Mass.'

Miss Merriton didn't care for the tables being turned on her. Pointing a trembling finger at a tarnished silver tea service on the oak dresser, she played her trump card. 'That has been in my family since the Mutiny. I always intended that one day Darryl's family would inherit, but now never will I permit that to pass to the children of a Hindu mother.' Her strength of opposition to Darryl marrying out was reinforced by three loud thumps of her walking stick on the cement floor.

They sat enveloped in a chill silence, avoiding each other's eyes.

'And what have you seen of India so far?' Miss Merriton asked Kay eventually. Having won the shoot-out, she could afford to sound gracious.

Kay said the first thing that came into her head. 'I've just visited Walipur.'

Miss Merriton gave a sniff. 'Walipur I don't know but way back when I was a nurse - you know all those handsome doctors battled to date me - I worked in the hospital in Ajeemkot that isn't far from there.'

On a mad impulse Kay delved into her handbag and showed her the wedding photo of Iris and Ashley. 'You wouldn't happen to know them, would you? Like you she was a nurse there.' It had said as much on the marriage certificate.

Miss Merriton held it up to the light and peered at it with the small magnifying glass she wore on a chain round her neck. 'Let me see... Oh my goodness - this takes me back. Of course, that's my nice colleague Iris Quinn, and she married whatshisname...yes, Ashley. That's it, Ashley Blake, a loco driver. My, he was dark. You know, I was a guest at their wedding - a fine do that was - but shortly afterwards I was promoted to a higher grade and posted elsewhere. Oh yes, I always won promotion. And then in the way of things somehow we lost touch.' She handed it back and Kay noticed that Miss Merriton had large, ugly hands. 'How did you come by it?'

'Er, um, a friend in England suggested that I might want to ...look them up.'

Miss Merriton gave a short rasping laugh. 'Dig them up, you mean. I hear they perished in a cholera epidemic. Dead as doornails.'

Kay glanced at Renee. Miss Merriton had her facts right. 'Did Ashley have brothers and sisters?'

' Just the one. Iris used to say she was a proper little madam.'

'Do you think you could remember her name?'

'Wash out your mouth. Don't you go maligning me. There's nothing wrong with my memory.' Miss Merriton's anger spewed out again. 'That's the trouble with you young ones - no respect. I haven't got Alzheimer's. Now let my grey cells do the talking.' She reached for the last piece of burfee and chewed it very slowly, savouring it down to the last crumb.

They were all leaning forward Kay suddenly realised, watching as the cogwheels engaged.

'It begins with an H. Yes, that's right, I'm sure. H is for hellish as Iris used to say. Now is it Hyacinth? No, because I wouldn't have forgotten it was flowery, like Iris's, so it can't be. Helen? No, though she fancied she had the face that would launch a thousand ships. Hazel? No. No.' Miss Merriton gave a cackle. 'That's pussy's name. Wait...it's coming to me, it's coming, it's on the tip of my tongue. Oh... it's gone.' She slumped back in the chair. 'It was something fancy, that much I grant you.'

Bitterly disappointed, Kay caught Renee's sympathetic eye. *We'll keep trying,* she mouthed.

Tony coughed and checked the time. 'My shift starts in an hour, so we'll have to head off.' It was a diplomatic excuse because he never worked on Sundays, but Miss Merriton wasn't to know that. It was a signal for them to leave. Renee kissed her and Kay, who couldn't remember when anyone had displayed quite so many un-redeeming features as Miss Merriton, shook her hand while Tony and Darryl patted her briefly on the shoulder drawing their hands away quickly as if from a fire.

'Whew!' Tony said as they strolled across the pretty courtyard and smiled at some residents seated on benches. 'She'd make a mint curdling milk.'

'Are your parents opposed to the marriage?' Kay asked Darryl tentatively.

'Not at all. They're very fond of Jyoti and accept that I have the maturity and the right to choose for myself. Jyoti's folks were a little troubled at first but I've won them round. So that leaves Aunty who's a pain in the proverbial.'

'The standoff with Aunty will last to the end,' Renee said gloomily. 'When they're at the altar rail she'll be calling Mum and demanding that she comes round and helps her to dress.' They'd seen it all before.

'And Mum, bless her, won't have the heart to refuse and the whole event will be delayed with us waiting like sheep.' Darryl shuddered at the prospect. 'Count yourself lucky Kay, you don't have the same problem.'

But Kay did have a problem - the problem of her growing fondness for Rahul and whether he reciprocated. And there was also her quest blighted by the absence of living relatives. Was it really worthwhile staying in India any longer but who'd look after Hermie? She couldn't break her promise to her.

CHAPTER 22

The spring festival of Holi descended and an unsuspecting Kay was ambushed by revellers and daubed with coloured dust and dyes.

'And when it becomes a furnace, *Bonnie Brae's* my seasonal lifeline,' Hermie declared.

Renee was touring with *The Shakers* and Kay missed her friendship. And as for Rahul - Kay sighed. *In Walipur he was holding my hand. What has changed?*

'I've noticed with growing concern that Hermie's becoming rather dependent on you. Do you think it's fair to let her become so attached when you'll be leaving at the end of the year?' Rahul had said pointedly

'Well, there's not much I can do about that. I was hired as a companion, remember? It's really up to Hermie to keep me at arm's length or, as she'd put it, keep me in my place. I think you'd agree she's capable of that.'

He'd grunted and abandoned the subject.

***

The temperature soared and Kay felt drained. May brought the loo - the grit-laden burning wind raging up from the Thar Desert keeping Gopi in perpetual motion dusting the house three times a day. At night, during power outages, beds were moved out into the garden where it was cooler but Kay still spent restless hours, her eyes following shooting stars. The rain-starved earth cracked, flowers withered and fruit rotted quickly.

'I'll head up to *Bonnie Brae* and get things ship shape,' Kay offered, 'so which of the servants shall I take?'

'None,' Hermie said flatly. '*Queen of the hills*, Sivalik may well call herself but they don't like it since it's too far from their villages. They're crafty devils. In the past, when I didn't know better, I insisted they accompanied me only to find they primed relatives to summon them home with anguished telegrams announcing that some cousin or ageing uncle had breathed his last. I took the hint and their folks have kept remarkably healthy ever since.'

'You mean they'd rather stay down in the blistering heat near kith and kin than trade it for the mountains?' Kay was incredulous. Left to their own devices she could imagine standards slipping. Gopi as she well knew was an arch backslider.

Hermie sighed. 'I know exactly what they get up to when I'm away. But what can I do about it? If I put them under any compulsion, I'd risk losing them.' Her brow crinkled. 'I couldn't bear that at my time of life.'

During the winter the six-person alliance of householders to which Hermie belonged employed a local chowkidar to police the vacant hill cottages. 'And in the summer he engages a temporary servant for me. But this year as I have you, I'll do without.'

'Er... er...'Kay wondered how to put it tactfully. Now fully accustomed to domestic help, she didn't relish household chores in an unfamiliar setting, however lyrical. 'It would help to have someone for the rough work and the bazaaring,' she ventured. When the idyllic beauty of the Himalayas beckoned how could she condemn herself to two months of drudgery? She looked hopefully at Hermie.

Hermie briefly shut her eyes. 'Well, perhaps not.' It had been an unfair wheeze but this way, with help in the cottage, she hoped to enjoy more of Kay's lively company.

***

Rahul was going ahead of Amrita to sort out their summer retreat since the days were long gone when the Ratan Singhs had a Comptroller and a fifty strong entourage to oversee the exodus and prevailed on by Hermie to give Kay a lift, he could hardly refuse. He'd been ready to be polite but indifferent but the sight of her in a cream cotton sundress, with her tanned legs, shining cloud of hair and Jackie O sunglasses disarmed him.

'You look so cool and I love that scent. What is it?'

Kay felt an easing of the tension and settled in the front passenger seat with Gertrude in the back breathing down her neck. '*Interdit* by Givenchy. Dammit must he always smoulder?

He laughed and she was pleased that a kind of accord had been restored between them.

They left the sun-girt city by the suspension bridge that spanned the muddy brown waters of the Jumna. The going was slow through scorching villages but gradually the dusty plains ebbed away and as they began the curling ascent past the deeply forested folds of the National Park a russet shadow darted across their path.

'A fox.' Rahul smiled and braked gently. 'The road we're on was completed in 1929,' he said as he niftily negotiated one of its 275 right angle turns and 25 dizzying hairpin bends.

They zigzagged up the steep climb, heavily overhung with wooded hills on one side, a precipitous khud on the other. It was not a drive she cared to see herself tackling.

'It's vertiginous,' Kay gasped clinging to her seat, scarcely able to bring herself to look down. 'Watch it!'   One false move and they'd be hurtling over into the deep valley below. 'It's not exactly for the weak-kneed.'

Seeing a rickety bus hurtling down towards them crammed with rustics, Kay closed her eyes and said faintly. 'The road's too narrow . One of us will have to back up.'

'And it won't be me.' Rahul laughed unkindly at her ashen face. ' Look, you're safely anchored in your seat so just sit back, admire the scenery and fear not, I've made this journey so many times I can do it with my eyes shut.'

'I hope not,' Kay murmured and digging her fingernails into her palms, she averted her head, past thinking what might happen if he miscalculated. Rahul sped past the oncoming vehicle with just millimetres to spare.

Here and there remote ashrams lay hidden amongst mottled hills and Kay glimpsed tumbling silver streams and breathed the freshness of the air. Eventually they emerged from the twisting climb and drew up in Sivalik's open square.

'I can put you out of your misery. We're arrived and this is Laurel Chowk,' Rahul said. Ahead of them on a slope of wild cherry trees the pastel yellow church of *Christ The King* lifted its smooth dome. 'Shall we stretch our legs?'

Kay got out. The air was pure and sharp with the scent of pines. 'It's heavenly after the unforgiving heat.' She looked about her. The mountains kissed the sky, verges sparkled with yellow and pink flowers and overhead thrushes curvetted, whistling their sweet song. Children with round, black eyes and rosy brown skin, skirmishing under a full-leafed lyre-tree, its shape deciding its name, Kay remembered, and unique to Sivalik, ran up and swarmed over the bonnet.

Kay caught Rahul's smile and smiled back. 'Nobody told me it was so divine,'

'Yes, isn't that awful? One tends to take these things for granted. Now, I'll drop you off at *Bonnie Brae*,' he said after they'd drunk several tumblers of sweet tea brought to them courtesy of the prime-sited *High Peaks Cafe*, 'which is something that couldn't be done in earlier times when cars, well, except the

Maharajah's, were banned. Even now, it's still pretty traffic free and really the best way to get around is on a motor scooter.'

'That sounds my kind of thing; perhaps you'd tell me where I could hire one. And enlighten me,' Kay got back into the car, 'I meant to ask Hermie, but *Bonnie Brae* sounds very Scottish.   I'd have expected something more Indian flavoured.'

'Ah. Intimations of homesickness. Sivalik was a popular spot with the British during the Raj and probably reminded the man who built the cottage of the Scottish Highlands so he did the next best thing - named this piece of heaven after it.' His glance brushed her before switching back to the road ahead.

'According to Hermie, Hartley went leopard shooting up here but it did occur to me that that might simply be poetic licence.'

They were climbing up a narrow ribbon of road, shaded on the off- side by the mighty Himalayan oak, the thick trunk white-washed to a few feet, while on the other only an occasional two- strand wire fence separated them from a plunge into a deep gorge of conifers.

'Alas, no.' Rahul gestured deprecatingly. 'Hartley and Father, although they'd never met, were both keen shots. I can't think why. Nowadays, the only shooting permitted is with a camera.' He must have recollected something for he began to laugh.

'Share the joke?'

'One vacation when I was a boy some friends and I were up here and we were mucking about driving everyone mad. One was a really cool mimic - there was no sound, human or animal he couldn't replicate - so late one night, when everyone had gone to bed, we crept out, hid behind a boulder and he imitated to perfection that weird sawing sound a leopard makes. You'd honestly think it was lurking offstage ready to pounce. Lights came on in the palace; in those cottages on that hillside, more lights. The sawing went on and on. Then, creeping towards us in the gloom, we made out several figures - seasoned field sport types, mind you - with loaded shotguns. We were so terrified they were going to let fly we gave ourselves up and got a through lambasting for our sins - not so much, I suspect, for larking about when we ought to have been asleep, but for humbugging the experts.'

Kay laughed and swinging round another deep curve, they crested a great slope of shapely walnut.

'Welcome to *Bonnie Brae.* '

Framed by scented grey-blue pines and whispering silver birch, it overhung the curving road. Kay gazed spellbound.

Rahul opened the car door then cupping his hands shouted for the chowkidar and the sound echoed cleanly across the silent valley. There was an answering call. 'Good, he's only just below us at *The Dell.'*

A few minutes elapsed and then from rustling undergrowth a man with a stout carved stick wearing a grey pullover over flapping trousers, materialised.

'Salaam rajah-ji, salaam madam.'

They namastaed back and he heaved Kay's case onto his shoulder.

'Goodbye for now, Kay. You're in good hands but if you need anything urgently just send him over to me with a chit. There's a landline phone but one tends to lose a connection after fifteen minutes and the mobile signal can be patchy.'

'Thanks for the lift.' Kay wondered at the slight feeling of isolation that had suddenly descended on her, watching till Rahul had bobbed away out of sight behind great-girthed Himalayan deodars thick in leaf. In that moment she knew she'd fallen in love with him, arrogant and difficult though he was but what she was going to do about that she'd no idea. Then she turned round and followed the chowkidar up a stone-strewn path bordered by a tangle of wild flowers.

She paused to get the cottage's perspective. Built, she guessed, in the 1850s, of lime mortar and stone, it had a red sloping corrugated iron roof and parrot green exterior woodwork. Fretted dark oak arches shaded an oak- planked porch, where umbrellas and carved walking sticks stood with a stiff broom, a double row of red-earthenware plant pots and garden tools. On a nail above the door hung a horseshoe, a relic of Ajeemkot, Hermie having whisked it off its peg on the last visit home.

The chowkidar smiled at her encouragingly and taking a bunch of keys from her pocket, Kay turned the doorknob, hearing a faint squeak. There was no hall and she found herself in a large square room with a pink washed ceiling. At the far end four straight-backed chairs were grouped round a circular polished walnut-wood table and beyond it a pine-wood dresser held rows of pink and white plates and, the usual precaution against power cuts, a big beeswax candle and a box of matches.

Pleasingly chintzy and comfortable, the old-fashioned furniture was in keeping with the style of *Bonnie Brae.* Bright dhurries covered dark oak floors, white washed walls bore photographs of Putch and Suzie, a corner held a solemnly ticking cuckoo clock and a picture of Hartley as a young officer in his sappers uniform stood on the carved mantelpiece above the fireplace, while on a shelf, gathering dust, lay his regimental hat and back copies of the National Geographic Magazine. Kay moved across to a window and looked down the little path and across to a valley flaming with rhododendrons.

She attacked the stairs. The creaking timber staircase gave onto a lozenge of a landing, two simple, pretty bedrooms, both similar with cushioned window-seats, chests of drawers, deep almirahs and squashy chairs, and a bathroom with blessed modern plumbing. She found herself grinning with relief that she'd been delivered from emptying a thunder box that Renee had warned her about, or heaving buckets of water from a mountain stream.

'You are liking?' An anxious voice floated up.

She'd forgotten all about the chowkidar and turned swiftly from the view. 'I could live here forever.' She clattered down to the kitchen where the chowkidar was busying himself with a battered tea caddy. Well-worn daykchies lined a shelf in an alcove and a glimpse in the cupboard showed chipped crockery, cutlery in need of a shine, and a pile of yellowing table linen. Kay was relieved she wasn't expected to perform miracles with a primitive sigri for there was a neat little calor gas cooker, a gleaming stainless steel sink, a microwave and a compact fridge/freezer. It seemed as though *Bonnie Brae* had been quietly waiting to be brought to life again after a long hibernation.

'I am engaging Meena, young Pahari, to be starting when Hollingberry madam is arriving.' He handed Kay a cup of tea and she helped herself to a ginger biscuit from a packet she'd bought in the *High Peaks Cafe.*

'Where are we going to put her?' she asked puzzled, struck by the apparent absence of living quarters for the maid from the mountains.

He pointed through the window to what had appeared to her to be a cowshed at a respectable distance from the cottage and investigating, Kay was satisfied that the accommodation was adequate although simple.

'You wanting me tomorrow?'

'No thanks.'

He namastaed and hobbling down the hillside shouted up to say that if she had any problems he would be at *Larkspur* for the next few days, pointing vaguely in the direction of nowhere. Vague gestures in the direction of nowhere were, she was to learn later, a distinct and infuriating characteristic of Sivalik folk.

It had been a long day so, unpacking quickly, Kay decided on a bowl of vegetable soup and an early night.   The bed had been made up, soft and downy, the sheets immaculately ironed but country sounds kept her awake for a while - the hoot of the pygmy owl from its perch in a chir pine, the distant call of a barking deer above the growl of a solitary black bear, the haunting whisper of wind through the trees.

The crowing of a rooster and a rhythmic drumming above her head jarred her awake. *Dammit, what's that?* Getting up, Kay drew the curtain and peered out, bursting into laughter as she glimpsed several red-bottomed, long-tailed, pewter-grey lunghi monkeys prancing across the iron roof. The sun had risen, staining the jagged white teeth of the mountains into strawberry ice cream. Kay stretched and yawned feeling utterly and satisfyingly at home.

Pity Hermie was due soon. That thought brought her swiftly down to earth. She finished breakfast that she'd pleasingly dawdled over and, walking to the coop to scatter grain for the hens, realised that *Bonnie Brae* was open on all sides, surrounded by deep bushes of lavender and creeping plants, some ablaze with flowers. In a sunny spot stood a sundial, its plinth inscribed with the words: *Remembering Hartley who always found time*. Woodland and mountain stretched as far as the eye could see and all the while there was a faint but constant whirring of cicadas. It was, Kay felt, a little rural bubble of serenity. More immediately though, there was the larder to be re-stocked, batteries for the radio and logs for the fire when it turned cold in the evenings. There were sheets to be darned and knives to be sharpened. And the garden, much tangled and overgrown, to be tidied up, but Kay decided to leave that to Meena.

The ring of the telephone startled her with its unexpectedness. 'Are you all right?' asked Rahul.

'It couldn't be better. What a place, it's simply wonderful. I can't think why Hermie doesn't live here all the year round.   I'm just off to the bazaar to get in some supplies.'

'Which one?'

'What do you mean?'

'There're two - one each end. Dufferin - that's bigger - is in the older part of Sivalik and then there's Redburn. And you'll find a few covered shops along the Mall.'

'Which would you say's nearer?'

' Dufferin, easily.'

Picking up her jute shopping bag Kay stepped into a fresh and bracing morning. Her way dropped down past an old school and eventually she began the climb up to Dufferin bazaar. Somewhere birds sang and through thick drifts of spruce the sunlight spangled down over winding moss walled paths edged with bright blue Himalayan poppies as butterflies danced over a bank of mauve lilac. The general effect was like having stumbled into a beautiful fairy-tale.   But a moment later the spell was broken as a threadbare, baggy trousered coolie, humping a heavy load tied to his back with lengths of rope, shuffled past her round a bend.

The furrowed lane stretched up growing progressively steeper and when Kay found herself by an old clock tower she paused, suddenly dizzy, and it took several moments to catch her breath. So this was what Hermie had meant about gradually acclimatising oneself to the rarefied mountain air.

Two grey donkeys and a scooter were all the rush hour she'd had to contend with. From the bazaar came the buzz of laughter and talk but there was not the same rough, raucous sound of city crowds or importuning street pedlars that Kay had found so irritating in Delhi. No one seemed the slightest bit interested in her. The facial features to which she'd become accustomed in the last few months had altered for here many were apple-cheeked Paharis - mountain dwellers - with strong limbs and high cheek bones.

Shopping list in hand, Kay moved purposefully along. Open fronted stalls were doing a roaring trade in a variety of items from fresh vegetables to rosewood walking sticks, watches, table tennis bats, sewing needles and textbooks on particle physics. She fingered some pretty cotton fabrics meaning to run up new curtains for the sitting room to replace those that had faded badly where caught by the sun. And some crockery, she thought, remembering the oddments.

'All fast,' the shopkeeper assured her sensing her interest.

'What?' she said startled.

'It no run,' he explained and she nodded in sudden comprehension.

'How much?'

He told her and she gasped. She'd seen another shopper paying nothing like that. 'You can't be serious.'

The sharp-eyed man shrugged as if he didn't care whether or not he had her custom and Kay floundering, upped her offer but he refused to budge. Kay thought she detected a gleam in his eyes.

Then just as she was about to tell him to shove it, she'd take her business elsewhere, there was a voice at her shoulder.

'I'll take that, that and that... and that's all you'll get and not a paisa more,' the deep tone said with finality.

Kay turned round with mixed feelings, glad to be rescued yet resentful that Rahul had had to. 'I can manage,' she said stiffly.

'Not as well as I can,' Rahul remarked cheerfully as he paid the shopkeeper who tossed in several reels of cotton thread as a bonus. 'Anything else?'

Rather woodenly Kay admitted she needed a frying pan, a sharp vegetable knife, a lemon squeezer and a new kerosene lamp to hang outside at night.

'Come on then.'

With the ease of a skilled huckster, Rahul was driving more hard bargains. 'I'm enjoying this,' he said with a grin. 'I've never shopped for household goods in a bazaar in my life.'

'They're just giving everything away,' Kay grumbled.

'Perhaps they are; after all, I'm a V.I.P.'

She gave him a sharp look but he looked unrepentant.

'Anything else while I'm about it?'

'No.' Kay suppressed a sharp annoyance at his presumption. 'I suppose I ought to say that it was good of you to help, but I really wanted to do some haggling myself,' she said a little resentful that he'd excluded her from the fun of that.

'You're an ungrateful wretch,' he retorted cheerfully. 'By the way did you tell them you were shopping for Hollingberry madam? They'd have quoted the right price had they known, to save themselves an ear-blasting.'

'I didn't.' Kay was rather nettled she hadn't thought of that. 'Now have you finished? Should I don a hair shirt?'

'I can multi-task but being a fashion guru isn't one of them,' he teased. 'Look Kay, that's what Hermie's addicted to.'

Kay glanced across to where a rickety trestle table was set up. 'Honey. '

'Not just any common or garden honey,' Rahul said as they crossed over. He picked up a jar that looked as if it was filled with thick cream. 'This is lotus honey and that coppery gold is saffron honey.'

The honey wallah dipped a tiny wooden spatula into a jar and handed it to Kay.

'Ooh, it's delicious - so red and sweet. Now hang on a moment. Yes, I think its hibiscus.'

'Well guessed. 'Rahul smiled. 'And here's what we call *dirty* honey...'

'To be avoided like the plague?'

'No, no. Granted it's the cheapest honey but that's only because you have to boil and strain it at home yourself. Once that's done, it's as delicious as standard honey.'

'Ji!' The honey wallah was offering them shots of something. Rahul knocked his back in one gulp and Kay did likewise.

'It's mulberry wine, one of Hermie's favourite tipples.' He began to laugh. 'I remember she and Hartley were convinced they could make a better job of it themselves so one year they bought sacks of mulberries and set to bottling it - only once it had fermented the bottles exploded and the stuff was all over *Bonnie Brae*. It was weeks before the cottage was the same again.'

'So lots of honey and lots of mulberry wine for Hermie. I do want everything perfect for her She brought me a charming gift from Mumbai.'

There was a pause. 'You don't say. How atypical.' A curious light had entered Rahul's eyes. 'Hermie's generally very parsimonious. I haven't had as much as a bottle of vinegar from her in all these years. So it's just as well I'm here to help you out,' he said with a maddening grin, recovering himself quickly. 'And now...'

Ignoring Kay's protests that she could manage the parcels herself, he summoned a coolie and she found herself meekly handing them over watching as his sturdy legs sprinted ahead of them, the bundle perched on his shoulder.

Sunlight filtered through interlacing trees and they trudged along in silence. Off the leash, Gertrude bounded ahead and they followed her onto a rugged path that sliced through the hillside and up and ever upwards past *Bryn Mawr, Killarney* and *Tara's Hall* nestling among giant maple and horse chestnut.

Rahul stopped and leaning against a rough wall of fern and moss gazed across to Gun Hill. 'Admire the view.' For seconds neither said anything, their eyes locking.

Kay dragged her gaze away and said quickly. 'I'm beginning to recognise a few landmarks but what's that desolate ruin in that hollow?'

' Well spotted. That's the haunted lodge of Sir George Everest - only he pronounced it Eve-rest - after whom the mountain's named. He was the first Surveyor- General of India with a brilliant mind but ferociously bad tempered from all accounts, who remained a bachelor until well into his sixties. He was so enamoured of his Indian mistress that he tacked on a bibikhana – lady's annexe. Look, you can still see bits of it. He was an absolute martinet and a stickler for perfection, his English subordinates simply loathed him. He'd turn in his grave if he knew Everest is pronounced the way it is today, so perhaps the haunting is him wreaking retribution.'

They'd come full circle. Kay unlocked the cottage door and the coolie left the shopping on the porch.

'I'm sure Hermie will keep you jumping.' He hesitated fractionally. 'I'm heading up home as I'm expecting a call from Powley and since cell phone reception is unreliable here, I have to yoke myself to a semi-functioning land line.'

Kay nodded and smiled trying to make light of the fact that he hadn't suggested a date. One step forward, three backwards.

***

Hermie cast a beady eye over *Bonnie Brae.* 'It's all spick and span I grant you but I hope that in realising perfection you haven't allowed yourself to be fleeced,' she said spikely.

Kay gave a hollow laugh acknowledging to herself that the trouble with Hermie was that she liked things nice but refused to accept how much that could cost. She was a bean counter, although when it came to Putch and Suzie with their plaited leather silver thonged leashes and china bowls, she didn't hesitate to splash the cash.

'No problem, Rahul saw to it that I wasn't.'

Hermie raised her eyebrows but said nothing and Kay saw that she'd slotted the information away.

'So who has chowkidar employed?'

Kay told her about Meena who'd happily taken up residence in the cowshed.

'That's good. I like her. She's been with me three years running save when that witch from *Larkspur* beat me to it. I didn't expect to see her back this year, though.'

'Why ever not?' Kay cut a wedge of chocolate cake.

'I thought she might have become a mother. She's been trying for a baby ever since her marriage some years ago. At one stage she was even considering fertility treatment, but couldn't afford it.'

Kay looked at her flabbergasted. It made no sense to her when there was a population explosion in the sub-continent. 'Hasn't she considered adopting?'

'Out of the question.' Hermie pursed her lips. 'This horrible caste system makes it impossible. What if the baby turned out to be from a dalit background?' '

Kay shuddered, appalled that this sort of mindless discrimination was still all pervasive.

'Meena,' Hermie called, 'are you going to tell me what mischief you've been up to these last few months?'

Giggling shyly behind her hand Meena came running. A broad-hipped girl, she wore traditional dress from the Garwal hills - a yellow bordered, ankle-length full black skirt below a yellow over blouse, her long black hair scooped neatly back in a scarf. Despite the fact that she'd spent several summers in the service of exacting hill householders, she was still jungly. She beamed her pleasure at seeing Hollingberry madam again and Hermie launched into rambling conversation with her in kitchen Hindi. To Kay's horror, tears began to roll down Meena's cheeks and heaving herself up Hermie placed an arm round her shaking shoulders.

Kay started. 'What on earth's the matter?' She hoped Meena wasn't complaining about her. Not that she had grounds to but one never knew...

Hermie's face was grim. 'Poor mite, she's unable to conceive. In her village, fingers are being pointed and people are whispering as rumours are spreading that she's barren because she's possessed by the devil.' Hermie reached over for the telephone book and looked up the number of the cottage hospital. 'I can't stand by and see her suffer. I'm sending her for tests straight away. It's the least I can do and whatever it costs I can afford.' She clenched her hands in a blaze of anger. 'The poor girl's being shunned, her husband has threatened to throw her out and her mother-in-law has been beating her up.'

Kay was taken aback at Hermie's generosity towards Meena, which appeared out of character.

Hermie kept her word. The next day Kay found herself walking with Meena down the stone strewn path. The pines sang and from the distance came the tinkle of cowbells. They parted at a dilapidated signpost *Private Road to Hotel Belvedere.* Kay paused for a moment looking across at the building shadowed with heavy trees; the rusting metal, decaying woodwork, cracked and crumbling stonework bearing witness to its former pomp and glory in the palmy days of the Raj. With a shy smile Meena turned off to the right to the cottage hospital and

Kay scrambled on uphill to the palace. Sheer curiosity and a determination to explore every inch of Sivalik brought her there.

Designed in the style of a French chateau and surrounded by high walls topped with jagged slivers of green glass, the palace, deep windowed, gloriously turreted, stood astride a forested ridge. But weeds choked the side entrance and getting no sense out of doodwallah who was busy un-strapping heavy churns from his scooter Kay trudged round to the big, main entrance. It was ornate, with stone elephants mounted on stone gateposts, the once Venetian-red wrought iron railings bleached to pale rust. A brass nameplate bore the Ratan Singh coat of arms and an inscription redolent of the past – HH The Maharajah of Walipur and someone, with more zeal than success, had attempted to obliterate the words *Pro Rege et Patria.*

Kay stood for a long time absorbed by the picture and the sharp scents of the hillside before retracing her steps along the sunny track to *Bonnie Brae.*

***

Another fortnight of clear skies and crystal air slipped slowly away although Kay didn't think she'd ever forget that morning when the aerial ropeway that swung her up to Gun Hill dangled her over sheer nothingness for a heart-stopping thirty minutes during one of Sivalik's power cuts.

' Delhi was an oven and I'm no hot house plant - just a lily of the valley.' Hermie was sitting in her favourite chair looking at her favourite view - the wooded valley against a backdrop of soaring peaks. The resinous smell of pines poured in through the open window. She smiled at Kay and raised a glass of lager to her lips. 'The simple pleasures of life.'

'Becoming your companion meant that I could stay on to tackle a family riddle and when you were in Mumbai, I kick-started some fieldwork.' What finally sparked Kay to confide in Hermie was the knowledge that she and Hartley had toured the country extensively and she'd shown herself to possess an elephantine memory for names and faces. There was an outside chance she might have heard of the wayward Blake girl.

'Oh, and what's that?' Hermie threw her an encouraging glance.

'Amongst Mum's things I found some photos that made me think I may have Indian links.'

Hermie sat up interested and reached for a cigarette. 'Lots of English people have family ties from way back with India.'

335

'My digging has been useful but I've still a long way to go. But first...' Kay exited the room hurrying back with a large buff envelope. She knelt by Hermie's chair. 'Now this one shows Dad and Mum, Leslie and Delphine Forrester, on their wedding day. Mum's maiden name was Blake.'

Hermie made a sharp audible intake of breath.

'Are you all right?' Kay looked at her anxiously. 'Shall I fetch the brandy?'

'Don't mind me. Go on. What else is there?'

'From various official papers, I've worked out that these people,' Kay pointed to the group photo, 'are Mum's parents and grandparents.' She turned the photo over. 'Look, someone has pencilled initials.'

Kay told Hermie about her conclusions. 'But who and where is Ashley's sister? I assume she's the girl H, the one who seems to have decamped.'

Hermie made no comment and taking up a large magnifying glass to scrutinise the photographs registered with shock the faces of her family in this, a photo belonging to a complete stranger. Her heart was pounding. 'Mmm' she said forcing her tone to sound casual, 'Anything else?'

'Yes. This.'

Tears pricked the back of Hermie's eyes but she kept herself banked down. What a pretty girl Delphine had grown into Hermie thought, glancing back again at the wedding snapshot, but then she'd been a pretty child.   'And this must be your Mum as a baby with her parents.'

'Right first time.'

The years scrolled back and all at once Hermie was in Ajeemkot, long forgotten until this moment, and she saw herself sitting in the tonga bouncing little Delphine on her knee. 'Now remind me - where did you say you found this lot?'

'In Mum's trunk. I was sorting out her belongings after the funeral. I know nothing about Dad's family, although records suggest he was a love child. And these may also interest you...'

Fixated by the certificates Hermie heard Kay babbling like a stream that had burst about her visit to Ajeemkot and much else besides. And when she shuffled through the cemetery photos and read the epitaphs, Hermie felt herself go cold, as though the blood was draining from her, and for a moment she thought she might break down. Then faintly as if from afar she heard Kay's voice.

'But despite all this, the mystery has deepened. I haven't been able to plug the gap with a single living relative and I don't know what to do next.'

Hermie lifted the lager glass to her lips, then realising it was empty placed it on the table with trembling hands. She slanted a glance at Kay and said, 'I think I'll go up to my room and have a shut-eye.' She pressed the back of her hand to her mouth wanting more than anything else to be alone.

Kay regarded her with a concerned look. 'How awful of me to have gone on like that and now I've tired you out.'

'No, no.' Hermie managed a smile. 'I blame this potent cocktail of mountain air and lager.' She rose stiffly. 'Let me have a ponder about your little problem and we can discuss it again later.'

A deep shadow of disappointment clouded Kay's eyes and Hermie unable to bear it turned her gaze away quickly.

Somehow Hermie got upstairs and slumped down in the chair. She shut her eyes and reached for her hairbrush. *I can keep quiet and know that I have a great niece, or I can tell Kay the truth about myself. I won't be hasty.*

***

Over the next few days, Kay observed Hermie looking at her with a curious expression in her eyes and it seemed to Rahul, who noticed the affectionate gaze that followed Kay's movements, that the demanding Hermie was very solicitous of little comforts for Kay almost like that of a mother for her daughter.

'Any one at home?' Rahul's voice from the porch penetrated Kay's racing thoughts.

'Coming,' she shouted, unable to believe that in the fortnight since their last meeting she could miss someone so much. And just what exactly she was going to do about that, she hadn't the slightest idea. Her heart skidded when she caught sight of him in faded blue jeans and tee shirt, a cable knit flung across his shoulders. Gertrude was wagging her tail.

'Hello, ladies.' His hawkish glance flickered curiously between the two women, as if he were assessing something. 'I come from Mother with an invitation for **you,** Hermie '– the stress on her name didn't escape Kay – 'to dine with us tonight. Edith's our houseguest. I'll send the car for you.'

'That sounds very nice. I'd be delighted. Are you going back home now?'

Rahul shook his head. 'My tenants have convened a meeting - no doubt to take me to task for some perceived neglect - so I'm off to Dufferin to be horse whipped. Fancy a walk, Kay?'

'Yes, you run along,' Hermie said unexpectedly, before Kay could invent a diplomatic excuse, and somewhat amazed, recalling Hermie's earlier warnings, she found herself negotiating the downhill track behind him.

'You've quite won over the old girl,' he said.

'Have I?' Kay said sweetly, 'I really wouldn't know.'

'Both Mother and I can't be wrong. But as I've told you before you're only temporary here and old people are very impressionable. We don't want to have to pick up the pieces when you've gone.'

'I can't help it if Hermie likes me.' Kay met his gaze squarely seeing no reason why she shouldn't get that message across.

Rahul halted in his stride beneath a clump of fir trees and swung her round to face him. His eyes were flinty. 'Elderly women are very susceptible to anyone who shows them a bit of attention and kindness and Hermie's no different.'

Kay tried to pull away but his fingers tightened on her shoulders. 'I'm fond of Hermie and I wouldn't do anything to hurt her.' But she herself was worried about a situation that could get out of control.

Rahul kept staring at her in the manner of a prosecutor to an accused. After a few moments his eyes fell away and he let her loose so suddenly Kay almost lost her balance, then turning on his heel he was gone, striding across the hill after Gertrude, the crunch of pine needles underfoot very loud in the still air.

***

Hermie hadn't spoken to Kay again about her findings and Kay had not raised it. But she spent as much time as she could in the reassuring and undemanding company of Tony and Renee, who'd secured a gig at the crumbling *Belvedere* and who knew the hill station well.

Dodging lunghis that swung through the horse chestnut trees pelting passers-by with conkers, the threesome picnicked at moss- curtained waterfalls; another day they browsed through Tibetan handicrafts at the tiny Tibetan township in Jolly Valley with its fluttering pennants, tiny teahouse and Buddhist temple. Kay got the impression that the Tibetans were unpopular with the locals since they thieved the gelignite that was used for blasting limestone, and tossed it into the river to kill the trout.

One long weekend they trekked through breath taking scenery to Gangotri, the source of the holy Ganges River high in the Himalayas. Back in Sivalik, in the endless mountain twilight as distant trumpet notes blown by Tibetan monks echoed sombrely across the mountains Kay, in the depths of a moth-eaten armchair at the *Belvedere* found herself flipping through her friends photos of the many mountain peaks - *Lady Hood 1814*, still legible, boldly graffitied across a rocky flank of Bhardwar.

Renee and *The Shakers* thumped and throbbed, although Kay hoped she wouldn't be expected to sit through another evening of pop rock ballads, for despite her defence of Renee's vocals to Rahul, she thought she was an ear-drum blaster and tended to wave her arms about like a semaphore. And there was a minor tragedy when a cruel-beaked vulture with a nine-foot wingspan swooped down over *Bonnie Brae* and bore away one their chicks.

***

Hermie felt more alone than she'd ever felt before as she battled with herself. She felt as if she'd been dropped into a pit. *Oh Hartley, tell me what to do.* Hartley always so straight and honest would have said, brace yourself Hermione dear, face the truth and be done with subterfuge. *But I'm not going to tell the whole story. That's mine and mine alone.*

It was a seraphic morning. Swathes of light poured through the trees dappling the ground and an occasional bee zoomed through the air. Meena sang to herself as she swept the porch and the clip clop of ponies' hooves sounded very loud in the still air.

Kay sat curled up in a sitting room chair, at her elbow a pile of books authored during the Raj, borrowed from the raftered public library in Laurel Chowk. Entitled *The Owl Taxi, An Averted Marriage* and *Rescuing Rupert*, Kay was laughing immoderately to herself at something in *Thanks to Sanderson.*

'You must have been the best Christmas present for Delphine and Leslie.'

Kay's head jerked up; there was a curious mix of exultation and tenderness in Hermie's tone she'd never heard before.

'And, dear,' Hermie added in a choked voice, as if she was struggling to find the right words, 'I've been meaning to show you something.' She was on her feet and crossing over to a small desk, that she always kept locked, lifted out a tooled-leather photo album. She unsealed an envelope and from it withdrew two black and white snapshots, both slightly cracked down the centre, and handed them to Kay.

Kay studied them in silence for a moment conscious of Hermie's watching eyes.

'They're identical to mine. How...what...?'

'That girl is Ashley's sister. She is Hermione. Hermie.'

'But that's your name.' Kay heard her voice squeak in surprise.

Still with that strained look about her eyes Hermie said, ' I am that girl.'

Aghast, Kay looked down again at the photo and back to Hermie's face. This woman was her great aunt. Her window to the past. It was like tunnelling out of the dark into sunshine.

Hermie reached over and took Kay's small hands in her own and Kay saw that her eyes had filled with tears.

There was a long silence. Kay gently disengaged herself and went to the window, leaning out and taking deep gulps of fresh air. She turned round and heard herself murmuring, a deep apology in her tone, 'But can we be certain?'

Hermie became tight-lipped and her face set. 'You are my biological great niece. But for those of little faith, safely tucked away among my private papers is all the ammunition we'll ever need to satisfy a Judge.'

Then Hermie was hugging Kay tightly as if she never wanted to let her go. 'You've come into my life at a time when I sorely need family, pet.' Hermie lifted a hand and ran it over Kay's hair and cheeks. 'You've got my hair and my smile and my complexion and Ma's little tip-tilted nose and when you're vexed, your frown says Blake all over again. '

Kay started to say something about Leslie but Hermie waved it aside and with a sudden base thought Kay wondered if Hermie would have felt the same way about her if she'd been dark-skinned like Renee, or indeed if she herself would have felt any different if Hermie had been anything like old Miss Merriton.

'Could we talk about how it all happened?' Kay probed gently when they'd both wiped their eyes, wondering if she should address her as Aunty.

Hermie's mouth tightened then she gave a little shrug. 'Why not? What's done is done.' The shuttered look faded. 'Days ago when you started talking, I knew immediately but I wanted time to consider.' She paused. 'If you really want to know... '

'I want to hear if you want to tell.'

Hermie munched meditatively on a marron glace, her feet on a footstool. 'As you know, I'm getting on now although' she added with a touch of vanity, 'I don't look it. There was a seven-year gap between Ashley and me. Ma was pregnant with me when she and Pa went on holiday down south and I decided to put in an appearance a little earlier than expected.'

'Ooh,' said Kay, realisation dawning, 'that explains why there was no trace of you in the Ajeemkot records office.'

'Hermie perverse as ever.' Hermie gave a roguish laugh and jangled her bangles. 'We lived in Ajeemkot's Railway Lines.' She was sketching a picture of the Blakes and Kay drew closer.

'Shall I bring tea, madam?' Meena popped her little head round the door.

'That'll be very nice,' Hermie said, 'and some of those coconut biscuits Kay baked yesterday. Now... where was I?' She picked up her knitting and a far away look came into her eyes as voices from the past echoed in her thoughts.

The floodgates had opened and Kay realised there was no stopping her. 'I was rebellious and swore to pull myself out of the rut. I didn't want to end up like Ma and I could see what was happening to my contemporaries.'

Kay was puzzled. 'You've lost me. What was the problem?'

'The problem?' Hermie blazed. 'I'll tell you. You don't know, can't know, won't know how it was like for AI families like us all those years ago. The British ruling class excluded us socially although they feigned our worth to them by making skivvies of us. We were second-class citizens. Marginalised, I think's the jargon for it. They bought our loyalty with a promise of jobs and pitted us against the Indians, who despised us for being the stooges of the imperial power. We were patriotic to the British and protected their interests, yet they treated us shamefully and abandoned us like an unwanted child when they were forced to pull out. There was deep pay disparity and, with rare exceptions, opportunities for AIs to advance were limited. The old, old ploy of divide and rule.' Her knitting needles click, clicked. 'But Pa and Ashley didn't understand, couldn't see what was happening under their noses. They were content and expected me to conform. We argued and I was rebuked.' She flashed a victory sign. 'But I got my way.'

'And your Mum?' Kay poured a cup of tea and handed it to her with a slice of lemon and Hermie took a few sips, her pinky finger crooked.

'Dear, sweet Ma. I was her princess. She was so anxious for me to do well, to marry well, to be happy.' She sighed. 'How proud she would be if she saw me now. She knew something was pulling me away and I tell a lie when I say she wasn't heart broken when I cut loose.'

Re-living the past was making Hermie emotional and her voice rose and shrilled. 'Poor darling Ma.' Tears sprang to her eyes. 'I was so young, so ...hard. When one's that age one's so single-minded and so...ignorant about life. All I saw was me stepping into delicious freedom. I hurt the very person I never meant to, the very person who meant the world to me. Ma.'

All of a sudden Kay became very conscious that Hermie's voice had taken on the same strong inflexions, the same singsong, as Renee's. Gone was the upper-class English drawl.

'You...' Kay was on sensitive ground and hoped Hermie wouldn't take offence at the past tense, '... were a very attractive young woman.'

Hermie's expression implied that she'd never thought otherwise and she gave that smile that must have brought many a man to his knees. 'Live long enough Kay and you'll grow old gracefully like me. I was sharp-witted, mind. Not bookish or brainy but what yawl call streetwise. I was the last to deny that freedom also spelled danger.'

It was obvious to Kay that Hermie played the starring role in the drama and she suspected that Hermie's story was laced with the wisdom of hindsight, a large dollop of dramatic licence and even greater selective editing as she recounted domestic disputes, her life in Delhi and her meeting and marriage to Hartley. It was like TV soap, and when Hermie paused from time to time to check the knitting pattern or select another piece of crystallised fruit, Kay found herself fidgeting, hardly able to contain herself, for the next episode.

'Did Hartley meet the family... mind about...your being AI?'

Hermie obviously didn't care for this remark for her face went an unhealthy shade of brick. She paused and said coolly. 'That was all nicely tucked away and, besides, I never found the right moment.' Kay sensed she'd ventured into forbidden territory and didn't pursue it.

'I was young and personable and at home in Ajeemkot we lived very much according to the upper class English way of life.'

This was, Kay knew, another whopper. She'd realised from Renee and from her own research, how things were like in those days for families such as the

Blakes, and wondered if she could ever untangle the fiction from the truth in Hermie's account of her past.

'You'd never have guessed I was AI and country born - that was a crude expression coined by the Brits to mean us persons of mixed-descent. I was ashamed of being that, of being off-white, another pejorative they used, but it was caused by their attitude towards us.' Hermie was still prepared to lay the blame elsewhere. 'They got us to do their dirty work; to run the essentials and services that enriched them, drove a wedge between us and the Indians and mocked us behind our backs. I've never forgotten the day Mr Armitage, my boss, forbade me to play in the club tennis tournament. And then when Ma was on her deathbed,' she dabbed her eyes, ' she let me into a secret. About the dashing Englishman who jilted her when she was seventeen. They got engaged - she was so happy she'd never have to ride in a tonga again - and he wrote her such romantic letters about picking the loveliest flower in the meadow only to demand the ring back when he discovered she was chee-chee.'

Kay was shaken, prepared for nothing like this. It was easy, she supposed, with hindsight, to accuse Hermie of selling out.

Hermie turned her gaze to the valley and Kay realised she'd persuaded herself that the family rift was entirely of Pa and Ashley's making and that she was a victim. 'With Hartley I had status, a lovely home, a nicely defined niche in society.'

'Did you and Hartley have any children?'

Hermie sighed. 'Alas, no.' She lowered her voice. 'The specialist told me Hartley had a low sperm count, but I never let on that I knew. I allowed him to think that it was I who was incapable of conceiving. But he never once threw it up in my face.' She stared unblinking at Kay. 'He loved India so, when he decided to stay on, I didn't begrudge him. I was the last person to deny him that wish. Indeed I fully supported and respected his decision even though by doing so I was sacrificing the chance to go **home,** to a nice town in the Home Counties, to a comfortable life-style and as the wife of a war hero. I was never embittered.' The glib lies tripped effortlessly off her tongue.

'And you lived the sort of life you'd aspired to?'

' Absolutely. Hartley made sure I was well looked after.' Indeed she'd made sure that he did.

Hermie stretched out a hand and patted Kay on the arm. 'Even now luck hasn't deserted me. It's so good to know we have ties of kinship. What more could I ask for?'

Hermie leaned back in her chair and smiled contentedly as though some heavy load had dropped from her. At last, without lifting a finger, she'd acquired a relative and a charming one at that.

'You'd have loved Hartley - the pair of you would have got on like a house on fire.'

Hermie, you've still not acknowledged all the facts for what they truly are, Kay nearly said but what was the point? She wondered again if Hermie would've been so quick to claim kinship with her if she'd been anything like Renee. Hermie had ruthlessly axed her family. But Kay's heart ached for her. She couldn't abandon her now. She didn't want to. She'd meddled with Pandora's Box and having lifted the lid knew she must accept what lay inside.

'Why do you think Dad and Mum told me nothing?' Kay wondered why they'd tottered along on this tightrope of secrecy.

Hermie gave a deep sigh. 'Who knows? Maybe they felt they'd left all that behind and were starting a new life. Maybe they didn't want to burden you with all that ethnic baggage.'

They were ashamed of being AI, Kay realised. 'This is the end of my odyssey,' she said sombrely.

'Dear, you must promise me something.' Hermie's hand tightened over her wrist. 'You're not to breathe a word about this to anyone,' she said almost fiercely. 'I don't want to rake over old coals. It's our secret and I want it kept that way. No gossiping. No pillow talk with Rahul. Is that understood? Now, I don't know about you, but I'm gasping for another cuppa.'

Is that all? For a moment Kay had expected an unsavoury disclosure - the neat dispatch of a jealous lover or blackmailer in a convenient shooting accident. Or something spicy – like a love child. *What was it Yvonne said when her own sister, single and sixteen, became pregnant: a child does not wait to be invited. With Hermie anything was possible.*

Kay nodded vigorously and Hermie's face relaxed. Kay was about to add something when Hermie frowned, her face growing frosty and folding the newspaper into a square, she turned to the crossword as if she regarded the conversation as closed, pondering 1 down, 6 across.

Her thoughts spinning, Kay darted to the kitchen to ask Meena to brew a fresh pot of tea. In her heart she supposed she'd known that fate would take a hand but never, ever like this. She wanted desperately to confide in someone but had to keep her promise to Hermie. But what would Rahul make of it, Kay wondered, when he did hear of it, as he was bound to?

In bed that night unable to sleep Kay rolled back the events of the day. She hadn't found relations of her own age but an elderly aunt who'd come to depend on her. To go back to England at the end of the year would be unnecessarily cruel to Hermie. On the other hand, Hermie might be quite content to let her leave. Kay couldn't see any long-term prospects for herself in India. She'd need to kick-start her own life, her career and in due course look forward to having a husband and family of her own. As far as she was concerned, her quest was over. But if she was truthful with herself her feelings for Rahul were not.

***

Hermie mulled over the revelation for several days saying nothing further to Kay about it again, nor without any change in her attitude towards her. She was the same old Hermie, up and down, crotchety, irritable and affectionate. Finally she telephoned Edith at the palace.

'Do come over later if you're free. Something personal has come up and I'd appreciate your advice.'

Edith racked her brains as she walked the half-hour it took to reach *Bonnie Brae*. 'You've not got your colour back, Hermie.'

'Unfortunately I still get some unpleasant spasms.'

'You ought to have taken the doctor's advice and undergone angioplasty. Now you're having more warning signs and you must admit yourself to hospital when you get home. Where's our Kay?'

'I've given her the afternoon off and she's gone for a ride round Camel's Back.'

'If I'd known she could ride, I'd have gone with her.'

'She can't, but she'll try anything once. Now Edith takes a look at this and tell me what you think.'

Somewhat surprised, Edith dropped her head to the bundle of papers while Hermie sat quietly, the only sound the crash of lunghis swinging through the trees.

Twenty minutes later, Edith lifted her eyes. 'Very, very interesting, and although it's a truly remarkable coincidence I don't think there's any doubt about

345

the relationship. However,' she held up a cautionary finger, 'if I were you, I'd run it past Yusuf just to be on the safe side.'

Yusuf had acted for the Hollingberrys for many years. Clever and discreet, he ran a flourishing practice and counted Barry Maddox, the Ratan Singhs, Edith and a host of moneyed Delhi-ites amongst his clientele.

'I was hoping you'd suggest that,' Hermie said. 'That's exactly what I propose to do.'

Edith smiled. *Hermie is no fool.* 'And assuming he okays it what then?'

'Let me say that I've become rather fond of Kay and I'm very pleased it has turned out like this. She's a modern, independent girl, capable of leading her own life.'

Edith reached over for her bag and extracted a packet of cigarettes. 'If proven, then Kay is your next of kin unless...'

'Unless, what?'

'Ashley had other children.'

'Rubbish.' Hermie would have none of it. 'Bernadette maintained her links with Ajeemkot. She'd have known and would almost certainly have told me. Kay's clearly an only child.' Her eyes met those of her friend. 'You know Edith, I can hardly believe it - with Kay I've been given a second chance. Yusuf will find he has some drafting to do.'

Edith picked up her handbag. 'It's not mandatory.'

'You don't have to tell me that. I've never done anything under compulsion.'

Edith said bluntly. 'How much exactly have you told Kay?'

'Only as much as she needs to know,' Hermie said evasively.

'Come on,' Edith said impatiently. 'What do you mean by that?'

'Well you know perfectly well...'

That Hermie didn't care to be reminded by her friend of that chapter of her youth and the way she skirted round the subject convinced Edith that Hermie had suppressed the HH episode. Edith wasn't surprised that Hermie had only told Kay half a tale.

Hermie's mood was very light hearted that evening as she joked her way through dinner. She squeezed Kay's hand tightly before she went upstairs, tackling the stairs with unusual weariness, Kay noticed with a pang of concern. Kay sat motionless for a long time. The revelation of the relationship hadn't been entirely the welcome surprise she'd anticipated. Cousins of her own age with families of their own were one thing; an elderly, infirm widowed great aunt was quite another.

***

Kay saw little of Rahul for just over a week until the morning she was on her way to the Post Office with Hermie's letters, one addressed to Mr Yusuf Khan, Senior Advocate and the other to H.E. The American Ambassador. She'd reached the top of a little hill and had looked back the way she'd come. And then there he was striding up behind her, Gertrude loitering behind on a frolic of her own.

'We meet again.' Rahul's glance drifted from the envelopes to her face.

'Is it such a surprise considering we live not a million miles away from each other?' In spite of herself, Kay felt the colour rise in her cheeks and heard her heart beating like a drum.

He held open the Post Office door and she preceded him inside. *He's being rather off-hand and that's unpleasant. But no matter.* She allowed herself a small smile. *Little does he know!*

Like other things in Sivalik the Post Office was charmingly eccentric. On the counter lay a *Complaints and Suggestions* book alongside a pastry brush stuck in a large pot of gum used liberally by customers to seal their envelopes. And black ink was available on demand.   Behind a counter sat a man at a telephone putting through trunk calls for queuing customers.

'Is Hermie having problems?' It was obvious Rahul was referring to the letter addressed to Yusuf.

'Not that I know of,' Kay replied truthfully for she hadn't typed it. 'Besides, it would be rather rude of me to pry and I'm sure you wouldn't want me to do that.' She licked the stamp and stuck it on, the letter feeling like a burning torch in her hand, and hastily popped it through the slot only too aware of Rahul's eyes watching it slide through.

'Had you thought of asking?' Rahul persisted. 'Perhaps I could help. I usually do; she invariably asks me to draft her letters to him.'

Wisely biting back the retort that it was none of his business, Kay said lightly, 'It can't be important, then. If she needed your help or advice I'm sure she'd have asked.' She added with a slightly mocking echo of his own, 'she usually does.' Kay slung her jute bag over her shoulder and began walking away from him. 'I've no idea what the letter says and I'm not in the least bit interested. Why don't you quiz Hermie herself?'

347

'I fully intend to.' Rahul's eyes narrowed as he followed her out of the door, his big body only a hair's breath away, and Kay realised that he who'd up to now had always been consulted by Hermie about her business affairs found her sudden by-passing of him distinctly out of character.

'But I can tell you about her rather trenchant letter to the Ambassador. '

'Oh, that old book chase,' Rahul said dismissively. 'Personally, I think she can whistle goodbye to them.'

Kay gave a sudden derisive snort and as a thunderclap rang out, scuttled into the nearest tea shack as a sudden shower took everyone unawares, making her hair stick to her scalp and her clothes to her skin.

It was another sparkling day; the air had that effervescence and snap that reminded Kay of the Swiss Alps. Hermie was poring over the morning's mail that had brought Yusuf's assurances that Kay's evidence was incontrovertible, but that Hermie herself would need to satisfy any third party that she was whom she claimed to be by producing not only her marriage certificate but also, more importantly, her birth certificate. It was exactly as Hermie had hoped he'd say.

* * *

Troubles don't come singly. Rahul had cause to remember that nearly three weeks later when the much-vaunted chemical plant in a densely populated, poor sector of Walipur exploded, releasing toxic gas. Thousands succumbed at a stroke to lung-corroding fumes; the death toll rose daily. Corpses littered the streets, family pets lay where they'd collapsed, vultures circled their prey. Hospitals burst at the seams with the dead, the dying and terrified survivors. Pre-occupied with leading a massive relief effort in which Amrita and Edith were embroiled, Rahul, as he'd been meaning to, had no chance to pursue with Hermie his growing suspicions about Kay's motives.

Several days had passed since the catastrophe struck. Wilting from lack of sleep, but angry at the municipality's slowness in ridding the area of decomposing livestock and sick to the stomach with the smell of putrefying animal flesh, Rahul personally commandeered a truck with lifting gear, removed the dead cattle and after dousing them in salt and lime flung them into deep, earth-covered pits. Districts on higher ground and the more salubrious parts of Walipur were unaffected, but even from here, on hearing the news, frightened families had evacuated themselves to outlying towns in panic-stricken flight leaving homes unlocked.

'And what's more, sir,' Steve Powley, whose voice was reduced to a croak, reported to Rahul, 'everywhere looters have had a field day.'

Compensation was demanded at American levels, but Rahul feared that even if it were forthcoming, it would be fraudulently siphoned off leaving nothing for the victims.

Reading media accounts and watching the nightmare situation enfold on TV, Kay began to understand why Rahul had made the ascent to high political office so quickly. At first she'd assumed it was privilege that had won him his rank, but it was clear that sheer merit had played by far the greater part.

AFPP dissidents had seized on the crisis in Walipur to mount a challenge to Rahul's leadership. 'And now, if you can,' Edith advised after the immediate aftermath had ebbed away, 'focus on restoring your flagging fortunes in the Party.'

'I'll be Leader unless and until I choose to stand down,' Rahul retorted. 'My supporters and I have decided to call the rebels bluff and to put it to a vote. They'll be sorry they didn't back me.'

Edith took his hands in hers and squeezed them. 'Somewhere I read that *Life is in Two Acts - it's all about surviving the intermission.*'

***

Hermie was ordered complete bed rest. Edith who'd returned to Sivalik from Delhi could never remember her friend looking so wan, so grey, with deep, dark rings under her eyes.

With an air of one who is much pre-occupied Hermie said slowly, 'under those lace hankies, you know the ones I keep for best, is a silk jewel pouch.'

Edith raised her eyebrows. 'Odd place to keep a piece of jewellery.' It was so unlike Hermie who had a tidy mind. 'Shouldn't it be with the rest of your baubles?'

'Just get it and I'll tell you - and I don't have baubles as you so flippantly put it,' Hermie said irritably.

Edith did as she was asked.

Hermie removed the copper bangle worn to ward off rheumatism and her gold bangles and opening the pouch, slipped a jewelled enamel bangle over her wrist, snapping the clasp fast with a resounding click. 'There!' She smiled broadly. 'See for yourself.' She twisted it round and round and the gems caught the light, then undoing it handed it reverently to Edith who gazed at her friend, puzzled at the little turn. 'Just read that but be careful, it's very precious to me.'

Edith peered at the inscription and gave a soft gasp, her eyes meeting Hermie's.

' I kept it secret all these years.' Edith sensed that Hermie was enjoying herself. 'A little secret between HH and me that no one, not even Parvati, who was inclined to believe she was omniscient, knew about.' Hermie murmured the inscription to herself and HH's regard for her bloomed afresh.

Adjusting the pillows at her back, Hermie's eyes shone with the memory. 'We had such fun together - how we laughed and loved.' Fiercely she added as if even after all these years she had a need to justify her actions, 'there was never anything cheap or sleazy – we both had high standards and I was hand-picked by Parvati - and do you know Edith, it's only since discovering that Kay's my great niece that I've felt an almost overwhelming need to learn about our little boy and what became of him. Not that I want to contact him, or see him,' she added swiftly, misreading the expression on Edith's face, 'oh, none of that, because now Kay is like a precious daughter to me, just as I was to Ma. I'd simply like to know how he fared. How has life treated him?' Hermie was a little breathless with the exertion of talking and clasped Edith's hand. 'I can honestly say my life was supremely happy once I met Hartley and I hope my son has been as blest. I suppose this longing to know is only natural?'

'Perfectly natural. Hermie, my dear, do you honestly want to know?' Edith's voice was muffled in a fearful crescendo of lunghis gymnastics across the roof. She felt in a trap. Would the shock of revelation be too much for Hermie in her current state of health or should she lie and say nothing?

There was a pause.

'Could you cope?' Edith said eventually in a voice that sounded rather odd to her.

Hermie nodded vigorously. 'In my head and in my heart my little boy has been with me every single day. Every moment I've ached for him.'

Edith wondered if she was exaggerating just a little.

Hermie gave a deep sigh, 'But I expect it's impossible. I'm too late. He has gone from me forever and I will have to live, and die, with that.'

'Don't sound so keen to meet the grim reaper,' Edith scolded her. Then, more gently, she added, 'it's not impossible.'

Hermie's head jerked up, and she seemed to grasp perfectly what Edith was saying. 'You know something. Go on, I'm up for it.'

'If he chooses...not to know you, you must promise not to interfere in his life.'

'Ah, so I'm not wrong. You do know!' Hermie closed her eyes and clasped her hands together as if in silent prayer. 'I promise, I promise, I promise on Ma's grave. I was all he had. My dearest wish is only to know that...he has done well.' A sudden thought occurred to her and she said quickly, 'If he's a bankrupt or a jailbird, or a...gay, don't bother to tell me.'

Edith raised her eyebrows and Hermie said hastily, 'I'm only joking.'

Many a true word is spoken in jest murmured Edith to herself.

While she fetched Hermie a glass of brandy, Edith pondered on the wisdom of revealing all. 'Drink up, it'll do you a power of good.'

'Are you, aren't you, will you, won't you...?' Hermie said.

Edith opened her handbag and withdrew a newspaper cutting of Louis shaking hands with the President of India after he'd presented his Letters of Credence as the U.S. envoy. He was facing the camera and looking straight at Hermie.

'This man, Louis Addison - the American Ambassador… '

'Edith, I always suspected you were an oddball and this irrelevance proves it. All right, I know the man's written me a nice letter telling me that that my book problem is at the top of his agenda -'

'- Louis is your son.' Edith pressed the cutting into Hermie's outstretched hand and passed her the magnifying glass.

Hermie smoothed the cutting with a finger seeing a tall, broad-shouldered figure with a strong, good-humoured face. She didn't speak for a moment or two. Then she said in a choked little voice, 'that's my handsome boy.' She gave it a little kiss and raised her head and looked at Edith, the hand that held the cutting, was shaking. 'And my God, he has the same smile as HH.'

Edith didn't like to add that there was also a look of Rahul about him in the forehead.

'I left the bunderbust to you so what happened?'

Edith told her and Hermie said softly, 'I don't know what I'd have done without you. You've been a good friend to me.' As if mesmerised, Hermie was still looking down at the picture then slowly and very reluctantly made to give it back.

Edith shook her head and patted Hermie's hand. 'No, no. You keep it; it's yours.'

Hermie leaned back on the pillows looking quite smug. 'He has done brilliantly,' she said with a pleased air.

'Yes.' Edith smiled back highly relieved that the disclosure had been painless. 'He has a very happy family life. You gave him the precious gift of loving and responsible parents and he became one himself.'

Hermie couldn't have been more delighted with the way Louis had turned out if she'd orchestrated it herself. 'I did my best for him; he deserved that. I was in a financial and social bind at the time. I had no expectations at all, and I couldn't have given him the secure background that his adopters were able to. He has fulfilled my every dream and I'm so happy. So very, very happy.' Tears of joy trickled down her face. 'Now answer this. Have you told anyone else?'

'Of course not.'

Hermie's voice was unsteady. 'Good. That's how it shall remain.' She pressed the clipping to her heart. 'I am well content,' she told the picture softly and pressed her lips to it. She was at peace. She leaned back against the headboard and closed her eyes. 'Those are Kay's footsteps.' She hastily slipped the cutting under the pillow meaning to place it with the baby photo in her purse.

'Don't mind me.' Kay bounced in. 'I've just brought your pills and Edith can make sure you take them while you both natter away.'

'I was just leaving,' Edith said. 'I've another invalid to look after.'

Hermie and Kay raised their eyebrows.

'Andy has developed canker in the left ear and is in doleful mood, so the vet's promised to look in on him. Goodbye, my dear.'

Hermie muttered a pre-occupied goodbye. She waited until she could hear them moving around downstairs then felt for the cutting, gazing down with a smile at the pictured face as if she'd never seen it before, and Louis smiled up at her. Yet Louis was a fast retreating yesterday and Hermie felt she could happily lock the door on it and throw away the key. *Kay is my wonderful today, my wonderful new tomorrow.*

***

Now that Vimla and Rahul were, according to Mrs Vohra, virtually betrothed, Amrita's animosity towards Kay softened, Rahul noticed with some amusement.

'She's nursing Hermie very well, and Edith has told me how patient and willing she has been during the past few months putting up with Hermie's

352

cantankerous ways. She seems to possess an in-built nurturing instinct. I wonder if she could be persuaded to be my companion, if I doubled her salary.'

Rahul suppressed a choke of mirth. 'Hardly...' he mumbled. 'It's probable she may simply decide to go home when her contract expires. She hasn't spoken of renewing it.' Indeed Kay had not spoken at all, or rather he hadn't seen her for some considerable time so embroiled had he been in the chemical affair and internal AFPP squabbles.

'Hermie will be very disappointed when that day comes.' Amrita didn't look forward to bearing the brunt of Hermie's displeasure. 'Do you - ?'

'Mother, please. Can't we leave it till later?' If he didn't cut her short he could be sitting there all day while she maundered on and on. 'There's a helluva mountain to climb before the ballot. There are two other very strong contenders and it's crucial Powley and I leave no stone unturned.'

***

Hermie died in her sleep. Meena had come up with chota hazri and had found her quite still and cold.

'Poor Kay,' Rahul said gently as she wept against his shoulder. 'What a shock. I'm so very sorry.' He was kindness itself, insisting on relieving her of the arrangements.

Kay was numb. She remembered how inexplicably happy Hermie had been the previous evening as she kissed her goodnight.

In accordance with her wishes, Hermie was laid to rest beside Hartley in the cone-strewn cemetery beneath the whispering spires of the pines. Kay wore a sombre dark-blue dress and the servants, standing a few paces behind, came to Sivalik to pay their respects and bid their employer a final salaam, Gopi blubbering like a child. Gerald read the Lesson and Barry gave the Eulogy whilst Bernadette, choked with tears, clung to a grim-faced Edith.

'I can't quite believe it,' Edith had told Kay drearily. 'I'm older than she was and in the natural order of things I expected her to outlive me.'

After the funeral when people came back to *Bonnie Brae,* complete strangers came up to Kay saying how much they'd always enjoyed Hermie's company. Kay turned over the cottage keys to Yusuf and forlornly returned to Delhi with the bewildered dogs, but without Hermie the bungalow felt empty and impersonal.

***

The heat hammered down but with recently installed air-conditioning Kay hardly noticed it. The previous day she'd received a letter from Yusuf whom she remembered from the funeral ten days earlier as a bearded, hollow-cheeked man, asking her to call at his office in connection with Hermie's Will.

Kay half-wondered if perhaps Edith would come with her but could not find it in herself to disturb her, for she'd last seen her sitting in a crumpled heap, still dazed with grief at the sudden death of an old and treasured friend.

'I believe you're acquainted with Rahul Ratan Singh.' Yusuf motioned Kay to a chair after the usual civilities.

'Yes, of course.' Kay wondered what Rahul's interest was in what she regarded as a purely family matter. 'Rahul it's nice to see you again,' Kay said with a smile.   Apart from the funeral when she'd exchanged a few words with him, she'd not seen him for weeks and Edith had volunteered, sensing Kay's disquiet, that he was still embroiled in pressing constituency and Party business.

And there was Vimla. For a moment everything went black before her and she briefly closed her eyes as she felt a sharp pain of the most primitive jealousy.

Rahul gave a curt nod and Kay found herself flushing at his cold politeness. Sensing an atmosphere, Yusuf cleared his throat and told Kay that Rahul was Hermie's Executor and that apart from sizeable legacies to Edith, Gopi, other servants and to friends, Hermie had bequeathed her valuable portfolio of shares to Edith and Kay on a 50:50 basis, and the residuary estate to *my beloved great niece Kay Forrester.*

 Yusuf darted her quick look and from the expression on his face Kay could tell he was uncertain if she'd grasped the implications so bemused did she probably appear.

'Now,' Yusuf said briskly. ' WORTH. CONSIDERABLE. Two unencumbered prime-site freeholds. A half-share in the equities -' he rubbed his hands, '- blue-chip companies. Many outstanding pieces of jewellery and valuable miscellaneous personal effects. Hefty liquid assets in several high-interest bearing savings accounts.'

Kay tried desperately to marshal her thoughts utterly unable to grasp the reality of her changed situation – that it had changed there was no doubt - it was bittersweet coming so soon after Hermie's sudden death. She stole a look at Rahul but could divine nothing from his expression.

'I don't know what to say,' Kay said shakily.

Yusuf allowed himself a small smile. 'Testators enjoy the rare privilege of being able to surprise relatives and the even rarer one of damning the consequences. And it was always my client's intention to surprise. She told me how very fond she was of you and what you meant to her.' His glance flitted between Kay and Rahul and he almost winced at the other man's cold expression. 'She was delighted to discover you were a close relative.'

'Thank you,' Kay said quietly.

'When probate is granted I can start to administer Hermie's estate. I'll keep you informed.' Yusuf gave a sigh. 'Unfortunately, I can't say when title will pass to you. In India the grant of probate can take many months - sometimes years - it's a cumbersome and bureaucratic procedure. For what reason, who knows? I suspect for no good reason at all save the wielding of petty authority that's so prevalent in this country. But Rahul will undoubtedly use his influence to expedite matters and will, dare I say it, be impelled to introduce a Bill to right this most grievous wrong. Eh, my friend?'

Rahul got to his feet, his eyes hard. ' Thank you Yusuf, I believe we're done and that's all for the time being. May I give you a lift, Ms Forrester?'

There was an edge to his voice that made Kay's nerves curl. Outside Kay said quietly, 'What's all this Ms Forrester nonsense?'

Rahul's voice was flat. 'You schemed your way into Hermie's confidence. She'd originally left her estate to various charities but let me disabuse you - you won't see a rupee of it. I shall instruct Yusuf to contest the Will on the grounds of undue influence.' He saw quite clearly where he thought his duty lay. 'And bogus claims of relationship. Great niece, my foot,' he added with icy contempt. 'You won't get far with that scam.'

Kay drew back as if from a blow. He was talking nonsense and she had to defend herself. 'I'm not the stranger - the imposter - you take me for. I **am** Hermie's great niece. My Mum Delphine was her niece - her brother Ashley's daughter- and the relationship came to light when I decided to enlist Hermie's help. Hermie knew about it before she changed her Will.' Kay felt her cheeks flame. 'That's exactly why it seems she did alter it. She wasn't gaga. I'm family and she wanted me to inherit. I didn't pressure her but I can and will prove our ties - that much we owe each other. We can't deny our kinship.' *Hermie, Hermie, she thought, what a trail of trouble you've left behind.*

Rahul gave a derisive snort. 'A lonely old woman's fantasy. How do you explain why Hermie said nothing to Mother and me? We were close to her. The whole business sounds fishy -'

'- Hermie wanted it kept secret. Is that so hard to believe? But I'm sure she told Edith -'

'That proves nothing. Hermie couldn't bear to see you go and would've done anything to anchor you. So until you can substantiate your claim by documentary evidence keep your pilfering hands to yourself.'

'I don't care about the estate,' Kay cried. 'I know only what the truth is.' Her legs felt like pulp. 'Your threats don't scare me.' Almost as an afterthought she added with some satisfaction, 'you're piqued Hermie never consulted you, that you had to take second billing. It's all been a big blow to your ego because you've always managed her affairs.'

'If you want to find out if I'm serious just try me -'

'- You must know that I will.' Kay made a brave attempt to match his determination.

They'd pulled up at Hermie's house and as she got out he delivered a parting shot. 'You'll be hearing from the Court.' Then he was gone in a whirl of dust.

Defeated, Kay went into the sitting room, out of the gaudy sunlight, the killing heat. She sat for a very long time, shaking a little. The meeting in Yusuf's office had forced Kay to this exploration of her feelings of Rahul. She'd responded to that strange pull of his, that mix of sexuality and intellect and it had grown into love and in the whole wide world he was the only man for her - the man she longed for and couldn't have. The strength of her own feelings had tricked her into dreaming that he'd return her love.

***

The servants' tempers frayed and just when Kay thought that she'd go mad with the heat, the monsoon broke - torrential cloudbursts, bloated grey skies, squadrons of ugly frogs, but the bulbul never faltered in its sweet song.

Proof, evidence. The words hammered in Kay's mind and she could think of nothing else. Enquiries of Hermie's bank and a search of both properties yielded nothing. Renee and Tony were all set to trawl through church records in Delhi but learned that the registers had been sent for digitisation and it would be months before data could be downloaded. With no clues as to where exactly down south Hermie was born, and neither Barry nor Edith being any the wiser, Kay could take it no further, although Barry, true to form, had promptly offered to *arrange* whatever she needed.

***

Sighing, Kay sat for a while longer then snapped shut her book, a collection of verse by the nineteenth century AI poet, Henry Derozio. She could scarcely grasp his meaning and wondered if he was a genius like Tennyson or simply downright awful. And did it matter?

A sudden terrific thunderclap made her jump sending Putch and Suzie, in a doze at her feet, into a fit of hysterical barking. She crossed to the window and stood there, looking for a long time at lightning shredding the night sky. As she came back out of her thoughts and turned away, a dark streak on the ceiling had resolved itself into a cascade.

Kay shrieked and, to his credit, Gopi came running.

'Don't just stand there - do something. Call Ratan Singh-ji,' Kay cried as the servants stood wailing and impotently wringing their hands.   But the phone was dead, the landline disabled by the storm and she'd forgotten to re-charge her mobile so she despatched the sweeper to Rahul's.

'Thanks for rescuing me,' Kay said gratefully, slightly more composed as Rahul quickly materialised with a workman who administered first aid to the roof.

Rahul dismissed it with a little gesture. 'The property has to be kept properly maintained until the estate's administered. And I suppose we'd better mop up,' he said with his customary briskness, gazing at the sodden scene. 'Those books look as if they could do with a spot of drip drying.' He wrinkled his nose.

Kay pushed her hair back out of her eyes. 'I spent many happy hours browsing through those shelves.' They held a row of Hermie's thrillers - she shared Kay's taste for them - and her much read torrid romances, a well thumbed volume of homoeopathic remedies, Hartley's substantial and, Kay imagined, valuable, collection of rare first editions on shikar and field sports, regimental memoirs, a treatise on theosophy by Annie Besant and several on Indian butterflies, fungi, and bats. *Minutes of the Himalayan Conservation Society.* Books on flowers and trees and English folk songs and half a shelf of Victorian travellers' accounts of darkest Africa. All were sodden as though they'd fallen into a swamp.

Kay put a hand to her mouth. 'Books are so personal, so special. I'd hate to have to throw anything out.'

357

'I don't think you'll need to.' Rahul pulled out a title at random. 'Oh, very Hermie,' he murmured and Kay craning over his shoulder saw that it was *The Memsahib Book of Cookery*. 'And that's an intriguing title – God, how meanings change. He gestured to *Camp Recipes for Camp People, 1913* and the author is...' he laughed, 'or rather, calls himself *Chota Sahib*. Now,' Rahul was his practical self. 'Run and find some bed sheets.'

'That's easily done.' Old sheets and old tablecloths Hermie hoarded in abundance, Kay remembered wryly, darned and patched.

Laying the books down in neat rows, they aimed short bursts with a hairdryer, crisping the pages and dislodging old cinema tickets, dried flowers, bookmarks, the occasional foreign bank note. It was slow going and the steam given off made the room smell like a laundry. Once or twice Kay felt Rahul's lingering glance, but he said nothing and she wondered about Vimla and his outburst over the Will.

Kay reached up for a soggy volume on Indian birds that looked impressively comprehensive and seemed to be the first of three companion volumes. Beautifully illustrated, it would eventually need specialist handling for the binding had split. Under a warm jet the pages separated and thin sheets of folded paper slid free from the section on bulbuls.

'Another lump of rubbish to be got rid of,' Rahul said a little sourly. Snatching it up and crushing it into a ball he tossed it into the waste paper basket. 'We're already knee deep in extraneous material.'

'You're very hasty,' Kay said lightly and some impulse made her retrieve it. She smoothed it out. It felt and looked different from the rest - coarse yellowing paper, torn at a corner, purplish ink. 'Throw it away unread, unremarked? That's very unscientific of you. It could be important.' She gasped. *It couldn't be. It was.* 'It is. Her heart was beating very fast.

'What's up?' He'd seen her trembling.

Kay pushed across two splodgy sheets folded up inside each other. After a short pause Rahul said, 'the answer to your prayers.' He gave her a look she couldn't read. *'Hermione Delicia Blake, daughter of Wilburt and Noreen Blake born Ootacamund 21 May at 10:01 p.m. Caste: Anglo-Indian.* **And** her marriage certificate.' His voice was bland.

'I'm glad you're so quick on the uptake. Yes. The evidence you wanted.' Kay felt a sudden acid lump in her throat.

They stared at each other.

'It's not what I wanted. That was never the issue. Don't condemn me. You should understand that a Court would have required proper verification of the kinship and knowing this I was trying to save you from a great deal of embarrassment.' Rahul looked acutely uncomfortable.

Kay flew to her feet. The reprieve was nothing to her. She'd always known the truth. 'Don't wriggle,' she said furiously. 'You can't really expect me to believe that. Don't try to excuse yourself...to justify yourself to me. You should've trusted me - why didn't you? You'd no right to expose me to this. To jeopardise my future. You shit.'

He'd scrambled to his feet, his face pale, dodging the blows she was aiming against his chest. Catching hold of her wrists, he muttered lamely, 'I don't want to hear any more of this nonsense. You won't lecture me as what I did was from the best of motives. You can manage on your own; I'm leaving now.'

'Yes, do that. Get out, stay out.' Something deep inside her seemed to snap. 'I never want to see you again.' Kay was past thinking, past caring what she said or did.

Rahul let go of her then strode from the room and vaulted the verandah steps.

Kay ran out into the compound. 'And don't you ever darken this doorstep, *my doorstep,* again.' Her shout was drowned in the growl of a car engine.

Wet through, her head throbbing, she went to her room and slamming the door collapsed in a chair, her face in her hands. Hot tears coursed down her cheeks. All she wanted to do was to clear out. *Out of this wretched house, this wretched country.*

***

On a cold, grey London evening Kay, home for some months, felt a sudden pang for the light and sun of India. She'd decided that there was nothing to tie her to Delhi as she had then still no legal right to the house; her funds had run low as probate was still pending and she'd not liked to ask Yusuf for any monies on account of herself. She longed for the comfort of old friends and familiar surroundings and would need to find a job and pick up the threads of her old life.

She had a sudden vivid recollection of Vimla's lovely neck and kohl-rimmed eyes, remembering that rumours strongly suggested that she and Rahul planned to marry soon. Renee had only managed a couple of text messages as she was busy promoting her new album and touring Sri Lanka with the band. Edith had surprised her with a signed copy of *Der Morgenstern - My Indian Journal,* her reminiscences quirkily self-illustrated that, within days of publication, had gone straight to No 1 in Germany's bestseller list.

Kay found it painful to remind herself that she'd actively initiated the separation from Rahul and that he was out of her life. That she'd eventually be very comfortably off was no consolation. It had been a bitter harvest.

Not for the first time Kay found herself turning to the laminated card bearing an inspirational verse that Renee had pressed into her hand at the airport.

My life is but a weaving
Between my Lord and me,
I cannot choose the colours
He works steadily.
Often He weaves sorrow
And I in foolish pride
Forget that He sees the upper,
And I the underside.
Not till the loom is silent
And the shuttles cease to fly,
Shall God unroll the canvas
And explain the reason why.
The dark threads are as needful
In the weaver's skilful hand,
As the threads of gold and silver
In the pattern He has planned.

Her birthday passed uncelebrated and Christmas was a week away. In an effort to bring seasonal cheer to the shabby flat, Kay had maxed her credit card on new carpets and a new sofa, run up new curtains and had set to with paint and roller brush. Wearing tartan trousers and red jumper, she mounted a stepladder to dress the six foot high Christmas tree with lights and ornaments and to tie on the Christmas fairy. *Is that the doorbell?*

Slowly climbing down, Kay went into the narrow hall and undid the door chain.

After a moment's gaping silence she said slowly, 'Rahul... well...' In an impeccably cut charcoal suit and toning silk tie, he looked immorally attractive.

'Hello, Kay.' He sounded tentative. He held out his hand and with the briefest of pauses she took it. 'You're looking very nice.'

Kay's heart fluttered in her throat. 'Thanks. Er...won't you come in?' Her hospitable instincts came to the fore. 'Do sit down. Can I ...er.. offer you a drink? This is a surprise.' Kay busied herself with bottles and glasses, her heart pounding.

'Perhaps I should have let you know.' Rahul was looking round the sitting room, personal possessions marking it all her own. 'What a cosy nest this is.' He sank onto the sofa, closing his eyes for a moment, his shoulders hunched, exhaustion marking the lines of his mouth. 'Have you heard from Yusuf? He told me he'd emailed you.'

'I expect he has but my pc has crashed and my mobile was nicked. I'm waiting for the insurance to come through so that I can buy a replacement.' Kay handed him a glass of Argentinian malbec.

'Ah, perfect.' He buried his nose in its bouquet. 'Yusuf has been a miracle worker. Probate has been granted.' He was studying her intently.

'That's very quick isn't it? But I feel better already,' Kay said coolly. 'I couldn't make any plans till I knew. How is Amrita?' Not that she actually cared a damn about her, but Kay was desperately trying not to stall, desperately trying to keep her features and voice under control, desperately wondering what Rahul was doing there.

Rahul stood up and walked restlessly to the window, glass in hand. 'After the Vimla business...'

'What business?'

'She eloped with her Judah,' he blurted out, 'and they married in New York.'

'What!' Kay was flabbergasted. 'But I understood you and Vimla ...'

'NEVER. Not in a million years. To cut a long story very short, Vimla and Judah, a medical colleague, were an item - they were crazy about each other. He's a member of the Bene-Israel, an ancient Indian Jewish community, but Mrs Vohra refused to countenance Vimla marrying out. So I hatched a little bluff.'

'And I assumed...' Kay didn't know whether to laugh or cry. 'Oh, Rahul, dare I ask how Amrita and Mrs Vohra took it?'

His eyes crinkled. 'Very, very badly I'm afraid.' Mischief danced in his eyes.. 'Both women are united in misery.' He crossed back to the sofa. 'Mrs Vohra is hysterical and blames her husband for giving his daughter a liberal education, but worse still, if truth be known, she is bemoaning lavish past wedding gifts to daughters of friends and sees no hope of reciprocity.'

'And Mr Vohra?' Kay wanted to hear the male angle.

'His attitude was that Vimla has undermined his authority and he ordered her never to set foot in his house again. But he's coming round, the old softie. And pragmatic to boot. What is done is done and can't be undone, so make the best of it. Anyway, like him, Judah plays a mean game of snooker so I predict a grand reconciliation after a decent stand-off period.' He gave a sudden warm smile and Kay's heart jolted.

'Vimla's younger sister finds the romantic splicing utterly sensational, although Mrs Vohra is absolutely mortified and despairs of finding the right boy for her owing to the precedent set by her sister.'

'And what,' Kay asked wickedly, wishing she'd been there to witness the drama, 'is Amrita plotting for you now?'

'Oh, she's given up on me. I gave an Oscar winning performance as the jilted suitor and am wallowing in a torrent of sympathy,' Rahul said basely, 'and showered with congratulations.'

Kay lifted her eyebrows.

'You see before you the leader of the AFPP.' Rahul grinned. 'Yes, thank God I was re-elected. It was a brutal, bruising fight. Very dirty, very ugly, very close at the first ballot. I was advised to stand down for the sake of Party unity, but I refused. With dogged Powley in the wings, I was determined to soldier on and see off the rebellion. And then I thought *I'm whacked.* I need to get away from it all. And what better place than here - with you.'

She thought he looked thinner and suddenly his eyes were full of such anguish that she looked away.

'Is it a bad moment? Should I have warned you first?' Rahul stretched out his hand and took hers. Her face must have changed for he added sharply, 'Kay, listen to me, please. I know you're mad at me and you've every right to be. But we can't leave it like this. I've missed you terribly. I've been a bloody fool.' His features were bleak with self-condemnation.

Could something be salvaged from the shreds? There could be no going back, of that Kay was sure, but could they go forward? She'd banished him from her home but hadn't succeeded in banishing him from her heart. But she was wary.

'Darling, listen, I can't go on being so feebly wishy-washy. Don't close yourself to me.' His voice was a little despairing. 'It's been hell without you. The sweetness left my life when you quit.'

'I don't want things to fall apart because you're playing games,' Kay said a little miserably. 'Oh, I don't know...'

Rahul regarded her sombrely. 'I'm almost too frightened to find out but I have to, for ignorance is not bliss and it's folly not to be wise.' His eyes were a curious mixture of passion and vulnerability. This was a new, more humble Rahul.

'But Amrita...' Kay couldn't bear any more skirmishes and enmities.

'Well, yes. Mother.' He looked a little shamefaced. 'She couldn't stand idly by and see her precious son rejected by Vimla Vohra so she's already dropping hints about a charming daughter-in-law, the great niece of a Colonel's widow.' He thought it prudent not to mention that Amrita had conveniently skirted around Kay's AI heritage whilst stressing her considerable means and assets.

'Indeed.' Kay was speechless. Amrita had taken a great deal for granted. She wondered if there'd been anything else.

Rahul caught her quizzical look. He couldn't tell her that when he'd announced to Amrita that he meant to marry Kay she'd threatened to disinherit him - *spare me the cliché, Mother* — that she'd hinted darkly at a terminal medical condition - *there're some things stronger than apron strings, Mother.* That she'd locked herself in her room, doing puja, weeping non-stop and going on hunger strike, the melodrama ending when Edith rammed a German fencing sword through her window pane and over the sound of breaking glass yelled at her to swallow her pride and prejudice.

He kissed the tip of her nose. 'I committed a bad error of judgment. I know sweetheart, I hurt you dreadfully, but I suppose it's a question of being wise after the event.' His voice tautened. 'When you came into my life and disrupted it like that, I should've known. And I've been so stupid I fear I'm going to lose you — that I had the chance of a lifetime and blew it.'

Kay's heart was racing knowing that they'd reached the point where matters had to be resolved.

'Persuade me my inheritance has nothing to do with all this'. she said a little wickedly, keeping him dangling.

His eyes took on a wounded look, but then he must have seen the glint in hers for he grinned.

'I'm glad you have some pin money of your own.' His retort was tinged with uncustomary tenderness. 'Kay darling, I'm nothing without you.'

His voice dissolved her. 'I've always loved you.' His love was the best inheritance of all. She pummelled his chest with her fists and as he caught them and pulled her into his arms they kissed.

'Does that mean what I think it does?'

'I can't answer a question I haven't been asked.'

A small frown appeared between his eyebrows. 'I thought you'd know me by now. I don't usually ask - ' He kissed her again. 'I give orders.'

Kay laughed and sank against his chest. All the doubts she'd had seemed suddenly, incredibly, to have resolved themselves.

'I'm the luckiest man alive.' Then he said quickly, 'Is it all settled'?'

'If you say so.'

'Right, that's that then.' Rahul grinned, his relief only too obvious and extracted two first class airline tickets from his jacket pocket. 'Darling, we leave tomorrow.'

They stepped off the flight to be met and garlanded by the chauffeur, Rahul's hand slipping into hers as they walked towards the Merceces. They turned into Hermie's driveway. The sun slanted in deep gold bars against the newly whitewashed house. The lawn had been mowed. Putch and Suzie, tails wagging furiously, performed their welcoming gambits. Up in a peepul tree a bulbul began to sing.

'Wouldn't you rather go to your place?' Kay asked surprised.

Rahul shook his head and smiled and the tenderness in his gaze made her realise there was no need for him to say more. Holding hands they made their way up the verandah steps.

'My dears!' It was Amrita, smiling and very gracious. It was a great concession, Kay knew, on the Rajmata's part to be there.

'Mother.' Rahul bent down to kiss his mother's feet and Kay instinctively followed suit to her future mother-in-law.

Amrita embraced them both. 'And see who else is here.'

Edith, indomitable as ever, came forward, her hands outstretched. 'Welcome home, Kay.' She'd always felt that a period of contemplation and detachment would bring Kay and Rahul together again.

Something turned over in Kay's heart and she realised quite suddenly that she was glad to be back - that her roots were here, that it was home. 'It's lovely to see you all.'

They trooped into the sitting room, no one sitting in Hermie's chair by unspoken common consent. Kay looked around approvingly. The furniture had been polished, the terrazzo floor shone, roses and violets scented the air, everything was spick and span, as Hermie would have wished. Dear, impossible Hermie. And there she was beaming down from a silver photograph frame standing on the mantelpiece.

Edith followed her glance. 'I thought you might like to have that.'

'How very thoughtful. It's just what I want. It makes everything sort of complete.'

They went silent, thinking of the woman who'd delighted in doing exactly as she wished. 'And what's **this?**' Kay's eyes alighted on a tray. **This** was a selection of delectable English cakes and pastries served on Hermie's best Copenhagen porcelain with her Swiss embroidered table linen.

'What a treat.' Kay glimpsed a coffee-brown face peeping round the door. 'Gopi! You old rascal!' Who'd have believed it of her old adversary?

He shuffled into the room. 'Salaam madam,' and grinned a little sheepishly, then turning to Amrita addressed her in Hindi, muttering something about shaadhi.

'Do you want to know what he says?' Edith translated with a smile. 'He says he hopes you'll let him to cook for your wedding.'

They laughed. *Over my dead body*, Kay thought.

Edith looked round for her bag. 'Come along Amrita, we'll leave these two love-birds to get re-acquainted.'

'Oh don't go yet,' Kay said and meant it, but they were already making for the door. She stood on the verandah waving them off then turned quickly back into the sitting room that echoed with the bulbul's song.

'You've been away far too long.' Rahul stretched out a hand. 'Come over here Kay darling.' He made her name sound so beautiful. 'You are my jewel of Walipur - my present, my future, my always.'

'That doesn't sound like the Rahul I know,' Kay moved to the man who meant everything to her and his lips met hers, 'but it is the Rahul I love.'

THE END